FEAST OF THE FLESH

Taking my arm, Sandy led me from the lounge into the dining room and stood me before a large table. 'Lie on the table,' she instructed. 'And we'll get started.'

'But, I thought we were eating first?' I demurred, wondering why the table wasn't laid.

'We are, in a few minutes,' she replied mysteriously. 'Tom, I'll go and organize the food while you prepare Sue for the sex-banquet.'

When Sandy had left the room, Tom lifted me onto the table and spread my limbs. I didn't protest, thinking that they were going to eat my pussy for starters. But when he secured my wrists and ankles to the table legs with handcuffs, I became apprehensive and asked him what he was up to.

'You're going to enjoy this,' he grinned, running a finger up my wet slit. 'You'll see what we have planned for you in a minute,' he added as Sandy wheeled the food in on a trolley.

'Starters,' she smiled, placing two pineapple rings over my erect nipples. 'You like bananas, Sue?' she asked, passing Tom the fruit . . .

Also by Ray Gordon in New English Library paperback

Arousal
House of Lust
The Uninhibited
Submission!
Haunting Lust
Depravicus

The Splits

Ray Gordon

NEW ENGLISH LIBRARY
Hodder and Stoughton

First published in 1996
by Hodder and Stoughton
A division of Hodder Headline PLC
A New English Library paperback

10 9 8 7 6 5 4 3 2

All characters in this publication are fictitious and any resemblance to real persons, living or dead, is purely coincidental.

British Library Cataloguing in Publication Data
A CIP catalogue record for this title is available from the British Library

Gordon, Ray
The Splits
1. English fiction - 20th Century
I. Title
823.9'14[F]

ISBN 0 340 66055 4

Typeset by Avon Dataset Ltd, Bidford-on-Avon, Warks
Printed and bound in Great Britain by
Mackays of Chatham PLC, Chatham, Kent

Hodder and Stoughton
A division of Hodder Headline PLC
338 Euston Road
London NW1 3BH

Chapter One

He was around twenty-five – married, good-looking, with a rugged, masculine body and long black hair cascading over his forehead.

He was also my latest sexual conquest. As I knelt before him and sucked his huge purple knob deep into my hot mouth, I laughed inwardly. *Another married man falls*, I exulted as he shuddered in his adultery, his penis twitching, his silky knob swelling dangerously.

As his sperm gushed, filling my cheeks, waking my taste buds, I kneaded his heavy balls and took him even deeper into my mouth. Gasping, trembling, he clung to my head to steady himself as his knees sagged and his bollocks drained.

Making her timely entrance, his pretty, young wife screamed hysterically as I looked up at her, her husband's sperm glistening on my lips, dribbling down my chin. She'd expected to have coffee with me – a chat and a giggle as we caught up on the latest gossip. But, taking the bait, she'd discovered instead her husband's infidelity. Now their marriage was over – destroyed in a few seconds of mindless lust. As she fled, her flushed cheeks streaked with tears, he pulled his trousers on and gave chase, desperate to explain that it had been a mistake, that he really did love her, that I had meant nothing to him.

Too late, I gloated wickedly as I slipped my panties up my long legs to cover my wet, inflamed pussy – my weapon. *Too much water under the bridge, too much sperm in another woman's mouth*. Another conquest, another broken marriage to add to my ever growing list. The wedding vows had been broken. Now the tears, the pain, the hurt would come. *As they had to me.*

I'll never forget that fateful morning last summer when my husband, Jim, stood before me in the lounge – and glibly destroyed me. In seconds, from being happily married, I became a deserted, betrayed, broken woman.

I hadn't believed the anonymous note lying on the doormat that morning. Until I'd opened that white envelope and playfully confronted Jim, I'd thought that we were together, that things were fine between us. Reading the scribbled words about an alleged affair to him, I'd laughed, thinking that he'd laugh too and offer a reassuring explanation. He didn't. And my stomach sank, fell like a stone as his riposte pierced my soul.

'I'm sorry, Sue. I'm leaving you.' He was standing on the hearth rug we'd bought only three weeks previously – the rug I'd anticipated us spending long winter evenings on, sprawled out naked by the coal fire.

Shock registered first – and a frightening sense of total devastation. I could barely comprehend what he was saying, let alone reply. My mind reeled with obscene images of my naked husband in another woman's bed – my best friend's bed – entwined in lust, loving her, writhing in the lewd act of adultery, his penis penetrating her young pussy, filling her with his sperm as she gasped her illicit love for him.

My hands trembled, my heart beat wildly. Parts of my life flashed before me – our first meeting in the small coffee shop off the High Street. Our Greek island honeymoon – the orange glow of the setting sun bathing our naked bodies as we made perfect, idyllic love on that sandy Andros shore.

'Sue!' he called through the mist of my tormented mind. My legs were shaking and my head swimming as I focused my tearful eyes on him.

He was a stranger to me now. His black hair hanging over his unusually lined forehead, his crisp, white shirt open, displaying his hard, bronzed chest – he wasn't the man I'd known and loved. He lifted his head, his dark eyes gazing into mine as he attempted a slight smile. Opening his mouth as if about to speak, he sighed. Usually positive, a pillar of strength in a crisis, now I saw before me a wimp.

'Sue, I'm sorry,' he mumbled, his head hanging low. Sorry? Was that it? After what I'd thought had been three years of happiness married to the man I loved . . . sorry? 'It's not your fault . . .' Not *my* fault? He screws my best friend, says he's leaving me for her, wrecks my life – then tells me that it's not my fault?

'How long have you been lying to me, cheating on me, betraying me?' I finally managed to blubber through my tears. The stark reality of my words had hit home, I knew. He winced slightly, biting his lip as he searched for an appeasing answer – a lie. Obviously realizing that I at least deserved the truth, that I'd eventually discover the truth if he were to lie to me, he hung his head again.

'All along, I suppose,' he mumbled.

'All along? You mean you've been screwing that little tart throughout our entire marriage?'

'I was seeing her before we married, Sue. I tried to end it but . . .'

'Good in bed, is she?' I interrupted the pathetic figure standing before me. He looked like a dishevelled schoolboy who'd been caught wanking. Holding his hand to his forehead, he screwed his eyes shut as if trying to black out the truth. 'Got a nice fanny, has she?' I persisted, imagining him kissing her there, loving her there – slipping his penis into her. 'Tighter than mine, is it?'

'No! It's just that . . .'

'Just that *what*, Jim? That she's a better fuck than me?'

I screamed hysterically. 'Is that it? You'd rather fuck her dirty little cunt? Get out! Get out of this house and never come back!'

As he turned and left the room, my stomach churned. I felt dizzy with fear, sadness, anger, grief. Bastard! The front door banged shut, loudly, and that was it – he'd gone. I thought he'd come crawling back to me before long – pleading, begging me for forgiveness. Once he'd realized what he was giving up – me, the house, our future – I thought he'd be back. But I was wrong.

For several days after Jim's departure I stayed in bed and mooched around the house in my dressing gown, asking myself *why*? Where had I gone wrong? Could I have been a better wife? In my despair, I blamed myself for the note. If I hadn't confronted him, I'd never have known that he was fucking another woman behind my back. In my ignorance, things would have been all right.

I didn't eat, or sleep. Sobbing into my pillow in the early hours of the morning, I'd come to, puffy-eyed, cheeks wet, drowning in my sorrow. Letting myself go, I wallowed in grief – anger. Lost in self-pity, injured pride, there seemed little point in dressing, bothering to put make-up on. My world had gone, spun off out of orbit into oblivion.

For a while, I blamed myself for his affair. I remembered the times I'd said no to sex, the times I'd known he was feeling randy and I'd turned my back on him in bed. But, on those rare occasions, I'd felt tired. I couldn't force myself to make love when I was too tired even to think straight! *Perhaps I should have done?*

But, as the days passed, I recalled the times when I'd eagerly said *yes* to sex – many, many times. And the times I'd begged him for sex, instigated nights of wild and desperate passion. Wet with excitement at the little surprise in store for my husband, I'd climb into bed with him, knowing that he was longing to lick my pussy, drink my come.

Between my thighs, he'd lick, suck, and then gasp with delight as a banana popped out between my cunt lips. Extracting the delicacy from my pussy with his teeth, he'd savour the creamy fruit before sucking a beautiful orgasm from my clitoris.

I thought long and hard about those heady days, those frantic nights we'd spent making love, doing anything and everything, fulfilling each other's every whim, every desire, every sexual fantasy. Only the night before he'd dropped his bombshell we'd spent hours making close, passionate love.

And to think I'd had no idea that he'd been screwing my so-called best friend all along! Bitch! Bastard! Why had he said that it wasn't my fault? Was it some kind of psychological ploy to have me believe that I really *was* to blame?

I began to think of *her*, my best bloody friend. At twenty-six, Caroline was two years older than me, shy, unimposing, with her dull, wispy blonde hair tied back in a ponytail. My own luxuriant blonde tresses were thick, long, crimped. What the hell did she have that I didn't? What was the attraction? She had to have *something* to offer, *something* to lure my husband away from me. But what?

Sensible, well-educated, I'd thought she was my friend. I'd never have imagined her offering her body to my husband, making love to him behind my back. I'd never have imagined my husband making love to *anyone* behind my back, let alone Caroline! She was a bitch, I decided – a whore, a tart. *But she had Jim.*

The house was quiet. Only my thoughts, swirling thoughts, thoughts of hatred and revenge disturbed the peace. It would always be quiet now that it wasn't a family home, I reflected, sitting in the lounge one evening. We'd planned to have children, or, at least, I had. Obviously the patter of tiny feet couldn't have been further from Jim's mind as he sank his solid penis into Caroline's wet pussy and gave her his sperm – *my* sperm.

Alone, I felt as if I was in a void. A huge, black hole – empty, bottomless, meaningless, pointless. After a month, I felt worse. I'd thought that time would heal my wounds, take the pain away, but the passing weeks, and another note describing in graphic detail how Jim and Caroline would be making love, had only heightened my anger, hatred, and bitterness.

Trying to come to terms with what had happened, I'd go for long walks. I'd sit in the park watching couples walking hand in hand – and despise them for the love they shared. I'd watch couples in the supermarket buying the weekend shopping, as we used to – and detest the very idea of marriage. I became obsessed. The bitterness eating away inside me, I grew bent on destroying relationships. If I couldn't have a relationship, then no one else would.

I started writing anonymous letters – scathing, libellous letters to Caroline telling of Jim's unfaithfulness to her. To ease my pain, I'd tell her that hers wasn't the only fanny he was screwing. I'd conjure graphic descriptions of his penis entering other women's pussies – their slippery juices glistening on his shaft as he fucked them behind her back.

She'd have known that the letters were from me, of course, but I didn't care. It made me feel better just to think that I'd planted the seed of doubt in her mind. A seed that would grow and grow until, like ivy creeping up a tree, it strangled the bitch!

'You'll soon find yourself a nice man,' my friends would console me smugly in front of their husbands. It's funny how human nature works – how people seem to derive satisfaction from other people's misfortune. Perhaps my sadness served to remind them how lucky they were, how happy they were? They had their husbands, their love, their sex-lives. *I had nothing.*

My friends began to pity me. They'd call in for coffee, trying to cheer me up with their incessant drivel. I suppose they meant well, but I sensed that they were curious about my state of mind rather than genuinely wanting to help me. I felt like a freak on parade at a circus, and they'd all come to look, to point. When they'd had their fill, they'd go home laughing, cracking jokes at my expense.

But even worse than my so-called friends were the notes, the relentless notes, relating in explicit detail what Jim and the bitch got up to in bed. Caroline wouldn't lower herself to such deranged behaviour, I knew. She'd won, after all – she had Jim. The only reason she'd bother sending notes of that kind would be to rub salt into my wounds.

I knew that I had to shake off my depression. Despite the cosy couples, the pitying wives, the notes, I had to take control of my emotions, free my mind of Jim – and the bitch. And then it happened. Quite clinically, the healing process was set in motion one Saturday evening, when Tony materialized on my doorstep clutching a screwdriver.

Tony belonged to Sally, a friend from down the road, who'd generously dispatched her husband upon hearing that my washing machine had broken. In his early thirties with dark, swept-back hair, brown eyes, perfect white teeth and a suntan from the recent family holiday in Gran Canaria, he was an attractive man – a good catch, I surmised. *Sally was a lucky woman.*

She'd told me, proudly, smugly, how Tony had never strayed, how faithful he was. But I'd always thought Jim to be faithful. Perhaps Sally's husband was the same as Jim – deceitful? Perhaps all men were the same as Jim? Bastards!

'Come in, Tony!' I invited with a warm smile. Not having expected him to come galloping that very evening like a knight on a white charger, I was wearing my red miniskirt and silk blouse in readiness to go out for a drink. It was to be the first time I'd ventured out into the night, into a bar, on my own. I'd had the crazy idea of getting drunk and trying to blot out the world. But I knew that blotting things out wasn't the answer – the world was here to stay. I could try to change the world – my world – but not obliterate it.

Tony stepped into the hall, gazing down between my breasts at my deep cleavage as I closed the front door. I was aware of his eyes on the back of my legs as he followed me into the kitchen. What was he thinking? I wondered, imagining his eyes transfixed on my rounded buttocks as I walked.

'It washes, but it won't spin,' I said, waving my hand at the aging Bendix. He pulled the machine out and took the back off. Whether or not he knew what he was doing, I didn't know or care. I hated men but, strangely, it was nice to have a male in the house for a change.

I made coffee and sat at the kitchen table while he fiddled around with the machine. Gazing at Tony, I remembered when Jim had tried to repair the dishwasher, and blown it up. We'd laughed and ended up making love on the kitchen floor.

My mind drifting, I began to picture Tony screwing his wife. I'd always had difficulty imagining other couples making love, writhing in orgasm, gasping, panting. But when it came to Tony and Sally, I found that I could easily picture them naked in bed – entwined in their marital lovemaking. I suppose I found the exercise simple because Sally had always said how good her sex life was, how she never failed to have at least half a dozen good orgasms.

A wave of jealousy gushed over me. My mind began to reel with thoughts of my ex-husband in Caroline's bed, kissing her naked body, mouthing and licking between her legs as he used to mine. I felt my stomach twist into a tight knot of jealousy – complete and utter hatred. Then I pictured Sally – Tony licking and mouthing between her thighs as she gasped her satisfaction. *Millions of couples were making love – as I lay alone in the loneliness of my big, cold bed.*

It was then that something gripped me – urged me to destroy Tony's and Sally's twee family unit. Although I'd grown to despise relationships, I'd thought I'd felt like that because of my crazy state of mind. I suppose I hadn't expected to actually vent my hatred. Sally was a friend – I couldn't wreck her marriage just because mine was over! But now, I twisted round in my chair and parted my legs slightly.

Tony focused his eyes between my thighs, gazing at my panties – and froze. I knew then that, friend or not, I wanted to hit out at Sally, at Tony, at any and every married couple and shatter their dreams. Pretending not to notice his amorous gaze as I fiddled with my teaspoon, I parted my legs further. His eyes transfixed on my red panties, I knew what he was thinking, what he'd like to do – and that's when the realization hit me. *During those few moments, my life changed dramatically. My world, with all its painful devastation, had changed.*

I caught Tony's gaze, and smiled. Returning my smile, he mumbled something about the washing machine as he reached for his screwdriver. For the first time in weeks I felt elated, excited, a sense of danger mixed with sexual arousal. My panties wet, I became aware of my clitoris, throbbing as I discreetly pulled my skirt up higher and parted my thighs even more.

I could feel his eyes there, between my thighs, burning, piercing, as, my elbows on the table, my chin resting on my fist, I browsed, apparently nonchalantly, through a magazine. Was his penis stiff? I wondered. Would he charge home and make love with Sally, picturing the triangle of wet, swelling material between my thighs? Would he imagine me in her place as he moaned his sexual satisfaction and his penis throbbed and jetted his sperm deep inside her cunt?

No doubt Jim had imagined Caroline squirming in orgasm beneath him as he'd come inside me. Bastard! Perhaps Tony would picture me naked, my long hair cascading over my breasts, my nipples, while he secretly masturbated?

I speculated whether Caroline took Jim into her mouth and drank his sperm or not. Whether she rested her head on his stomach and gently sucked him into her mouth. He'd always liked that, and so had I. Perhaps I hadn't been good enough? Perhaps I hadn't done it properly? But I'd always thought that I'd brought him immense pleasure during those most intimate, private moments. As he came in my mouth and I swallowed his sperm, I'd thought that we were somehow unique, that no one else had ever even imagined the loving intimacy we were experiencing.

I'd thought that Jim's penis was mine, all mine. But I'd been sharing it with another woman! The thought sickened me. I'd taken him into my mouth after he'd penetrated her vagina. I'd given my body to him, entirely. I'd never dreamed of sharing my body, my vagina, with another man. It had been his, and his only.

What had the bitch got that I hadn't? Even though I say it myself, I was attractive, feminine, sexy – slim, well proportioned, curvy in the right places. Jim had liked me to appear feminine in the extreme and I'd always dressed sexily for him. Many a man had turned his head as I'd walked down the street and, even on Jim's arm, I'd never been short of wolf whistles or tooting car horns. Looking back, I think he enjoyed watching men watching me. But, seeing as he was screwing Caroline behind my back, he couldn't have been that proud of me! I suppose he got some kind of kick out of other men thinking about my body, gazing at my long legs, picturing my pussy.

I grew accustomed to dressing in revealing tops, miniskirts and high heels – for Jim. I remember the day he arrived home with a surprise present of silk stockings and a suspender belt for me shortly after our honeymoon. I'd barely rolled the stockings up my long legs before he pulled me onto the bed and ravished me, licking between my thighs, sucking my inner pussy lips into his hot mouth. Fool that I was, I didn't know that the bastard ravished Caroline like that, too!

'It needs a new part,' Tony sighed as he emerged from behind the washing machine, his eyes glued between my thighs. 'I'll have to come back tomorrow evening and fix it.'

'There's your coffee,' I smiled sweetly, not wanting him to leave. 'How's Sally?'

'She's fine,' he replied as he sat down. 'More to the point, how are you now that . . . Well, now that you're . . .'

'On my own?'

'Yes.'

'I won't be on my own for long, I'm letting the spare room to a college girl. It's not so much for the money, it's to help her out, really – and for the company. I've known her for some time and . . . Well, you don't want to hear about that.'

'When's she moving in?'

'Monday, hopefully.'

'So you're OK now that Jim's . . .'

'Couldn't be better,' I replied cheerily – I lied. 'I'm single, carefree, happy . . . I can go where I want, when I want, do what I like, when I like. Looking back, I don't know how I put up with being tied down! I realize now that having to think of someone else all the time, never being able to make decisions on my own, plan things without having to consult someone else, was such a weight on me. It was like walking around in chains! I can honestly say that I've never been happier.'

'I'm pleased to hear it, Sue. I know what you mean about having to consider someone else all the time. Only the other day I was invited out with the lads, a stag night, and Sally wouldn't hear of it! I suppose marriage stifles the individual to an extent.'

'Stifles? More like bloody suffocates!' I laughed.

Lowering his eyes, Tony gazed at my firm, rounded breasts as I leaned forward to stir my coffee. They were in good shape – nicely formed, full, pert. My areolae were dark, topped with long, sensitive nipples. For some reason, then, I desperately wanted to show Tony. To open my blouse, lift my bra up and show him my breasts. I felt strangely alive – powerful, elated, wickedly alive with sex.

It was then that I knew I could lure any man I wanted into my bed. Suddenly, I realized the power I had as a woman. I'd been used by a man, and thrown away, tossed aside like a piece of rubbish when he'd finished playing with me. But now, *I* had power!

Sally had made one or two cutting remarks concerning my marriage and now I found myself burning with a strange desire for revenge. She was a friend, and a good one, but that didn't seem to matter as I gazed into her husband's eyes and licked my lips provocatively. All my morals, my conception of right and wrong, melted, trickled away, leaving me free of guilt as I undid the top three buttons of my blouse.

'It's hot tonight,' I remarked, fanning myself with my blouse, revealing my full bra straining to contain my heavy breasts.

'It's going to get hotter, according to the weather forecast,' he replied, trying to avert his eyes. 'I . . . I'd better be going, I suppose,' he mumbled awkwardly, glancing at his watch.

'So soon?' I asked, adding impishly, 'Oh, of course, Sally will want you back at your post, back by her side where she can keep an eye on you – stifle you.'

He frowned and pursed his lips. Gazing at me with a pained expression, I knew that he wanted to prove that he wasn't under his wife's thumb – that, although he'd not been allowed to go on the stag night, he wasn't completely under her control.

Standing up, I took my empty cup to the sink, hoisting my skirt up as I reached up to the cupboard for two wine glasses.

Placing the glasses on the table, I opened the fridge door, bending over further than necessary, keeping my long legs straight as I took a bottle of wine from the shelf. I could feel his eyes on my thighs, my buttocks, and a shot of adrenalin coursed its way through my veins. *I had power!*

'You'll stay for a glass of wine, won't you?' I smiled, my blouse falling open, exposing my half-cup bra, my deep cleavage, as I turned to face him.

'Er . . . Just one glass, then,' he replied hesitantly, glancing at his watch again.

'Phone her, if you're worried about the time,' I suggested with a hint of sarcasm. 'Use the one in the hall.'

'Yes, I . . . I think I will,' he stammered, rising to his feet. 'I'll just let her know that I'm . . . that I won't be too long.'

I listened at the door as he made his excuses, told his male lies. 'I shouldn't be too much longer, love. I've got the machine in bits, it needs quite a lot doing to it. Well, it was *your* idea! I wish you wouldn't volunteer me for this sort of thing! OK, love. No, not much longer than half an hour. Yes, me, too.'

Returning to the kitchen, he stood in the doorway, a look of relief in his expression as I passed him his wine and suggested that we sit in the lounge. Placing the wine bottle on the coffee table as he followed me into the lounge, I sensed that he felt awkward. He obviously wasn't used to being alone with a single woman, a woman flashing her bedroom eyes – her wet panties.

We sat on the sofa, sipping our wine, talking about the weather and how nice it would be to have a barbecue. The inane conversation continued as I reclined, relaxing, my skirt riding up my thighs. He gazed nonchalantly around the room, pretending not to notice, admiring one of Jim's awful paintings of a ship enduring a raging storm.

Seizing the opportunity, I discreetly pulled my skirt higher

– perhaps a little higher than I'd intended. Turning his head to look at me, Tony's eyes widened as he glanced down at the swell of my panties, scarlet now with my copious juices. Another shot of adrenalin coursed its way through my body and my stomach somersaulted as I realized what I was doing to him.

'You've changed since . . .' he began hesitantly. 'Since you and Jim . . .'

'Yes, I have. As I said, I'm free now, single – and happy.'

'I'm happy, too,' he declared unconvincingly.

'Are you?' I asked. 'Are you happy knowing that the lads enjoyed a stag night, and you weren't allowed to go?'

'Happiness doesn't depend on whether or not you're allowed . . . I mean, able to go out on your own, without your partner – it's not like that.'

'Would you stop Sally from going on a hen night?'

'No, I don't think so.'

'There's an imbalance, then. It's one-sided, as most relationships are,' I proffered.

'No, I . . . I wouldn't say that, exactly!' he returned awkwardly, his eyes darting from mine to my drenched panties.

'Then, what *would* you say?'

'I . . . I don't know. I mean, there's got to be give and take in a marriage. Compromise, that's the word.'

'So, you're not allowed to go out on a stag night, but she can go out on a hen night. Is that compromise? Is that fair? Is that what you'd call a balance?'

Tony shifted awkwardly on the sofa, his eyes between my thighs again as he nervously rolled his wine glass between his palms. I was enjoying my wicked game. The sense of power was incredible, overwhelming. I – a mere woman – was in control, while he, a man in a man's world, was confused, weakening, floundering.

I could so easily wreak havoc between him and his wife. Even without using my body I could keep him chatting, compliment him, play on boosting his male ego – and he'd be late home. Not only did I have the power between my legs, but in my mouth. What man could resist listening to my flirtatious words?

'I wish Jim had been more like you,' I sighed, sipping my wine. 'You're such an understanding man. Sally's a lucky woman – I hope she appreciates you.' He smiled again. I knew what he was thinking – Sally didn't appreciate him at all!

'It's not always easy to . . .' he began.

I smiled sweetly. 'After several years of marriage, you take for granted and you're taken for granted. That's the way it is. Does she *genuinely* appreciate you?' I prodded as he glanced at his watch yet again. 'Does she know how lucky she is to have an understanding and extremely attractive man like you?'

Tony sighed and finished his wine. Placing his glass on the coffee table, he moved forward, sitting on the edge of the sofa as if about to leave. My words were playing on his mind, I knew. He was thinking, wondering about Sally. He was also thinking about my panties, and what lay beneath the thin, wet, scarlet material.

'I think we both appreciate each other,' he said after some deliberation.

'She doesn't take you for granted, then?' I persisted.

'No, she . . . As you said, after several years of marriage, an element of taking things for granted creeps in, but . . .'

'Too many women ignore their husband's basic needs, their desires,' I interrupted, taking the bottle and filling his glass. 'I don't only mean sex, of course. Take the stag night, for example. You needed to go, to join your male friends, to escape for a while, to have a little fun – and you were denied that basic need.'

'I wasn't *denied* . . . It wasn't a case of my not being *allowed* to go!'

'You mean, you could have gone – but it would have caused problems?'

'Yes . . . No, no, not really! It's just that Sally doesn't always see my point of view. She said that I hadn't considered her when I'd arranged to go out with the lads, which is true, I suppose.'

'You'd *arranged* it?'

'Well, I'd said that I'd be going, yes.'

'God, you are under the thumb, aren't you? I wonder what your friends thought when you didn't turn up? I'll bet they all had a good laugh!'

Tony frowned, pondering my words as he sat back on the sofa. I was winning the battle, although I wasn't sure at that time exactly what the battle was about. Did I really want to destroy his marriage? I wasn't sure what I wanted – until I thought of him leaving, going home to Sally, kissing her, making love to her, leaving me alone in the loneliness of my quiet house.

I knew that the time had come to use my pussy power, to put it to the test and determine its true potential. Where to start? Grab him? Pull him close and kiss him? Stand before him and slip out of my clothes? The game was new to me. How should the seduction begin?

'It's getting hotter,' I sighed as he gulped his wine. 'Are you hot?' I asked, placing my hand on his knee. He looked down at my slender fingers as I moved my hand up his leg and gently squeezed his inner thigh. Was his penis stiffening now? Gazing at his trousers, I imagined that it was.

Sliding my hand further up his thigh, closer to his crotch, I looked into Tony's brown eyes. What was he thinking? What were his male thoughts? So close now to breaking him, I mustered all my courage and grabbed his crotch, squeezing the hardness in my hand. He closed his eyes and sighed, wondering, no doubt, whether he had the power to resist. He was obviously fighting a raging battle with his conscience. His thoughts would be swirling, lurching between my hand, the pleasure, the excitement, the danger – and his wife.

Gently kneading his hard bulge, locating what I imagined to be the end of his penis, I leaned forward and kissed him. He responded, pushing his tongue deep into my mouth and groping beneath my skirt as if he'd been nowhere near a woman for months. Parting my legs, I felt his fingers pulling my panties aside, exploring me there – the soft warmth, the feminine wetness. *I desperately wanted him deep inside my vagina.*

My hand trembling, I tugged his zip down and groped my way into his trousers. I was burning with passion, lust – a rampant desire for revenge and sexual satisfaction. Suddenly, I found myself gripping Tony's warm, hard shaft. My heart pounding as he tasted my saliva, sucked my tongue into his mouth, I moved the loose skin back and forth over the hardness of his knob.

It had been a long time since I'd held a penis in my hand, and I found myself squeezing it as if it were the first one I'd ever held. It was hard, warm, powerful, and I wanted it in my mouth, pumping, sperming over my tongue.

Tony's fingers located the entrance to my vagina, spread my inner folds, opened the portal to my inner sanctum. I felt exhilaratingly rude, dirty, obscene. As his intruding finger circled the soft, pink flesh surrounding my hole, inducing my cunt milk to trickle, I prayed that he'd explore my tunnel, push his way deep into my cunt and finger me.

Then, suddenly, he *was* inside me, massaging my inner flesh, caressing the drenched walls of my neglected vagina. My clitoris ached, throbbed for his massaging attention, but he only fingered me, inducing my cunt milk to flow in torrents and bathe his hand.

'This is wrong!' he gasped, pulling away and gazing into my eyes. Was his conscience winning? 'Sally . . . My wife . . . She'll be expecting me and . . .' As he made his futile attempts to win his inner battle, to cling to his treasured fidelity, I lowered my head. Gazing at his penis, the huge, purple knob, I grinned as I pulled the skin back to capacity. *If only Jim could see me now*, I thought as I opened my mouth and moved nearer to my friend's husband's penis. If only Jim could watch me sucking another man's cock into my mouth! *If only* Sally *could see me now!*

Tony breathed heavily, trembling with expectation as I moved even closer – teasing, tantalizing. I'd never taken another man into my mouth and I was wild with excitement – frenzied with lust. What would it taste like, his knob, his sperm – pumping, gushing? Did they all taste the same? How much cream would he pump into my mouth as I sucked?

Pushing my tongue out, I licked the tip of his hard knob – warm, salty. His penis twitched in my hand and he shuddered, reclining on the sofa and pushing his hips forward, waiting for the inevitable – my lips closing around his glans, my tongue rolling.

I had power, power to tease and tantalize, to break his marriage vows, to destroy his fidelity, to tear down the flimsy walls protecting his precious family unit. And I used that power!

Taking his knob into my hot mouth, I lowered my head, sucking in his shaft, taking in as much of his massive penis as I could manage. Tony let out a long, low moan of male pleasure as I moved my head up and down, using my mouth as I would my vagina. Savouring the salty taste of his silky glans, my thoughts turned to his wife, Sally – my friend. This was *her* penis, *her* possession. This was the penis that had assuaged the cravings of her vagina, pummelled her cervix, brought her untold pleasure – anointed her sacred receptacle with its love.

This was the penis, *her* penis, that she'd sucked into her mouth, loved, fondled, kissed, treasured. But now it was mine – all mine!

A thrilling sense of satisfaction coursed its way through me, waking my body, stimulating my mind. Not only sexual satisfaction, but an inner satisfaction – the satisfaction that comes with power. I could hardly believe what I was doing to my friend's husband, how easy it was to break a married man, to bring him crashing to his knees. Were all men so weak, so eager to succumb to women? I wondered as he gasped, my snaking tongue bringing him nearer to his climax. Was it really this easy to demolish years of marriage?

Intoxicated with the ease of destruction, I moved my head up and down faster, gripping his hardness by the base and using my tongue to bring out his sperm – Sally's sperm. Holding my head, Tony shuddered and cried out. 'I'm coming!' I was in two minds as to whether to leave him in that state, abandon him on the verge of orgasm. But no, I wanted my pleasure, too. 'Coming!' he groaned again as his knob exploded in my mouth and his sperm jetted, splashing the back of my throat, bathing my tongue. God, how I'd missed the taste of sex!

Savouring his male come, I sucked and tongued his pulsating, purple knob as he filled my cheeks with his white liquid. Swallowing hard, I slowed my rhythm as he tried to still me, to put an end to the beautiful sexual torture. Holding back a mouthful of sperm, in my wickedness I deliberately allowed it to dribble from my lips and run down my chin as I sat up and gazed into his deep eyes, my finger running over his wet glans. Licking my lips, allowing him to glimpse his sperm glistening on the tip of my tongue, I returned his smile.

'Was that all right?' I asked, knowing full well that it was more than all right!

'That was . . . God, that was . . .' he gasped as he lay back, waiting for the last ripples of pleasure to leave his trembling body.

As I released his knob, his penis fell and lay limp over his trousers, and I thought again of Sally. What would she say, what would she *do* if she could see her husband now? She would feel as I had when Jim had dropped his bombshell – only worse, I imagined. At least I hadn't actually seen Jim with Caroline, I had no lewd picture etched in my mind as Sally would have if she were to see her beloved husband on my sofa, his penis glistening with my saliva – his sperm running down my chin.

Glancing at his watch, his face lined with guilt, his eyes frowning with anguish, Tony concealed his penis in his trousers and pulled his zip up. The evidence, I mused. He'd wash the minute he got home, wash away my saliva, his sperm, the proof of his infidelity. But the memory of what he'd done would remain forever, swirling in the dark corners of his mind – nagging, consuming his conscience.

Sally would notice a change in him. She'd notice a subtle change in his manner, in his lovemaking. She might even talk to me about it. I'd plant the seed of doubt in her mind, give her cause to worry, tell her that, contrary to what she believed, her husband might well be the same as mine was – a cheating, two-timing, adulterous bastard who couldn't control his base desires.

'I'd better go,' Tony said guiltily, standing up.

'Yes, go home to your wife,' I grinned. 'She'll be worrying about you, wondering why you're taking so long.'

He half smiled. I knew that the cold reality of what he'd done hadn't hit him yet. But it would, later that night, or in the morning: it would come crashing into his mind like a tidal wave. And Sally would notice the change.

Rising, I pulled my skirt down, covering my thighs. He watched as I buttoned my blouse. Hesitating as he opened the door, he was in two minds. Didn't he want my body? He'd felt the wet heat of my vagina, slipped his finger deep into my inner sanctum, massaged my inner flesh – didn't he want to taste me, lick me there? *My cunt ached for him.*

He was torn, I could see that. His thoughts would be lurching again, lurching between me, my body, the dangerous excitement of adultery – and his little wife.

'You'll be back tomorrow to fix the machine?' I asked, my eyes wide with expectation.

'It's Sunday, so . . . I'll need to get the spare part and the shops are closed.'

'Oh, I see,' I replied, dropping my head in disappointment.

'I'll come and take another look at it. Perhaps I can repair the broken part and . . .'

'Oh, good!' I grinned. 'I'll get some more wine in, shall I?'

'No, no, I'll bring the wine,' he replied.

'But, Sally . . . She'll . . .'

'It's all right. I'll tell her that I'm going to see a friend or something.'

'Lie to her, you mean?'

He winced and bit his lip. But he'd soon be a regular visitor, I knew. Soon, he'd be only too happy to come and see me, to cheat on his wife, to lie to her, to betray her. Once his guilt had subsided and his male desires had risen, he'd be round to see me, to fuck me, at every opportunity.

As I lay in my bed that night, I thought of Jim sleeping with Caroline – and Tony, cuddled up beside Sally. Happy couples, happy in their love, happy in the belief that their partners were faithful. *Happy in their ignorance.*

Sally would grope for Tony's penis, not knowing where it had been. She would stiffen her male possession, slip it into her wet vagina, not knowing that I'd sucked the sperm from her cherished monument. But Tony would know – would recall his knob pulsating in orgasm against my tongue, his sperm filling my cheeks. He'd picture me, think of my wet vagina, my creamy sex-liquid, oozing, bathing his invading finger.

Guilt? Yes, he'd feel guilty for a while. He'd feel the piercing stab of guilt as he penetrated his wife, thrust his shaft deep into her hot pussy and thought of me as he fucked her. But I'd soon put an end to that destructive emotion – replace his puerile guilt with a thirst for adulterous lust.

And when the time was right, when his marriage was beyond redemption, I'd dismiss him, cast him aside and leave him to wallow in his lonely, empty world. *As I'd been left alone in mine.*

I imagined enticing Jim to the house, and seducing him. What better way to score over that bitch of bitches, Caroline? What better way than to seduce my ex-husband – her man? After all, he wasn't past committing adultery! A leopard doesn't change its spots. An adulterous bastard is an adulterous bastard – nothing can change that!

Jim would be easy enough to lure into my bed – an easy lay. He enjoyed sex as much as any other man, so why not with me, his ex-wife? If I could convince him that all I wanted was wild sex, with no strings, he'd be round like a shot.

I planned my new life as I lay on my pillow and closed my eyes. My slim, curvaceous body, my bedroom eyes, my wet panties, my words of seduction would entice man after man, husband after husband into my bed. And I'd find satisfaction in the knowledge that all men were equally weak. Jim had cheated on me, discarded me, pushed me aside for a tart – but I had power now. And, as with all men, his weakness would be his downfall. I would destroy relationships – corrupt husbands, watch fidelity crumble, shred wedding vows. *Wreak havoc amongst the hand-holding loving couples.*

I'd have to change my image, I decided. Already, I dressed sexily, but to play the role of a tart, I needed to *look* tarty. I'd wear even shorter skirts – *micro*skirts. Tighter, more revealing tops, stockings, suspender belts and, of course, six-inch, red stilettoes. And thigh-length, red leather boots . . .

I also needed to be well-practised in the fine art of body language – learn to flash bedroom eyes at my friends' husbands, use my eyes to invite, to lure. I needed to practise flashing my panties, too – innocently display my tight, wet, bulging panties to married men.

Tony coming to repair my washing machine had changed my way of thinking, lifted me out of the rut of depression and despair that had swallowed me up. Tony had changed my life. And now I was ready to change the lives of the people I knew – destroy the lives of the people around me by way of revenge for the pain, the hurt, that life itself had hurled at me for no apparent reason.

But I would have to put a stop to the notes. Shadows of those white envelopes, the crude words so cruel against the virginal white paper, lurked in the dark depths of my subconscious, destroying my plans, torturing my soul.

Pulling the quilt over my shoulder, I slept well that night. For the first time in weeks, I slept really well.

Chapter Two

Sally phoned me on Sunday morning asking if she could borrow a bag of flour. I guessed that it was a lame excuse to come round and see me, and I wondered whether she'd already noticed a change in Tony. If they'd made love when he'd arrived home, she would have noticed the difference, the guilt mirrored in his guilty eyes.

Trying to conceal my excitement, I told her to come over straight away. I said that I'd be delighted to see her, and I filled the kettle as soon as I'd put the phone down.

I felt elated, like a child waiting to open my birthday presents. My stomach somersaulted with anticipation, with the prospect of talking to my lover's wife. I was alive with life! At last, *I* was the other woman, the woman who could feel no hurt, no pain. I was removed, and yet crucially involved – the third point on the triangle. I held the key – and my friend's marriage in the balance.

I could seduce her husband again, or leave him to her – the choice was mine, and mine alone. I could lure him away from her, snatch him from their marital home, play with him as a cat plays with a bird, until I grew bored. And then I'd discard him, as I'd been discarded. The tables had turned, as they always do, although we never know which way, or when.

Sally arrived wearing a long summer skirt and flimsy top. As she stood in the doorway with the sun behind her, I discerned her shapely thighs through her skirt. I could clearly see the outline of the small indentations at the top of her inner legs. I'd always imagined the indentations to be a wonderful design feature to accommodate testicles during intercourse. I imagine many things, but I wasn't imagining the outline of her panties – curved, bulging with her full pussy lips!

She wasn't unattractive – far from it, in fact, which only heightened my sense of power. Her dark hair was long and thick, shining in the sunlight streaming in through the kitchen window as she sat at the pine table. Her make-up had been carefully applied, not that she really needed any. She was pretty. With huge hazel eyes, she was extremely feminine, inordinately sensual.

But no matter how beautiful, how stunningly attractive women were, I knew I could snatch their husbands from under their noses – and they were powerless to stop me! Without a tiara, I had the pulling-power of Princess Diana – the jewel between my legs!

'How's the washing machine?' she asked as she rested her arms on the table and looked up at me.

'Tony said that it needs a spare part,' I replied, pouring the coffee. 'Anyway, is everything all right with you two?'

'Why do you ask?'

'Oh, I don't know. Perhaps I'm wrong, but you seem to be worried.'

'I think we're all right,' she smiled, but I could see that something was bothering her.

I wanted her to open up, to talk about Tony, the way she felt about him, the things they did in bed together. I wanted to discover the intimate details of their sex-life. If I could determine what she wouldn't do for him in bed, what sexual act she wouldn't perform, I could fill that void, ensure that he got what he wanted from me – and turn him from her.

'Is there anything wrong, Sally?' I asked concernedly. 'I've known you for some time, and I can't help feeling that something's bothering you.'

'I'm not sure. Tony . . . He seemed different last night.'

'Different?' I frowned, my heart beating wildly with excitement.

'Yes, he was . . . I don't know, I can't quite put my finger on it. He seemed to have something on his mind. When I asked him what was wrong, he shied away from me, as if he were guilty.'

'That's odd. Perhaps he's worried about money?' I suggested nonchalantly.

'No, no, it's not money. He came in and made straight for the bathroom, which I thought strange.'

'Perhaps he needed the loo?' I laughed.

'No, the loo's separate. He had a wash, I heard him. He was in there for some time, and when he came out, he couldn't look me in the eye.'

Time to sow a seed of doubt!

'Ah, that reminds me of Jim. I should have seen the signs, heard the warning bells – but I didn't. Not until it was too late, that is. You don't suppose Tony's got another woman, do you?' I ventured boldly as I joined her at the table and passed her coffee to her.

She flinched, gazing at me with her big eyes as if asking *me* whether I thought Tony had another woman or not. I recalled the times she'd sat in my kitchen telling me how faithful Tony was, how he would never dream of even looking at another woman, let alone go off with one, as Jim had. She'd almost revelled in my plight, delighted in my agony. But now, as we both sat at the very same table, the whole thing had turned round.

It wasn't that I wanted to get even with her, to hurt her. Nothing personal. I suppose I just wanted to hit back at *someone* for the pain and suffering I'd endured. From the minute I began to seduce Tony, I realized that I'd changed, that what I was doing wasn't particularly nice. I'd thought that, after the previous night's events, I'd wake in the morning dripping with the sweat of guilt – remorse. But the long, dark night had roused hidden monsters within me – evil monsters – which only strengthened my resolve. Heightened my desire to wreck marriages.

I didn't want another man, a permanent relationship. As far as I was concerned, men were all lying, cheating bastards! But I didn't want anyone else to have a man, either. Perhaps, subconsciously, I was trying to save my friends from men? Perhaps, by wrecking their marriages, I'd save them from the unexpected and sudden pain of adultery? Best to get it over with, while they were young, and able to cope. *In reality, I didn't give a shit for my so-called friends.*

'Of course he hasn't got another woman!' she laughed, obviously trying to make light of my suggestion. 'I mean, I'd know if he had, wouldn't I?'

No one ever knows – until the end.

'Would you?' I returned. 'Jim was screwing another woman for years, and I'd never have known unless I'd confronted him with that first note. Having experienced a cheating man, I know what the signs are. With the benefit of hindsight, I can see that all the signs, the clues, were there, staring me in the face. For example, when we made love, he was . . . How can I put it? He was good, we were very good together but, looking back, he was sort of removed. The reason being that he was thinking of her! Have you noticed that with Tony?'

It was pretty obvious that she had! She gazed into her coffee cup, deep in thought, probably trying to piece the signs together, the clues. She'd never suspect me, of course, not good old Suzanne Millington. I was the last person in the world that anyone would believe capable of husband snatching!

'When did you last have sex with Tony?' I asked.

'Last night. I was in my nightdress ready for bed when he came home and . . . Oh, I meant to ask you – what time did he leave here?'

'About eight, I think.' *Nine!* 'Why?'

'I just wondered. He was rather late home. Anyway, he joined me on the sofa, after he'd spent some time washing, and, feeling randy, I . . . Well, you know.'

'And what was his reaction? I mean, was he different in any way?'

'He didn't seem to want me near him at first. I persisted and he eventually gave in. The strange thing is that . . . I don't really want to go into the details of my sex life.'

'Go on. It helps to talk.'

'Well, I've never let him come in my mouth. I just don't like the idea of it. Anyway, I was giving him . . . I was doing oral sex, and he said that there must be something wrong with me. He said that other women love their husbands coming in their mouths and that I had a weird hang-up about it. It was unlike him to be so cruel.'

'It sounds as if he's recently experienced it with another woman and . . .'

'I don't know, maybe.'

'What else don't you like doing – sexually, I mean?'

'I won't shave my pubic hair off for him! He can't understand why I won't do it, but it would look awful!'

'He wants you to shave?' I asked incredulously.

'Yes, it's ridiculous, isn't it? I think he must want me to look like a schoolgirl!'

'I'll tell you this, Sally – I'd never have a man come in my mouth, and I'd *never* shave!'

'I'm glad I'm not alone. I was beginning to think that there *was* something wrong with me!'

'No, not at all! Never do anything you don't want to.'

So, I thought as she sipped her coffee. *She won't let him come in her mouth.* In that case, Tony would definitely be round again! But shaving? I wasn't sure that I would go that far! It would certainly please him, turn him on, but . . . I decided to give it some thought later. For now, I wanted to discover as much as I could about Tony, his likes and dislikes, so that I could entice him into my bed – destroy his marriage.

'Jim used to want me to masturbate in front of him,' I continued, eagerly awaiting her reaction.

'Tony bought me a vibrator some time ago. I've never used it, though,' she confessed.

I was enjoying our intimate chat and, as I toyed with my coffee cup, I wondered why we'd never talked like this before.

'You don't masturbate, then?' I pursued, picturing her fingers frantically massaging her clitoris.

'No, I don't. And if I did, I wouldn't let him watch!'

'No, neither would I!' I laughed. 'God, men are weird, aren't they?'

'They seem to be!' she giggled.

She was relaxing, at last, and I decided to continue questioning her, discover more about her sex life. Jim had once suggested that we try anal intercourse. I'd agreed, and quite enjoyed it, but it wasn't something that we'd indulged in very often. I couldn't imagine Sally allowing Tony to stick it up her bum, though! But I asked her, all the same.

'God, yes, he has asked me!' she laughed. 'But there was no way I was going to do *that*!'

'I don't blame you! I suppose there must be some women who enjoy it. Perhaps Tony has found someone who . . .'

'No, no! I'm sure that Tony's faithful. I must have been imagining things last night – blown it up out of all proportion. Anyway, it's been good chatting to you, Sue. It's helped me a lot – thanks for listening.'

'Any time. Keep me posted, won't you?'

'Yes, I will. Any idea who wrote those terrible notes, yet?'

'No, not yet,' I replied dolefully.

'It's awful, writing stuff like that to you. I can't imagine the pain it must bring you.'

'No one can imagine what those notes do to me. Anyway, I'd rather not talk about it.'

'Oh, yes, of course. Well, I'd better be going. I've got the Sunday lunch to prepare.'

'OK. And don't worry, I'm sure Tony's not screwing anyone else.'

'I hope not!'

I needed one last line to shatter her confidence, one last comment to plant the seed of doubt firmly in her mind – but what? Seeing her out, I suddenly had an idea.

'I'll tell you one little trick that might help you,' I proffered conspiratorially. 'Should you suspect that he's been messing around, as you did last night, make him come, and see how much sperm he produces.'

'That's an awful thing to have to do!' she giggled.

'It's a simple test, that's all. It will prove whether he's come recently or not. Try it and see.'

'OK, I will. See you, Sue. And thanks again for being there, for listening.'

'You wanted some flour,' I reminded her, grabbing a bag from the cupboard.

'Flour? Oh, yes – thanks.'

I knew that I'd got it made as I saw her out. What finer way to have her suspect her husband of screwing around than for me to bring him off – and off and off and off – before sending him home? He wouldn't have one drop of sperm to dribble after I'd finished with him! Jubilant, I decided to prepare for the evening, to plan the seduction.

Shave? I was still in two minds. It was something that I'd never contemplated, let alone done! But the hair would soon grow back again. If I went ahead and shaved my pussy, and it really turned me off, my pubes would soon grow again.

Slipping my clothes off in the bathroom, I contemplated my body in the mirror. My pubic bush was dark gold, thick, and completely concealed my pink crack. I wondered whether I was normal as I reached for the can of shaving foam that Jim had left behind. But, normal or not, this was all part of my game of seduction, I reasoned, as I squirted a mountain of froth over my bush and rubbed it in.

Sitting on the bathroom stool with my legs splayed, I grabbed a razor from the basin and began to drag it over the pubic vegetation. Surprisingly, as I scraped the springy curls away, leaving strips of smooth, baby-soft, white skin, I became highly aroused. My clitoris throbbed and I wondered about masturbation.

I'd given up masturbating just before I'd left school at sixteen. It was something that I'd always thought to be very wrong, and potentially damaging! But now, as I carefully shaved my mound, my swelling pussy lips, I decided that there was nothing wrong with indulging in a little self-pleasure. Besides, Tony would love to watch me bring myself off, so I had to get some practice in!

Pulling my outer lips apart, I shaved off the last few sprouting hairs and wiped myself with a warm flannel. This is it! I thought as I stood up and turned to face the mirror. My moment of truth – and what a moment! Gazing at my naked slit, my pouting pussy lips, I gasped, wondering what the hell I'd done. Smooth, soft, hairless, defenceless, my once shrouded femininity was on blatant display.

The sight brought memories flooding back, memories of my schooldays, of lying in my bed at night rubbing my clitoris until I'd reach my secret heaven. Those were heady days of sexual discovery, and I'd loved them. But now, with my ultimate discovery of sex, the power it held for me, I anticipated even more intoxicating days – days of destruction.

Wandering into my bedroom, I lay on the bed, my legs spread, my fingers exploring my naked pussy lips – smooth, soft, warm. Running a finger up my creamy slit, I realized how wet I was. My cunt yearned for attention, ached for an inquisitive tongue. My juices pouring from my hole, I speculated how long it had been since I'd last come. Weeks? Months? It had been too long, I knew that, as I dragged my slippery cream up my sex valley and rubbed it around my erect bud.

I imagined Tony standing at the end of the bed watching me masturbate. He'd like that. The sight would stiffen his penis until he had no choice other than to dive between my naked legs and lick me, drink the come from my hot vagina and then fuck me as I'd never been fucked before.

I wanted Tony *now*! The evening was a long way off – I needed him *now*! I needed to feel his long, thick penis deep inside me, throbbing inside my tightening cunt. I felt dirty, perverted, obscene – sexually excited as never before. I was rapidly changing from an innocent little housewife into a whore – and I loved it.

As I held my fanny open and vibrated my fingertips over my hard clitoris, my legs began to twitch, my stomach rising and falling as the sensations of impending orgasm stirred deep within my womb. I could feel my vaginal sheath rhythmically tightening, spasming, and I imagined Tony's massive cock jetting its spunk inside me – filling me to the brim.

Suddenly, the sensations welled up, exploding between my cunt lips, gripping my entire body, lifting me from the bed and floating me high in the air. My cunt burned with sex, desire, passion as it squeezed out its hot juices, my clitoris throbbing, pumping out waves of incredible sexual pleasure. In my sexual frenzy I pinched my nipples, hardened, ultra-sensitive, squeezing them, milking magical sensations from them as my climax rolled on and on.

Trembling uncontrollably, gasping, squeezing my eyes shut, I eventually brought my knees up to my chest and rolled onto my side. I'd done it, released the pressure, the tension, masturbated, fingered my clitoris to a beautiful orgasm. Fantasizing about Tony, it was one of the best orgasms I'd ever elicited from my clitoris – my beautiful cunt. Thinking of his hard penis driving in and out of my wet pussy had heightened my pleasure incredibly and, again, I found myself longing for him, craving his cock, his cream.

As I rolled onto my back, relaxing, twisting and pulling my wet inner lips, I recalled his knob in my mouth, his sperm gushing, bathing my tongue, filling my cheeks as his heavy balls drained. I wanted to keep his sperm, save some in a jar by my bed so that I could dip my tongue into it and taste him. I craved sex now – cold, crude, dirty sex with a married man.

At least Jim was further from my mind now. Once the only man I'd ever share my body with, the only man I'd suck, he was fast becoming nothing more than some tart's lover. The world was full of married men, and I wanted them all! The pain had subsided – but the anger, the desire for revenge rode on.

As I dressed, I convinced myself that I was trying to make up for those monogamous years, years of thinking only of one man, giving my body to one man. But now, after devouring the fruits of Tony's throbbing cock, shaving my pubic hair, masturbating, and coming as never before, I was on an exciting path of discovery. Where that path would take me, I had no idea, or care. *All I cared for was power, and I had it – cunt power!*

I spent the day thinking about the evening, praying that Tony would come round. Anything might crop up, and he'd not be able to make it. What would I do? Should he not come, how would I get through the evening? As the sun fell gently from the sky I became almost paranoid and began to think that Sally had enticed him into her bed. My mind reeled with confused thoughts. He was her husband, he belonged to her, but I wanted him – desperately needed him. If he didn't turn up, I'd go there, to his house and . . . I didn't know what I'd do. I even considered going to the local pub and pulling a man, any man, to use, to suck, to fuck. But I was desperate for Tony, a married man. Desperate to fuck him – ruin him!

My head aching, I slipped my panties off and pulled my miniskirt up to reveal as much of my thighs as possible. I took my bra off, too. My nipples pressed invitingly through my tight T-shirt – beautifully alluring! He'd notice them, and his penis would stiffen. I'd sit with my legs open and allow him to look up my skirt at my shaven pussy lips. I'd pretend not to notice as he feasted his eyes on my sweet, alluring cunt, gazed at my naked femininity – dreaming of fucking me. Then, I'd lure him to the bedroom, use his body, offer him *my* body – and think of Sally at home waiting for her man. *As I used to wait for mine.*

The doorbell rang at seven o'clock, and I was almost a nervous wreck with excitement and sexual arousal. I could feel my juices seeping from my vagina, running down my inner thighs as I opened the door and gazed into Tony's deep brown eyes. He half smiled as he held out a bottle of wine and swept his dark hair back.

Neither of us spoke as he followed me into the lounge. There were no words, I suppose. He knew that he shouldn't be there with me, but he couldn't help himself. I knew that I shouldn't have my friend's husband there with me, but I was desperate – desperate to come, to feel *him* coming inside my mouth, my cunt. *And desperate to wreck his marriage, as mine had been wrecked by that little tart, Caroline.*

Jim had once brought home a couple of dirty video tapes and we'd watched them together before making love. I knew from watching the girls on the tape how to behave, what men wanted to see and hear – how they wanted a tart to behave. Now *I* was the little tart and, God, was I going to play the part!

Tony sat in the armchair opposite the sofa as I poured the

chilled wine. Passing him a glass, I sat on the sofa and relaxed, parting my legs in the hope that he'd glimpse my naked pussy. His eyes widened visibly and he gasped as I parted my legs a little further, displaying my smiling pussy-crack. Sitting on the edge of his chair, his trousers bulging, he grinned.

'You certainly know what a man likes!' he breathed, his eyes transfixed between my legs as I opened them even more.

'*You* chose the Blue Nun! But I agree, it is quite delectable,' I replied innocently, licking my lips provocatively.

'Most delectable!' he enthused, dragging his eyes from my fleshly epicentre to meet my teasing gaze.

'How's Sally?'

'She's . . . she's all right. She said that she'd been to see you this morning. You didn't . . .'

'What? Tell her what I did to you last night? Of course not!'

'No, no . . . I meant . . . If she were to find out about us, she'd kick me out.'

The poor dear! He wanted me to suck the sperm from his throbbing knob, something that his wife wouldn't do, and still keep his precious marriage intact! Talk about having your cake and eating it! I was convinced – all men were the same. They all profess to love their wives, but one sniff of some extamarital fanny and they're overpowered! I felt hatred for Tony then – for myself, too, for what I was doing. But I was only playing the game, the game of life, the game all married men play – and, probably, most married women.

What was it that drove people to commit adultery? I wondered. Sex? Nothing more, nothing less. I'd always thought that a pussy was a pussy, but men seemed to think that they had to collect them like conkers. Why? They're all the same, aren't they? A cock is a cock. Well, some are bigger than others – Tony's was bigger than Jim's, which pleased me. I supposed it boiled down to the excitement of being with the forbidden person – the danger of being caught with someone you're not supposed to be with. Even though I had no ties, I still felt the danger, the excitement of being with another woman's husband. It was like a tonic, a drug – and I exulted in every treacherous minute of it!

Lying back on the sofa, I pulled my skirt up over my stomach and opened my legs as wide as I could, blatantly displaying my shaven slit to his disbelieving eyes. Parting my pussy lips with my fingers, I exposed my inner folds of wet flesh, the drenched entrance to my hot vagina. Remembering Sally's words about her not masturbating in front of her husband, I massaged my stiffening clitoris and gasped a little, playing perfectly, I hoped, the role of the tart.

But soon, my gasps were for real. No longer did I have to fake the immense pleasure my clitoris was bringing me. Closing my eyes, I was aware of Tony at my feet, gazing at my open cunt as I wantonly frigged. Having a man watch me during my most intimate moments heightened my pleasure incredibly. I felt dirty, crude, as I worked my fingers faster between my swelling pussy lips. It was heaven! There I was, legs rudely asunder, my shaved pussy lips spread, peeled back to expose my innermost femininity, masturbating as a man sat at my feet watching me.

My climax came quickly. Shuddering, I was virtually unaware of Tony as my body became rigid and I cried out as my very being seemed to pivot on my cunt. Unable to control himself, Tony thrust a finger deep into my open hole, heightening and sustaining my incredible orgasm as I vibrated my pulsating bud with my wet fingertips. I thought I was going to die as the waves of sheer bliss erupted from my swollen clitoris. The incessant, shuddering orgasm had me in its grip, and there was no way I could roll off the crest of pleasure as it took me higher and higher.

At last, the waves of sex subsided and I began to slip back into my quivering body. I lay there, my burning pussy open,

Tony's fingers exploring my drenched cavern, my clitoris inflamed and still aching with pleasure. My eyes closed, my hands limp by my sides, I relaxed completely, slipping into a warm pool of lust as I felt Tony's hot breath between my legs as his tongue lapped up my slippery come.

Probing, licking, he cleansed me, drinking my juice as it trickled from my body. Moving up my valley, he centred his attention on my sex-bud, sucking it into his hot mouth and flicking his tongue over the sensitive tip, re-ripening it magically. I imagined him licking Sally's clitoris, sucking out her orgasm as she writhed in ecstasy. I wanted to ask him about her, what she was like in bed, how many times she came, how wet she was, how hard her nipples were when sucked into his mouth. But, sensing the birth of another eruption swirling in my womb, I opened my legs wider, surrendering my intimacy completely to Tony.

Pulling my T-shirt over my head, I circled my hard nipples with my fingertips as he worked expertly on my swelling clitoris. I knew that his penis would be as hard as rock and I heightened his arousal by gasping crude instructions. 'Finger my wet cunt!' I ordered, much to his delight. 'That's it! Finger my cunt and lick me! God, yes! Ah, ah! Coming! Coming in your mouth!'

The waves of lust crashing over me, sweeping me up and sucking me into a sea of pure sexual ecstasy, I let go completely. My entire body trembled violently, my mind swirled as I lay there with my clitoris pulsating in Tony's mouth. His fingers deep inside my tight vagina, he thrust his hand back and forth, maintaining the incredible pleasure emanating from between my splayed pussy lips. I could barely catch my breath. My stomach rising and falling, my breasts heaving, I could only cling to the sofa and arch my back until the inconceivable bliss began to slip away, leaving me panting, my head tossing maniacally, my eyes rolling in my illicit euphoria.

'Nice?' he whispered as he scooped the hot come from my hole with his tongue.

'Yes! Yes!' I gasped, still trying to steady my quivering body. 'Did Sally teach you how to lick a girl's cunt like that?'

'No, she didn't,' he replied, lifting his head and gazing into my eyes as I managed to focus on him. 'Sally didn't teach me anything.'

'Does she like you coming in her mouth?' I persisted, knowing full well that she wouldn't allow him that intimate pleasure.

'Yes, she loves it!' he lied. 'She begs to suck my cock and drink my sperm,' he added – for good measure, I supposed. 'In fact, she can't get enough of the stuff!'

Now he was going too far! Who was he trying to kid? Pathetic man! I smiled sweetly at him, wondering how hard his penis was, and when he'd push it deep into my aching pussy-hole. Unbuckling his jeans, he tugged them down, his penis catapulting proudly to attention. He was big, bloody big, I'll give him that! The previous night I hadn't realized just how mighty his weapon really was. Now I was desperate to have him stretch my cunt wide open, fill it to capacity and fuck me with his magnificent organ. *Sally's organ.*

'Sally's a lucky girl!' I trilled, taking his penis in my hand. 'I'm not surprised that she begs to suck your knob and drink your come!' He smiled, revelling in his boosted male ego as I pulled the loose skin back and admired his purple knob. Cupping his heavy balls in my other hand, I weighed them, kneaded them. 'You're all man, aren't you?' I gasped admiringly.

'And you're all woman,' he replied, eyeing my pinken, open crack – oozing, dripping, sodden.

'Do you like me shaved?' I asked impishly.

'God, yes! Sally shaves, too.'

'Does she?' I smiled, wondering why he had to lie, why he

had to make out that she was so bloody good, so perfect for him. If that were the case, then what the hell was he doing here with me?

He was beginning to annoy me. I know I should have just shut up and let him wallow in his fantasy about his bloody perfect wife, but I couldn't. I needed to fight back, to attack. Perhaps I was jealous? I don't know. Why the hell should I be jealous when he was cheating on her, when I had his hard penis wavering between my legs, ready to sink deep into my tight vaginal sheath? When she was at home waiting for him? I decided to take a shot at him, bring him down a peg or two – once he'd pushed his rod deep into my ravenous hole, of course.

Walking on his knees, he moved nearer to my open body and pressed the purple head of his solid penis between my reddening pussy lips. I looked down, watching as his knob drove into my cunt-hole, dragging my inner lips deep into my hot sheath. His poker slipped into the heat of my furnace, slowly, gently, opening me, filling me, until his balls came to rest against my buttocks. It was heaven, having a married man inside me! I could feel him, his hard knob pressed against my cervix, and I could hardly wait for his sperm to spurt and fill me.

As he began to move his hips back and forth, his huge cock gently fucking me, I smiled. The time was right – he was gasping, gazing down at our coupling, my shaven girl-lips encompassing the base of his massive shaft, my clitoris exposed, hard, ripe. The time had come to strike.

'I saw Sally in the park the other day,' I breathed.

'Oh, did you?' he spluttered, not really wanting to discuss his wife while he fucked me.

'Yes, I thought she was with you at first, but then I realized that it was someone else – another man.'

His eyes caught mine. They mirrored worry, jealousy,

anger. He couldn't bear the thought of another man's penis deep inside his wife's cunt, but he thought nothing of sticking his into mine! The game was improving nicely.

'Who was that, then?' he asked, still working his hips, driving his piston deep into my cylinder.

'Ah, that's nice!' I gasped. 'God, you're big! I love being fucked by you!'

'Who was the man you saw her with?' he repeated.

'I don't know, just some young man. They wandered off into the trees before I had the chance to say hallo. Perhaps she has a bit on the side, like you!' I laughed.

He began fucking me harder, pummelling my cervix, kneading my firm breasts, tweaking my nipples painfully as if trying to vent his anger on me. My body rocking to and fro as his shaft repeatedly withdrew and sank into my tightening hole, I closed my eyes, desperate for his fruits to fill me. Putting all his effort into his adultery, he seemed to forget about Sally. Peeling my pussy lips open, he watched his shaft, glistening with my juices, as it slipped in and out of my trembling body.

I moaned and pushed my hips forward to meet his thrusts as my orgasm neared. He was good, very good, and he knew it! Expertly massaging my clitoris with his thumb, he quickened his rhythm, battering my cervix harder, faster, as he grimaced. I knew that this was it as I began to tremble all over. He was going to come inside me, fill my aching cunt-sheath with his sperm – the sperm Sally awaited.

'Coming!' he cried as his knob ballooned inside me. I could feel his sex-liquid, gushing, squirting, filling my rhythmically spasming cunt. My shuddering climax came, too. My clitoris throbbing with pleasure under his caressing thumb, my cunt gripping his pistoning shaft like a vice, I lay back, opening my legs even further to take him deeper inside me. On and on he thrust, his sperm jetting, his knob throbbing, his balls slapping my taut buttocks until he collapsed over my heaving breasts, his adultery complete – sealed. *Marriage vows shattered!*

We lay there, his penis shrinking within my hot, wet vagina, his muscular trembling body crushing mine. I had set out purely to destroy, but I was finding forbidden pleasure from our union, a kind of inner warmth that I remembered having with Jim. *God, I hope I'm not falling in love!* I thought as I ran my fingers through his hair. *That's all I bloody well need!* Was I frightened of falling in love?

His penis finally slipping out of my sodden hole, he sat back on his heels and gazed into my eyes. 'That was nice,' he murmured, finally pulling his jeans up.

'It was,' I smiled. 'But you're not finished with me yet, are you?'

'You mean, you want more?'

'We've only just started!' I laughed. 'Or have you got to get home to your wife?' I added sarcastically.

'No, no. She thinks I'm going to a friend's after I've done your washing machine.'

'Then you'll fuck me again in a minute?'

'Yes, of course I will!' he enthused, leaning forward and kissing my naked mound.

As Tony kissed and licked my crack, pulled and stretched my aching nipples, I thought again of Jim. I'd entice him round and seduce him, shatter his brave new little world with my shaven fanny. He'd succumb, I knew. He'd wonder at the change in me, of course, and I'd tell him that I had several men all fighting to get into my knickers. I'd also tell him that I'd seen Caroline walking with another man, kissing another man – just to stir things up a little! Whether he believed me or not wouldn't matter – the seed of doubt, of destruction, would be planted and watered.

'I love your smooth, soft cunt,' Tony mumbled through a mouthful of my pink girl-flesh. I gazed down at him. Poor man

– he had no idea of my game, no conception of my intentions. There he was, sucking my pussy folds into his mouth, lapping up my come, his sperm, and there was I – planning his come-uppance. But he wouldn't be alone – just the first of many to fall.

'And I like you nibbling my cunt,' I smiled, pulling my pussy lips wide open for him. 'I want you to fuck me every day, eat my pussy, make me come in your mouth every day.'

'I will! I'll be round every day to fuck you!'

How fascinating, I thought, that a woman's pussy, the soft pads of flesh either side of the dividing groove between her legs, attracted men in their droves. Men paid for it, fought for it, killed for it, even! But even with my new-found awareness, I still couldn't comprehend the real power between my legs, the implications. It was incomprehensible that a simple crack, a hole between my legs, held more power than money – than anything.

But it didn't matter why. The point was that I owned a pussy, an all-powerful pussy, and I was going to use that power to my advantage. To destroy marriages!

'Why don't you kneel astride me so that I can suck you?' I suggested as my clitoris throbbed within Tony's mouth. He looked up, gazing at me between the swell of my firm breasts, and smiled. I knew he'd enjoy that again, seeing as his wife wouldn't allow him to come in her mouth, let alone savour and swallow his sperm. Climbing to his feet, he slipped his jeans off and, kneeling either side of my hips, presented me with his huge penis – solid, thick, beautiful. Pulling the loose skin back, exposing his purple knob, I parted my lips and engulfed him within the heat of my mouth.

'Ah, that's nice!' he gasped, gazing down at my lips stretched around his thick shaft as I swept my tongue over his silky glans. Determined to make it really good for him, so that he'd pester Sally to allow him to sperm in her mouth, I cupped his balls, gently kneading them as I moved my head back and forth, taking his glans to the back of my throat and then squeezing it between my lips. There was a serene satisfaction on his face as he watched my lips roll over his wet shaft – an expression of complete and utter sexual satisfaction.

'You *are* hungry, aren't you?' he laughed as his penis twitched and his knob ballooned.

'Mmm!' I breathed though my nose, closing my eyes as I waited for him to explode in a gush of salty sperm. Sucking him deep into my mouth again, I wondered whether Sally would be suspicious when her husband returned home. Hopefully, she'd attack him, pull his penis out and try to wank some life into it. If he managed to come at all, he'd only dribble a little sperm, confirming her suspicion – and then all hell would be let loose! I'd phone her later, I decided as Tony suddenly gasped and gripped my head.

Moaning through my nose, I savoured his salty come as it filled my cheeks. Surprised at the sheer volume he was pumping out, I had to swallow hard, almost choking as he thrust in and out of my mouth, fucking me like a rag doll. Again and again he rammed the back of my throat, his sperm jetting from his knob, filling my mouth until it dribbled down my chin and splattered over my breasts. Desperately trying to pull away, coughing, spluttering, I finally managed to slip his massive organ from my mouth and gasp for air.

The thing wavered before my eyes, sperm dribbling from its small slit, running down the wet shaft. He was, indeed, a big man! Gazing in awe at the monster as it began to shrink, I wondered how the hell he'd managed to get the whole thing into my tight little cunt-hole. His balls were massive, too. Hanging beneath the base of his cock, swinging from side to side, they beckoned for attention. I leaned forward, cupping them in my hand and kissing them lovingly.

His shaft began to harden as I licked around the head of his penis and I wondered whether he'd be able to come again. Twitching, the thing grew even more, and I took his knob into my hot mouth again and gently sucked.

'I can't come again!' he laughed as I rolled my tongue around his solid knob.

'Why not?' I asked, pulling away to look up into his soul mirrors. 'Or are you saving your next load for Sally?'

'No, of course I'm not! God, that's a thought! I hope she doesn't expect me to perform the minute I get home!'

'What will you do if she does?'

'God knows!' he sighed as I took him into my mouth again. 'Fake it, I suppose!'

I was determined to make him come again, and I licked and sucked his knob until he began to breathe deeply. Three times! I thought jubilantly as he neared his climax. Grimacing, he seemed to be in pain as I gripped his shaft, wanking him as I continued to suck and lick his swollen knob. Shoot! I urged in the conniving recesses of my mind as his body tautened. He was trying, I knew, as he reached down and pinched my nipples. In his treacherous, pathetic adultery, he was striving to give me his sperm – unknowing that Sally would demand it when he got home sweet home.

My mouth suddenly engorging with my spoils, he moaned, cried out that he'd come three times. *That's nothing!* I thought as I swallowed. *I can come three times in as many minutes!* Poor Tony, he was done, finished. Grimacing, gasping, he pulled away, his knob shrinking quickly as he climbed from the sofa and stood before me. Licking my lips, I looked up and smiled. He'd had enough, I knew. I'd save my greatest delight for another time, I decided.

Maybe tomorrow, maybe the next day, I'd allow him to push his massive organ deep into my bottom-hole. That would seal our adulterous relationship. After that, he'd have no option other than to return for more and more lewd sex, until Sally discovered his secret and called time. *Threw him out!*

Making his excuses, he pulled his jeans on and fled the house, barely managing to say goodbye as he slammed the front door shut and ran home, covered in guilt, to his wife. Grabbing the phone, I rang her, just to see how she was, if she'd been missing her precious possession.

'What time did Tony leave your place?' she asked peevishly. 'He was going to pop in to see Steve after, but he's still not home.'

'Ages ago!' I lied, the taste of his sperm lingering on my wicked tongue. 'He couldn't fix the machine so he left, ages ago.'

'I rang Steve, and he's not been there,' she confided with some anxiety in her voice.

'I don't want to sound crude, Sally,' I said firmly as I fingered my sperm-drenched pussy-hole. 'But give him a good wank when he gets in. That'll prove it one way or another.'

'I'll give him a bloody good wank, all right!' she fumed. 'I'll wank him to death if he's been screwing around!'

Relaxing on the sofa, my fingers caressing the wet folds between my pouting pussy lips, I smiled. A good day, I decided – a very good day! But tomorrow would be even better! I'd discover the outcome of the wanking session, and I'd have Tony again.

I'd give Jim a call at work – ask him round to discuss something. I didn't know what, but I'd make up some excuse or other to bring him round to the house. He'd lie to Caroline, of course, as he used to lie to me. And then he'd come round – and come! *Another death knell for the dishonourable institution of marriage!*

Chapter Three

Ten o'clock Monday morning and I was already an hour late for work. *Sod the library!* I cursed as I climbed from my bed to answer the front door.

I wasn't too badly off, cash-wise, and there and then, I decided to quit my part-time job and put all my efforts into screwing my friends' husbands. Should money become tight I could even charge them for sex, I mused as I slipped my dressing gown on and bounded downstairs.

'I saw your car and wondered why you weren't at work,' Jilly, my neighbour, smiled as I opened the door and picked up my mail. 'Is everything all right? You're not ill, are you?'

'No, I'm not ill, I just overslept, that's all,' I replied. 'Come in, I'll put the kettle on.'

'No, I can't. Derek's got the day off to do some decorating so, rather than get under his feet, I'm going to my mother's for the day,' she trilled happily.

'Oh – OK, then. But do come round for coffee one morning.'

'Yes, I will. Maybe tomorrow. Well, I'd better go, I promised her that I'd be there by ten.'

'All right, Jilly. See you tomorrow, perhaps – bye.'

So, Derek's got the day off, I thought wickedly as I skipped upstairs. And Jilly's out for the day – how interesting! Another conquest? Why not? Derek was in his early twenties, not bad looking, and a dab hand at DIY – the wallpaper and paint brush variety, that is! Deciding to pay him a visit, I took a quick shower and slipped into my miniskirt and T-shirt – braless and knickerless, of course.

I felt no guilt. Jilly was about nineteen, naive, and very attractive – model material by anyone's book. But instead of pursuing a glamorous career, the poor girl had gone and got married. She'd been a good neighbour to me, but that wasn't going to stop me using her husband for sex – destroying her marriage!

I tried to convince myself that I felt sorry for her. I knew that the time would come when she would announce proudly that she was pregnant and, inevitably, Derek would be pushed into the back seat. He'd start cheating on her, lying to her, screwing around – and I had to save her from that! Didn't I?

I was sure that, at her tender age, Jilly would have no real experience of men. She wouldn't know how to pleasure her husband properly – suck his penis into her mouth, roll her tongue over his purple knob, swallow his come. I was also sure that, although only recently married, Derek would fall prey to my priceless, shaven pussy – my secret weapon!

Opening my mail before visiting Derek, I was horrified to discover another anonymous note – posted, this time, from my own town. Reading the words through carefully, I immediately read them again. The scrawl was almost like a child's handwriting – but the words were adult enough.

They told of Jim and Caroline – how they were having magnificent sex, how Jim had left me because I was no good in bed, how my cunt was too slack. They crudely depicted Caroline's cunt – her hot, tight, wet pussy and how, during the evenings, she would become Jim's sex slave, doing anything and everything, to and for him. I felt sick, angry, bitter.

I couldn't get the notes out of my mind. Tormenting me, my very being, I despised them! My marriage was over, for good. What was the point in writing hateful letters? I *had* to clear my mind and put a stop to the notes. For my sanity, I had to! But how?

Derek smiled as he opened the back door to me. His blue

eyes met mine, and I felt embryonic arousal stir in my womb. Many times we'd met, chatted over the garden fence, enjoyed a barbecue. But now I was looking at him in a new light – the light of potential seduction. *Destruction!*

He was well built, and I imagined his body to be hard and muscular. I noticed his eyes gazing at my stiffening nipples pressing through my tight T-shirt as I stood there wondering how long, solid and thick his penis would be when aroused.

He was a man, a male with male thoughts, needs and desires. How easily would he fall? I wondered in my wickedness. How long would it take before I had him where I wanted him, grovelling between my legs, licking my cunt, attending my most intimate feminine needs?

'I'm afraid she's out,' he apologized, his jeans covered in paint, his checked shirt tattered and torn. 'I'm doing some decorating,' he explained, looking down at his clothes.

'Oh, I won't bother you, then,' I replied, praying that he'd ask me in.

'No, it's all right – I need a break, anyway. Want some coffee?'

'If you're sure that . . .'

'Yes, course I'm sure. Grab a chair and I'll put the kettle on.'

Poised at the table, my skirt suitably riding my thighs, my smooth pussy lips inadvertently on display, I prattled that I'd wanted to ask Jilly about a recipe. Rattling cups and saucers, he didn't turn as he explained that she'd gone to see her mother. Then, grabbing a biscuit tin from a shelf, he swung round on his heels to face me.

I knew what he could see. Gazing seemingly nonchalantly out of the window, I knew he was confronting my young pussy-crack, smiling innocently out at him. My might, my power, my weapon, was on trial, and I trembled inwardly. How would he react?

The biscuit tin dropped to the floor, loudly. Bursting open, the custard creams spewed over the vinyl tiling like a shower of sperm from a pulsating knob.

'Sorry,' he smiled distractedly, kneeling down and scooping up the broken biscuits.

'What a mess!' I gasped, gazing down at him. 'Here, let me help.'

'No, you stay where you are,' he declared, looking up, his eyes level with my gaping pussy.

Doing my best to appear oblivious to the fact that he was devouring my shaved mound, my naked crack, with his incredulous gaze, I turned my head and gazed out of the window again, mumbling something about the geraniums. He took an eternity to clear up and I wondered what he was thinking, what thoughts permeated the vile swamp of his male mind as he beheld my crudely displayed womanhood.

He'd be thinking about his wife, Jilly – about remaining faithful to her. And wondering at me – why I'd shaved, why I was knickerless. He wouldn't guess that I'd set out to seduce him – not yet, anyway. And in his wildest dreams, he'd never imagine that my mission was to destroy his marriage!

He was just another man, I ruminated, my stomach somersaulting with sexual excitement as I felt a little juice trickle over my inner lips. Another man with male thoughts and base desires that he couldn't control. Fidelity was a meaningless word when it came to the male species. It might mean something initially, during the first flush weeks of marriage when wives are young, fresh and exciting. But the word soon paled into insignificance as their ever-rampant cocks ruled their heads.

And when they confronted me, the unlikely Suzanne Millington, the serial marriage-wrecker, they would be swallowed up in the filthy mire of their own corruption!

'How's Jilly?' I enquired sweetly as he eventually stood up

and tipped the contents of the biscuit tin into the new pedal-bin – a wedding present, no doubt. His face was flushed, his jeans full with his obvious arousal.

'She's fine. Er . . . What was I doing? Oh, yes, coffee.'

'You're enjoying married life, then?' I probed. 'It's been six months now, hasn't it?'

'Yes, six months last week. Money's tight, which doesn't help, but we're getting by.'

'Lack of money causes arguments,' I broached.

'You can say that again!' he groaned.

'Oh, I didn't mean . . .'

'It's all right. No doubt you've heard us rowing over money.'

'Jim and I used to argue about money, not so much the lack of it, but how to spend it!' I laughed, remembering how bloody tight Jim was with his cash.

'How are things with you, now? Now that you're on your own, I mean?' he asked as he placed a cup of coffee before me and sat down, strategically distanced from the table to afford himself a good view of my delicious girl-crack.

'I've been receiving anonymous notes – terrible notes about Jim and Caroline, the things they get up to in bed.'

'God, that's wicked! Any idea who's sending them?'

'I don't want to know – a monster, probably. I just want them to stop.'

He wasn't interested in the notes, I realized that! He couldn't keep his eyes off my pussy. I could see that he was trying desperately not to look, but his gaze was dragged back to my gaping cunt by the magnetic force there – the power. Shifting his chair for a better view, he stifled a gasp as I twisted round to admire the garden again – opening my legs wide.

My excitement was raging now, my womb fluttering, my hands trembling, my expectant clitoris throbbing. Not sure of my strategy, I turned quickly to face him, catching his gaze – shock in my wide eyes.

'Oh!' I exclaimed, looking between my legs shamefully. 'God, I'm sorry! I thought . . . I thought I'd put my panties on! What must you think of me?'

I knew what he thought of me – a tart, a woman, an object to be used. Fucked.

'I think you're a very attractive, sexy, young lady,' he smiled.

Beginning to slip and slide from his bedrock of fidelity!

'God! I'm so embarrassed! I really didn't . . .'

'Don't worry! I've seen it all before, I can assure you!' he laughed, his jeans almost bursting open.

'It's a good job Jilly isn't here. God knows what she'd think!' I smiled.

'I know what she'd think!' he retorted with a hint of anger.

'What?' I asked innocently, treacherously, sipping my coffee.

'She'd react the same way she always does when it comes to sex. She'd . . . No, I'd better not say anything.'

I knew that I'd hooked him! They were having problems, sexual problems. At last, I'd discovered the way in, uncovered the chink in the fragile shell of their marriage. And, like a termite, all I had to do was crawl in and slowly chew away at the foundations. Then, at a certain point of weakness, the marriage would crumble.

I still couldn't believe how easy it was to infiltrate relationships, divide couples, drive a wedge between them, set them apart from each other. My power was almost frightening and I began to question my actions, my motives. My aim had been purely to seek revenge for the way I'd been treated, but now I was enjoying my conquests. The desire for revenge was still there, still an obsession – but the desire for sexual satisfaction was as strong. After my sheltered upbringing, and then my boringly monogamous marriage to Jim, I was becoming a nymphomaniac. I *was* a nymphomaniac!

'Do you want to talk about it?' I asked softly, trying to sound understanding.

'I really don't know,' he sighed despondently. 'It's just that . . . Before we were married, things seemed to be OK, but after the wedding, everything went downhill. I can't remember when we last did it!'

'Oh, I *am* sorry. What's causing the problem? I mean, there must be a reason.'

'Jilly's the problem! She's either too tired, too bloody hot . . . And when we *have* done it, it's been pretty hopeless. She won't see anyone about it. In fact, she just pretends that everything's fine. She kids herself that we haven't got a problem.'

'God, you must feel awful! I mean, a young man like you, with no sex life! You must feel . . .'

'I don't know what I feel. I've told her that we'll have to sort it out. We can't go on like this. Well, *I* can't, anyway!'

He was in dire need of physical contact, and so was I – preferably his penis in contact with the dripping walls of my steaming vagina! I had what he wanted, what he was being denied – a hot, tight, wet cunt. And he had what I wanted – a hard throbbing penis. He also had a marriage. I didn't want that – but I wanted to destroy it! The thought suddenly struck me that my desire for revenge was getting out of hand, that perhaps I needed to see a psychiatrist. But I'd probably only open my legs and seduce him on his couch!

'It's not easy for me, either,' I smiled. 'I've been alone now for some time and . . . Well, you don't want to hear about my problems, you've got enough of your own, by the sound of it.'

'No, please . . . We both have something in common, we're both lonely,' he confided, exuding a yearning for someone to listen to him, to understand.

'Perhaps we should get to know each other a little better?' I suggested, winking at him and licking my lips provocatively.

'What do you mean?' he asked, his blue eyes frowning now, for some reason, almost fearful.

'Well, I need sex as much as . . .'

'No, no . . . I'm sorry, I didn't mean to infer . . .'

'What's the matter, Derek?'

'It's Jilly. I can't commit . . .'

'Adultery? Why not? She doesn't want you, sexually. Besides, she wouldn't know. What she doesn't know can't hurt her, can it?'

But she'll find out, of course!

He was proving a tough cookie. I'd thought he'd have dived between my legs at the first opportunity, but obviously not. I decided to call his bluff, make out that I was going home, leaving him with no option other than to picture my naked, open slit and masturbate. I'd give him one last glimpse at what he'd be turning down, I decided, opening my thighs and looking down to my gaping, pink crack.

His hands were trembling as he gazed open-mouthed at my hairless pussy, my pink inner lips protruding so invitingly. Could he really say no? Subdue his base, male desires, his instincts, and deny himself the pleasure of my young body? Abstain from the sex, the lust, that my wet, smiling pussy lips were offering him?

'I must go,' I said, rising to my feet and pulling my skirt down. He looked up at me, his eyes brimming over with confusion, longing, arousal. Aware of a flow of warm, sticky juice running down my thighs, I moved closer to him. God, how I needed his penis thrusting, pulsating inside me! 'You'd better get on with the decorating, you naughty boy!' I giggled impishly, jutting my hips. 'Thanks for the coffee.'

He looked straight ahead, gazing at my tight skirt following the slight swell of my stomach. This was it, I thought methodically. It was now or never. His thoughts must have been swirling around between my legs, my wet cunt, his penis aching in his tight jeans – and his new wife. Suddenly, he thrust his hand up my skirt and parted my hot pussy lips. Before I could speak, he'd pressed his fingers into the tightness of my saturated vagina, exploring my inner flesh, massaging the silky walls of my sex-sheath.

Lifting my T-shirt over my head, I exposed my rounded breasts to his wide eyes. Firm, ample, topped with long buds, they were fine specimens, aching to be sucked. Would he like to eat my nipples? I wondered. Or would he prefer to slip his penis between my breasts? I'd pull my tits together, crushing his hard cock between them as he fucked me there. He'd come, shoot his cream over my neck, my face – and like a good pussycat, I'd lap it up. I desperately wanted him now, coming inside me, coming over my nipples – coming all over my naked body.

Leaning back on the table to steady my trembling legs, I lifted my skirt up over my stomach and stood with my feet wide apart, exposing my shaved mound, my juicy crack, to his ravenous eyes. Another man had succumbed, fallen prey to my hot, tight pussy! I gazed down at him, fingering me, exploring me, using me – cheating on his wife. He was staring at my swollen outer lips encompassing his fingers, my slippery girl-juices decanting from my tightening sheath, trickling down his hand.

My intimacy open, exposed to my neighbour's husband, I grinned wickedly. I imagined myself working as a prostitute, preying on men's greatest weakness, taking their money in return for opening my body to their male eyes, their male organs. But my returns would be more than mere money – my rewards would be sexual satisfaction, and destruction!

As Derek moved forward on his chair, his mouth ever closer to the open centre of my quivering body, I half hoped that his wife would come home and catch him in his lewd act of adultery. She'd scream hysterically, go wild – psycho! The picture of her husband fingering my cunt would be branded into her memory, burnt into the very fibres of her mind – forever. After the courting, the engagement, the wedding, the home-building, their marriage would crumble in seconds. The dust would rise, like the Phoenix from the ashes. But there could be no new life for the relationship. There'd be nothing left to salvage.

As Derek continued his manual excavation of my cunt, his mouth drooling, I resolved to be caught – caught with a husband in an obscene entanglement of naked limbs, by an unsuspecting wife – or an unsuspecting Caroline! She'd discover me with Jim, my ex-husband, her live-in lover. I'd be sucking sperm from his pulsating penis and he'd be lapping at the wet folds between my swollen pussy lips with his tongue, when she'd discover us. Screams would rend the air – Caroline's hysterical screams of insufferable mental pain!

'You've got a lovely cunt,' Derek breathed, kissing my smooth mound, licking the soft skin just above my alluring pussy-crack. Peeling my swollen lips apart, he licked the glistening hood of my clitoris, breathing in the scent of my female sex-juices.

'Does Jilly enjoy you opening her pussy lips and licking her cunt out?' I asked crudely.

'No, she won't let me,' he sighed unhappily.

'Does she suck your cock?'

'No, we don't have oral sex – we don't have sex!'

'Then you'd better use *me* to satisfy yourself, use *me* for sex. I only live next door, so my cunt will never be far away from you. All you have to do is ask, and my cunt is yours, and yours only.'

'Don't you have other men?' he asked, his wide eyes looking up at me, praying that he was the only one.

'There's no one else,' I smiled as he popped my clitoris out from its protective cover and sucked it into his mouth. 'I only want you, Derek. No one else.'

His eyes smiled as he swept his tongue over the tip of my clitoris. The poor, foolish man! He thought that I was his, that I belonged to him. He thought he was special to me, that I felt something for him. I felt something for him all right – complete and utter contempt!

His wife obviously wasn't special to him. She was nothing now that he had the use of my body, my cunt. He didn't need to turn to her and beg for sex any more. He must have thought it was his lucky day – but luck didn't come into it! He was merely a pawn in my wicked game, nothing more. And when I'd finished with him, wrecked his marriage, destroyed him, I'd knock him off the board and find another pawn to play with.

'Perhaps Jilly's a lesbian!' I giggled as he slurped and licked the inner folds of my pinken slit. I can't think why I said it, the words just tumbled from my mouth. He didn't answer – he couldn't, his mouth was full of my wet, fleshy folds.

In my perverse thinking, I imagined licking between Jilly's cunt lips, bringing her clitoris to orgasm with my tongue as she lay naked on my bed. I imagined Derek walking in, catching us in our lewd, lesbian coupling. Perhaps it would work both ways? Why lure only husbands into my lair? Why not wives, too?

There must be some married women who were latent lesbians, I reflected. Tracy, a friend I'd known since my school-days, had once told me that she'd had lesbian tendencies. Apparently, during her teens, she'd had some sort of relationship with another girl. She'd eventually married Craig, a handsome hunk, and they'd bought a house not far away from mine. Must add the happy couple to my list! Perhaps I could entice her to have lesbian sex with me – and Craig would discover us, licking each other's cunts, mouthing, lapping – coming. God, my thinking was going way off course!

'Jilly won't let me spank her,' Derek confessed unexpectedly in an odd tone as he forced his fingers deeper into my cunt, gripping my buttock tightly with his other hand. 'I like spanking women,' he added wickedly, a strange glint in his eye as he looked up at me. 'I like thrashing their buttocks.'

'Do you?' I asked, somewhat astonished. 'Why?'

'I don't know why – I just like it. I like putting girls across my knee and thrashing their bare bottoms until they scream and beg for mercy.'

I was more surprised than shocked – spanking was something I'd never contemplated. Jim had never suggested it, but I'd read about it, of course, heard about it – but never considered it. My hot juices were flowing in torrents now, my mind reeling with images of me lying over Derek's knee as he spanked my burning buttocks. Wondering how many men were into spanking, and how many wives weren't, I decided to make it my forte.

'Would you like to spank *me*?' I asked, running my fingers through his blond hair as he licked the length of my inflamed sex valley. He looked up again, his eyes wild with excitement – almost evil. 'Well, *would* you like to smack my bare bottom?' I repeated, licking my full lips.

'Yes, I would!' he breathed as he stood up, the fire of uncontrollable passion burning in his deep blue eyes. 'Bend over the table and lift your skirt up!' he instructed in a low, husky voice.

'Like this?' I taunted, leaning over the table, my feet apart, my skirt high over my back.

God, if Jilly were to walk in now! I thought as he cupped my buttocks in his hands as if weighing melons. She'd scream, rant, rave, sob hysterically – lose all control! Kneeling behind me, her husband kissed my taut buttocks, licked the dark, sensitive crease between them, stimulating me as never before. I sensed his tongue nearing my small hole and I shuddered. He wouldn't lick me there, surely? But he did. Pulling my buttocks wide apart, he probed around my bottom-hole with his tongue, tasting me there, exciting me, waking sleeping nerve endings until I gasped with the immense pleasure and begged him to make me come.

Pressing his tongue against the tight ring of brown tissue, he managed to push the tip inside and a wonderful shiver crept up my spine. It was as if I were giving not only my body, my cunt, to this man – but my very being.

As he tongued my bottom-hole, my mind went off on a weird tangent and I thought again of a lesbian relationship – licking a girl's bottom, groping between her legs. We'd lie head-to-toe on the bed, both drinking the slippery cream from each other's vaginas. The thought sent a delightful quiver through my pelvis and my womb trembled and convulsed.

Lost in my lesbian reverie, imagining that Derek was a girl licking my bottom, I wasn't prepared for the first hard slap across my buttocks, and I jumped, almost falling from the table.

'You're a naughty little schoolgirl!' he cried as he slapped me again. 'You wet yourself in class and you deserve to have your bottom smacked!'

Some fantasy! I thought as he slapped my stinging buttocks even harder. Did Jilly know of his inner desires? Did she know that he fantazied about spanking schoolgirls?

'I'm going to thrash your bottom until you come!' he cried, spanking me again.

The burning sensation was heavenly. My whole body seemed to respond as I imagined that I *was* a schoolgirl with my navy-blue knickers around my knees and my gymslip up over my back. Clinging to the table, I felt my juices pouring from my hot cunt, my clitoris stiffening, aching for relief, as I remembered my dishy school teacher, pictured him behind me spanking my bare bottom with a ruler.

Derek stopped the thrashing abruptly and moved away. Was that it? Was it over so soon? I hadn't come, and I desperately needed to! I lay over the table, wondering what he was up to, whether he was about to push his penis deep into my hot, tight pussy or not. Perhaps he was gazing at my crimson orbs, my pussy lips dangling tantalizingly from my body, dripping with my slippery cream?

'Don't move!' he instructed. I didn't want to move, or speak. I just wanted to stay like that, my femininity crudely exposed, enticingly bared before a man – another woman's husband. Moving my feet further apart and pushing my bottom out, I pictured the view he'd have of my rudely open body, and shuddered. I'd never been spanked before and the experience had woken another side of me. I felt dirty, like a common whore, as I thrust my bottom out even further.

I sensed him behind me, moving about. Was he pulling his penis out – his long, hard, thick penis? My eyes closed, my mind reeling with sex as he lay something across my back, I grinned. 'What are you up to?' I murmured. He said nothing. Suddenly, I realized what he was doing and a bolt of terror shot through me.

The rope tightened across my back, pinning me down as he crawled under the table and tied the ends. 'Derek!' I cried, trying to lift myself up as he secured my ankles to the table legs. 'Derek, what the fuck are you doing?'

Grabbing my hand, he bound it with rope and stretched my arm out. Taking the rope under the table, he bound my other hand. I was his prisoner! 'Derek!' I cried again, fearful now of his intentions. 'I'll tell Jilly!' I threatened pathetically, but he only laughed as he moved behind me and pulled my buttocks apart, stretching the delicate skin within my crease.

My heart leapt as he took a tub from the fridge and smeared a handful of cooling cream between my buttocks. Presenting something to my small hole, he began to push and twist. Hard and cold, I knew it wasn't his penis as the thing slipped past my tightening muscles and sank deep into my bowels. Further he pushed the invader home, and I imagined it to be at least a foot long as I sensed it driving deeper into my trembling body. I cried out in terror as he smeared more cream between my legs. 'Please, Derek! Take it out! It hurts, please!'

Laughing wickedly, he moved around the table, kneeling down and gazing into my wide eyes. 'I've always wanted to tie a woman down!' he confessed, leering at me. 'Jilly won't let me do anything to her, but now I've got you, Sue – and I'm going to live out every fantasy I've ever had!'

'I'll tell Jilly! Unless you let me go now, I'll tell her!'

'She'd never believe you! Naive, trusting little bitch that she is – she'd never believe you!'

My game, my resolve to destroy marriages, had backfired on me. Where was the power now? I'd picked the wrong man, I knew. I'd picked a bloody pervert, an animal! I remembered reading somewhere about a man who lured women to his flat, stripped them, tied them down and lived out his sadistic fantasies. Was Derek like that? I wondered fearfully. He looked normal enough, had always seemed pleasant enough. Quiet, polite, unassuming, he'd been a good neighbour. But wasn't it always the quiet types? With their hidden desires, their suppressed animal instincts, wasn't it always the quiet ones?

Standing up, he slipped his jeans down and exhibited his huge, hard penis. 'Nice, isn't it?' he asked proudly, waving the massive thing threateningly under my nose. 'Now, where do you want it first? Your bum's already full, so that only leaves your mouth or your shaved cunt! What's it to be?'

I said nothing as he pulled his foreskin back and brushed my lips, my chin, my nose, with his purple knob. Should I open my mouth and suck him? I wondered. Better to play along with him than rile him. But what had changed him? All right, I'd provoked him by exhibiting my shaved pussy, but what evil monster had I stirred? I'd expected to turn him on – not turn him into some kind of fiend!

'Why don't you take that thing, whatever it is, out of my bum, and then make love to me properly?' I suggested calmly, trying to appear eager.

'Properly? What, you want it up your bum?' he leered, a wicked glint in his evil eye.

'No, no! In my pussy!' I cried in my terror.

'Your bum it is, then!' he shrieked triumphantly as he leapt around the table and stood behind me.

Pulling the cold object from my bottom-hole, he dropped it to the floor and yanked my buttocks apart. This was it, I knew, as he applied another handful of cream to my anal entrance – but I'd asked for it! I felt his knob there, pressing against my tightly closed ring – pushing, twisting, trying to gain entry to my bowels. His breathing was heavy, deep, and I wondered what else he planned to do to me as his knob slipped past my muscles and invaded the portal to my sacrosanct flesh chasm.

My bottom was stretched open, painfully but arousingly engorged by his massive knob. Fearfully, I waited for him to enter me fully, to push the entire length of his huge weapon deep into my hot bowels and impale me completely.

'You've a tight little bum!' he cried gleefully as he pushed his shaft an inch or so further into my constricted, hot bum-sheath. Saying nothing, I closed my eyes, trying to allow my arousal to outweigh my fear as he pressed his weapon deeper into my quivering body.

Suddenly, he slapped my buttock and I yelped. Again, he slapped me, only harder, and I screamed. He was obviously delighting in my plight. My yelps and screams only serving to drive him on, he spanked me again and again as he finally pushed the entire length of his thick, hard cock deep into my bum. I could feel his heavy balls resting against my cunt lips, his belly pressed against my buttocks. The sensation was heavenly, but still my arousal was suppressed by fear.

Gripping my hips, he began his male thrusting, driving his piston deep into my tight anal sheath, filling my entire pelvic cavity with his huge organ. My body rocked with each thrust, the table gliding across the floor as he took me with a vengeance. Pummelling me, almost splitting me open, he slapped my buttocks again, grunting, groaning, as he lost himself in some weird and frightening fantasy.

'Coming!' he cried as my clitoris throbbed with the beginnings of my own climax. 'Dirty little whore!' he breathed, slapping me again. 'Filthy tart!' I knew then that Jilly had married a monster. I knew why she didn't want sex with him! Suddenly, his body became rigid, my tight anal sheath expanding, dilating to take his ballooning shaft. And then I sensed his sperm gushing into me, filling my bottom-hole, lubricating the obscene, forced coupling.

My clitoris erupted in orgasm as he thrust and pumped me full. My juices pouring down my inner thighs, my cunt spasming, aching to grip on a hard cock, I almost passed out in my sexual delirium. On and on he thrust, his spunk jetting into me, his knob distending my tight tube.

'My clit!' I begged involuntarily. 'Rub my clit!' But he ignored me, my female needs, as he made his last hammering thrusts, draining his huge balls until his heaving body finally stilled.

He remained motionless, his huge shaft impaling me, absorbing the inner heat of my bowels, his sperm swimming inside me. Was he satisfied now? I wondered. Now that he'd come, quelled his sexual force, used me, would he untie me, let me go? As he slipped his shaft from my aching bottom-hole, I gasped. The pleasure had been intense, my climax almost frightening. But my clitoris had been sadly neglected and I needed to come again, properly – in his mouth.

He began spanking me again, slapping my taut buttocks

harder and harder, and I knew that my ordeal was far from over! My mind spun with thoughts of Jilly, the poor young thing who'd probably been put through sexual hell by her evil husband. Why was she still with him? Why on earth live with a man like this? Perhaps he'd threatened her? Forced her to stay with him with his threats of spanking sessions? I'd save her from this evil monster if it was the last thing I did!

At last he stopped his thrashing and moved away. Trying to turn my head to see what he was doing, what vile fantasy he was planning to live out next, I asked him whether Jilly knew about his spanking fantasy.

'Yes, she does. I used to give her a good spanking,' he said, taking the leather belt from his jeans. 'I still do, sometimes.'

'But, you said that she won't allow you to . . .'

'Her allowing me to spank her or not doesn't come into it! If she fucks me about, she gets a good thrashing!'

'Fucks you about?' I asked anxiously.

'Yes, if my food's not ready on time, or if she hasn't bothered to do the shopping properly, I give the little bitch a damn good thrashing!'

'But you don't have sex with her?'

'Mind your own business!'

'You want to have sex with her, don't you?' I asked, wondering what weird relationship they really had.

'Just shut up about Jilly!' he blasted, lashing my inflamed buttocks with the belt.

I took the thrashing – I had no choice! But, strangely, although the belt stung like hell and my buttocks burned, I found myself enjoying it. My clitoris throbbed again. My vagina spasmed, squeezing out my juices as he whipped me. I was dazed, intoxicated with lust – giddy with the sensations emanating from my buttocks, from between my legs. My mind seemed to drift, to float away from me as the pain turned into incredible pleasure – frightening pleasure. With each lash, I jolted, my cunt tightened, my clitoris pulsated, my buttocks twitched.

'Don't stop!' I heard myself cry in my delirium as he dropped the belt. 'Please, whip me again!' He moved round the table and stood before me, his jeans around his ankles, his penis pointing skywards, hard, solid, ready – for what? Turning, he opened the fridge and took a large cucumber from the shelf.

'No!' I screamed as he waved it in my face.

'Do you reckon I could get this up your cunt?' he asked, his eyes glowing, mirroring his inner wickedness.

'No, please! Derek, what the hell's happened to you? Why are you . . .'

'Shut up! Or I'll shove this up your arse!'

Kneeling behind me, he forced the massive cucumber into my hot vagina, filling me, stretching me open so wide that I really thought that I was going to split open! Pushing, twisting, he forced the green phallus deep into my cunt, grunting expletives as he stood up. I felt his penis, his hard knob, between my buttocks again, pressing against my small inflamed hole. Squeezing my eyes shut, I grimaced as he pushed his shaft deep into my bowels again. My pelvis full, bloated, he began fucking me, ramming my tethered body, forcing the table across the floor again until it hit the sink.

Reaching between my legs, he massaged my aching clitoris, hardening my little nodule until, gasping in my sexual frenzy, I reached my trembling climax. 'God, yes!' I screamed. 'Coming! Fuck me harder!' I felt as if the earth was shuddering with me as the table jolted and rocked. On and on the waves of incredible pleasure crashed over me. My entire body was afire with lust, every nerve-ending tingling, every muscle tightening. Then his sperm came again. Gushing, jetting into my sore bottom-hole, filling me, lubricating his pistoning shaft, I could feel the male come – wet, slippery, heavenly.

At last, my climax subsided, leaving me quivering with satisfaction. Slowing his rhythm as his orgasm receded, he finally slipped his penis from my bottom-hole and sat on the chair, exhausted – I prayed! The cucumber shot across the room and hit the floor as I contracted my muscles. My aching holes vacant, gently closing, I lay there, perspiration stinging my eyes, my breathing heavy.

'Want it again?' he asked, rising to his feet.

'God, no!' I cried. 'Please, Derek – leave me now. Let me go, please!'

'I might, if you promise me something,' he grinned menacingly, kneeling before me and looking into my tearful eyes.

'What?' I whimpered.

'Promise me that you'll come back and let me tie you down again.'

'Yes, all right,' I agreed. I had no choice, I knew. All I wanted was to get out of that house and wash my used body, cleanse my aching holes.

As he untied the ropes, I thought of Jilly. I'd talk to her, get her to open up and admit that she was living in constant fear of her evil husband. As I stood up, my back, my limbs aching, I pulled my skirt down and grabbed my T-shirt, staggering to the back door – to freedom. He watched me, his eyes piercing, burning into my very soul as I stepped out into the garden and ran home.

As I showered my aching body, washing away the sperm and cream oozing from my inflamed bottom-hole, I wondered if I'd met my match. Derek was a weird one, to say the least! Or was he simply the same as any other man? Had he just found the courage, the nerve to live out the fantasies that all men secretly harbour in the recesses of their vile minds? If all men harboured such fantasies then, with my body, my offer of crude sex, it would be child's play to bring them to their knees, to drag them away from their wives – and destroy them!

But what about Jilly? I felt sorry for her, anxious for her. I realized then that of all the marriages I'd planned to destroy, Jilly and Derek's simply couldn't continue. For her sake, I *had* to end it!

Spending most of the day gazing out of the lounge window, looking out for Jilly, I tried to make my plans. Confront her? I didn't know what to do. As Derek had said, she wouldn't believe me if I told her that her husband had tied me over the kitchen table and whipped and fucked my bottom. But I felt that I had to do *something*! Apart from the way he treated Jilly, Derek expected me to go there again, to allow him to tie me over the table and repeatedly defile me.

As Jilly walked past my house, I called out of the window and beckoned her in. She smiled sweetly, naively, as I opened the front door. She was pretty, very pretty. Her long dark hair cascading over the swell of her young breasts, her big brown eyes sparkling with life, I could hardly believe that she lived in fear of her husband. She seemed so happy – it just didn't fit.

'I wonder how Derek got on with the decorating,' she smiled as she sat on the sofa. I wondered too! Having spent so much time fucking and whipping me over the kitchen table, I doubted very much that he'd have done any work at all!

'You'll soon find out,' I replied. 'Anyway, I wanted to ask you if you're happy, Jilly.'

'Happy? Yes, of course I am!' she giggled. 'Why do you ask?'

'Because I've heard you both arguing and I . . .'

'Everyone argues!' she interrupted.

'Yes, I know but . . . I hope you don't mind me asking you this, Jilly, but . . . does he hit you?'

'Hit me? No, of course he doesn't hit me! Good God, do you think I'd stay with him if he hit me?'

'Does he whip you, thrash you with his belt?'

She looked down at the floor, her face reddening slightly. I suddenly realized that she'd wonder how I knew about it, how I'd discovered her awful secret. Gazing at her short skirt, her shapely thighs, I wondered what it must be like for her, married to a weirdo – never having sex. All she had to look forward to was a thrashing!

'You can tell me about it, if you want to,' I coaxed gently.

'There's nothing to tell, Sue. We have our secrets, our sexual secrets and . . . How do you know, anyway?'

'I . . . I've heard him. The walls are thin, and I've heard him whipping you.'

'I enjoy it. It's not one-sided, honestly! I love it! I don't mean to be rude, but it's our business, Sue. I think you've got the wrong end of the stick.'

'Are you sure? I mean, you'd tell me if you . . .'

'It's something we enjoy, it's all part of our great sex life – and that's all there is to it.'

Great sex life? I didn't believe her. Convinced that she really despised his leather belt, I decided I'd try to spy on them, get some evidence so that I could help her. At least she now knew that I knew. If ever she really did need help, I hoped that she'd come to me.

'I must go, or . . .' she began hesitantly as she stood up.

'Or what, Jilly?' I asked accusingly.

'Or he'll wonder where I've got to. Don't worry about me, I'm fine, honestly!' she assured me as I saw her out.

'If you ever need me, you know where to find me!' I called as she wandered down the path. Smiling, she waved goodbye and I closed the door, praying that the adulterous bastard wouldn't thrash her for being late or something.

Slipping into the back garden, I wondered whether I would be able to see them in their kitchen if I peered through the hedge. Making a hole in the thick privet, I could see the kitchen quite clearly – Derek talking to Jilly, pointing to something, a tin of paint, I think it was. She seemed happy, smiling, laughing as they chatted. If only she knew that he'd screwed me over the kitchen table! I thought as he took her in his arms and kissed her.

As I watched them, feeling sorry for Jilly, the way he treated her, I tried to think of a way she could catch him screwing me. I wasn't bothered about her feelings for me when she caught us red-handed, I just wanted to see their marriage in ruins. She'd never speak to me again but, in my heart, I'd know that I'd saved her from that monstrous husband of hers.

What I saw next almost stopped my heart. Falling to her knees, Jilly tugged Derek's jeans down and began sucking on his huge penis. Closing his eyes, he leaned on the table as she moved her head back and forth, taking his massive knob to the back of her throat. I could hardly believe my eyes! No sex, he'd said. *The lying bastard!* I thought as I watched her moving her hand up and down his shaft as she sucked on his knob. He'd tricked me, tried to make me feel sorry for him – used me.

Slipping his knob from her mouth, Jilly moved her hand faster up and down his shaft, her tongue licking his glans as his sperm jetted, covering her pretty face, splattering her hair. Sucking him into her mouth again, I could see that she was delighting in drinking his come. Delirious with lust, even when he tried to restrain her she wouldn't let go, sucking him deeper into her mouth, her hand wanking him as if it was the last time she'd ever see him.

Back in the lounge, I sat down and listed all my friends – their addresses, their husbands' names. I was incensed with what I'd seen. Derek had lied to me, used me. They were at the top of my hit-list, Derek and Jilly – their marriage would fall first, I'd see to that! I'd visit Derek again, allow him to tie me over the table and whip me, fuck me. Or perhaps I'd invite him round and ask him to tie me over my kitchen table? Yes, that was the answer. Make sure that Jilly called round at the crucial moment. Leave the back door conveniently open and she'd walk right in on her husband's evil betrayal!

As I wrote my ex-husband's name next to Caroline's, I grinned. It was their turn to savour the bitter taste of infidelity – of lies and deceit. It was late afternoon, and I knew that Jim got home from work before she did – around six o'clock. I'd ring him, make up some excuse or other and ask him round. And, with my pretty pussy on display, smiling at him invitingly, I'd seduce him!

He'd come in my mouth, in my wet vagina, and then go home to *her*. He'd tell his lies, concoct his stories about being caught in traffic, leaving the office late, having to visit someone on the way home. Then he'd slink into the bathroom and wash away the sperm, the saliva, the girl-juice from his penis.

He'd lied to me, betrayed me, and now he was going to do the same to Caroline. The tables had turned. I was winning!

Chapter Four

I wasn't sure how Jim would react when I phoned him. I thought he'd either hang up, or start rowing with me for ringing him at Caroline's place. But I had to try. Somehow, I had to get him round to my house.

Once he saw the naked bait ensconced between my thighs, he'd swallow it, I knew. He was a man, after all! Lifting the phone, my hands trembling, my heart racing, I dialled the bitch's number.

'Jim, it's me – Sue,' I said when he answered.

'Oh, Sue. How . . . how are you?' he asked cautiously.

'Fine! Couldn't be better!' I trilled. 'Listen, sorry to trouble you, but I need to discuss something with you. It's to do with the life assurance we had. I've had this letter, and I can't make head or tail of it. I don't suppose you could pop round this evening and have a look?'

'Er . . . I don't know if . . . I thought all that had been dealt with?'

'That's what I thought. I can't understand it at all. It seems that they want some money . . .'

'From us? They want money from us?'

'It looks that way. I'm sorry to have to call you, Jim, but I don't know what to do.'

'I'll be there in an hour. I won't be able to stay for too . . . I've got to go!'

Banging the phone down, he was obviously frightened of something. That bitch, Caroline, must have come in, and he'd nearly had a heart attack! Talking to his ex-wife on the phone wouldn't be acceptable to her, I knew. Already, he'd be lying to her, telling her that it had been a wrong number. Already he'd be mouthing his male lies!

I'd started the ball of deceit rolling. The trap was set. All I had to do now was spring it at the right moment, and he'd fall prey to my beautiful pussy. My bum still stinging from Derek's bloody leather belt, I tidied the lounge, did my hair and make-up, and sat down to await Jim – my next victim.

It was the first time we'd spoken since he'd walked out and I wondered what he'd thought, hearing my voice after all those weeks. I wondered if he was missing me, my body – my cunt. But no, he had the bitch to service him. He'd be lying to her again by now, making his excuses about going out to see a friend, as he used to with me. God, the tables have turned all right! I reflected happily as I lifted my skirt to monitor my smiling pussy-crack – my bait.

'Come in!' I invited cheerily as I opened the door to find Jim standing on the step, looking nervously this way and that to make sure the coast was clear. He looked just the same – the same clothes, the same Jim, although his hair was a little longer. It was peculiar opening the door to my ex-husband – almost as if we were strangers. After all the intimate times we'd shared, we could have been from different planets.

Although I'd made my plans, and I didn't want Jim back, my stomach churned and knotted as I gazed dreamily into his dark eyes. Fighting off whatever emotion it was, I led the way through the hall. In the lounge, I sat opposite him on the sofa and asked how he was.

'All right,' he smiled, looking around the room – memories flooding back, no doubt.

'And Caroline? Is she all right?'

'Yes, she's fine. Where's this letter, Sue? Only, I don't have much time.'

'I can't find it. I've been searching high and low, and it's disappeared! I had it this morning, but now . . .'

'Well, when you find it, I'll come back,' he said a little impatiently, moving to the edge of the armchair.

'You couldn't take your paintings, could you? Only I don't really want them here,' I said, stalling for time.

'I don't want them. Throw them out, or take them to a charity shop,' he replied indifferently.

Acting quickly, I lay back on the sofa, my legs open just enough for him to glimpse my shaved crack. Praying that he'd notice, I parted my thighs a little further, commenting on the weather and how hot it had been recently. My head turned slightly, I could see him looking up my skirt, his eyes bulging with confusion and desire.

He'd wonder why I'd shaved, of course – but would he ask? He'd probably think that I had another man who liked me naked, hairless between my legs. He'd wonder, too, why I wasn't wearing my panties.

Trying to avert his gaze, he checked his watch and frowned. I knew that he didn't want to go, not yet, anyway. But he'd be worrying about *her*.

'Are you seeing anyone?' he asked, a hint of jealousy in his voice as he gazed between my thighs.

'Why do you ask that?' I smiled, twisting my long blonde hair round my fingers and licking my lips seductively.

'Because . . . I just wondered, that's all.'

'I did sleep with one man, but that was just a passing thing, a mistake,' I confessed.

'A mistake?'

'Yes, I thought it would nice to have a boyfriend, but he was no good in bed. Bloody useless, in fact!' I laughed.

He frowned again as I reclined on the sofa, relaxing, with my pussy on full display. He was confused, and definitely jealous: I could see it, feel it. I knew that he couldn't understand the change in me. He'd probably thought that I'd burst into tears, break down in hysterics and beg him to come back to me. But no, this was the *new* Suzanne Millington – the marriage wrecker!

'By the way, I've got some good news – I got my decree absolute through the other week,' I said cheerily.

'Yes, so did I,' he sighed.

'Are you going to marry Caroline, or just live together?' I probed.

'We plan to marry, later this year.'

'Oh, good! I'm pleased for you, Jim – I really am!'

He couldn't begin to understand why I was so happy, relaxed, so very different than he'd expected me to be. One of my greatest attributes, I decided, apart from my pretty pussy, was my ability to totally confuse people. When confused, confronted with the antithesis of what they'd expected, they floundered hopelessly.

The game was going well, but I needed him to drop to his knees and suck my pussy lips into his mouth. If I was going to destroy his relationship with Caroline, he had to fall clean into the trap. Once he'd tasted, he'd be back for more. Again and again he'd be back, until I tired of him – and arranged his downfall!

'So, you're not seeing anyone at the moment?' he pursued, his eyes still transfixed by my swelling labia.

'No, I'm not. I wish I was, though – I feel so randy these days! Whatever we did or didn't have, Jim – the sex was good, wasn't it?'

'Yes, it was,' he smiled – more memories flooding back?

'Anyway, I'll find someone to satisfy me soon, no doubt. Presumably, sex is good with Caroline? Sorry, I shouldn't have asked you that – it wasn't fair of me.'

'No, it's all right. Sex is OK with her, I suppose.'

'Only OK?'

'Well, it's all right. It's just that . . . It doesn't matter. Anyway, I'd better be going.'

Where was the chink, the vulnerability in this relationship? I wondered. The sex was *OK.* What did he mean by that, exactly? I didn't want to blatantly pry into his sex life, but I desperately needed to know what the problem was. Until I'd discovered his Achilles heel, I couldn't move in for the kill.

'The sexual side of our relationship was so good that I doubt if I'll find anyone to match it,' I continued, watching his eyes for a reaction.

'Yes, I know what you mean,' he sighed.

'Still, you've got Caroline, so at least you're all right.'

'She . . . Yes, I've got Caroline.'

'Things *are* all right with you two, aren't they?' I persisted.

'She works long hours. By the time she gets home, she's tired and . . . Anyway, I really must be going.'

'All right, Jim,' I conceded, wondering how the hell to make him stay. 'You know, since we split up, I've felt alive with life! I'm never tired, never depressed – always happy, in fact! I've given up the library, by the way.'

'Oh, have you? Look, I've got to get back. Let me know when you find the letter, won't you?'

'Yes, I will,' I smiled, standing up with him.

Moving towards him, I reached out and clutched his bulge, and grinned. 'The sex *was* good, Jim!' I whispered huskily, kneading his stiffening penis. 'It was the best!' He glanced at the mantelpiece clock, and then looked into my bedroom eyes. He was near to succumbing to my body, to my pretty crack, to my tight wet vagina, I knew, as his penis continued to harden while I massaged him through his trousers. Imagining Caroline sucking him, swallowing his sperm as he came in her mouth, I fell to my knees and tugged his zip down.

'Sue! I . . . I don't want this! I don't want us to get back together again!' he protested.

'Back together again?' I echoed with a laugh. 'Neither do I, Jim! That's the last thing I want!'

'But . . . but I thought that you . . .'

'Surely I can suck your lovely penis into my mouth, just for old times' sake?' I grinned, pulling his weapon out and engulfing his ballooning knob in my hot mouth.

'God, that's good!' he groaned as I ran my tongue over his silky glans. 'Caroline, she . . . she won't do this.'

Got him! I knew there had to be something missing! Sex is *OK*? How the hell could it be OK when the oral side was non-existent? What had been the attraction? I wondered. How the hell had Caroline lured him away from me in the first place? Oral sex had always been a vital part of our lovemaking, the essence of our sex life, so what the hell had made him leave me for her?

'Sue . . . Sue, I . . .' he gasped as I pulled his trousers down and cupped his heavy balls in my hand. I did my best, put every effort into pleasuring him – sucking, licking, mouthing – and he was loving it! Gripping my head, he swayed, his body trembling as he came ever nearer to jetting his sperm into my hot mouth. 'Sue . . . Ah! God!' he breathed as his shaft twitched. 'Coming! God, I'm coming!'

Gyrating his hips, he fucked my mouth, pumping out his come, filling my cheeks, douching my tongue. I swallowed hard, rolling my tongue over his glans, giving him what he wanted – giving him what she couldn't, or wouldn't, give him. His penis slipping from my mouth as he crumpled to the floor, he lay on the carpet, satisfied, done in his coming. His penis, Caroline's penis, lay invitingly over his huge balls – glistening, long, thick, spent.

So? I wondered. Whose penis was it now – hers or mine? The notes I'd sent her had been futile, I realized that. The weeks I'd spent crying, sobbing into my pillow, had been pointless. And all the time, I'd held the key. All along, I'd had what it took to destroy her, their relationship – and I'd missed it. Through the mist of my tears, my confusion, I hadn't seen the key! That was my pussy, my all-powerful pussy. Now I was using that key!

'God, that was good, Sue!' he beamed as he lay there, tugging his trousers up.

'Come back for more – if you want to, that is,' I suggested.

'I . . . I don't know. I mean . . .'

'It's up to you. I'm here – I'll always be here, ready for you.'

'I don't want things to go too far, Sue. I've moved on now, I don't want to go back to . . .'

'To what, Jim?' I prompted, hoping that he'd reveal why he'd left me for her.

'I don't know. Look, I will see you again. I'll call round from time to time for . . .'

'For sex, Jim?'

'Yes, no, I mean . . . Well, not only sex, I suppose.'

'Be honest, Jim. You only want me for sex. I don't mind that. I'll be honest with you – *I* only want *you* for sex, so things are equal. As I said, sex is good with you. It's the best.'

Climbing to his feet, he stood before me, thinking, wondering. I could almost hear his thoughts crashing around in the ruins of his poor mind. Slipping his hand up my skirt, he cupped my naked pussy lips in his palm. 'Why have you shaved?' he asked softly, feeling my wetness.

'Because I've changed, Jim. I masturbate every day, I never wear panties . . . Like you, I've moved on – I'm enjoying life.'

'But shaving your . . .'

'Don't you like it?'

'Yes, very much! You're not seeing anyone, are you?'

'No, I'm not.'

'Then, where did you get the idea from?'

'I was taking a shower one day, after I'd spent an hour or so masturbating, thinking about your huge cock, and I decided my pussy needed her freedom. It's cleaner, far more hygienic – and very sexy!'

Slipping his finger into my hot cunt, he nibbled my ear. I breathed heavily, letting out a long, low moan of pleasure as he massaged my inner sanctum. 'Fuck me, Jim!' I gasped as he slipped another finger into my cuntal sheath. 'Please, fuck me!' He moved back, gazing into my eyes as he pulled his hard penis out of his trousers and slipped it under my skirt. I felt his solid knob, running up and down my drenched valley, between my inner lips, probing around the entrance to my wet cunt. Standing on my toes, I aligned my hole with his probing cock and gently lowered my body. At last, he was slipping his organ into my cunt, opening me, filling me as he gasped and clung to me.

He was breaking his trust! I'd done it! I'd taken his penis into my pussy-hole – his fidelity was shattered. Caroline was the stooge now, the one betrayed, lied to, cheated on. The sense of satisfaction was immense, incredible, as I bobbed up and down on his long, treacherous shaft. There was sexual satisfaction, yes, but more: an overwhelming sense of victory.

As he lifted me from the floor, I wrapped my legs around him, sitting on his massive rod as he bounced me up and down, fucking me. My arms around his neck, I clung to him, my head back, my eyes rolling as he impaled me, took me to my sexual heaven.

'Coming!' I cried as my clitoris throbbed. 'God, I'm coming!' My juices poured from my quivering vagina, lubricated our perfidious coupling, and I imagined Caroline questioning him. Why had he dashed into the bathroom the minute he'd got home? Why were his underpants stained – white girl-juice, sperm-stained? He'd lie and lie to convince her that his penis was hers and hers only – but he would share it with me now. Whenever he felt the need, he'd come to me – and treacherously fuck me!

Groaning, he bounced me up and down like a rag doll. 'Come . . . coming!' he gasped as his sperm flooded my vaginal sheath. My clitoris erupted again, in unison with his knob, and we melted into a simultaneous ecstasy of release – of heaven. Finally collapsing to the floor, me on top of him, his cock still lodged in my roost, we lay there, panting, gasping, trembling.

'I've missed that!' he gasped as I wiggled my hips and squeezed my cunt muscles.

'So have I!' I replied, kissing his mouth, pushing my tongue between his lips.

'I'll come round again, if that's what you . . .'

'Yes, do! Come and fuck me again and again, Jim! Fuck my cunt, my mouth, my bottom-hole!'

As I crawled from his hard body, his shaft slipping from my drenched cavern, I stood up and adjusted my skirt. He climbed to his feet and pulled his trousers up, glancing at his watch and sighing. 'I really must be going,' he mumbled, combing his dark hair back with his fingers.

'Thanks, Jim,' I smiled. 'That was heavenly.'

'Tomorrow, perhaps?' he grinned as he left the room.

'Yes, tomorrow.'

When Jim had gone, I sat in the lounge and rang Caroline, a huge grin lighting my face as she answered the phone. 'May I speak to Jim, please?' I asked, disguising my voice as best I could.

'He's out, can I take a message?' she replied.

'Er . . . Is that his mother?'

'His *mother*? No, it's not!' she snapped.

'Oh, he told me that he lived with his mother. Er . . . Perhaps I shouldn't have . . .'

'Who is this?'

'Er . . . It's all right, I'll catch him at his office tomorrow.'

'Can I ask who's calling?'

'It's personal . . . I shouldn't have . . . I'm sorry to have bothered you.'

Nice one, Sue! I congratulated myself as I hung up. That'll get her thinking! He gets home late, stinking of sex and perfume, guilt mirrored in his guilty eyes as he dives for the bathroom . . . The phone call, his stammered lies – that'll get the bitch thinking! *Again, the stench of adultery swirls and billows!*

Wondering whether Sally had discovered Tony's sperm shortfall yet, I lifted the phone and dialled her number. Tony answered, his voice guilty, grumpy, as he asked what I wanted.

'Just thought I'd give Sally a call,' I said cheerfully. 'Is she there?'

'Yes, she is,' he mumbled. 'We're not speaking at the moment,' he added dolefully.

'Why ever not?'

'She . . . It's a long story. I'll get her, hang on.'

So the poor man had been caught spermless! No doubt he'd tried to make light of it, lied to her, bleated that men didn't always produce copious quantities of sperm – but she'd not have believed him. With me continually planting seeds of doubt in her mind, telling her about the signs, the signs of adultery, she'd never believe him.

'Hello, Sue,' she said softly.

'Sally, how are you?' I asked cheerily.

'So so.'

'What's the problem? You sound down.'

'I did what you suggested and . . . Well, there was hardly any . . .'

'Oh, Sally, I'm so sorry! Oh, God! You poor thing!'

'He dashed into the bathroom when he got in. I . . . I feel so . . .'

'I know how you feel – I've been there, remember?'

'I don't know what to do, Sue. He said that he'd been to Steve's after he'd left your house, and when I told him that I'd phoned Steve and knew he hadn't been there he started mumbling something about another Steve. It was obvious that he was lying.'

'What are you going to do?'

'God knows! I don't want him anywhere near me, I know that much!'

'Come round and we'll talk about it, Sally,' I prompted, wondering what other seeds to plant.

'No, not now. He's just gone out, I heard the front door slam shut. I'll see you tomorrow, perhaps. I've got some serious thinking to do right now!'

'All right – and try not to worry too much. I mean, we may be wrong about this.'

'No, I know he's been up to something. I'll see you tomorrow. Bye.'

Grinning, I replaced the receiver and sat back with a great sense of satisfaction. There I was, systematically eating away at their marriage, and yet, in Sally's eyes, I was completely innocent! The feeling warmed me, excited me, quenched my thirst for destruction. First Tony, then Derek, and now Jim had succumbed to my sweet pussy. How many more men would there be? I wondered. How many more cocks could my shaved cunt lure to my den of moral destruction?

Thinking about the situation, I decided that, although my shorn pussy had more than enough magnetic pull over married men, I needed another weapon to hand. Men bored quickly with the same old thing, I knew. I needed something to complement my hot, tight cunt – but what?

Whipping was something that Derek had obviously enjoyed. I'd enjoyed it, too! I'd loved being tied down and whipped – used as a sexual object, purely for cold sex. I wanted to open my body to men, lie over a table, my buttocks splayed, my small, once-so-private hole on display, my wet labia hanging, gaping – dripping with sex!

I needed to play on men's fantasies, their weird and

wonderful sexual desires. That was it – I needed a sex room! A room dedicated to sex – whipping, bondage, and anything else I could dream up. Men would come in their droves to see me, to whip me – to fuck me.

What with Sharon, the college girl, moving into the spare room, the room next to my bedroom was my only choice. It had been going to be the nursery but . . . I decided to start making the necessary changes straight away. The dressing table would have to go, and the wardrobe. The single bed, too. I'd need a table, ropes – handcuffs, perhaps? I needed anything and everything to do with bondage. Chains? Yes. But where to find the equipment? I'd have to look into it. A house clearance firm would take the furniture away, leaving the room vacant for my tools of sex. I'd call someone the next day and arrange it, I decided as the front doorbell rang.

Tony stood on the step, forlorn, his hair dishevelled – a broken man. I smiled, inviting him into my lair. 'Sally doesn't sound too happy!' I quipped as he followed me into the lounge – Jim's sperm tracing my inner thighs.

'Did she tell you *why* she's not happy?' he asked, sitting down.

'No – I assumed that you'd had a row or something. What's happened?'

'When I left here, I went straight home and . . . She decided that she wanted sex. After my session with you, I could barely get it up! Anyway, she grabbed me and . . . There wasn't much in the way of spunk. She suspected me of screwing someone else.'

'You *had* screwed someone else, so she was right, wasn't she?' I laughed.

'Yes, but I didn't want her to know, did I? It was if she was testing me, for Christ's sake!'

'Things will be all right. I mean, she's got no proof, has she?'

'No, but . . . Sally doesn't need proof. She's been talking to someone, I know it! Someone's been putting ideas into her head. It's not you, is it?'

'*Me*? Christ, Tony! I'd hardly be having an affair with you, and then put ideas into your wife's head, would I?'

'No, I suppose not. It's just that she . . . I don't know, perhaps I'm imagining things.'

'I think you must be! And if you're not, then you must bear in mind that she has other friends, besides me. She could have been talking to anyone. Adultery is a dangerous game, Tony! But we won't get caught – we can't, can we?'

'I hope not!'

'There's no way she'll discover that we're having an affair! Anyway, have you come round for sex?'

He smiled at me, his eyes gazing at the swell of my breasts, my erect nipples outlined by my tight T-shirt. Of course he'd come round for sex! Now that Sally had cut him off, barricaded her cunt, he'd *have* to come to me for sex, almost daily! Sitting next to him on the sofa, I lifted my T-shirt over my head and tossed it across the room. Gazing at my firm breasts, my long nipples, he grinned.

Tentatively reaching out, he stroked my breasts with the back of his hand. Closing my eyes, I reclined, relaxing completely as he leaned forward and sucked my nipple into his mouth. I felt his tongue, rolling, licking, snaking around my hardening budlette. I wanted him to sperm over my tits, shoot his male cream over my milk buds. And when he'd done, I'd lap it up like a starving cat.

'Come over my tits!' I whispered, running my fingers through his hair as he suckled on me like a baby. 'Please, Tony, I want your sperm dripping from my nipples.' He looked up, my wet milk bud slipping from his mouth as he grinned. Standing up, he slipped his trousers off and climbed astride me, his long penis wavering before my wide eyes. Taking his hard knob into my mouth, I gently sucked, gripping his shaft by its base as I savoured his salty glans.

'That's good!' he breathed as I moved my head back and forth. 'God, you're good!'

I *was* good, I knew that! The more practice I was getting, the better I was becoming. Again, I relished the thought of being the other woman, rather than the little wife at home, waiting for her adulterous husband to come sneaking back, reeking of sex. Caroline was probably beside herself with anguish. Sally was so suspicious she wasn't even speaking to Tony! And me? I was enjoying every minute of it! Sucking Tony's cock, waiting for his sperm to shoot from his knob and splatter my tits, my nipples, I hadn't a care in the world! *No one could hurt me now – no one!*

Suddenly, Tony gasped as his knob exploded in my mouth. Pulling away, I wanked him, licking his shiny knob as his sperm squirted, splashing over my breasts, dripping from my hard nipples. On and on his stream flowed, soaking me, covering me, until he moved back to end the beautiful torture. Gasping as I massaged the last ripples of pleasure from his throbbing cock, he looked down at me, at his white spunk, baptizing my areolae.

'Go on, then, lick your tits!' he breathed, rubbing his knob against my nipple. Lifting my breast, I sucked my hard bud into my mouth and savoured his salty come, licking, slurping until my breast was clean. 'And now the other one,' he instructed. Lifting my heavy tit, I cleansed the smooth skin, the hard nipple, fervently lapping up his cream as he watched. 'You're a sexy bitch!' he cried as I took his flaccid shaft into my mouth and sucked. 'God, you just can't get enough, can you?'

'No, I can't,' I replied truthfully as his knob slipped from my mouth. 'I'll tell you what we'll do next . . .'

'I'd better get back to Sally,' he sighed.

'What for? She's not speaking to you, so why go dashing back to her?'

The poor dear was too worried about his future to stay with me any longer. I was going to suggest that he give me a good spanking, but I knew that he wanted to rush back to his crumbling marriage, to see if he couldn't prop it up as it tottered in the wind of adultery.

He'd be careful now, I knew. Sally wouldn't throw him out on a suspicion. She'd collect her proof, her evidence, before she went running to a solicitor crying her accusations of betrayal – adultery. While things were rough for Tony, he wouldn't rock the boat too much. But as soon as the waters had calmed, I knew he'd be back, his stiff penis in his hand, his heavy balls aching for relief.

When he'd gone sneaking back to his wife, I made myself a cup of coffee and grinned as I surveyed my hit-list. I needed a system, a method of noting the degree of decay against each crumbling marriage. A points system was the answer, I decided. Nought to ten – nought being a good, strong marriage, five, pretty rocky, and ten, the maximum – divorce. I wrote number one beside Jim and Caroline, and two beside Tony and Sally. Derek and Jilly being an unknown quantity, I left them blank. But I swore the day would come when number ten would be written by every name in that book!

Hiding it under the sofa, I went to answer the doorbell. I was surprised to find Sally, her eyes tearful, her face flushed, standing on the doorstep. Was she ripe for three points? I speculated, inviting her into the lounge. I knew that there had been another row, that the marriage had suffered yet another blow. Surely she hadn't tried the sperm test again? They weren't speaking, so she'd hardly have tried bringing him off! Fidgeting nervously on the sofa, she looked up at me and half smiled.

'He came home a while ago,' she began. 'I know that he

went to see someone this evening, but I don't know who.'

'Look, Sally, it doesn't matter who it is – the point is that he *is* seeing someone,' I smiled as I sat down and put my arm round her. 'Answer me this – do you want to hang on to him, or do you want to let him go?'

'I . . . Well, I want him, I suppose. But I don't want him if he's screwing around!'

'OK, so you want to hang on to him, keep the marriage going. In that case, you'll have to work at it. I don't mean to be crude but, although the way to a man's heart is through his dick, it's no good trying to compete with whoever he's seeing. She's probably young, eager to please him, a gymnast in bed – you can't compete. Cut him off, sexually. You might think that you'd only drive him further away by doing that, but it's the other way round – he'll want you all the more. You'll have to make him jealous, too. Make him think that you're . . .'

'That would only make matters worse!'

Exactly!

'No, it wouldn't. He thinks that he can get away with his adultery. All the time you're at home happily getting on with the cooking and housework, he thinks that he can nip off and play the field. You'll have to lead him to believe that you . . . Give him reason to be suspicious.'

'What, perhaps the odd suspicious phone call or something?'

'Yes. If he believes that you're seeing someone, or at least has his suspicions, it will make him think again. He'll realize that he might lose you, that he's not the only man in the world.'

'Yes, I see what you're getting at. But . . . what if it backfires?'

'It won't. Look, if he's planning to leave you for another woman, which I doubt he is, then you'll not be able to stop him. But if he believes that there's a chance that you might leave him for another man, he'll shape up and behave himself, won't he?'

'I suppose you're right. I'll tell you what – give me five minutes to get home, and then ring me. I'll grab the phone and make out that I'm speaking to a man. I'll whisper and appear nervy.'

'Great! That'll get him thinking!'

'Thanks, Sue. I don't know what I'd do without you, I really don't. You're a good friend.'

'That's what friends are for. Now, off you go, and I'll ring you in five minutes.'

I made the phone call and listened to Sally's giggles and whisperings. I could hear Tony in the background, asking who she was talking to – his suspicion rising, hopefully. It wasn't time to award them three points yet, but that time was fast approaching!

Unfortunately, the front doorbell rang and I had to hang up, leaving Sally whispering to the dialling tone. Forgetting that Sharon had said that she might be moving in that day, I was surprised to see her.

'I know it's pretty late in the day,' she smiled, dumping her huge shoulder bag on the hall floor. 'But I got held up, what with one thing and another, and . . .'

'Don't worry. Take your bag into the spare room, the room I showed you, and I'll make us some coffee while you unpack,' I replied, wishing that I hadn't offered her the room at all. I could hardly entertain married men in the house with Sharon lurking! There again, she'd be at college most of the time and, no doubt, she'd be out having fun during the evenings. And if not, then I'd just have to make other plans for my seductions.

After unpacking, Sharon eventually joined me in the lounge for coffee. Wearing high lace-up boots, a short, tartan skirt and a Rolling Stones *Voodoo Lounge* T-shirt, she was a typical teenager. Her hair – much longer than mine – was a lovely natural blonde. Feminine in the extreme, her blue eyes sparkling with life, her full mouth always smiling, she was a glowing picture of girlish youth.

'Sue, there's something you'd better know,' she murmured mysteriously as I passed her her coffee. Sitting facing her, I smiled, waiting for her to tell me her secret. Probably something to do with a boyfriend staying the odd night, I thought as she twisted her hair nervously round her finger.

'This won't affect you, but . . .' she began awkwardly, her happy face now anguished.

'What is it, Sharon? What's the problem?' I coaxed.

'I'm . . . I'm a lesbian,' she finally announced.

I must admit that I was shocked, although I don't know why. There were plenty of lesbians in the world, so why not Sharon? But she was so pretty, so attractive – so young. How could she say that she was a lesbian at her tender age? She'd have barely had any experience with boys, so how could she decide that she was a dyke?

'Are you sure?' I asked stupidly, as if asking if she were pregnant.

'Yes, one hundred per cent,' she replied firmly.

'How do you know? I mean, you're so young!'

'I know what I am. Age has nothing to do with it, anyway.'

'I realize that, but . . . What I mean is, you've hardly had the time to gain any experience with boys, let alone girls.'

'I discovered that I was a lesbian two years ago. I'd been seeing this boy and . . . well, we split up because he wanted me to do this and that sexually, and I wouldn't. Anyway, his sister and I became friends and . . . well, it went from there. She'd missed the last train home one weekend and we slept together at my parents' house. By the time the sun had come up, I knew that I was a lesbian.'

Incredible! I thought as I gazed into her deep blue eyes. A lesbian! I still couldn't believe it. She was so feminine. But, I realized, all lesbians weren't necessarily butch. It seemed sad in a way, but it wasn't until I imagined her naked with another girl that I thought that she was probably better off without men. Perhaps her way was the answer? Men were all lying, cheating, two-timing bastards. What better countermeasure than to do without them completely, finding love – and sex – with another woman? But I wasn't a lesbian. The idea intrigued me – but I wasn't a bloody dyke!

'Why tell me?' I asked as she sipped her coffee.

'I don't know. I suppose I thought that you might find out and be upset or something.'

'I wouldn't have been upset. Although I'm pleased that you told me. Do you have a . . . do you have a girlfriend?'

'No, not at the moment. I did have a good relationship with a girl from college but . . . Well, it didn't work out. How about you?'

'No! I haven't got a . . . Oh, I see what you mean! No, I haven't got a man at the moment. I'm not looking, really. I'm just trying to recover from the divorce, I suppose.'

'An attractive girl like you! You'll soon be snapped up!' she giggled, leaving me wondering fearfully if she might fancy me.

Although the thought of a young girl coming on to me quite shocked me, it also excited me somehow, and I became curious as to how our relationship might develop. I mean, living together, sharing the same bathroom, the same lounge, how long would it be before . . . My mind was veering off course again. There was no way she'd fancy me! But, somewhere, deep in the dark shadows of my mind, I hoped that she did.

I found myself wondering what lesbians did, exactly. Licking, sucking orgasms from each other's clitorises, yes, but what else? Did they use dildos? I supposed that they did, and pictured Sharon lying naked with her legs open, another girl ramming a huge candle in and out of her fresh, young pussy.

I suspected that they found some kind of love, too. The attraction wasn't only each other's pussies, I was sure!

Observing Sharon's rounded breasts, I began to imagine her nipples. Did her own body turn her on? If she was sexually aroused by the female form rather than the male, then, surely, she found her own body arousing? Lesbians must suck each other's nipples – do all the things that men like doing to breasts.

I wanted to ask the girl – ask her what she got up to, what it was like to lick another girl's cunny. Although the thought sent a shudder up my spine, it also aroused me. I didn't want to lick her, but I imagined her licking me, my open cunt. The thought of her deriving pleasure from my wet pussy was quite thrilling, and I pictured her head between my legs, her long blonde hair cascading over my stomach as she peeled my pussy lips apart and lapped up my come.

'I'll go to bed now,' she declared, finishing her coffee. 'I've got a class first thing in the morning and I'm feeling pretty tired.'

'OK. I'm tired, too. The bed's made up, but the table lamp doesn't work, I'm afraid.'

'That doesn't matter,' she yawned as she stood up.

'See you in the morning – sleep well.'

Watching her leave the room, I wondered again about her preference for her own sex. Having a strange fascination about lesbians now, I wanted to discover what her thoughts were as she walked down the street eyeing the pretty girls. She must look at girls the same way as men do, I mused. Did she look at the swell of their breasts and wonder how hard and long their nipples were? Did she wonder about their hot, wet pussies beneath their short skirts?

As I climbed into my bed, I pulled the quilt up, realizing that my own pussy was wet – very wet! Was it thinking about Sharon licking me there that had caused my girl-juice to decant? Or perhaps just the thought of being licked there by anyone, having my clitoris sucked into a hot mouth? Whatever, I'd discover all there was to know about young Sharon – and her lesbian thoughts.

Chapter Five

Sharon was up early the following morning, taking a shower and preparing for college. Climbing from my bed, I slipped my dressing gown on and wandered downstairs to the kitchen to find her sitting at the table in her bra and panties, munching cornflakes.

She had a good body – slim, curvaceous, with youthful, taut, unblemished skin. Her breasts were full, well rounded, and, I imagined, very firm. As she rose and took her bowl to the sink I glimpsed the swell of her red panties, and strange thoughts surfaced – thoughts of her pussy lips, the wet, pink girl-flesh nestling between them, her clitoris, her tight vagina.

My thinking was changing – my attitudes, my outlook shifting from the straight and narrow social norm I'd been indoctrinated with. Her young sex-sheath would be hot, wet, and very tight – her inner lips small, protruding only slightly from her pretty slit, her clitoris, protected by its pretty pink bonnet, hard, ever-ready for masturbation, for exciting to orgasm. Had she trimmed her pubic hair? Or shaved completely, as I had?

But why was I thinking like this? I asked myself. What was happening to me, changing me from a heterosexual woman into someone who thought of young girls' pussies and firm breasts, as well as men's long, thick penises?

'Did you sleep well?' I asked as I filled the kettle, wondering whether she'd masturbated before getting up – slipped her slender fingers between her swelling cunny lips and massaged her clitoris to fruition as she'd fantasized about my wet pussy.

'Yes, very well,' she replied, turning to face me, her shining golden tresses cascading over her naked shoulders. 'I must get the bedside lamp fixed so that I can read in bed.'

'It's probably only the bulb,' I replied. 'There are some spare ones somewhere – under the stairs, I think.'

'I'll have a look later.'

Her nipples pressing through her red lace bra, I wondered what it would be like to lick them, suck them, stiffen them in my mouth. I thought again of luring wives, as well as husbands, to my lair, and seducing them. But I'd need experience – sexual experience with a woman before I could seduce women. I needed, desperately craved, a clitoris throbbing in orgasm in my hot mouth. Vivid images of Sharon's open cunt pressed against my mouth swirling in my mind, I sensed my pussy lips swelling, my stomach somersaulting. I wanted Sharon, her body – her cunt. I didn't understand my thoughts, the way I was thinking. What the hell was I becoming?

'I'd better be going,' she said, smiling at me, brushing her hair away from her sparkling blue eyes.

'When do you finish?' I asked, trying to stop myself from reaching out and squeezing her breast, cupping her bulging panties in my palm.

'I'm not sure. Either lunch time, or late afternoon. I don't know which classes I've got today. By the way, there's the post,' she added, pointing to the table as she left the room.

The plain white envelope lay ominously on the table. I instinctively knew what it was as I ripped it open and read the psychopathic words:

I'll bet you miss Jim fucking your wet cunt! He prefers Caroline's, you know that, don't you? You were never any good in bed, you know that, too. You've lost!

Screwing the sheet of paper up, I threw it into the bin. What was the bloody point of these notes? I hated them, detested them! I wanted to rid my mind of Jim and Caroline once and for all – put all the pain behind me. Their destruction would come. But my tormented mind, the evil notes, could go on forever.

Sharon left the house wearing cut-off jeans and her Stones T-shirt. Wondering, again, if she could fancy me, I watched her walk down the road from the lounge window, her youthful thighs smooth, unblemished, her taut buttocks stretching her denim shorts. Contemplating letting her in on my plans of marital destruction, my thoughts turned to the spare room and I grabbed the phone book.

'There's not much call for beds and wardrobes at the moment,' the man from the secondhand furniture shop informed me bluntly.

'You mean, there is a call, but you're *saying* that there isn't so that you can get the stuff cheap and make a bloody good profit?' I returned.

'Let's have your address, and if it's all right with you, I'll be round in half an hour to give you a price,' he replied indifferently.

I knew I was about to be ripped off. The rogue was obviously keen to earn a quick buck, but I had no choice. The room had to be cleared before I could transform it into my den of iniquity – my lair.

He was keen all right, arriving ten minutes early. Surveying the furniture, he sucked air in through his pursed lips and shook his head as if to infer that it wasn't worth a penny. In his mid-twenties, and not bad-looking, I was in two minds as whether or not to seduce him. His jeans were tight – too tight, judging by the size of his bulge. Would he like me to slip his cock out and suck his knob, drain his balls and drink his come? I wondered. Undoubtedly!

Trying to make me feel guilty for dragging him out to view what he seemed to think was a pile of junk, he offered me twenty pounds for the lot, mumbling something about losing money. Bastard! I thought as I eyed the nearly-new divan. Wonder if he's married?

'Make it fifty and I'll throw something else in,' I grinned, my dressing gown falling open at the front.

'Fifty? What else . . . What will you throw in?' he echoed, his disbelieving eyes transfixed on my crack, my naked, bulging pussy lips.

'What do you want?' I asked impishly, raising my eyebrows and grinning.

'Er . . . I haven't got fifty on me.'

'You'd better just take the furniture and give me twenty, then,' I smiled, pulling my gown together – concealing my wares.

'I've got thirty,' he said enthusiastically, holding out three ten-pound notes.

'That's more like it!' I exclaimed, grabbing the notes and stuffing them into my dressing gown pocket. 'I'll leave you to get on with it, then,' I added, leaving the room.

'But I thought . . .'

'Mind the paintwork, won't you!' I called from the kitchen.

Thirty pounds for the furniture *and* my beautiful young body? He must be bloody joking! I thought as I listened to him groaning as he cleared the room. A typical man! He wants to use me, to satisfy his male lust, but he won't pay for the pleasure!

When he'd finished lugging the furniture out to his van, he called me from the empty room, probably expecting to glimpse my naked slit again.

'All done, love,' he said, gazing at my breasts jutting under my dressing gown.

'Good,' I smiled. 'Are you married?'

'What?'

'Are you married?' I repeated.

'Yes, I am – why?'

'Just wondered. I was thinking of giving you a ring and inviting you round for an evening, but if you're married, your wife might answer the phone so . . .'

'I'll ring you,' he interrupted eagerly.

'No, I'll ring you – if you want me to,' I grinned, allowing my gown to fall open again.

Gazing at my naked crack, my *femme fatale*, he told me his phone number. Another one hooked, I mused, allowing my gown to open a little more. 'I'll ring you, then,' I said. 'If your wife answers, I'll tell her that I've got the wrong number. What's her name?'

'Hazel,' he replied, looking up and smiling. 'And I'm Dave. When will you phone me?'

'I'm not sure. My name's Sue, by the way. Where do you live?'

'Goldsmith Crescent, a few blocks away – number twenty-two.'

'Oh, yes, I know it. I might ring you tonight, I'll see how I feel.'

'I'll look forward to it,' he smiled as we walked down the hall to the front door.

'And so will I!' I breathed huskily as he took one last lingering look at my body, my gown now far enough open to expose my long nipples.

I'll bet you'll look forward to it! I thought as I closed the door, imagining his wife waiting for him to come home while he was screwing me. Adulterous bastard! He didn't deserve a wife! And he wouldn't have one, by the time I'd finished with him! Wasn't there a man in the world who'd remain faithful to his wife in the face of my pretty, hairless pussy? I couldn't believe that *all* men would plunge so easily into the murky depths of adultery at the first glimpse of another woman's tight slit! Was there no fidelity? No, there wasn't, I decided – the word meant nothing. It might as well be deleted from the dictionary.

If anything, the secondhand-furniture man had strengthened my resolve to seek and destroy marriages, and my thoughts turned to the spare room again. Trying to imagine it transformed into a sex den, I wondered what to do. Chains hanging from the walls, a rack for stretching people . . . No, it was supposed to be for sex, not torture! But where to start? Wandering out into the garden, I conjured my imagination and tried to think along the same filthy lines as men.

Men were all perverts, I decided – not that *I* could talk! They liked the darker, colder side of sex. They enjoyed unusual, distorted, corrupt sex. Soothing background music, subdued lighting and a soft bed with a naked woman reclining, ready and waiting for love, wasn't what they wanted. They craved hard-core, dirty sex, and there in the garden, I formulated an idea that met that criterion admirably.

Taking Jim's exercise bench from the garage, I placed it in the centre of the spare room. Slipping out of my dressing gown, I sat on the padded top of the narrow bench and reclined, resting my back on the sloping section with my head on the floor. My feet on the carpet, my legs spread, my pussy lips gaping, I was the picture of female obscenity. Perfect, I thought, my arms on the floor, my hands gripping the tubular frame. My wrists cuffed or tied with rope, men could use me as they wished – fuck me, lick me, wank over my tits, or whatever other fantasy they wished to live out. And if I were to turn over, they could take my bottom-hole, slip their hard penises deep into my bowels, or thrash me with a leather whip and watch my come spewing from my open vagina.

Fingering the soft, wet flesh between my swelling outer lips, I gently caressed my clitoris, massaging the small protrusion as it grew and pulsated. Closing my eyes, I imagined a man kneeling between my legs, his hard penis driving deep into my hot vagina, his sperm gushing, filling me.

As I masturbated, opening my eyes now and then to gaze at the upside down window, I imagined the window cleaner having the time of his life, wanking up his ladder as he watched me come. What I didn't realize was that my fantasy voyeur was for real – not up a ladder, but standing quietly in the bedroom doorway.

The first I knew of Sharon watching me – watching me frig as my phantom window-cleaner drove me wild – was when she knelt softly between my legs and planted a kiss on my inflamed pussy lips. Jumping up, I stared at her in horror. What must she have thought? There I was, lying back on the exercise bench, my legs splayed, my cunny lips spread, my fingers massaging my clitoris . . . My face flushed with embarrassment, I was about to leap from the bench and grab my dressing gown when she gently pushed me back down.

There were no words. I knew what was coming, what she'd do to me, but I had no power to resist. Now, like the men I'd seduced, I was fighting a raging mind battle. The power I'd enjoyed wielding over men was useless now – now I was the seducee! My mind whirled. My senses numb, I felt giddy with confusion, my head spinning with expectation, apprehension. My clitoris had been close to orgasm, my sex-juices pouring from my hot vagina, and I desperately needed to finish what I had started. But this was another girl kneeling between my legs, gazing at the most intimate part of my body.

My eyes closed, I pretended that it was Tony there, opening my pussy lips, examining my wet, inner flesh. Working silently, Sharon gently pushed her fingers into my tight sheath – female fingers. Kissing and licking my inner thigh, she tasted me, teased me. The sensations were incredible, and I began to writhe and breathe heavily. My body trembled expectantly as I sensed her hot breath between my legs, on my swollen pussy lips. I knew that she was going to lick my naked pussy, suck my inner folds into her hot mouth, engulf my clitoris and make me come, and I shuddered in delight.

Desperately trying to blank out the image of Sharon's mouth, her full lips kissing me there, stirring a base desire that lay sleeping in a dark corner of my subconscious, I switched from Tony and tried to picture Jim between my legs as she ran her tongue up my open groove. But Jim's image soon faded as vivid pictures of Sharon's female tongue probing between my pussy lips filled my mind.

What the hell was I doing? What was I? A lesbian? My head on the floor, I couldn't see her – I could just feel her nuzzling, nibbling my swelling outer lips. Was this what I wanted? I wondered as she sucked my inner labia into her mouth. I tried to imagine Jim again, any man, fingering me, sucking on my very femininity. But the reality wouldn't fade away – it was Sharon.

Her full lips pressed between my pussy lips, her tongue wiggled and wormed its way into my vagina – tasting, licking, exploring my secret flesh. Gasping, I gripped the tubular frame of the exercise bench. Strange thoughts swirled, drifted – heterosexual, lesbian, male-female, right-wrong, female-female. Would she expect me to kiss her pussy, to push my tongue into her open vagina? I wondered as she opened my cunny wide with her thumbs, exposing more of my sensitive flesh to her inquisitive tongue. Did I want to lick her pussy, slip my tongue into her hot hole? I didn't know what I wanted. I needed to experience the ultimate lesbian act, but I was sure that I would shy away from it at the very last minute.

Sharon moaned as she moved her tongue up my sex valley and ran it round the base of my yearning clitoris. Her breath seemed hotter now as my clitoris stiffened in response to her caresses. Picturing her wet, pink tongue – a female tongue –

licking my clitoris, I let go, released my mind and sank into the comforting warmth of the forbidden coupling.

The room seemed to darken, my mind floating above my body as Sharon sucked my blossoming nodule into her mouth. My entire being centred on her mouth engulfing my most private spot – the epitome of my femininity. I was about to come in a girl's mouth.

Expertly, as only another girl knows how, she fingered me, massaged the walls of my vagina as she sucked and licked my pulsating nodule. Her long blonde hair cascading over my stomach, caressing me, I began to shudder with the birth of my first lesbian-induced climax. Opening my thighs wider, I gave myself completely to Sharon, gave her my body, my mind, my very being.

My hands over my face, trying to conceal my ecstasy, I trembled uncontrollably as my clitoris swelled and throbbed. I was there, at last, my climax coming, gripping me, ripping through my nervous system. Crying out, I opened my legs wider, pushing the open centre of my body harder into Sharon's face, her hot mouth.

At the crest of my orgasm, she slipped a finger deep into my bottom, heightening my pleasure until I thought that I was going to pass out. Rhythmically massaging the sensitive inner flesh of my holes, working on my clitoris with her darting tongue, she took me to the most incredible climax imaginable. Gasping, shaking violently, I thought that I'd never come down from the orgasmic tidal wave I was riding. On and on I floated on the surf of lust, my head tossing wildly from side to side, my whole being flying up to wonderful new heights of consciousness.

At last, my quivering pleasure subsided, the incredible climax gently bringing me down from my sexual heaven. Trembling, I lay there as Sharon lapped up the milky come flowing from my trembling, consumed body, drank the juices of lesbian love flowing from my very being.

Suddenly, I was overwhelmed with feelings of guilt, embarrassment, and degradation. What had I done? Allowing another girl to masturbate me with her mouth, her tongue, was immoral, vile. I couldn't begin to comprehend my wanton lust as I'd allowed her to push her tongue into my vagina and drink my come. But I couldn't deny the pleasure, the immense feeling of sexual satisfaction that our union had brought me. Torn between right and wrong, between what was socially accepted and what was viewed with horror, I sat upright, facing, at last, my lesbian partner.

She smiled, her face still wet with my pussy juice, her eyes alive with the lust of life. 'Did you enjoy that as much as I did?' she whispered, her sea eyes penetrating mine. Steeped in guilt, embarrassment, I opened my mouth to speak, but the words wouldn't come. What could I say? The pretty college girl kneeling before me had just buried her face between my legs, opened my pussy lips, sucked an orgasm from my pulsating clitoris, swallowed my sticky come-juice. What could I say?

'Your first time?' she asked, her eyes still gazing deep into mine. My first time? Yes, with another girl, it was! I felt as I had after school one hot summer's day when I'd allowed a boy to pull my navy-blue knickers down and examine my naked crack – shy, naive, stupid in my innocence. He'd fingered me, watching my face for a reaction, waiting for me to come – but I hadn't. Then, he'd pulled his penis out, the first one I'd ever seen, and asked me to wank him. It was stiff and, I'd thought at the time, huge! I'd run – my knickers around my knees, I'd run across the field, crying, sobbing, wondering why I'd let him touch me there. But now, there was nowhere to run, no hiding place.

Stunned, I watched Sharon as she stood up and slipped her T-shirt off. Her red lace bra came into view – the very same one she'd been wearing earlier when I'd had to restrain myself from reaching out and squeezing her breast. My eyes wide with fear and excitement as she reached behind her back and unclipped her bra, I held my breath. Slowly, provocatively, she peeled the cups away from her firm spheres. Semicircles of her areolae came into view, and then her long, brown nipples.

Dropping the garment to the floor, she unbuckled her belt and tugged her cut-off jeans down her long, slender legs. Her red panties bulged with her pussy lips. Wet, stained with her juices of arousal, the material followed the contours of her femininity, outlining the cleft where her clitoris lay – hard, no doubt, in expectation of orgasm.

Kicking her shorts aside, she placed her thumbs between her hips and her tight panties and slowly pulled the material down. With bated breath, I watched as her scanty blonde pubic growth came into view, the small curls springing to life as they were freed from the confines of her tight panties, fanning out from her groove like fern leaves. Trembling now, I gazed in trepidation at the summit of her crack, knowing that she'd want me to reciprocate, to kiss, lick and suck her there.

Further Sharon pulled the red material down, revealing her full pussy lips, her opening groove, her glistening, pink inner lips protruding exotically from her sex valley. Finally, she slipped her panties off and stood before me – naked.

Not one word had passed my lips since she'd caught me masturbating, and still I didn't know what to say. As she walked towards me, her sweet pussy only inches from my face, I felt trapped. I couldn't turn and run. Besides, I wasn't sure whether I wanted to run or not. I wanted to touch her there, between her legs, but I wanted her to go and leave me alone. I'd thought about seducing wives as well as husbands, and this was my chance to discover another woman's body, to masturbate another woman. I had to take that chance – or spend forever wondering what I'd missed.

'Just stroke me there, if you feel nervous,' Sharon coaxed, looking down at me as she ran her fingers around her elongated nipples. I wasn't suffering from nerves – just torn between right and wrong, moral and immoral, normal and abnormal. But I'd enjoyed her mouth, her tongue between my legs, swirling around my clitoris, so why not reciprocate? I asked myself as she jutted her hips expectantly. 'It won't bite!' she giggled as she reached down and parted her swelling pussy lips to expose her intimate, pinken flesh to my ever-widening eyes.

I'd never seen another girl's open pussy before, and I found myself comparing, adjudicating. Hers was the same as mine, of course, but her outer lips were smaller, less developed – her vaginal sheath tighter, no doubt. Tentatively moving my trembling hand towards her glistening offering, I stroked her pink inner lips. They were rubbery, slippery, wet with her love-juice. No one would know, I reasoned as I contemplated pushing my finger deep into her body. Jim, Tony, Derek . . . No one would ever know what I'd done.

'Please!' she breathed, standing with her feet wider apart and stretching her cunny lips open further. I knew what she wanted as I moved the tip of my finger around the wet entrance to her young vagina. Whatever happened now, I decided, I *had* to finger her, I *had* to experience the emotion, the sensation, the feel of another girl's inner flesh gripping my finger.

Pushing my digit up, I watched it disappear into the heat of her tightening vagina. Her juices decanted, bathing me, running down my hand as I impaled her completely. She shuddered, rocking her hips slightly to slip my finger in and out of her lesbian love-hole. Looking up, I gazed at her pretty face. Her eyes closed, her lips open slightly as she breathed deeply, slowly, she appeared to be lost in her lesbian heaven, drifting in her sea of female pleasure.

Inserting another finger into Sharon's spasming vagina, I

began to thrust as a man would his penis. She swayed, tottering a little as the pleasure permeated her body – infiltrated her mind. As I watched her wet inner lips rolling in and out of her hole in time with my fingers, I wondered how her juices tasted. I'd never sampled my own slippery come, let alone another girl's, and I found myself thirsty for knowledge.

Gripping my head, she pulled me closer. My face pressing against the contour of her belly, I breathed in the scent of her warm skin. Kissing her navel, I explored the small indentation with my tongue as I fingered her, massaged her love-sheath. Pushing down on my head, she gasped. I knew what she wanted me to do but I felt that I wasn't ready, the time wasn't right. *Is there ever a right time?*

Moving down, I kissed the soft, warm skin edging her crack. Her sex perfume filling my nostrils as I tentatively licked the top of her slit, I felt a pang of arousal deep within my womb. Opening her cunny lips further, Sharon gasped again as I pushed my tongue out and licked around her clitoris. The small nodule hardened, swelled in response to my caressing tongue. Pressing the pink flesh surrounding her bud, she popped it out, exposing its full length to my hungry mouth. Sucking, licking, I wanted to lose myself in her hot cunt, swirl in her come, drown in her sex. Right or wrong, it didn't matter as I moved further down, licking the entire length of her open sex valley, tasting her girl-cream, breathing in her female fragrance as I closed my eyes and pushed my mouth hard against her wet flesh.

'Ah, yes!' she breathed as I slipped my fingers from her hole and licked around her entrance, drinking her milky fluid as it oozed from her sex-sheath. She tasted of sex, female sex – warm, oily, creamy. My own juices flowing, seeping from my vagina, wetting the exercise bench, I desperately needed to come again, to feel her tongue there, licking, sucking on my flowering cherry.

Slipping off the bench, I lay on the floor, smiling up at Sharon, indicating for her to join me. Kneeling astride my head, her gaping pussy soft and warm against my mouth, she lay on top of me and buried her face between my legs. Both licking, nibbling, we seemed to melt into each other, become one as we entwined our bodies in lesbian lust. Never before had I experienced the electrifying sensations, the feeling of complete and utter sexual fulfilment as we drank from each other's sanctums, surrendered to each other our naked bodies.

Our breasts, our hard nipples, each other's arms embracing naked female flesh, our legs wide, our tongues darting, seeking out clitorises, we began to shudder. Praying that we'd make it together, I sucked her nodule into my mouth, flicking my tongue over the hard, sensitive tip. Reciprocating, she mouthed and licked my own pleasure-button, bringing me exquisite sensations that coursed their way deep into my womb.

Her wet pubic curls brushing my cheeks, her juices gushing from her tight hole, I sensed Sharon's muscles tighten, her body become rigid. My own muscles tensed, my legs twitching as my orgasm rose from the hot, quivering depths of my pelvis. We were about to come together – our illicit union taking us ever higher, we were rising together, exquisitely, to an untenable peak of sexual fulfilment.

In a wild sexual frenzy we licked, sucked, mouthed each other's femininity – brought out each other's orgasms. Her body hot, perspiring, heavy on mine, her pussy inflamed, burning with desire, I worked on her budding clitoris, fingered her tight hole, sustaining Sharon's climax as she sustained mine.

Our pussies in each other's mouths, our tongues licking, slurping, in my wildest dreams I could never have imagined the immense pleasure, the total satisfaction, another woman could bring me. As only one woman could do to another, she duplicated my every move, my every kiss, lick, nibble. Whatever I wanted from her, whatever pleasure, I had only to give her that pleasure.

Breathing in her cunt scent, I licked between her legs, her thighs, the crease between her taut buttocks, the small strip of sensitive skin between her two beautiful holes. Parting her buttocks, I gazed at her small hole. Pushing my tongue out, I tasted her there, licking around the most private entrance to her young body. Raising my buttocks as she parted them to reciprocate, I sensed her tongue, darting, exploring, licking my bottom-hole. The sensations driving me wild, I started to shudder uncontrollably.

Moving back to her clitoris, I swept my tongue over its sensitive tip, bringing out another orgasm as she followed suit and elicited mine. Clinging to each other, shuddering, we sucked the pleasure from each other's naked bodies before finally falling limp – spent, panting, gasping, perspiring, drifting in a pool of lesbian lust.

As Sharon climbed from my quivering body, I wondered what to say. What *could* I say? She'd think that I was a lesbian – perhaps I was! My mind reeling, I felt giddy with shame. What I had done was immoral, shameful – but beautifully feminine.

And it wasn't over yet. Moving between my open thighs, Sharon took her breast in her hand and ran her long nipple the length of my slit, wetting her milk bud with my slippery juices. Massaging my clitoris with her breast bud, she smiled, moving up my body and offering her wet nipple to my mouth. I took it – like a baby suckling its life-force, I lapped up my own juices from her breast as she fed me.

When I'd cleansed her, she knelt astride my body, sliding her wet crack over my nipple, decanting her juices, bathing my milk bud. Smiling at me again, she moved beside me and licked my brown bud, lapping up her cunt milk, stiffening my nipple delightfully. Sucking hard on my breast, she closed her eyes, lost in her lesbian fantasy. Then she sucked harder, causing me to cry out as she bit my brown bud. Lifting her head, she smiled and licked her full lips, before moving away.

'That was nice,' she murmured as she gathered her clothes and dressed. I smiled as I climbed to my feet and grabbed my dressing gown, covering my glowing body.

'Coffee?' I asked, rather stupidly.

'Thanks,' she replied, covering her young breasts with her T-shirt as if nothing had happened. Fraught with guilt and shame, I set little store on her nonchalance, supposing that she was well used to lesbian encounters.

As I filled the kettle, contemplating exactly what I'd done, and whether I'd do it again or not, Sharon wandered up behind me and stroked my hair. 'That was really nice,' she breathed as I turned to face her. Her blue eyes shone, sparkling with youth as she gazed at me. Her full lips furled into a smile as she leaned forward and kissed my mouth.

My heart racing, I moved away, unsure of what I was doing, what she wanted from me. I couldn't form a relationship with her, I knew that much. But, there again, what we had done had woken something inside me, stirred some sleeping instinct. I didn't understand my feelings for her. She was living with me now, and I was uneasy about the future.

Leaving her to make the coffee, I dashed into the hall to answer the phone. 'It's me,' came Jim's low voice.

'Oh, hi!' I replied, wondering what had happened when Caroline had quizzed him about the mysterious phone call from another woman.

'Are you free this evening?' he asked.

'Free for what?'

'I've had some trouble, I just wondered . . . I need someone to talk to.'

'Why, what's happened?'

'It's Caroline. Apparently, someone rang and . . . A woman phoned, asking for me. Christ knows who it was! Anyway, Caroline's got the wrong end of the stick. You know how jealous she is. Well, perhaps you don't.'

'And you want to talk to *me* about it?'

'Yes. I just thought that . . . You didn't call her, did you?'

'Why on earth would *I* call her?'

'I don't know. Can I come round this evening?'

'Yes, all right – about seven.'

'The sex we had *was* good, Sue.'

'I know it was! And we'll have lots more – if you want to?'

'I do! Look, someone's just come into the office, I'll see you at seven.'

Poor Jim! I thought as I hung up. My phone call had obviously worked a treat! My first phone call, that was – I'd decided to make many, many more to Caroline. But I had to play the game carefully. If she suspected that it was me, it could end before I'd ended her relationship with Jim.

Finding Sharon sitting at the kitchen table sipping her coffee, I suddenly had an idea – get *her* to call Caroline. But it wasn't the right time to talk about Caroline, there were other things to discuss. Still confused, riddled with guilt, I sat opposite her and smiled.

'I'm pleased that I moved in with you,' she volunteered.

'I'm pleased, too,' I replied. 'Why did you come home early?'

'I'd mixed my classes up. What are you going to do with the spare room?'

'Er . . . I've cleared it out ready for . . . Sharon, what we did together was nice, but I don't want . . .'

'A relationship?'

'Yes.'

'Don't worry, Sue. It was nice loving you like that, and I'd like us to do it again. There are no strings, I only want sex with you, so don't worry.'

I only want sex with you. The words cut through me like a knife! *Sex with you.* This was a girl talking to me! Again, I seemed to be floundering in a deep pool of confusion. I didn't know what to say. Suddenly, I realized that I couldn't fight my inner desire – the ever-rising desire I had to lick between her thighs again, to feel her tongue caressing my clitoris. Right or wrong, it didn't matter – no one would know, no one could judge.

Perhaps I shouldn't have, but I told her about my plans to destroy marriages – about Jim, Tony, Derek, and the things I'd done. I suppose I wanted to change the subject, to get away from sex – lesbian sex, anyway.

'God!' she breathed in response. 'You can't go around wrecking people's lives like that!'

'Why not?' I asked indifferently.

'Because . . . because it's not right! I know what your husband did to you was wrong, but two wrongs don't make a right!'

'Two? There are going to be dozens of wrongs before I've finished! By the way, I've been receiving notes, telling me in explicit detail about Jim and Caroline, what they do in bed together.'

'God! That's an evil thing to do!'

'It's awful! I want them to stop. I'll never rid my mind of those people all the time the notes keep coming – I just want them to stop!'

'Whoever it is will give up. They can't go on forever, can they?'

'No, I suppose not – I hope not! Anyway, I need a favour from you.'

'What?'

'Phone that bitch, Caroline, and pretend that you're a mysterious woman after Jim. Ask if he's in, and sound sexy.'

'What, now?'

'No, she'll be at work. This evening. Phone her this evening.'

'I don't know, Sue.'

'You do want us to . . . you do want sex with me again, don't you?'

'Yes, but . . .'

'Good, that's settled, then.'

'No, it's not! Look, I'll make a deal with you. I'll go along with your games, ring whoever you want me to, do whatever you want me to do, but only if you allow me to pleasure you whenever I want to.'

'How often will that be?'

'Every day, if not more.'

Diving again into a sea of confusion, I eventually agreed to her deal. I desperately wanted sex with Sharon, but I couldn't allow my feelings for her to get in the way of my plans. Love? I didn't know what I felt for her. She was so young, and so very pretty. Her smile was bright, her eyes full of life. But what were my real feelings for her?

The afternoon passed quickly. Sharon spent hours in her room studying, thank God, while I went out and bought some items for my sex den – rope, a body massager and, embarrassingly, lots of KY-Gel from Boots. I also bought some huge candles from a gift shop. I'd wanted handcuffs and chains and leather whips, but I didn't know where to get them from. Mail order, I supposed as I dumped the stuff in the spare room and checked my watch, wondering how to explain my purchases to Sharon. Six o'clock.

Wearing a miniskirt and loose blouse, Sharon was standing in the kitchen preparing a meal – ham salad. She turned and grinned as I entered, obviously seeking praise for her efforts.

'I hope you're hungry!' she beamed.

'Starving!' I enthused, admiring the way she'd cut the tomatoes into interesting shapes. 'You've done well,' I added.

'Perhaps you should take over in the kitchen.'

'I'm no good at cooking,' she declared, placing the plates on the table. 'But salads are a speciality of mine.'

As we ate, I talked of my plans, and the phone call I wanted her to make to Caroline. Sharon was far from happy about it, complaining that it was wrong to destroy marriages, but I reminded her of our time in the spare room, and our deal, and she agreed to help me in my quest. After the meal, I led her to the phone and grinned.

'Right, you know what to say,' I said, praying that Caroline would answer the phone as I dialled the number. Hearing the ringing tone, I passed the phone to Sharon and waited with bated breath.

'Is Jim there?' Sharon asked, much to my delight. If he was there, the idea was that Sharon hang up before he reached the phone, fuelling Caroline's suspicion. 'Oh, when will he be back?' she asked. 'No, there's no message, thanks. No, I don't want to leave my name. No, it's a personal call, I'm a friend of his. I'll try again later.'

Replacing the receiver, she frowned at me. 'The poor woman must be writhing in anguish now!' she complained.

'That's nothing, you wait until she discovers Jim screwing me!'

'You don't really plan to have her catch you red-handed, do you?' she asked.

'Too right, I do! Anyway, he'll be here soon, so . . .'

'I'll stay in my room, I've a lot of studying to get on with.'

'Why not join in?'

'What?'

'Join in the sexy fun. Let's give him a lesbian show.'

'Christ, no! If you think I'm going to . . .'

'You *do* want me again, don't you?'

'Christ, Sue, that's emotional blackmail!'

'Yes, you're right. So, how about joining in? Or are you

completely averse to having some sexy fun with a long, hard penis?'

'I'm not averse to it, it's just that I prefer my own sex.'

'Then you'll join in? I'll tell you what – you join in, and you can live here rent-free.'

I knew that would sway her. On her meagre grant, she could barely afford to survive. I was sure that she couldn't turn down an offer like that!

'All right,' she sighed. 'But I'm not having him up me!'

'Agreed. We'll give him a lesbian show, and I'll have him up *me*, as you put it. Right, this is the plan. When he's here and you can hear that things are well under way, come into the lounge, naked, and appear surprised, embarrassed, and . . .'

'I will be bloody embarrassed!'

'No, you won't. Now, go and wait in your room. I'll leave the lounge door open so you can hear what's going on.'

Disgruntled, Sharon made for her room to prepare for her timely entrance. Jim would be back for sex again and again once he'd sampled two women, I knew. The plan was going well – too well, perhaps. The thought suddenly struck me that Caroline might follow Jim to my house and the relationship would be over before I'd had my fun. I wanted the chance to enjoy the sport before I moved in for the kill! All I could do was pray that he'd been clever enough with his lies to escape the bitch.

Sitting in the lounge, knickerless and braless, in my miniskirt and open blouse, I awaited my prey. Grabbing my notebook, I grinned as I crossed out number one and scribbled number three by Jim's and Caroline's names, promoting them to leaders in the wrecked marriage stakes. The rot was setting in, the decay crumbling the very foundations of their relationship. And by the time Sharon and I had dealt with Jim that evening, I reckoned they'd be halfway to the finishing post.

Checking my list, I realized that there were so many couples that I hadn't even started on. But there was no rush – I had all the time in the world to bring them all to their knees. All the time in the world!

Chapter Six

Jim finally arrived, cowering on the doorstep like a frightened rabbit, his eyes darting this way and that. 'What's all this about?' I asked as we entered the lounge.

'Someone phoned *again* – a woman!' he moaned as he sat beside me on the sofa.

'Well, if you're going to screw around, you'll just have to be more careful,' I imparted impishly.

'I *am* careful – and I'm not screwing around!'

'You're screwing *me*! Anyway, someone's obviously got your phone number. Are you sure you haven't slipped up and given it to some girl or other?'

'Positive! Caroline's *really* suspicious now. Christ, I don't know what's going on! Who the hell's been ringing me?'

'I don't know. Perhaps someone knows that you come here to see me?'

'No, of course no one knows! Anyway, she's not suspicious about me going out, it's the bloody phone calls.'

'Why don't *you* answer the phone?'

'I haven't been there when whoever it is rings.'

It seemed strange talking to my ex-husband about the problems he was having in his relationship. There he was, opening up to me about his troubles as if I were an old friend. I suppose that's how he viewed me – as well as a sex object, of course. If only Caroline knew! If only she could see him sitting on my sofa, listen to him confiding to me about their relationship!

After the scathing notes I'd sent to Caroline, Jim had

obviously suspected me of making the phone calls, but I was pretty sure that I'd allayed his suspicions – for a while, at least. I knew that I had to be careful, play the game vigilantly, sow small seeds of doubt in the bitch's mind – and lots of them. The day would come, of course, when the whole thing came out into the open. Caroline would catch us naked, entwined in lust, fucking – and she'd throw him out. He'd go mad at me – and I'd laugh in his face! *Bastard!*

'How would you like me to wash away all your worries?' I purred as I reclined on the sofa and pulled my skirt up over my stomach. He gazed at my smooth pussy lips, my pink, inner flesh protruding alluringly from my open crack, and smiled. 'It's yours for the taking,' I proffered, opening my legs even wider.

'I don't know what I'd do without you,' he breathed as he cupped my swelling cunny lips in his hand. I laughed inwardly as I thought how much better off he'd be without me – the serial marriage-wrecker!

Tugging at his zip as he ran his finger up and down the length of my moistening sex valley, I pulled his hard penis out and squeezed the solid shaft. He sighed, lying back as I moved the loose skin back and forth over his plum. 'That's nice,' he gasped as I tugged his jeans down and fondled his penis with both hands, caressing, stroking, hardening him. Kicking his jeans aside, he almost ripped his shirt off and lay back on the sofa, his legs open, his heavy balls rolling, yearning to be drained.

'You have the best dick in the world,' I whispered. 'I hope Caroline appreciates it.'

'She used to,' he replied dolefully.

'Well, it doesn't matter whether she does or doesn't, because I do. Now, are you going to come in my mouth, or would you rather come in my wet cunny first?'

Suddenly, Sharon called out from the hall and opened the

lounge door. 'I'm ready for you, Sue, you sexy little lesbian!' she cried as she breezed into the room carrying the rope I'd bought. 'I found this in the spare room,' she giggled. Playing her role perfectly, she made for the mantelpiece and turned to face me, feigning astonishment to see Jim sitting next to me, naked.

Her young, naked body was a beautiful sight. Her elongated nipples, her darkening areolae, were just visible through the veil of long golden hair cascading over her firm breasts. The soft hair nestling between her shapely thighs appeared as if it had been brushed away from her groove, her tight crack seemingly smiling, impishly poking its pink tongue out.

'Oh, I'm so sorry!' she cried, folding her arms to cover her rounded breasts, the rope hanging down over her smooth stomach. 'I didn't realize . . .'

'That's all right, Sharon,' I smiled. 'This is Jim, my ex-husband.'

'Oh, hallo,' she murmured, gazing at his stiff penis. 'I'll leave you both in peace,' she added, looking at me.

'You don't have to go. She doesn't have to go, does she, Jim?' I asked, turning to face him.

He gazed at the girl, at her young crack, in amazement. Then, his penis harder than ever, he looked at me. 'No, she doesn't have to go,' he breathed. 'Sue, I didn't realize that you were . . .'

'A lesbian? No, I'm not, really. Sharon's my lodger, and we have some sexy fun now and then, that's all. Shall we show him what we get up to, Sharon?' I asked, beckoning her to join me as I slipped off the sofa and lay on the floor.

Sitting beside me, she leaned forward and sucked my nipple into her mouth as I opened my legs. Reaching down, she ran her finger up and down the length of my slit, lubricating my sex furrow with my slippery pussy milk. I breathed heavily, closing my eyes as she located my clitoris and sucked harder on my sensitive nipple. I heard Jim gasp as I parted my thighs further, allowing Sharon to push three fingers deep into my tightening cunt.

'Suck me!' I cried as she slipped her fingers from my hole and dragged my juice up my opening valley to my clitoris. Moving down, she flicked her tongue over my supple outer lips, wetting my intimate flesh with her warm saliva. Arching my back, I opened my eyes slightly and gazed at Jim through my lashes. He was visibly stunned, his eyes wide, his mouth hanging open in astonishment as Sharon stretched my pussy wide open and licked my hot, inner flesh.

My climax quickly approaching, I reached out, beckoning Jim to join us. Grinning, he knelt by my side, offering me his huge weapon. Taking his knob into my mouth, I ran my tongue in circles round his silky-smooth glans as Sharon continued to work on my ripening clitoris. Delirious with electrifying sensations of sex, I ran my hand up and down the shaft of Jim's twitching penis, desperate to bring out his sperm.

'I'll do that!' Sharon, cried, neglecting my clitoris and grabbing his penis. Pulling his knob from my mouth, she massaged the loose skin, moving it back and forth over his ballooning plum. I wanted to suck him, but she held my head down, grinning as she wanked his shaft. Gasping, Jim threw his head back as his sperm jetted, splashing my face. My mouth open, I tasted the salty drops as they cascaded, bathing my tongue, splattering over my cheeks, my nose.

Allowing me my pleasure, Sharon thrust Jim's knob into my mouth and moved down to my aching clitoris. I sucked, drank the milky come as it spurted from his beautiful knob. My body quivering uncontrollably as Jim pinched my nipples and Sharon sucked my clitoris into her hot mouth, my climax rose from my womb, tearing through my body, blowing my mind.

Shuddering, I sucked Jim's shaft deeper into my mouth until I sensed his knob at the back of my throat, felt his hairy balls resting against my face. My orgasm took me higher, on and on, gripping me as Sharon sucked and licked my throbbing clitoris. The rolling waves of pure sexual bliss crashing through my consumed body, I thought that the end had come. Holding my breath, my back arched, my fingernails gouging the carpet, I waited for my climax to release me from its beautiful, torturous grip.

At last, I fell limp. Jim's penis shrinking in my mouth, my clitoris fluttering delightfully in response to Sharon's darting tongue, I relaxed in the wake of the most heavenly, almost frightening, climax of my entire life. My slaves moving away, I opened my eyes slightly to see Jim's flaccid penis hovering above my face. Taking his spent member in her hand, Sharon fondled the shaft of male flesh, pulling the skin back and examining the purple knob as if she'd never before seen a male organ.

Would she suck it into her mouth? Would Sharon, the confirmed lesbian, take a penis into her mouth and drink its gushing sperm? Through my lashes, I watched her massaging the once again stiffening member. Only inches above my face, Jim's rod bulged, swelling in response to her kneading, fondling, caressing.

Manoeuvring her naked body, Sharon placed her knees either side of my head and leaned forward, burying her face between my legs, lapping up my hot come. Her young crack open, oozing with her cream, hovering above my mouth, I pushed my tongue out to taste her. But suddenly Jim was there, behind her, running his knob up and down her gaping crack, lubricating his swollen glans in readiness to penetrate her.

Would Sharon allow him to fill her lesbian girl-sheath with his huge male organ? I wondered as his hairy balls tickled my forehead. I watched with bated breath as he pushed his knob between her distended pussy lips, parting them, opening the entrance to her beautiful girlish love-tube. Slowly entering her,

Sharon's young cunt yielded as Jim sank his spectacular shaft.

Impaling her completely, her swollen cunt lips stretched around the base of his thick member, he slowly withdrew. The soft, veined skin of his bulging organ glistening with her cunt milk, he drove into her again. Withdrawing, he impaled her again and again, quickening his rhythm as Sharon mouthed between my pussy lips, stiffening my clitoris as my ex-husband took her young body from behind.

I'd never thought that I'd be watching Jim driving his cock deep into another girl's tight vagina. But there were no distressing emotions, no jealousy – only immense arousal as I watched his solid shaft fuck Sharon's wet cunt only inches from my face. I began to think that we should have invited another girl into our marriage to add a little spice to our sex lives. There again, before my metamorphosis, I'd have been riddled with jealousy at the merest thought of my husband screwing someone else.

Although my mission had been to destroy Jim's relationship with Caroline, I was beginning to think twice. Why put an end to his sex visits? Sharon was obviously having a ball! Why not continue to enjoy our three-D relationship?

My thoughts swirled – thoughts of Jim cheating on me, using me, discarding me for that bitch, Caroline. No, however good our sexual relationship, I would still destroy him, see him fall, break him for what he'd done to me.

Sharon suddenly gasped and Jim grunted, bringing me back from my thoughts of destruction. His huge shaft was thrusting into her young body, threatening to split her tight vagina open as he neared his coming. My clitoris throbbing, my cunt burning, yearning to be fucked as Sharon was being fucked, I pushed my tongue out and tried to lick the juices glistening on Jim's driving shaft. But suddenly slipping the thrusting length of his penis from her hot cunt, he rubbed just his knob between her pouting pussy lips as his sperm spouted.

Bathing her rubicund inner lips, his come dripped into my mouth, splashing my tongue as I lapped up the exotic blend of their orgasmic juices. Managing to raise my head, I sucked his knob into my mouth and drank the last of his sperm as it jetted. Sharon's wet cunt dribbled its magical cream over my flushed face as I fervently mouthed and sucked. I was lost, delirious in my quivering pleasure as my clitoris exploded in her mouth. Licking her cunt, Jim's cock, gulping down the juices of their fucking, I pulled Sharon down on me, squashing Jim's penis between her hot cunt lips and my hungry mouth as my entire body shook with orgasm. Barely able to breathe, my face drenched with sex, my eyes rolling, I seemed to pass out, to slip into a strangely comforting state of semi-consciousness.

Finally coming round, I opened my eyes to see Jim and Sharon gazing down at me. 'Are you all right?' Jim asked, brushing my wet, matted hair from my face.

'Yes, I think so,' I murmured as my senses slowly returned.

'You were shaking so much!' Sharon exclaimed. 'I've never seen a girl come the way you did!'

'I've never come like that before!' I cried, trying to raise myself on my elbows.

'Did you like having Jim up you after all?'

'Yes, it was . . . it was so good because I had you to lick at the same time. I wouldn't want to be alone with a man, but I like the three of us together.'

'You're not a complete lesbian, then?' I smiled.

'I don't think she can be!' Jim rejoined. 'You were great, Sharon!'

Sitting up, I wiped the sperm from my face and tossed my hair back, wondering whether Jim could manage to fuck me so soon after taking Sharon. As I was about to get up, Sharon gently pushed me down and rolled me over. 'I'm not finished with you yet!' she giggled, sitting on my back to pin me down. Grabbing the rope, she bound my wrists behind my back as Jim took my feet and opened my legs wide.

'What are you going to do?' I asked, somewhat fearfully.

'You'll see!' Sharon chuckled, climbing off my back.

Taking two more lengths of rope, they bound my ankles, pulling my feet wide apart and fixing one rope to the sofa leg and the other to the armchair. My legs splayed, my wrists bound, my naked body defenceless – I was their prisoner.

Sharon pulled my buttocks apart, crudely exposing my bottom-hole to my ex-husband. I knew then that Jim was going to enter me there, push the entire length of his rock-hard penis deep into my bowels, and I protested. 'Not there!' I cried as I felt the hardness of his hot knob press against my small hole.

'Yes, there!' he laughed as Sharon opened my buttocks further, stretching my hole open.

Closing my eyes, I relaxed my muscles, allowing the massive knob to sink into my body. Sharon groped beneath me, locating the wet entrance to my pussy as Jim pushed his weapon deeper into me. The sensations were heavenly, and I raised my bottom to accommodate his huge organ. His balls finally coming to rest against my cunt lips, he'd impaled me completely. His warm belly pressing against my buttocks as Sharon's invading fingers twisted their way deep into my hot cunt, I gasped.

Never had I known such sensations! My entire pelvis stretched to capacity, my body began to rock as Jim swayed his hips, fucking my bottom-hole as Sharon pistoned my aching vagina with her fingers. Breathing deeply, my mind drifting, floating on a pool of carnal pleasure, I was in my sexual heaven as I was crudely taken, used by a man and a woman.

Knowing that I could do nothing to defend my body against Jim and Sharon heightened my arousal incredibly. My naked body tethered, my legs splayed, exposing the very centre of my femininity, I felt wonderfully dirty, crude.

'I want your cunt in my mouth!' I cried as Sharon located

my clitoris. 'I want to suck the juice from your cunt!' Ignoring my pleas, she massaged my clitoris, bringing me all-encompassing sensations, jolting every muscle in my body. Faster she masturbated me as Jim hammered his knob deep into my bowels, opening me as never before. Swirling feelings surfacing from deep within my womb, I knew I was on the verge of release.

'God, I'm coming!' Jim cried as he drove into me with a vengeance. As my clitoris erupted beneath Sharon's wet fingers, I sensed my anal sheath expand as Jim's offering gushed deep into my very being. On and on he pistoned his huge cock into my stretched anal sheath, filling my bowels with his slippery come. Quivering uncontrollably, I gasped, my eyes rolling, my face flushing as the blood rushed to my spinning head. Locating my sex centre again, Sharon thrust her fingers deep into me, stretching me again, bringing me exquisite sensations as Jim made his last pummelling thrust into my bum-hole before collapsing over my back.

I lay there trembling, panting in my exhaustion, his shrinking penis absorbing the heat of my bowels as Sharon brought out the last ripples of pleasure from my palpitating cunt. Sliding his shaft out of my aching bum-hole, I sensed my muscles close, sealing in his sex-liquid. Gently, sensitively, Sharon slipped her hand from beneath me, leaving me to relax in the aftermath of my incredible climax.

Finally untying my bonds, my abusers released my aching body and sat side by side on the sofa. Climbing to my feet, sperm oozing between my buttocks, I staggered across the room and collapsed into the armchair.

'God, that was good!' I gasped.

'We should have fucked like that when we were married,' Jim smiled as he reclined on the sofa, his penis lying over his heavy balls.

'We should!' I agreed as the phone rang.

'If that's Caroline . . .' Jim began, his expression anguished.

'She wouldn't ring here!' I laughed, dashing into the hall and closing the door behind me.

Grabbing the phone, I smiled to hear Tony's voice. 'How are things going?' I asked, my fingers appeasing my aching clitoris.

'She's speaking to me again, but I'm worried.'

'What about?'

'You two get on well. Has she ever mentioned a male friend of hers to you?'

'Well, I wouldn't like to say anything, Tony.'

'So she has told you?'

'I really don't think that I should discuss this. Besides, you have me: so what if she does have a male friend?'

'It's bloody adultery, that's what!'

'God, *you* can talk!'

'I know, but it's different for a man, isn't it?'

Different? What a bastard! Still, at least I could now give Tony and Sally three points! After listening to several minutes of his complaining, I told him that I really had to go.

'Can I come round and see you?' he pleaded.

'What, now?'

'Yes.'

'Give me an hour, and then come round,' I replied. 'By the way, where's Sally?'

'Over the road at that fat woman's house – you know, that ugly old cow. What's her name?'

'You mean Pauline?'

'Yes, that's her.'

'Oh. Anyway, I'll see you in an hour.'

'OK – look forward to it. Bye.'

Returning to the lounge, I told Jim, nicely, that he'd have to leave as a girlfriend was coming round to see me. Dressing, he smiled at Sharon and winked. Had the bastard planned to screw her? I wondered. Arranged to meet her behind my back and fuck her? Probably! But I didn't care. Sharon was my lodger, and a lesbian, and I doubted very much that she'd go sneaking off to meet my ex-husband for a quick fuck.

When Jim had gone, Sharon and I dressed and sat on the sofa. Showing her my notebook, I wrote number three beside Tony and Sally and grinned. 'He's coming round,' I said. 'In about half an hour.'

'God, you don't want me to join in *again*, do you?' she asked.

'Yes, but this time, it's going to be completely different. I have a plan. I know it's early in the game, but I'm going to arrange for his wife to catch her adulterous husband in the act.'

Sighing, Sharon raised her eyes to the ceiling. I knew that I was asking a lot of her but, after all, she was living in my house rent-free – and eating my food. Promising that it was the last time I'd ask a sexual favour of her, to my relief she agreed.

As Sharon showered, I rang Pauline and asked if Sally was still there – but she'd gone. Not wanting to ring her at home in case Tony answered, I waited until I saw him coming up the road before dialling her number. The phone rang and rang, but she didn't answer. My plan, it seemed, was doomed!

'Come in, Tony,' I invited with a welcoming smile as I opened the front door, wondering whether to ask him where Sally had gone. 'I've got to pick something up from the chemist, but I'll leave you in the capable hands of my lodger, Sharon,' I explained as we entered the lounge. 'She's having a shower, she won't be too long.'

'But I came to see *you*!' he groaned.

'I know that. I won't be long, Tony. Surely you can wait for me? Anyway, Sally's not at home, so what's the rush?'

Leaving him fuming in the lounge, I closed the door and grinned at Sharon as she bounded downstairs in her dressing gown. 'Seduce him good and proper,' I whispered. 'I'll go out and find his wife and bring her back here, OK?'

'I suppose so,' she mumbled. 'I'm not a bloody prostitute, Sue!'

'I know you're not. Look, this is the last time, I promise you.'

Leaving the house, I ran the short distance to Sally's place, only to find that she was still out. Over the road, Pauline invited me into her house and started rambling on about her kids. Telling her that I was in a hurry, I asked her where Sally'd gone, but she didn't know. In despair, I decided to go home and join in the fun. My plan was in ruins, but, no doubt, there'd be other opportunities.

As I reached my front door, I saw Sally coming down the street. Satan was with me! 'Hi, Sue!' she called.

'Oh, hi, Sally! How are you?' I asked.

'Not bad. You been out?'

'Er . . . Yes, I have. Fancy a glass of wine? You can come in and meet my new lodger, Sharon.'

'OK. I can't stay for long, though,' she replied, following me into the hall.

'Go into the lounge, and I'll get the wine,' I suggested, praying that Sharon had Tony in a compromising position – a lewd, filthy, disgusting position!

This was it, I thought as I uncorked the sparkling Lambrusco I knew Sally wouldn't be sharing – socially, anyway! The first of many marriages about to bite the dust! Waiting in the kitchen, I shuddered with delight as Sally's hysterical screams filled the house – and poor Sharon flew upstairs. Dashing into the lounge, I almost burst out laughing to see Tony standing before his distraught wife, his jeans around his ankles, his wet cock hanging limp over his balls.

'Did you know that he was here screwing that girl?' Sally sobbed through her tears.

'No, I didn't!' I gasped, glaring at Tony. 'Christ, Tony, that's my lodger! She's only a young girl, how could you?'

'She . . . she started it!' he returned pathetically.

'I knew there was someone!' Sally wailed, turning to me. Waving my hand at Tony, I indicated for him to go as Sally cried on my shoulder. The door closing, I sat her down to comfort her.

'He must have come round to finish the washing machine,' I said lamely, placing my arm round her shoulders.

'I walked in and . . . She was on all fours and he was kneeling behind her . . . God, I'll never forget the sight of them!'

'Stay here, and I'll go and ask Sharon what the hell happened!' I volunteered, leaving the room.

In the kitchen, I poured two glasses of wine before going upstairs to see Sharon. Cowering on her bed in her dressing gown, she looked up at me in disgust.

'You did well,' I praised her.

'Christ, Sue! That woman will blame *me*!'

'No, she won't. Come down in a few minutes and . . .'

'No way!'

'I'll tell her that Tony told you he was single, and that you fell for his charm. It'll be all right.'

'I might, I'm not sure.'

'Give me ten minutes, and then come down.'

Taking the wine into the lounge, I passed a glass to Sally and advised her to drink it. 'I've spoken to Sharon,' I began as I sat next to her. 'Apparently, she'd just taken a shower and, not knowing that Tony was here, she came into the lounge in her dressing gown. I'd left the front door open as I was only going out for a while and it was so hot. He must have walked in to fix the washing machine, thinking that I'd be back soon and . . . Anyway, he told Sharon that he was single and, using his charm, he seduced her. She said that she was very frightened at first, but he coaxed her and offered to take her out for a meal.'

'Did he rape her?'

'No, of course he didn't! I suppose she thought that . . . I don't know what she thought, the poor girl! She's very young and impressionable. Perhaps she fell for his charm and couldn't help . . .'

'So, you didn't know that Tony was coming round?'

'No, all he'd said was that he'd be round to fix the machine when he'd got the spare part. Presumably, that's what he was doing here.'

It was working like a dream! I couldn't believe how well it was going. There I was, still friends with Sally, and yet I'd destroyed her marriage. Within seconds, her marriage was over – smashed into a thousand tiny pieces! But, just to make sure, I planted another seed of doubt.

'Sharon isn't the one he's been seeing,' I said.

'Then there must be someone else?'

'There must be. That was the first time he'd met Sharon – she's only just moved in.'

'God, he's a bastard! I knew there was another woman, but I didn't realize that he'd screw anyone who he happened to bump into!'

'Just like Jim!' I quipped. 'They're all the bloody same!'

Obviously not able to pluck up the courage to confront Sally, Sharon didn't appear. Probably just as well, I mused, as the phone rang. Leaving Sally with her wine and her tears, I closed the lounge door and picked the receiver up.

'What's happening?' Tony asked shakily.

'You tell me! What the hell did you think you were doing?'

'She seduced me, Sue!'

'Don't talk bollocks, she's only a young girl!'

'She did! She opened her dressing gown and . . . Before I knew what was happening, she'd . . .'

'Well, you *are* a very attractive man!' I laughed.

'It's not bloody funny! What the hell am I going to do? Why

did you let Sally into the house knowing that I was there?'

'When I got back, she followed me up the path. There wasn't much I could do. Besides, I was going to say that you'd come to fix the washing machine – I didn't expect to find you fucking Sharon!'

'What the hell am I going to do?'

'There's nothing you *can* do. I'll talk to Sally and try to get you out of this mess, but I don't hold much hope.'

'Please, try! Do your best, Sue – I'm depending on you!'

Depend on me to finish your marriage off!

'Your marriage is over, Sally, you realize that, don't you?' I murmured softly, concernedly, as I joined her on the sofa. *The power of suggestion works wonders!*

'Yes, I know,' she whimpered wretchedly. 'I can never face him again.'

'I know how you must feel. After what Jim did to me, I know *exactly* how you feel.'

'How could he do it? We've been happily married for . . . Over the last few days, he's changed so much. He was fine until . . .'

'Until what?' I asked, praying that she wouldn't connect the change in her husband with my broken washing machine.

'I don't know, I'm confused!' she sobbed. 'How the hell could he do this to me?'

I was becoming bored. Tears, blubbering, I was becoming very bored. My own tears – tears for Jim – had drowned my emotion, frozen me. My plan had worked. The kill was over. Now I just wanted to plan my next victim's downfall – Jim's downfall.

'Look, you'd better go home,' I suggested. 'Try and sleep, Sally. Take a pill and try and sleep and we'll talk about it tomorrow.'

'Yes, you're right. Thanks, Sue. I'll see you tomorrow.'

'Right, and lock the bedroom door – you don't want that

adulterous bastard creeping in during the night. And don't listen to his excuses – there *is* no excuse for the way he's treated you.'

'I know that!' she returned, dabbing her face and climbing to her feet. 'I'll see you tomorrow.'

Joining me in the lounge, I could see that Sharon wasn't at all happy, although she did admit that Tony was a good fuck. 'What happened to the lesbian in you?' I laughed.

'It hasn't gone, it's just that . . .'

'That you like a hard cock up you for a change?'

'I suppose so. I can't get over that poor woman, Sue! What we did was so unfair!'

'Life's unfair! Life stinks! Anyway, forget about her! It's late, and I'm tired.'

'What time is it?'

'Half-eleven.'

'God, I'm totally shagged out, and I've got an early class tomorrow!'

'You'll be all right. Go on, get your beauty sleep and I'll see you in the morning.'

Sitting alone in the lounge, I contemplated my day's work. Strangely, I felt no guilt, no remorse. I'd deliberately set out to destroy Tony's and Sally's marriage, and had succeeded admirably. Opening my notepad, I wrote number nine by their names – ten being reserved for actual divorce. Glancing down the list, I added Tracy and Craig. Tracy was the girl I'd known from school who'd had a relationship with another girl. She'd married Craig, who was twenty-eight, bloody good-looking, and something in the City, and their relationship had been rock-strong. Although they only lived around the block, I hadn't seen either of them for a while. How was their marriage wearing after six years? I wondered. Knowing those two, it would be granite by now!

The taste of blood on my lips, I decided I wanted Craig. Fresh from the kill, I wanted him badly! But what story could I concoct to lure him to me? Although it was late, I felt a sudden rush of life course its way through my veins as I lifted the receiver and dialled Mr and Mrs Perfect's number.

'Trace, it's me, Sue,' I greeted her as she answered the phone.

'Oh, hello, Sue! Long time, no hear! I heard that you and Jim . . .'

'Yes, he's gone – we're divorced.'

'Oh dear! How are you coping?'

'I *was* all right. I was just going up to bed when I noticed water flooding out from under the kitchen sink. Now that Jim's not here . . . I know it's late, but is there any chance that Craig could nip round and take a look? I don't know anyone else I can ring for help at this time of night.'

'Yes, of course! He's watching TV. I'll send him round.'

'Thanks, Trace – I really appreciate it.'

'That's OK. Listen, I'll ring you tomorrow and we'll go out for lunch or something.'

'Right, we'll do that – thanks again.'

'No problem – bye.'

Standing at the kitchen sink with my skirt hoisted up and my feet wide apart, I splashed handfuls of water between my shaved pussy lips and my buttocks, washing away the sticky concoction of Jim's sperm and my pussy milk. Looking down at the water running across the floor, I smiled. A little more, I decided, pouring a saucepanful of water over the tiles. Craig wouldn't find a leaking pipe, of course, but that didn't matter. Drying myself with sheets of kitchen roll, I wondered how easily he would tumble into my trap – succumb to my pussy.

When he arrived, I led him into the kitchen and pointed to the floor. 'Oh!' he gasped, his brown eyes wide, his tawny hair swept back. Wearing well-cut grey trousers and a white, short-sleeved shirt, he looked a typical City type, and I wondered if he visited prostitutes or seedy bars while away from his pretty little wife and suburbia.

Squatting down, he opened the cupboard door under the sink and inspected the plumbing. 'Can't see a leak,' he said as I crouched beside him, my skirt high, my thighs open. My naked pussy lips would be bulging, forced to balloon between my thighs, I knew. Praying that my temptress wouldn't fail in her quest, I mumbled something unintelligible about the plumbing, complaining that it wasn't easy without a man in the house. Turning his head, he observed my femininity smiling at him from beneath my skirt, and grinned.

'You go around like that, and you'll get yourself into trouble!' he laughed, gazing between my legs. Obviously, my display hadn't been too subtle! Trying to appear innocent, I looked down and gasped.

'God! I didn't . . .'

'Like showing your pussy off, do you?' he mocked, his eyes still admiring my bulging cunt lips.

'I didn't do it deliberately!' I cried, standing up and pulling my skirt down. 'I was getting ready for bed and . . .'

'You've got a nice body,' he praised. 'You must be missing sex now that Jim's gone.'

This one didn't need encouraging! Who was trying to get whom into bed? I wondered. But did it really matter? As long as Craig became a regular visitor, a regular fuck – and I destroyed his marriage – did it really matter?

'You are awful! You're a married man!' I admonished.

'What's that got to do with it?' he quipped.

'Everything!'

'As far as I'm concerned, if a pretty little thing like you is crying out for sex, then I'll oblige.'

'I'm not crying out for sex!'

'Of course you are! All women are!'

God, a male chauvinist bastard if ever there was one! I

hadn't expected to come across anyone like Craig. I'd thought that I'd have to entice men, gently coax them, tempt them with my alluring pussy-crack. This one definitely deserved divorce – and I was going to make sure he got it!

'Fancy a glass of wine?' I asked, reaching for two glasses, my skirt riding high up my thighs.

'I fancy you!' he grinned, eyeing my swelling breasts.

'Don't be so naughty, Craig!' I giggled as he took me in his arms and tried to kiss me. 'Craig! What *are* you *doing*?' I cried as he thrust his hand up my skirt and cupped my swollen cunt lips in his palm.

'I like a shaved pussy,' he breathed in my ear. 'How about you taking me up to your bedroom?'

'We'll go into the lounge and have a glass of wine, and then you can go home to your wife,' I demurred, pulling away.

Grabbing the wine bottle from the fridge, I told Craig to bring the glasses. Placing the bottle on the coffee table, I sat on the sofa as he poured the wine. 'How's Tracy?'I asked as he sat beside me.

'She doesn't shave her pussy, if that's what you mean!' he laughed.

'I didn't mean that! God, don't you ever think about anything else?'

'Nope, all I think about is sex. When did you last have it? I'll bet it's been months!'

'About an hour ago, if you must know,' I replied, flashing him a wicked grin.

'Don't give me that! You're stuck here all alone: I'll bet you're dying for it.'

'*You* obviously are! Doesn't Tracy give it to you?'

'No, I give it to her.'

No messing around, I decided as I reached for his zip. Let's get straight down to it. The sooner I've got him eating out of my pussy, the sooner he'll regret the day he met me. Poor

Tracy, she'd be sitting at home waiting for her husband, not knowing that I was about to suck the sperm from his penis. Still, she'd be better off without a two-timing Casanova like Craig.

'I knew you were dying for it,' he breathed as I pulled his hard penis out. Saying nothing, I leaned over and kissed his swollen knob. 'God, that's nice,' he murmured as I gently sucked on his silky plum. Slipping his organ from my mouth, I looked into his brown eyes and grinned.

'I *am* dying for it,' I whispered. 'It's been weeks since I last . . .'

'Suck me again, and then I'll give you the fucking of your life,' he promised as I ran my finger over his glans.

'Does Tracy suck you?' I asked.

'Yes. But let's not talk about her.'

'Does she swallow your come?'

'No, she won't let me come in her mouth.'

'There's nothing I like better than drinking sperm from a big, throbbing cock. Let me drink yours, and then you can fuck me,' I whispered in my best husky voice. 'Stand up and pull your trousers down.'

Obediently, he stood before me and tugged his trousers down to his ankles. Desperate to see his manhood in all its erect glory, I dragged his boxer shorts down to his knees. His penis stood to attention, his heavy balls hanging below the root of his thick shaft, far larger than I'd ever imagined possible. Stroking his dark curls with my fingertip, I watched his mighty rod twitch in anticipation.

'You'll like this,' I smiled, looking up to his eyes as I sat on the edge of the sofa and pulled his foreskin back as far as I could. Licking the tip of his plum, savouring his salty glans, I knew that I'd trapped yet another married man. Another marriage would soon fall prey to my sensuous charm – my blatant whoring.

Engulfing his knob in my hot mouth, I moaned through my nose, kneading his balls as I mouthed and sucked. Gripping my head, he slowly moved his hips back and forth, groaning as he gently fucked my mouth with his huge organ. Raising my eyes, I smiled. His head thrown back, his mouth open, he was in his ecstasy – in my power.

Wanking him as I licked and sucked, I thought of Sharon sleeping in her room. Although I liked drinking sperm from orgasming cocks, I loved licking Sharon's youthful crack. Bisexual? I wondered as Craig began to tremble. Yes, I must be bisexual. Or just very sexual!

'Ah!' he gasped as his sperm jetted and he gripped my head harder. 'Ah, God!' He tasted wonderful – masculine, yang. Ramming his organ, thrusting in his coming, he fucked my mouth, filled my cheeks with his come until I sensed his wetness running down my chin. Swallowing hard, I drank his male fruits until I'd drained his balls. Slipping his knob out, I licked the small slit, ran my tongue round his swollen glans as he shuddered. Licking the length of his long, twitching shaft, I finally released him and looked up to see the satisfaction mirrored in his smiling eyes.

'You're good!' he gasped as he sat beside me.

'I know!' I giggled. 'You tasted lovely. Are you going to fuck me now?'

'Yes. I'll give you the best . . .'

His words tailed off as the phone rang.

'If that's Trace . . .' he began fearfully as I stood up.

'If that's Trace, I'll tell her that you've just fucked my mouth and that you'll be home after you've fucked my cunt!' I giggled as I left the room.

It *was* Tracy, wanting to know how the flood was. *The flood was beautiful, wonderful!* 'All under control,' I told her.

'Oh, that's good,' she replied. 'Is he on his way home?'

'He's just leaving,' I said, wondering whether she trusted

him or not. Sow a seed of doubt? Why not? 'He's a good-looking man, isn't he?'

'Yes, he . . . he is,' she replied uneasily.

'Anyway, I'll send him home to you. You don't want him out all hours of the night, do you?'

'Er . . . No, I don't.'

'OK, Trace, I'll talk to you tomorrow.'

'Yes, all right. I'm glad everything's OK now.'

'So am I. Thanks for lending your man to me – bye, Trace.'

Returning to the lounge, I smiled at Craig. 'She wants you to go home,' I said, joining him on the sofa, admiring his hard cock.

'What did you say?' he asked, taking my hand and placing it on his penis.

'I said that you wouldn't be long.'

'We've time for a fuck, then?'

'Yes, definitely!' I enthused, hoisting my skirt up and opening my legs. 'Come on, kneel between my feet and give me a good shafting!'

Taking his position, his solid rod in his hand, he stabbed his bulbous knob between my swollen cunt lips. Moving forward, my buttocks over the edge of the sofa, I lay back and closed my eyes. His huge shaft sank slowly into my cunny, opening me, stretching my young sheath. Further he pushed into me until I sensed his knob against my cervix. My pussy lips forced open, gripping the base of his shaft, I lay there in my bliss, waiting for the fucking to begin.

'Take your time,' I gasped as he began to ram into me.

'I don't *have* much time!' he panted as he quickened his rhythm. 'Trace will wonder what I'm doing.' Yes, she *will* be wondering! I thought as he grabbed my hips and thrust harder into my tightening cunt. 'God, you're a good fuck!' he cried, gripping my hips harder.

'Better than your wife?'

'Anyone's better than my wife!'

'I'll tell her you said that!'

'And I'll tell her that you're a whore!'

Pig!

Opening my thighs wider, my body rocking, I floated on the pleasure my cunt was bringing me. He was a good fuck, I admit, and I'd have enjoyed him, his penis, for many years to come. But I couldn't deviate from my plan. He was an adulterous bastard, and he was going to pay for it.

Pummelling my cervix, his knob ballooned and his cream squirted. 'I can feel it!' I cried as my clitoris exploded in its first throb of orgasm. 'I can feel your sperm coming!'

'God, you're good!' he praised. 'Tight, hot, wet . . . Ah!'

Gazing down, I watched my inner lips rolling along his veined shaft as he fucked me. My body trembling, I thought that the wonderful sensations of sex would never leave me as he continued his beautiful ramming. Suddenly, his knob slipped out of my inflamed hole and ran up my sex valley to my clitoris. Grabbing him, I massaged my nodule with his purple glans, sustaining my orgasm as the last of his sperm dribbled, lubricating the erogenous meeting.

Finally sitting back on his heels, his penis flaccid, his face grinning, he gazed between my legs at my open body. 'You've got the best fanny I've ever had the pleasure of fucking,' he said appreciatively.

'And you've got the best cock I've . . .'

'God, if that's her, tell her that I've left!' he breathed as the phone rang.

Slipping into the hall, I closed the lounge door behind me and grabbed the phone. 'Oh, hi, Trace!' I trilled, her husband's sperm coursing down my inner thighs.

'Has he left yet?' she asked accusingly.

'He's just going now,' I replied.

'He's been a long time, what's he been up to?'

'The leaking pipe, he . . .'

'You said that it was all right.'

'Yes, it is. He's been helping me to clear up.'

'Oh.'

'What are you worried about?' I asked.

'Nothing, it's just that . . .'

'Don't you trust him?'

'Yes, of course I do! It's just that he's been such a long time.'

'He'll be home soon, don't worry!' I giggled. 'Anyone would think that we'd been up to something naughty, the way you're going on!'

'No, I didn't mean to imply that . . .'

'I'm your friend, Trace – I wouldn't try to take your man away from you!'

'No, I know you wouldn't. Anyway, I'll call you tomorrow.'

'Okay, bye for now.'

Craig appeared in the lounge doorway and frowned. 'What did she say?' he asked.

'She doesn't trust you, does she?'

'No, she doesn't.'

'Why not?'

'I had an affair with . . . It's a long story. Anyway, I'd better be going. Can I see you again?'

'Whenever you want to. But ring me first.'

'Why, are you seeing someone else?'

Bloody typical!

'No, of course I'm not! It's just that I might be out, or busy.'

'Oh, right. I'll ring you, then.'

'OK, and thanks – that was great!'

'Thank *you*!' he smiled as I opened the front door.

'Bye, Craig. Hope you don't get told off!' I giggled as he walked down the path.

'So do I! See you!'

Filling in my notebook, I generously allocated Craig and Tracy three points. They would be an easy couple to tear apart. What with his previous affair, and her wildly suspicious mind, they'd be a pushover!

Chapter Seven

Sharon had taken herself off to college by the time I emerged from my bedroom the following morning. I'd been hoping for a good day but, to my horror, another white envelope lay on the kitchen table. My heart lurched as I read the scrawled handwriting:

I hope you are enjoying your lesbian friend's cunt as much as Caroline is enjoying Jim's cock!

Tearing the paper to pieces, I hurled it in the bin. To calm myself, I cleared up Sharon's breakfast things. *Lazy bitch!*

By nine-thirty, I'd eaten, showered and was in town browsing around the junk shops for equipment for my sex den. A leather whip caught my eye in one shop. Wooden handle, long, leather tails, worn but plenty of life left in them – five pounds. In another emporium I was lucky enough to discover an old, but working, pair of handcuffs – another fiver. No chastity belts – no problem!

Walking home with my spoils, the breeze cooling my naked, swollen pussy lips, drying my juices as they flowed, I'd just cut through the park and and was wondering about the sex den when I literally bumped into Caroline. Fortunately, the whip and handcuffs were concealed in a bag!

'Oh! Er . . . hallo, Sue,' she greeted me hesitantly, her face flushed with guilt.

'Caroline!' I beamed. 'How lovely to see you!'

Fucking bitch!

'Er . . . yes, nice to see you, too. How are you?'

'I'm fine, just been shopping. Why don't you come round for coffee some time?'

'Er . . . Well, I . . .'

'Oh, come on! Don't let what happened in the past spoil our friendship. I'm happier than I've ever been, I promise you. If anything, you did me a favour by taking Jim off my hands! Come round this evening for a drink and a chat.'

'All right, if you're sure that . . .'

'Course I'm sure! About eight?'

'OK, eight o'clock.'

'I'll look forward to it. See you this evening.'

Walking down the road, I felt alive, my mind buzzing with plans for the bitch's comeuppance. Fancy bumping into that cow! Must be fate, I decided as I opened the front door and climbed the stairs, dumping my equipment in the sex den.

Tracy turned up just as I'd filled the kettle. Gazing at her, I suddenly had vivid images of tying her over the exercise bench and licking her wet pussy, thrashing her beautifully rounded buttocks with my new whip, before forcing a candle deep into her bum-hole. God, how I'd changed! My thinking was becoming sexually perverse, to say the least!

Showing her into the kitchen, I noticed that she looked tired. Her pretty, jade eyes were heavy, blinking all the time, her forehead lined, her face sallow.

'You all right?' I asked, eyeing the tangled mass of brown hair that had always previously been so impeccably groomed into a boringly neat bob.

'Tired, that's all,' she sighed. 'I was up half the night rowing with Craig.'

Keeping him out late had obviously done the trick! Round one to me, as always! Poor cow, I'd sucked and fucked her husband, and she'd been up all night, floundering in her anxiety! She should have ignored him and masturbated herself to sleep – as I had in my schooldays.

'Rowing? What about?' I asked with as much concern as I could muster.

'Why he'd taken so long to fix your water leak. He didn't try anything, did he?'

'How do you mean?'

'Try and . . . Try it on, you know what I mean.'

Assuming my guilty look, averting my eyes, I sighed.

'He . . . Craig is Craig,' I expounded resignedly. 'He flirts, Trace – lots of men flirt.'

'He does more than flirt! I know him of old!'

'Well, he didn't do much, so don't worry.'

'What do you mean, "*he didn't do much*"?'

'He just tried to kiss me, that's all – it was only in fun.'

'Fun? I know that we haven't seen each other for a while, Sue, but you know about the affair he had, don't you?'

'Yes, I remember you telling me.'

'I don't trust him an inch! I hope you pushed him off!'

'Of course I did! I'll tell you something, Trace, when Jim left . . . I don't quite know how to put this so I'll just come out with it. I've discovered something about myself. You've no need to worry about Craig being here alone with me.'

'I've *every* need to worry!'

'No, you haven't. I'm a lesbian.'

The idea had been brewing. Why stop at husbands? In my quest to destroy marriages, why exclude wives? The time had come now to take my plan of combat a step further – to seduce Tracy. She was ripe for targeting – at odds with her husband, vulnerable, she'd also once mentioned a relationship with another girl. But I knew it was a gamble, and my heart was in my mouth as I awaited her reaction to my 'coming out'.

In those seconds – minutes, years! – of silence between us, I realized to what an extent I'd opened up sexually. In fact, I seemed to have no inhibitions at all! I could say and do anything I wanted, with men *and* women. Now, without the merest hint of embarrassment, I looked into Tracy's eyes and asked what she thought of my confession.

'Er . . . I don't know,' she began hesitantly, her jade eyes shining now, locked to mine. 'I suppose it's up to you, isn't it?'

'It's not up to me, it's the way things are. I have no choice in the matter – I fancy women instead of men.'

'I used to . . . Do you remember me telling you about that girlfriend of mine?'

'Oh, yes – vaguely.'

'I still feel . . .'

'Feel what?' I coaxed, my stomach leaping, my pussy dampening in arousal.

'We used to go for long walks in the country. We . . . we were both young, I suppose. We were walking one day and . . . we kissed – just playing around, really. But we both felt something. We had a kind of crush on each other, I'd thought at the time. Anyway, that was that.'

'That was that? What happened?'

'We made love.'

'Made love? But how?'

'Masturbated each other and . . .'

'And what? Tell me, Trace!'

'We did sixty-nine.'

'God! So, that's when you discovered that you were . . .'

'Many times we walked in the woods, and made love under the trees. They were the best days of my life. I'd thought that I'd found love – not sex, but genuine love.'

'Why did you stop seeing each other?'

'She discovered her true sexuality – and a boyfriend. Anyway, at least I now know that Craig is safe with you.'

'Couldn't be safer! It's *you* who should be worrying!'

'*Me*?'

'I've always liked you, Trace. I never realized what my feelings were, I never understood why my heart leapt whenever I saw you, why my stomach swirled – but now I understand.

Now that I've discovered my sexual preference, I understand my feelings for you.'

She half-smiled, fluttering her eyelids as she fiddled with her coffee cup. What was she thinking? Had I woken the sleeping lesbian in her? Had recalling those heady, teenage days of lesbian lust stirred something? Looking up at me, she opened her mouth and sighed. Was there a longing in her expression, an inner desire mirrored in her lovely eyes to have me love her, attend her clitoris? I wasn't sure, but I hoped so.

'It's not been easy,' she confessed. 'I've tried to be normal, if being heterosexual is normal, that is. But I still feel more comfortable in the company of women.'

'Comfortable?' I queried.

'Well . . . I suppose I feel . . . I don't know. Perhaps comfortable's the wrong word. I feel more at home with women, not having to put on a front, as I do with men.'

'But Craig . . .'

'Craig and I have a funny relationship. We get on well, I suppose, but the sex is what I'd expect with a man – wham, bam, thank you, ma'am.'

'Why have you never tried to find love with another woman?'

'Because it's not easy admitting it to myself, let alone others. Look, I like you very much, Sue – I always have. I've not been round to see you very often because . . .'

'You fancy me?' I proffered, my heart banging hard against my chest, my hands trembling.

'Yes, I suppose I do.'

In all the years I'd known Tracy, I'd never once imagined that she'd fancied me. There had never been a sign, a merest hint that she'd found me attractive. God! No wonder she'd kept away! Although I'd thought of luring wives as well as husbands into my lair, I hadn't believed for a minute that I'd actually do it. I didn't think I'd ever have the opportunity to destroy a marriage by seducing someone's wife!

'If you fancy me, then why not visit me more often?' I asked, deliberately naively.

'I had to fight against my feelings when the relationship I had in my teens ended. It was wrong to do what I did with another girl, I knew that. I have to fight against the feelings I have for you, can you understand that?'

'No, I can't! Listen, Trace – I like you very much, more than I should, and I realize now that I always have,' I said softly, taking her hand in mine as I sat opposite her. 'Can't we have something together?'

'But, Craig . . .'

'He won't know, will he? If you reckon that he's screwing around, then . . .'

'I don't really believe that he is, Sue. I'm just over-cautious after the affair he had.'

'Please, Tracy – listen to me. I'm lonely, I have no one. I need company, a relationship – I want us to have something, something we can share together. Even if it does have to remain our secret.'

She was weakening, I could see that – and so was I! She was very pretty, extremely feminine, with a full, sensual mouth, well-defined cheek bones and enormous green eyes set off by long, dark lashes. She dressed impeccably – in a turquoise lace blouse that outlined her feminine curves and a short turquoise skirt, she was definitely all female. Her hair and make-up were always immaculate – until now, that is. Until the row she'd had with Craig. Until her husband had confronted me.

My stomach swirling in arousal, anticipation, my clitoris stirring, I knew that the time had come to seduce her. This was to be my first seduction of a married woman, and I felt unsure, confused. My hands trembling, I couldn't believe that this was happening, that I was about to fulfil an inner desire – a desire I hadn't known existed.

Standing up, I took her hand and gently coaxed her to her feet. Leading her through the hall and up to my sex den, I wondered why she hadn't protested, even a little. Surely, she wouldn't allow me to take her upstairs and strip her beautiful body, examine the feminine intimacy between her legs? Saying nothing as I stood her by the exercise bench, I slowly unbuttoned her blouse.

Her eyes closing as I slipped the garment over her shoulders, I knew that I'd won – that she was mine for the taking. She could no longer fight her inner desires. Alone with me, there was no need for a front, for her to conceal her true sexual identity. Now, she could be herself – a lesbian.

Removing her bra, peeling the flimsy material away from her heavy globes, I gazed at her well-rounded breasts. The discs of her areolae were darker than mine – a rich, deep chestnut. Her nipples stood out, long, erect – suckable. They were fine breasts, and I nuzzled my face between them, breathing in her perfume as she sighed with pleasure.

This was a turn up for the books! I mused through my growing excitement. Craïg's wife in my sex den, her breasts bared, her nipples growing in her lesbian arousal! I could barely believe it. If only Craig could see me now, I thought as I sucked her long protrusion into my hot mouth and snaked my tongue round the sensitive tip. If only he could see me stripping his wife, sucking her nipple!

Dropping to my knees, I tugged her short skirt down to her ankles, admiring the swell of her tight, alluring pink panties hugging her swelling pussy lips. Kissing her thighs, I moved my attention up her warm, smooth skin to her panties, breathing in her sweet girl-fragrance through the soft material.

Looking down at me, watching me as I slipped her cover down, peeled the soft material from her mound, she smiled. 'Have you ever done this before?' she murmured. I nodded, not wanting to speak as I gazed at her dark pubes, her beautiful girl-crack – the crack that Craig's cock had opened many, many times.

Tugging her panties down her long legs, I realized just what it was that I was doing, and I began to think about the past. Never would I have believed that I'd ever be pulling another girl's panties down. If someone had told me only a couple of months previously that I'd be divorced, screwing as many of my friends' husbands as I could, licking a young college girl's cunt as she licked mine, licking a married woman's cunt the morning after her husband had fucked me, I'd never have believed it. But then, you never know what each day will bring!

'Do you know what to do?' Tracy asked unexpectedly. I nodded again as I peeled her generous outer lips apart, exposing the pink hood of her clitoris, neat, glistening – protecting. Further I parted her rubbery lips, opening her intricate folds of sex-flesh to my widening eyes. A globule of milky fluid clung invitingly to her inner lip like a tiny pearl drop. Homing in, I plucked the globule from her pink flesh with the tip of my tongue.

Slippery, tasting of sex, her milky fluid grew diluted with my saliva, and again I pushed my tongue out to replenish the flavour. 'You like lapping up my pussy juice?' she asked softly. I nodded again, poking my tongue into her open entrance, savouring her pearly liquid. 'Then you shall have more,' she breathed, sitting on the exercise bench and reclining, her head resting on the carpet, her thighs wide, her cunt open.

Repositioning myself between her legs, I resumed my pussy-juice tasting, opening her hole wide with my fingertips, pushing my tongue deep into the pink orifice, drinking from her hot well. She moaned and writhed as I moved my attention up her beautiful crack and flicked her erect clitoris with my tongue. Then she began twitching, gasping, as I ran my tongue round the base of her beautiful budling. I felt my own arousal mounting – a potent stimulus of sex and power. I was in control – her naked body was mine to use.

Would she scream in orgasm? I wondered. Or would she moan her satisfaction quietly as her climax lifted her from her trembling body? Her inner flesh reddening, her juices decanting, she breathed heavily, letting out a long, low moan of satisfaction as I swept my tongue over her erect clitoris.

Her arousal rising rapidly, I felt ever more powerful. First, I'd mouthed and sucked on Craig's hard cock and drunk his sperm. Now I was licking his wife's beautiful wet cunt, drinking her girl-juice. I could wield power over both men and women! I could do anything and everything! I was the devil's daughter!

Suddenly overwhelmed by a terrific desire to *use* Tracy, to commit some vile act of indecency on her naked body, I grabbed the rope and tied her ankles to the tubular frame of the exercise bench. Taking little notice of what I was doing, she opened her legs wider, gripping the frame as I bound her hands. Either she was lost in her arousal, or she trusted me completely!

Between her thighs again, I pushed three fingers deep into her hot, wet cunt, gazing in amazement as her juices flowed from her tight hole. Her pussy was mine now, mine to use – and abuse. I knew what I liked, how I liked my pussy attended – I knew what Tracy liked. Only a woman truly knows how to pleasure another woman.

Now she was my prisoner, I could do anything to Tracy, defile her, whip her, use her, love her beautiful body. My mind brimming with perverse creativity, I slipped my fingers from her hot vaginal sheath and dashed down to the kitchen. Grabbing the wine bottle from the fridge, I returned to my den of iniquity, grinning wickedly.

Settling between her legs, I pulled the cork from the bottle and sprinkled a little chilled white wine over her gaping pussy lips. Her inner flesh glistened as the wine trickled down her open groove, irrigating her furrow.

'Ah, that's nice!' she breathed as I lapped the wine from her pink crack. 'It's cooling, soothing,' she murmured as I poured a little more of the nectar over her mound and watched it trickle down her yawning sex-valley. When I'd cleansed her, lapped up the exotic cocktail of wine and pussy-juice, I took the bottle and pushed the neck into her tight vagina, wondering how she'd react.

She squirmed, rolled her head from side to side as I gently pushed the bottle further into her trembling body. The thick neck of the bottle parting her inner lips, stretching her vagina wide open, I delighted in my new-found debauchery, wondering what else I could do to her defenceless, tethered body.

The wine pouring into her cunt, cooling her, filling her, I wondered how much she could hold. Adjusting the angle of the bottle, I drained it, watching in awe as the offering disappeared into her cavern. The bottle had been about half full, and I held my breath as I watched it slowly empty into her quivering body.

'God, that's cold!' she gasped as I worked the bottle in and out of her bloated hole. 'Drink from me, drink from my cunt!' Slipping the bottle out, I watched the wine bubbling, flowing from her well, running down between her buttocks. Lapping up the heady nectar, I became aware of my own cunt, hot, wet, aching for attention – female attention. 'Suck it out of me,' she gasped as I licked her cold flesh, wondering whether to push the bottle into my own yearning orifice.

Tracy squeezed her muscles and I drank the wine as it flowed from her spring. Heady, mingling with her sex juices, the cocktail tantalized my taste buds, aroused me as never before. Her deep well completely drained, I moved up her glistening slit to her clitoris, erect and hard. Licking around its base, I imagined Craig there, teasing, stiffening the protrusion with his tongue as his wife gasped. But now it was me, another woman, there between his wife's thighs, bringing her beautiful sensations, arousing her, taking her ever closer to paradise with my tongue.

'Don't stop!' Tracy cried as her body began to tremble uncontrollably. 'God, don't stop!' Working expertly on her swelling bud with my tongue, I pulled her outer pussy lips wide apart, exposing as much of her wet, inner flesh as I could as she climbed ever higher to her peak. Her juices flowing in torrents, her pink inner flesh reddening as her orgasm built, she wailed her appreciation. 'Ah, ah, coming! Please, don't stop!' Her stomach rising and falling as her womb rhythmically contracted and relaxed, she finally reached her summit.

Slipping three fingers deep into her spasming cunt as I teased her orgasm from her clitoris with my tongue, I felt my own climax coming. Mouthing and sucking between her swollen lips, I reached down between my thighs and massaged my nodule, discharging my own powerful deliverance in unison with hers. Both writhing, decanting our hot come, we became one, locked in lust, a strange, consuming, lesbian love.

As our climaxes subsided, I laid my head on her mound, breathing in the sweet fragrance of her perspiring body as she trembled beneath me. 'Untie me and I'll do the same to you,' she whispered as I licked her matted, pubic bush. Untie her? Not yet, I decided – not yet.

I wanted to leave some evidence of her infidelity, some sign that would arouse Craig's suspicion – but what? Shaving her pubes crossed my mind, but no, I needed something more subtle. Besides, she could easily tell Craig that she had shaved herself. An idea came to me as I was sucking and nibbling on her wet pussy lips – love bites!

Sucking hard on the soft skin just above her mound, I knew

that Craig would see the marks and ask awkward questions – searching questions. Tracy could hardly do it to herself, so how would she explain the tell-tale signs of adultery? Sucking on her inner thighs, her stomach, her hips, as she trembled and squirmed, I stamped her with a dozen or more marks of lust before releasing her.

'God, why did you do that?' she gasped as she sat up and looked down in horror at her blemished skin. 'I didn't realize what you were doing to me! Craig will see and . . .'

'I wouldn't worry too much,' I smiled. 'He won't realize what they are.'

'I hope not! God, if he knew that . . .'

'Why don't you lie down again, on your stomach, and let me give you some more pleasure?' I interrupted.

'Don't you want me to suck you?' she asked, licking her pouting lips.

'Later,' I smiled. 'I haven't finished with you yet.'

Not by a long chalk!

Kneeling down, she draped her naked body over the bench, her buttocks splayed, exposing her small hole above her wet, gaping cunt lips. Tying her arms to the frame, I wound the rope around her knees, securing her young body in readiness for my every whim. The whip? I debated as I sucked on each buttock in turn, leaving more tell-tale marks of her lustful adultery – lesbian adultery. Yes, the whip – but not yet.

Grabbing the wine bottle, I dragged Tracy's slippery come from her gaping cunt with my fingertips and lubricated the ring of brown tissue surrounding her bottom-hole. Then, presenting the bottle to her small hole, I gently but firmly pushed, gazing as the delicate tissue opened and her anal sheath seemed to suck the neck of the bottle deep inside her hot body.

'Christ, not there!' she screamed as I drove the neck deeper into her bowels. 'Take it out! Argh! Take it out!'

'Enjoy it!' I giggled as her entrance was progressively

forced wider open by the increasing girth of the bottle neck. Soon, she stilled herself, breathing heavily as I groped beneath the bottle and slipped three fingers into the wet, slippery heat of her tightening cunt.

God, what a sight! The bottle protruding from between her splayed buttocks, her brown ring stretched, encompassing the thick glass neck, her cunt lips swollen, dripping with her hot come – she was, indeed, a sight!

'And now to bring your clitoris to orgasm again,' I chuckled, locating her hard bud and massaging her juices into its sensitive tip. She gasped, her body shaking violently as her climax rose from her quivering womb. 'You're going to come as you've never come before!' I laughed, manipulating the bottle, adding to the sensation of perverted sex.

'God, you're good at this!' she breathed.

'I get better!' I assured her as the doorbell rang. 'Shit! I'll get rid of them!' I whispered loudly, leaving the bottle buried in her bum-hole and climbing to my feet.

Craig stood on the doorstep, grinning. 'Thought I'd come and see you,' he smiled, swaggering past me into the hall.

'Christ, I told you to ring me first!' I complained as I followed him into the lounge, my heart beating wildly.

'I was just passing – you don't mind, do you?'

'Yes, I *do* mind, Craig – I'm busy!'

The thought struck me that I could take Craig up to my sex den and show him exactly what his wife got up to. Was I really that wicked? Yes, I was! Telling Craig to wait in the lounge, I bounded upstairs, grabbing the quilt from my bed before returning to Tracy.

'I've a surprise for you,' I declared, covering her with the quilt, leaving only her buttocks, the embedded wine bottle, her gaping cunt, on display.

'What are you *doing*?' she asked fearfully, trying to lift her head and shake the quilt off.

'Would you like a man to take you from behind?' I giggled.

'No! What the hell do you think I am?'

'A woman who loves sex! Anyway, he's a boyfriend of mine, and he's bloody good. Come on, Trace, let yourself go, get rid of your inhibitions and enjoy yourself.'

'I don't want some stranger screwing me, for God's sake!'

'Well, I really don't see that you have a choice. Either you agree, or you'll get this!' I threatened, grabbing my whip and giving her taut buttocks one hard lash.

I didn't really know what had come over me. I'd changed beyond all recognition, and I wasn't sure that I liked it. The worrying thing was that I seemed to have no control over my actions. Driven by a wild and frantic lust, I didn't even stop to consider the consequences. What the hell was I doing to Tracy, my friend? To destroy her marriage, to have her divorce her adulterous husband was one thing, but to tie her down and have her fucked by a man she thought was a total stranger was something else – evil!

A stifled yelp came from beneath the quilt as I lashed her buttocks again. 'Well? What's it to be?' I demanded. 'The whip again? And I'll ring Craig and tell him to come and see you tied up! Show him what you get up to behind his back!'

'Why are you doing this to me?' she sobbed.

'Sex, Trace, it's sex! I thought you liked sex?'

'With you, I do, but . . .'

'Let yourself go and have some fun. You'll like being fucked from behind as I rub your clitty and bring you off.'

'You wouldn't really get Craig round to see me like this, would you?'

'Damn right I would, so what's it to be?'

'I don't understand why you're doing this!'

'You'll soon find out why I'm doing this to you. You don't understand now, but you'll thank me for this in a few weeks' time, I know.'

'*Thank* you? Hardly!'

'OK, I'll ring Craig.'

'He's working in London, so . . .'

'No, he's not. I saw him drive past earlier. I'll ring him.'

'No! For God's sake, Sue! Look, I'll agree, but tell me who it is first.'

'I don't think you know each other, but keep quiet, just in case. Don't breathe a word while he's in here.'

'You're a bitch, Sue! You realize that I'll never come here again, don't you?'

'I don't really care whether you come here again or not. Anyway, I know you'll come back because you want my body. And, as I said, when all is revealed, you'll thank me!' I laughed as I left the room.

Craig grinned when I told him that I had a naked woman upstairs, waiting for his hard cock. 'Tied down?' he frowned.

'Yes, she's a lesbian friend of mine who likes a bit of cock now and then. Don't say a word in front of her as I don't want her to know who you are.'

'She'll see who I am!'

'No, her head's under my quilt, it's to be an anonymous fuck.'

'Who is she? Do I know her?'

'No, but she often visits me, and I don't want you recognizing each other should you happen to meet again.'

'God, you get worse!' he whispered as he followed me upstairs to my sex den.

'I get better, you mean! Anyway, no words, no talking, OK?'

'Whatever you say. I'm coming to like you, Sue, the way you think, the things you do.'

I didn't like myself – I hated myself, in fact. But I had to go ahead with my debauched plan and watch Craig screw his wife. I had to prove to her that he'd screw another woman, any woman, even a woman he didn't know, couldn't see – without a thought for his marriage. Craig would show his wife that fidelity meant nothing to him. And by allowing someone she thought to be a total stranger to fuck her, she'd prove the same to him – fidelity was dead.

Gasping as I opened the door and showed him into the room, Craig fell to his knees, stroking Tracy's buttocks, frowning at me as he pointed to the wine bottle, the thin weals patterned across her pale flesh. I smiled as I knelt beside him and unzipped his jeans, praying that he'd see the weals across Tracy's buttocks, the love bites, when she undressed for bed that night.

All hell would be let loose! There'd be questions, embarrassing questions. What was Tracy doing tied down naked in my house with a wine bottle sticking out of her bottom-hole? What was Craig doing, fucking someone he didn't think he knew? They'd both accuse each other of blatant adultery – and their marriage would be dead. A few choice lies from me would ensure there would be no chance of reconciliation. I'd tell Tracy that I'd been screwing Craig for months – and I'd tell him that she'd been to my sex den a hundred times, and screwed as many men!

'This is Carole,' I said, grinning at Craig and placing my finger over my lips as he pulled his hard penis out. 'She comes here for lesbian sex. She likes me to fuck her with a wine bottle and suck her clitoris. Carole, this is John, a friend of mine who visits me regularly for sex. His wife's no good in bed, so he comes to see me whenever he can for sex.'

Obviously, they'd know that I'd set them up, but I didn't care. The destruction of their marriage was the only thing of importance to me. Besides, what could they say to me? I was free, single, I could do what I liked, with whom I liked. They could hardly blame me for their adulterous ways.

Gently slipping the wine bottle from Tracy's bloated anal

sheath, I grabbed Craig's huge cock, aligning the purple knob with her open cunt. I watched with bated breath as he slipped his entire length deep into her quivering body.

'Take it out when you come and I'll wank you off all over her bum!' I instructed excitedly as he grabbed her hips and thrust into her again and again. Tracy whimpered, gasping as I reached beneath her body and rubbed her clitoris, stiffening her until she began to shake violently in her enforced lust. I desperately wanted her to express the pleasure he was bringing her, to display her sexual arousal, so that when all was revealed, Craig would look upon her as not only a lesbian, but a tart, a woman who didn't give a toss who fucked her tethered body.

I was surprised that he didn't recognize her as she began to gasp and moan her pleasure. But, I supposed, his wife was the last thing on his mind! Besides, one bum looks very much the same as another. Does one cunt feel much the same as any other to a man? I wondered. Does one cock feel much the same as another?

Watching Craig's hard rod slide in and out of Tracy's drenched tunnel, I myself became aroused, my juices flowing as I brought her clitoris to its summit. She writhed, squirming as Craig pulled his penis out of her wet sheath, sperm bubbling from the small slit on his deep purple knob.

Still massaging Tracy's throbbing spot, I grabbed Craig's twitching shaft and wanked him, showering his wife's buttocks with his sperm as he grimaced in his pleasure. 'You can fuck *me* next!' I cried, taking the couple to their respective sexual heavens. 'You can give me a good fucking like you did last night!'

Sucking the last of Craig's sperm from his throbbing knob, I brought out the final ripples of sex from Tracy's clitoris with my vibrating fingertip before lying on the floor and opening my legs. Tracy had remained silent, apart from her gasped whimperings of sex, and Craig hadn't spoken either. One word, I knew, and the game would have been over.

'Come on, then!' I cried as Craig settled between my legs and licked the juices from my open hole. 'Give me a good fucking!' Grinning, his penis incredibly stiff again, he drove into me, battering my cervix with his solid knob, shafting me as his wife lay there listening to his grunts and groans – the grunts and groans she should have known only too well!

God, how she'd recall every sound, every movement, every sensation when she discovered the truth! I could hardly wait for her phone call – her crying, sobbing phone call telling me what a bitch I was, what a bastard Craig was! She'd never speak to me again, let alone thank me. There again, I couldn't be sure. She might well come to me for lesbian sex once she and her adulterous husband had parted – divorced.

'God, you're good!' I cried as Craig grimaced and pumped his sperm deep into my tightening cunt. 'Yes, I'm there! Ah, yes, fuck me harder! Fuck my wet cunt harder!' She'd recall my words, my words of lust, and picture her husband fucking me – and I'd laugh wickedly!

Wrapping my legs around him, I pulled his body hard against mine, driving his cock deeper into my spasming vagina. Shuddering as my climax ripped through my body, I closed my eyes, revelling in my debauchery, my corruption. 'Come over my stomach!' I cried, pulling my skirt right up. Slipping his cock from my cunt, he wanked his wet shaft, shooting over me as I watched. His sperm splashing over me, coursing down my sides as he gasped and his balls drained, I reached between my legs and massaged another massive climax from my insatiable bud.

Recovering from my *grand mort*, I grabbed Craig's shaft and massaged the last of his jism from his purple knob. Smiling, I held my finger to my lips, indicating that he shouldn't speak. Then, finally releasing his spent cock, I staggered up and showed him from the room, leaving Tracy to wonder at her faceless adultery.

'Christ!' Craig gasped as we neared the front door. 'You're some bloody woman!'

'And you're some man!' I laughed, wiping the sperm from my stomach and licking my fingers.

'Who is she? She's a bloody good fuck!'

'No one you know,' I smiled, almost feeling sorry for him.

'I wish Trace was like that, into bondage and things!' he complained in his naivety.

'Do you?' I asked. 'Would you really like it if she were a lesbian who loved being tied down and fucked by women, as well as by any man who came her way?'

'No, definitely not!' he asserted as I opened the door. 'Women like that are just whores, they don't deserve husbands. Anyway, I'll see you tomorrow, perhaps,' he added as he stepped outside.

'Yes,' I grinned, knowing that tomorrow he'd be writhing in the agony of infidelity rather than orgasm.

Releasing Tracy, I helped her to her feet and smiled. 'You enjoyed that, didn't you?' I asked, stroking her breasts, tweaking her long nipples.

'Yes, I did,' she admitted softly. 'But I still say you're a bitch!'

'You'll be saying far more than that soon!' I giggled as she wiped the sperm from her buttocks and slipped into her clothes.

'What do you mean?' she asked, frowning at me.

'Nothing. No doubt you'll give me a ring later,' I added mysteriously as she followed me downstairs.

'I don't think so!' she remonstrated as I saw her out. 'I've got some serious thinking to do – about you, I mean!'

'Oh, yes, you'll have some very serious thinking to do later, I can assure you of that!'

'What *are* you talking about?'

'Let's just say that everything's going to change – everything's going to change dramatically!'

'*You've* changed dramatically, I know that! Anyway, I'll ring you sometime. Bye.'

When she'd gone, I sat in the lounge wondering why I'd done it, what had possessed me to behave the way I had. Tracy was right, I *had* changed dramatically, and I was beginning to worry about the consequences. Would I be cited in the divorce case? No, they could hardly both cite the same person! Craig might go mad and come round to see me. There again, he was the one who'd committed adultery, not me. I could always say that I didn't think that they'd find out who they'd been with. Perhaps they wouldn't? Unless Craig noticed the love bites, the weals across Tracy's buttocks, neither would know of the others' infidelity.

If he did discover the weals, and they divorced, what if word got around about me setting them up? No, Craig and Tracy knew very few of my other friends, so I would be safe enough to carry on wreaking havoc, destroying marriages.

It had been a good day, so far, and I still had Caroline to look forward to that evening. I could hardly tie her over the exercise bench and whip her, although I'd love to have done! What was my plan? I wondered. How could having her round for a drink help me in my quest to destroy her relationship with Jim? Feed her lies, plant seeds of doubt, yes – but I needed something far stronger than that.

Perhaps the time had come for her to catch Jim fucking me? I could always arrange for him to be at my place, between my thighs, screwing me. She'd arrive, see the open front door, walk in, and . . .

I made my decision – I would destroy their relationship that very evening. Why wait any longer? The opportunity might not arise again for some time, so why delay? I rang Jim at his office, praying that he'd be there, and that he was free that evening.

'I'd love to come round!' he enthused. 'What time?' That was a good question. I'd told Caroline to come round at about eight o'clock. I'd need a good hour with Jim to ensure that we were both naked, both delirious with lust by the time she put her head round the lounge door and discovered us.

'Seven o'clock,' I replied.

'Great, I'll bring some wine. We'll have a bloody good evening!'

'What will you tell Caroline?'

'I'll make up some story or other, don't worry.'

'Lie to her again, you mean?'

'Sort of. Anyway, it's my problem, don't worry about it.'

I did worry about it, because it suddenly occurred to me that she might tell him that she was going to see me, and the whole thing would be blown! But no, she wouldn't tell him, I was sure. If she were to say that she was visiting me, he'd try to stop her – she'd realize that. And I was certain that she really did want to come and see me, if only to gloat.

'All right, Jim, until seven,' I said, grinning.

'I can hardly wait!'

'No, neither can I!' I laughed. 'See you this evening.'

Thinking, planning, I suddenly realized that Jim would know that I'd set him up – and I didn't want that. I wanted him to come crying to me, pleading for me to take him back when his tart threw him out. That was to have been my *tour de force* – throwing Jim away, nonchalantly discarding him, as he had me.

I couldn't use Sharon again, it wouldn't be fair. Perhaps I could get away with telling Jim that I'd thought Caroline was coming round the following evening, and that I'd mixed the days up? I didn't know what to do. All I did know was that they were both coming round, and I'd be exposed for setting the whole thing up.

When Sharon came home at four, I *did* tentatively suggest that she seduce Jim as she had Tony. 'No way! I'm not here to be used as a weapon in your pathetic war games!' she stormed. I could see her point. I told her about Craig and Tracy, and she nearly hit the roof. 'When are you going to grow up?' she yelled. 'Can't you see that what you're doing is wrong?' I could see that it *was* wrong – very wrong. But I was hooked – addicted to destroying relationships. 'I thought we could have had something special,' Sharon said wistfully as she climbed the stairs to her room.

So, that was it – she was jealous. God, she'd probably fallen in love with me, daft bitch! That was all I needed – a love-struck, lesbian, teenage girl crying on her bed!

Sitting in the garden, I thought about my wrongdoing and wondered whether to call a halt to my treachery. After all, I'd wrecked two marriages, I'd had my fun, and I had plenty of studs willing to visit me at the drop of a hat. Perhaps the time had come to stop my evil games?

Chapter Eight

Caroline rang at six-thirty with her apologies. She couldn't make it that evening – shit! I'd so been looking forward to watching her crumple in the pain of her downfall. But, I consoled myself, there was still plenty of time to bring her down, plenty of time to watch the bitch fall from her pedestal.

By seven o'clock, I was ready and waiting for Jim to arrive. Although I was feeling down because my plan had gone so wrong, I was nevertheless looking forward to an evening of adulterous sex. Jim eventually turned up, thank God, but he was in a bad mood and started complaining about a row he'd had with Caroline – as if I was interested!

As we sat in the lounge, I wondered if the row had been over Caroline coming to visit me. For a dreadful moment, I thought he was going to ask me why I'd invited them both round, but he didn't. Apparently, the point of contention had been about him going out to visit some mysterious friend yet again. She'd said that she was suspicious, what with the phone calls, and accused him of seeing another woman.

'You two are in a mess, aren't you?' I laughed as I poured the wine, wondering whether he'd like to push the full bottle between my pussy lips and cool my hot cunt.

'I don't know what it is with her these days,' he sighed despondently. 'I know that the phone calls have pissed her off, but what I can't understand is why she's so suspicious all the bloody time.'

'Any woman would be suspicious if she kept having phone calls from a female asking after her man,' I reasoned.

'Yes, I suppose so. She said that she bumped into you by the park gates.'

'Er . . . Yes, we only passed by. It was rather awkward, as you can imagine.'

'She said that you'd invited her round for a drink.'

'No . . . I didn't actually *invite* her. She was so friendly . . . I didn't know what to say when she said that she'd call in to see me. I hadn't expected her to even speak to me, let alone . . .'

'Oh, I thought she said that you'd asked her round?'

'She sort of invited herself, really. Anyway, let's not talk about her.'

'Why ask me round if you knew that she was coming to see you this evening?' he asked accusingly.

'I . . . I didn't know that you were coming round when I spoke to her. I was going to call her and put her off, but she rang me and cancelled so . . . I didn't want her round here anyway! She's not exactly my flavour of the month, as you can imagine!'

'I thought for a minute that you'd planned the whole thing! Planned for her to discover me here with you!'

'God, no! Why the hell would I do that?'

'I was only joking!'

'Christ! That's the last thing I'd want – Caroline coming round and ruining our evening! Anyway, let's change the subject, shall we?'

I was disappointed that the evening had gone so horribly off course but, on the other hand, I was relieved to have escaped a possible inferno! Both Jim and Caroline had fiery tempers, and the last thing I wanted right now was the two of them going for me!

Relaxing with my wine, my pussy lips swelling, I decided to begin our soirée of rampant sex, and pulled my skirt up to display my shaved crack. Placing his glass on the table, Jim wasted no time, slipping his hand between my thighs and pushing his fingers deep into my hot vagina. I lay back on the sofa, my legs open wide, and closed my eyes as he massaged the slippery walls of my cunt, bringing out my juices, expertly stiffening my clitoris.

I thought of Derek as Jim worked between my legs. He'd enjoy another session over the kitchen table, and so would I! I pictured Jilly's face, imagining her expression as she walked into the kitchen and discovered her young husband with his penis thrust deep into my beautiful cunt. Tears would flow, hysterical screams would rend the air – and I'd laugh.

'You're very wet!' Jim remarked, forcing half his hand into my tight vaginal sheath, dragging my thoughts away from Derek and Jilly. 'God, you're a sexy little bitch! We had some good times in bed together, didn't we?'

Why *had* he left me for Caroline? I wondered. What had that cow got that I hadn't? But, whatever she did or didn't have, I didn't care any more. I had her man, in my lounge, fingering my open fanny while she sat at home alone – waiting.

Slipping my top off, baring my rounded breasts to Jim's appreciative gaze, I grinned. I felt wicked, sexual as never before, and I wanted him in my mouth, my cunt – my bottom-hole. I heard Sharon moving about in the hall as I opened my body to Jim, and I hoped that she'd come bounding in as he slipped his jeans off and stood before me, his hard dick standing to attention. I wanted her to join in again, slip her clothes off and allow Jim to fuck her as I sat over her pretty face and rubbed my open slit over her mouth. A delectable union!

'How do you want it?' Jim asked, pulling me to the floor and almost tearing my skirt off.

'Sixty-nine!' I grinned. 'Lie down, and I'll get on top of you!'

Settling over Jim's hard body, I pulled his foreskin back and sucked his beautiful knob into my hungry mouth as he peeled my pussy lips open and licked my wet inner folds. His penis soon began to twitch, his knob throbbing against my tongue as he sucked my clitoris into his mouth. Lost in my arousal, I heard the doorbell ring somewhere far off in the haze, but took no notice. Suddenly, my mouth was filling with sperm – pumping, gushing over my tongue as I sucked his knob and wanked his shaft.

Kneading his heavy balls as my clitoris exploded in orgasm against his caressing tongue, I slipped his knob from my mouth and watched his sperm jetting, splashing my face as I moved my hand faster up and down the length of his huge shaft. Licking, slurping, I didn't hear the door open – but I certainly heard the blood-curdling shriek!

Looking up, sperm dribbling down my chin, Jim's knob still squirting, bathing my hand, I smiled sweetly at Caroline. Her face flushed, her lips twisted in anger, her eyes afire with rage, her hands visibly trembling, she just stood there. Shocked, stunned, her mouth hanging open, she stood there like a statue.

Perfect! I purred inwardly. Sharon must have let the poor cow in thinking that I was watching TV or something. I couldn't have planned it better myself!

Pushing me off, Jim stood up, his half-erect penis wavering, glistening, dripping with sperm and saliva, his face reddening. 'Caroline!' he gasped. 'I . . .'

'You fucking bastard!' she screamed hysterically, lunging at him and pummelling his chest with her clenched fists.

'But, Caroline, I . . .'

'You fucking bastard!'

Not much of a conversation, I mused, sitting on the sofa, my legs open wide, my wet cunt blatantly on display to the unhappy couple. Jim tried to pull his jeans on, hopping around the room on one foot as he desperately tried to cover his deflated cock.

'Coffee, anyone?' I asked cheerily, leaping to my feet. Caroline flashed me a death-look, opening her mouth in disgust as she noticed my shorn pussy. 'I'll put the kettle on,' I smiled as I brushed past her and left the room. 'Do you still take sugar, Caroline?' I called sweetly from the hall.

'I knew you were up to something, Jim, so I followed you!' Caroline screamed as I stood outside the door. 'You'll find your things on the fucking pavement when you get back!'

'Caroline! You don't understand . . .' Jim began pathetically.

Doesn't understand? Give the bitch some credit, Jim – there's nothing to understand!

'You're a two-timing bastard!' she yelled. *Familiar words!* Flinging the door open, she stormed into the hall, glaring at me again. 'You're a fucking bitch!' she bellowed as she opened the front door. 'You can have him, I don't fucking want him!'

Neither do I!

Sharon had done a runner, obviously not wanting to hang around for the shrapnel as yet another relationship exploded into a thousand pieces. 'Well,' I smiled ruefully as I walked back into the lounge. 'That was a stroke of bad luck, Jim!'

'Bad luck! Fucking hell! How did she get in, for Christ's sake?'

'Sharon answered the door. I suppose she wasn't to know what we were up to. You should have been more careful, Jim. Fancy allowing her to follow you here!'

'I didn't allow her to follow me, for fuck's sake!'

'Well, you should have been more careful. Anyway, what are you going to do now?'

'What can I do? I've got nowhere to live – I'll have to move back here, I suppose.'

Slipping my skirt on, I wondered how to break the bad news to him. Sorry, but I have another man moving in. No. Oh, Jim, I forgot to mention it, but I'm getting married next month.

I didn't tell you, Jim, but I'm a lesbian – Sharon sleeps with me, so . . .

Move back here? What the fuck did he think I was? I knew what he was – a typical bloody man! How *dare* he think that he could just move back into the house – *my* house! I hated him, really despised him at that moment. As he flopped into a chair, distractedly running his fingers through his hair, his face anguished, I slipped my top on and stood before him. *The final blow – the kill!*

'What do you mean, you'll have to *move back here*?' I demanded angrily. 'You can't just move into other people's houses!'

'Other people's? But . . . but I thought . . .'

'Thought what, Jim? This is *my* house, now – it's in *my* name. It belongs to *me*!'

'But I've got nowhere to go, Sue! Can't I . . .'

'I'm sorry, but we both agreed at the outset that our relationship was to be purely sexual. That's all you wanted from me – sex. I remember you saying that you didn't want us to get back together again – you said that you'd moved on. And besides, all *I* wanted from *you* was sex. That's what we agreed, remember?'

'I know, but things have changed, haven't they?'

'Changed? Not for me, they haven't!'

'But we're good together, Sue. Can't we . . .'

'We are good, yes. But I have other men friends apart from you, Jim. I can't just end all my relationships because Caroline has discovered your infidelity.'

'Other men friends? But I thought . . .'

'Only two men at the moment. Well, three, including you. I see them a couple of times a week, just for some sexy fun, nothing else.'

'You bitch! You've been screwing me, and all along . . .'

'Hang on, Jim! You planned to marry Caroline, and yet you

were happy to sneak round here behind her back and screw me!'

'Yes, but that's different!'

Different?

'You were in a relationship, and you betrayed your partner, her trust in you – as you did with me. I'm free, single, so I can do what I like, with whom I like. I've cheated on no one, Jim! I can honestly say that I've never committed adultery. Anyway, I'm going out for a drink with Sharon, so if you don't mind . . .'

'Where can I go? Be reasonable, Sue!'

'Reasonable? You left me for Caroline, remember? Then you screw me behind her back, she finds out, so you think that you can move back in with me as if nothing's happened? I have my own life now. You didn't want me. When it suited you, you discarded me, tossed me aside like a piece of useless junk! I don't want you back, Jim! Please, don't tell me to be reasonable!'

'Can I still come and see you?' he pleaded, his head hanging low, his eyes frowning.

Talk about the clock turning back! He looked the way he had when he'd stood in the lounge and told me that he was leaving me for Caroline – pathetic! For a second, I felt that I should take him back. Recalling our good times together, the beautiful sex, the fun, the love I'd thought we'd shared . . . Christ, I was weakening! A second honeymoon? Re-discover the love we'd once had? Share our lives again? It sounded good.

But no – he'd cheated on me throughout our entire marriage. Lied to me, betrayed me, used me. He'd fucked Caroline! No! I'd definitely not have him back! I wouldn't take him back if he were the last man in the world!

'I must get ready to go out, Jim,' I sighed. 'Give me a ring some time and we'll enjoy an evening together.'

'A ring? Where the hell from – the phone box nearest to a fucking park bench?'

'You'll find a place, a nice little bedsit or something. And I'm sure you must have a friend who'll put you up in the meantime. Don't you know any other women who'll take you in for a while? Anyway, I have to get ready to go out.'

'Right, that's it then, I suppose. I'd better go and grab my belongings from the fucking pavement before they're stolen! And then find a park bench for the night!'

How sweet revenge! Seeing him out, a pang of guilt stabbed my conscience. I don't know why, because *he'd* cheated, not me. He was the betrayer, and he deserved whatever lay in store for him. Besides, I hadn't set him up – Caroline had followed him!

With a great sense of satisfaction, I called upstairs for Sharon, but she'd gone out. The night was young, and I was wondering what to do, how to spend my evening, when the phone rang.

'How could you do it!' Caroline stormed as I picked the receiver up. Oh God!

'I did exactly the same to you as you did to me!' I returned angrily. 'In fact, what you did was far worse: Jim and I were married, and you destroyed us – our marriage!'

'How long . . . how long has he been seeing you?'

'He never stopped seeing me, and several other women, from what I gather! He's a cheating bastard, Caroline! But you knew that, didn't you?'

'No, I didn't!'

'Yes, you did! He'd been cheating on me for years, fucking you behind my back. You knew what he was like, how he treated women!'

Bursting into tears, she hung up on me before I could ask her what she'd had to offer Jim that I hadn't, why he'd left me for her. Whatever the reason, it didn't matter any more. The point was that I'd won. But, looking at it another way, we'd both lost. In reality, we'd *all* lost – all three of us. But there were other relationships, other marriages to destroy, and I couldn't afford to dwell on Jim.

Ringing Sally, I wondered how she was feeling, whether Tony had left yet – been ousted from the marital home for his obscene sins. 'He's gone,' she snivelled. 'I threw him out, and I'm going to see a solicitor.'

'Good, you've done the right thing,' I assured her. 'I thought you were going to come round for a coffee this morning?'

'I did, but you were out. I've been wandering the streets aimlessly all day, trying to work things out, wondering why he did it.'

'That's how I felt when Jim . . . Did he give you an explanation? Not that there's much to explain!'

'He blamed the girl.'

'He would! I talked to Sharon again when you'd gone. She said that he came on strong, touching her up, fiddling with her, offering to take her out for a meal and generally using his charm. Being young, impressionable, naive, she fell for it.'

'I can't get the picture out of my head of him kneeling behind her with his . . . I'll never forget it – I'll never forget that awful sight!'

'You will, in time. Listen, when you feel like it, come round for a chat.'

'OK, Sue. I can't tell you how grateful I am, having a friend like you.'

'As I said, that's what friends are for. Give me a ring before you come round, just in case I'm out, or something.'

'All right. Bye. And thanks, Sue.'

'Any time, Sally. Bye – and try not to dwell on it.'

Retrieving my notebook from under the sofa, I wrote number ten by Sally's and Tony's names, seeing as divorce was imminent! I also awarded Jim and Caroline ten points. Derek and Jilly were still unnumbered, and I wondered how they were faring – whether she'd enjoyed a good whipping recently! Tracy and Craig would also have to remain an unknown quantity for the time being. Had Craig yet discovered the weals, the love bites, across his wife's buttocks? Surely, the tell-tale signs would last for several days, at least? Craig would notice them at some point – he had to!

Wandering into the kitchen, I found another plain white envelope lying ominously on the table. Tearing the envelope open, I read the familiar scribbled letters – the frightening words:

Your game will destroy you! You'll end up with nothing – no one!

My game? My quest to wreck marriages? Was that what the words meant? Yes, I was sure it was. *You'll end up with nothing – no one!* The words echoed around the canyons of my mind, maiming, disturbing my inner thoughts.

Relegating the note to the litter bin on my way into the hall, I grabbed the phone. Dialling Tracy's number, desperate to know whether or not Craig had discovered her weals, her adulterous ways, I tried to clear my mind. The bloody notes had to stop! They were ruining my life.

'Oh, hello, Sue,' Tracy replied flatly.

'You all right?' I asked.

'You know only too well that I'm far from all right!'

Oh, shit! What to say? There was no way out of this one! Still, my plan had been to destroy her relationship, so what the hell?

'What *are* you talking about?' I asked innocently.

'What you did earlier, your little game! That's what I'm talking about!'

'What did he say?'

'Who?'

'Craig, when he realized . . .'

'Craig? Now *I* don't know what *you're* talking about!'

'But . . . Didn't he . . .'

'Craig's not here, I haven't seen him since this morning.'

'So, he hasn't . . . Anyway, what's your complaint? You loved every minute of it!'

'Yes, but I've been thinking. There's something wrong with you, Sue. Tying me down, and letting some stranger use me like that was . . .'

'Was lovely! Go on, admit it, Trace!'

I wasn't convinced now that Craig would discover Tracy's weals. Perhaps a damn good whipping was the answer? Give her such a thrashing that the evidence would survive for weeks!

'He's not seen the love bites yet, then?' I asked.

'No, thank God! And as for my bum! God, you should see the marks! If he were to see them, I'd be in real trouble!'

'Then, why not show them to him before . . .'

'What? Tell him that you tied me down and whipped me?'

'No, of course not! What I mean is, show him before he sees them, and tell him that you fell over or something. If he discovers them, he'll wonder why you didn't mention it, won't he?'

'Yes, I see your point. I'll show him when he gets home. I hadn't thought of that, it's a good idea. Anyway, shall I come round and see you tomorrow?'

'Oh, you still like me, then?'

'Yes, but I can't think why!'

'In that case, yes, come round tomorrow.'

'All right. Sleep well, and I'll see you in the morning.'

'OK, Trace – bye.'

Things were getting better and better! God, the minute Craig saw Tracy's bum, he'd know whom he'd been fucking in my sex den and he'd go wild! But I hoped she wouldn't show him until I'd enjoyed the following morning's sex session with her. I was rather looking forward to licking her sweet pussy, making her come in my mouth again.

I did sleep well that night – so well that I didn't hear the phone ringing in the morning. 'Sue, it's for you!' Sharon called, shaking my shoulder to wake me up. 'Sue, there's a man on the phone for you!'

'Oh, right. Tell him I'm on my way,' I replied dreamily.

Slipping my dressing gown on, I dashed downstairs and took the phone from Sharon. 'Oh, Craig! How are you?' I asked apprehensively, realizing that he was fuming.

'Heading for divorce, thanks to you!' he raged.

'*Me*? Sorry, I'm not with you.'

'No, but *I* was with *you* yesterday – and with Tracy! What the hell did you think you were playing at? And how long have you been having a lesbian relationship with my bloody wife?'

'For as long as I've been having a heterosexual relationship with you. Anyway, you were both quite happy in the belief that you were committing adultery, so don't blame me!'

'I *do* blame you! Anyway, my marriage is over – finished!'

'Well, it serves you both right for playing around, doesn't it?'

'How could she do it? How the hell could she have a man fuck her from behind like that when she hadn't a clue who he was? God, she's a fucking whore!'

'And what are you? For doing exactly the same as Tracy did, what are you?'

'That's different. She's on her way to see you, by the way. She's hopping mad!'

'I don't give a toss! You both thought you were screwing someone else, proving that you're no better than each other!'

'You set us up, didn't you?'

'How could I have set you up? I didn't even know that you were going to come round, did I?'

'My life's ruined because of you!'

'You fucked your own life when you fucked Tracy and me!'

'Fuck off, Sue – just fuck off!'

Another marriage in ruins! 'I'm doing bloody well!' I breathed as I replaced the receiver.

'You're abominable!' Sharon bellowed, emerging from the kitchen. 'I heard what you said – you need psychiatric help!' I don't know about psychiatric help, but I needed the bloody notes to go away!

'Shut up, Sharon! You don't know what you're fucking talking about!' I blasted. 'You don't know what Jim put me through, what he did to me!'

'No, I don't, but why put others through it?'

'I *have* to – I *need* to. Anyway, are you off to college?'

'Yes, I'll see you later, after you've destroyed another half-dozen marriages, no doubt!'

Slamming the front door behind her, Sharon stomped off in a sulk. Oh, well, not to worry. It wasn't her business, anyway! And with that attitude, she should be paying me rent! I reflected as I wandered out into the back garden.

Another day, another broken marriage. Relaxing on the lawn with the sun shining down on me, I tried to take stock of my plans. So far, three relationships had fallen – how many more would there be? I knew so many couples and didn't really know where to stop. How many more marital paths would I cross? I didn't know, or care. I was finding a great sense of satisfaction from wrecking people's lives. Mine had been wrecked – now I was doing unto others as had been done unto me.

Through the hedge, I listened to Derek and Jilly in their kitchen, discussing breakfast. I'd made no headway with them at all – or with Dave, the man from the secondhand furniture shop. But he could wait. It was Derek and Jilly who deserved my attention next!

Hearing Derek leave for work, spoiling any fun I might have had there, I wondered what to do, how to spend the day. Sure that it was Tracy, I didn't bother to answer the doorbell and assumed that she'd sulked off, sobbing in her misery, no doubt. God, I was becoming a merciless bitch – and I loved it!

Suddenly, I had an idea. I had the day free, so why not go and visit my sister? She was married to a good-looking young man – a man who would be easy prey for my smiling, naked pussy! As I stood up and brushed the grass from my dressing gown, the side gate opened and Tracy stood there staring at me.

'Oh, Tracy!' I half smiled. 'Did you ring the doorbell? I . . . I can't have heard it.'

'Yes, I did. I want to know why you did it, Sue. I want to know how long you've been screwing Craig!'

'Twice, that's all. Once when he came to fix the water leak, and the other time was when you were tied . . . Well, you know about that.'

'Why, Sue? Why?'

'Why did you and I do what we did? It was just the same, just as bad.'

'That was different, and you know it! I thought you wanted something with me!'

Why was it always bloody different?

'I did! I mean, I do! I don't know what I mean. Anyway, Craig's just another conniving, two-timing bastard. All I did was prove that to you, so I don't know why you're so upset.'

'He's my husband!'

'And you're his wife – what's the difference? You're both as bad as each other. You both thought that you were committing adultery, and were more than happy to do so!'

'I wasn't more than happy . . .'

As my dressing gown fell open, Tracy's eyes lit up. God, was she still interested in me after what had happened? Surely not? Smiling now, she moved across the lawn towards me. I was about to open my gown further to entice her, to lure her to my sex den, when I heard a window open. Turning, I looked up to the house at the end of the garden.

'Listen Trace, I've got lots to do. Why don't you come back later?' I suggested, grinning at Tom, Jim's golfing friend, as he waved to me from the open window.

'I need to talk to you, Sue,' Tracy pleaded, placing her hand on my shoulder. 'Now that it's over with Craig, I'm free – we're both free, aren't we?'

'Yes, but . . . Please, Trace, come back tomorrow. I must go into town and . . .'

'All right, but promise me you'll be here.'

'Yes, about twelve – come for lunch.'

'OK, I'll see you tomorrow, and we'll . . .'

'We'll talk, Trace.'

God, she'd changed her tune quickly! I'd thought she was going to knock my head off or something, not accept an invitation to lunch! There again, she'd had enough of Craig and his bloody adulterous ways. To be honest, their marriage was over the minute she'd found out about his affair. Tracy could never trust him again, and without trust, there was nothing. All I'd done was speed things up a little.

'Hi, Tom!' I called, waving back to him the minute Tracy had gone, deliberately allowing my gown to fall wide open. I could see his expression change as my breasts, my shaved crack, came into view, and I felt a shot of adrenalin course its way through my quivering body.

'I'll come over!' he bellowed excitedly before closing the window.

My clitoris tingling in anticipation, I waited for Tom to emerge through the hole in the hedge at the end of the garden. Jim and Tom had used the hole as a rendez-vous when they were going off to play golf. Now and again, Tom's wife, Sandy, would pop through the hole for a chat and cup of tea, but since my break-up with Jim, I hadn't seen her, and I'd assumed she couldn't be bothered.

'Nice day!' Tom called as he appeared through the hedge.

'Yes, lovely, isn't it? You working hard?'

'Yes, catching up with paperwork. A few months ago, I turned the spare room into an office, rather than use the dining room. I was just opening the window to get some fresh air when I saw you. I often see you sunning yourself in your bikini.'

'Do you, now?' I laughed. 'Anyway, how's Sandy? I haven't seen her for some time.'

'She's fine! She's been meaning to come and see you.'

'But she didn't because she didn't know what to say about Jim leaving me for another woman, I suppose?'

'Something like that.'

'Tell her to come over now and have a coffee with me.'

'She's out – gone shopping.'

'Oh. Would you like a coffee?'

'OK, that would be nice,' he smiled, following me across the lawn and into the kitchen.

Tom was considerably older than me, in his mid-forties, in fact, but still a good-looking man. Tall and well-built, with a deep voice, he was *all* man. Surprisingly, I'd not thought of him as a potential victim, and I wondered why it hadn't occurred to me to add his name to my list. After all, hadn't he dragged Jim away from me most weekends, leaving me a lonely golf widow? I had to pay him back for that! Sandy had never done anything to hurt me, but what did that matter? Sentiment didn't come into it. Nothing was going to stop me from delivering a fatal blow to her marriage!

My dressing gown trick had worked a treat on the second-hand furniture man, and I knew it would prove to be a winner with Tom. I couldn't fail! My 'pre-pubescent' pussy, my omnipotent weapon, was like a magnet, attracting married men to me like bees to a honey-pot. As Tom sat at the kitchen table, I twirled round to grab the kettle, my gown opening, my erotic wares on blatant display.

'Sorry I'm not dressed yet, Tom,' I smiled. 'I've only just got up.'

'That's OK,' he murmured, his hazel eyes transfixed on my naked slit as I pulled my gown together. 'So, how are things?' he asked.

'Fine! I'm enjoying life, at last. How are things with you?'

'I've too much work on at the moment, but I'm coping.'

'Better to be busy than quiet, I suppose. It must be very interesting, being a private investigator.'

'It has its moments.'

'Is Sandy still doing bar work? Do you take sugar?'

'Yes, she loves it. Two, please. You still working at the library?'

'No, I gave it up when Jim left. Do you still play golf together?'

'Not so much now that he's . . . To be honest, I don't really have the time for golf any more.'

'No, I suppose not. You know the story, don't you – Jim going off with my best friend, Caroline?'

'Yes, he told me all about it.'

'Did he tell you that they've split up?'

'Split up?'

'Yes – things sort of went horribly wrong for them.'

'Oh! Where's he living now, then?'

'No idea! He's probably got himself a flat or something. There's your coffee.'

'Thanks. I wonder what went wrong between them?'

'I think he started cheating on her, as he did with me, and she found out.'

'God! Poor old Jim!'

'Yes, *poor old Jim*!' I snapped.

'Sorry . . . I didn't mean to . . .'

'That's OK. I still don't know why he left me for her. I'm all right now, it's history – but I'd still like to know why he left me for her.'

'He was . . . I'd better not say too much, I don't want to upset you.'

'No, go on – please.'

'Well, how can I put it? He was always a bit of a lad, as you know. He had another woman, apart from Caroline. The reason he left you for Caroline was because he thought he'd have more freedom living with her. Before he moved in with her, he told her a string of lies about working late in the evenings and at weekends and the like, and that she'd have to accept it. The idea being that he'd have plenty of freedom to meet this other woman.'

'But why not go and live with the other woman in the first place? Why bother to leave me and set up home with Caroline, just so he could see someone else? I don't understand.'

'The other woman's married. According to Jim, Caroline promised him the freedom he wanted, and the sex he wanted. Course, when he moved in with her, it was a completely different story – she clung to him like a leech, watched his every move! He needed the security of a home, a base, you see. He'd have his shirts washed and ironed, his meals cooked, a good sex life – and his freedom. Or so he'd thought!'

'Who's the married woman? Anyone I know?'

'I'd better not say.'

'Please, I'm intrigued.'

'Her name's Wendy . . . Wendy Dickinson or something. She lives . . .'

'Not Wendy Dixon?'

'Yes, that's it! Do you know her?'

'Yes, I do! God! Perhaps Jim's planning to set up home with her?'

'I don't know. Her husband's worth a fortune. I'm sure she wouldn't leave him for someone in a rented flat!'

'Unless she plans to divorce her husband and have Jim move in with her?' I speculated.

'Possibly. Jim did say that her husband was having an affair, so perhaps you're right.'

Another turn-up for the books! Wendy Dixon, of all people! She'd been a regular borrower at the library and we'd become friends – well, good acquaintances, really. But I hadn't realized that Jim knew her, let alone . . .

A double strike! Having wrecked Jim's and Caroline's relationship, how about Jim and Wendy – and her husband? I'd never met him. She'd told me that he worked away a lot, so that was probably why I'd never seen them together. My mind reeling with plans to attack yet another marriage, and deal Jim another blow, I seated myself opposite Tom.

'These married men all seem to have a bit on the side!' I laughed, allowing my gown to open slightly. 'Do you have a bit of spare, Tom?'

'Good God, no! There's no way I'd get away with it! To be honest, the adultery game just isn't worth playing – it can be a messy business. In my line of work, I deal with cheating husbands and wives every day! I'm on a case now. This chap is seeing someone, and his wife has hired me to nail him. The thing is, the woman he's seeing is a TV celebrity, so it's a bit awkward!'

'God! Who is she?'

'I can't say, but I'm not quite sure how to handle it.'

As I listened to his ramblings, I realized that Tom might not be such an easy lay after all. How to tempt him, crack him, other than to blatantly display my naked pussy slit and ask him to lick my clitoris to orgasm? Remembering a film I'd seen, I grinned discreetly.

'Sorry, Tom, but this heat gets to me,' I began, holding my

head. 'I just can't take it! I've been feeling quite ill recently. In fact, I feel a little faint.'

'Go and have a lie down. Some people can't . . .'

His words tailed off as I slipped from my chair and lay on the floor, my dressing gown doing nothing to conceal my breasts, my open thighs – my smiling pussy-crack. What would he do? Take advantage of me? Play the gentleman and cover me up? He'd certainly wonder why I'd shaved my pussy!

Dashing into the lounge, he returned with a cushion and placed it under my head – but he didn't rearrange my gown. Instinctively, though my eyes were closed, I knew that he was gazing at me, my open girl-slit, my nipples – but would he touch me? Suddenly I was aware of his finger running down my vaginal chasm and a shot of adrenalin, of sex, coursed through me. I desperately wanted him inside me, his finger exploring my wet pussy.

As he neared my entrance, he stopped, probably gauging my state of consciousness before trespassing into my fleshy cavern. Gently, slowly, his finger slid into me, and I tried not to gasp. Further his finger delved into my hot sheath, before withdrawing and circling my clitoris. Trembling, I couldn't help but sigh with the pleasure he was bringing me, and he recoiled, covering me with my gown before hurriedly returning to his chair.

Damn it! Why couldn't he have brought me to orgasm? But, I consoled myself, I'd hooked him. He'd seen my body, felt the inner heat of my wet vagina, and I prayed that that would be enough to seal our friendship. Slowly opening my eyes, I staggered to my feet and sat down.

'You fainted,' he said with concern. 'I thought I'd best leave you there. It must be the heat – are you OK?'

'I do feel a little strange. I haven't eaten properly for a day or two. God, I do feel dizzy!'

'Have some water. You're probably dehydrated.'

'Yes, I think I will,' I smiled, moving to the sink. 'How long was I out for?'

'Only a couple of minutes. Anyway, if you're sure you'll be all right, I'd better finish my coffee and get back to work.'

'Oh, don't go, Tom.'

'Well, I . . .'

'Sandy won't be back for a while, will she?'

'No, no, I suppose not. I'll stay for a while longer, if you want me to.'

'Do *you* want to?'

'I . . . Yes, of course I do.'

'Good. Where were we? Oh, yes. I was going to ask you whether you've ever committed adultery.'

'Er . . . No, not really.'

'Not really? What do you mean by that?'

What's the difference between a finger and a penis when it comes to adultery?

'I used to have a drink with someone on the odd occasion, but Sandy became suspicious. That was years ago. As I said, I'd never get away with it! Sandy and I have a special relationship, we have shared interests and . . . Anyway, I'd never commit adultery, as such.'

'Oh, that's a shame,' I grinned, licking my lips.

'A shame?' he echoed.

'Well, I rather like you, Tom – I always have.'

'Are you suggesting . . .'

'Yes, I suppose I am.'

His eyes met mine, and then fell to his coffee cup. Was he considering my proposal? Or was he highly embarrassed and wondering what excuses to make to get out of the house? Pulling on my gown, I bared a breast, an erect nipple, waiting for him to look up. Fiddling with his cup, he raised his head, his mouth hanging open as he gazed at my exposed tit.

'I'm a married man, Sue,' he sighed. 'You're a very attractive woman, but . . .'

'But what? We might as well use the hole in the hedge for something. Anyway, what do you do in the evenings while Sandy's working at the pub?'

'I work – sit up in my office working.'

'There you are, then. Why not pop through the hedge and come in for a drink now and then? I get bored sitting on my own, as you must do, so come in for a drink – or something.'

'Maybe . . .'

The damn phone always seemed to ring at the wrong moment! Telling Tom to wait there, I dashed into the hall and picked the receiver up to hear Tony's pathetic voice.

'Sue, can I come round?' he whined.

'No, I'm sorry, but I'm busy just now,' I snapped.

'I've had to move out of the house.'

'Yes, Sally told me.'

'What else did she say?'

'She said that she's seeing a solicitor.'

'Oh, God! I don't suppose you could speak to her, could you? Only, I don't want us to break up. I love her.'

Love? Huh! He didn't know the meaning of the word. *He lusts her, more like – lusts after her fanny, and mine!* To get rid of him, I told him that I'd do my very best to get Sally to take him back, which pleased him. In reality, I was going to do my very best to keep them apart! *Perhaps I should drive one last nail into his coffin? Arrange for Sally to come round just as Tony was screwing my bum!* That would seal his fate once and for all!

'Come round this afternoon, Tony – if you're free,' I suggested.

'Yes, I will – about three?'

'OK, I must go now, I'll see you later.'

'Thanks, Sue – I'll look forward to it!'

So will I!

Tom had gone, crept out of the house and slipped through the hole in the hedge, probably confused by his stiffening penis, my wet cunt – and his precious wife. Oh well, plenty of time to seduce him, screw him – wreck his marriage!

Before I showered and dressed, I rang Sally and invited her round. She readily accepted as she had some good news, although she didn't say what. All she would reveal was that she'd been talking to someone who'd once worked for Relate. Could she be having second thoughts about divorcing Tony? I wondered anxiously.

But it didn't matter – whatever the Relate person had told her, nothing would change her mind. Not after the scene she was going to witness that very afternoon!

Chapter Nine

I was quite surprised when Tom returned after lunch. There was I, sitting in the garden in my bikini reading a magazine when he came sneaking through the hedge like a naughty schoolboy stealing into an orchard. Praying that he'd decided to take me up on my adulterous offer, I patted the lawn and invited him to join me.

'Can't stay long,' he said guiltily, sitting beside me. 'Sandy thinks I'm working upstairs. Anyway, I'm free this evening – if your offer of a drink still stands, that is?'

Sandy thinks he's working – the lies begin!

'Yes, of course it does!' I enthused, noticing his eyes on my bikini bulging between the tops of my thighs.

'Good, I'll bring some gin – you do like gin, don't you?'

'Gin turns me on, you'll be pleased to hear! It's the juniper berries!' I giggled mischievously, sitting cross-legged, the thin strip of bikini material too narrow to conceal my swelling pussy lips. 'What time will you be round?'

'Sandy leaves at six-thirty, so is seven OK?'

'Fine! What time does she get in?'

'After the pub closes and she's cleared up – about midnight.'

'Good, we'll have plenty of time for some fun!'

'Right, I'd better get back. See you later, then.'

'Yes, I'll look forward to it, Tom.'

Watching him creep through the hedge, I grinned. This game was too easy – ridiculously easy! I felt that all I had to do was knock on every door and wave my magic pussy, and every marriage in the land would fall! Cunt-power!

Relaxing in the garden, I gave some serious thought to Jim and that bitch, Wendy Dixon. If Jim was still screwing her, he'd have no idea that I knew, let alone planned to wreck his relationship with her – and her marriage! It was time to make a move.

Wandering into the house, I grabbed the phone book and looked up Wendy's number. She was in, fortunately, and, to start up the conversation, I began by telling her that I'd left my part-time job at the library.

'I'd wondered where you'd got to,' she remarked.

'Still changing your books every week?' I asked.

'Yes, I am. Anyway, how are you?'

'Fine, and you?'

'Yes, I'm all right. My husband's away for a while, so I'm rather bored. I've got my books, but I do get lonely in this big house.'

'Yes, you must do. Listen, why not come round for a drink one evening?'

'I'd love to. When?'

'Tomorrow evening?'

'All right, that will be nice.'

'You know my address, don't you?'

'Yes, I do. I'll see you tomorrow, then.'

'OK, Wendy. It'll be nice to see you again – take care.'

She was a right bitch! I'd never given her my address – how the hell did she know it? Jim had probably screwed her in our bed while I was working at the library during the mornings. And why hadn't she mentioned my divorce? Surely, Jim would have told her? Unless he was living a massive lie! Bastard!

The day was getting hotter, and I was still wearing my bikini when Tony arrived. He looked me up and down as if I were an object for sale in a shop window as I pushed the front door to, making sure not to close it.

'Did you talk to Sally?' he asked, fondling my swelling pussy lips through my bikini.

'No, not yet. She said that she might pop round sometime for a chat, but I don't know when,' I replied, pulling away and walking into the kitchen.

'I hope you can help me, Sue. I really do want to get back with Sally again. I'm having to rent a bloody flat! I hate it! Still, I've got you, haven't I?'

'Indeed you have!' I smiled, checking my watch. Three-fifteen. Sally was due at three-thirty, so I didn't have a great deal of time to set the stage.

Feeling really randy, I slipped my bikini off and opened the fridge. Grabbing a cucumber, I tossed it to Tony and grinned. 'How about a nice cucumber sandwich?' I suggested provocatively, licking my lips.

Leaning over the table, I stood with my feet wide apart and my bottom pushed out. 'Well, aren't you going to fuck me with it?' I giggled as he pulled his clothes off.

'Too right I am!' he laughed excitedly. 'God, I wish Sally was like you, Sue! You certainly know how to have fun!'

'Indeed I do!' I gasped as he pushed the hard, cold phallus deep into my hot cunt, filling me, cooling me. 'Now fuck my bum!' I breathed as he rammed the cucumber in and out of my pussy hole. 'Grab some cream from the fridge for lubricant, and push your lovely cock deep into my bum-hole!'

The cooling cream was heavenly. Smearing it between my buttocks, he asked whether he could lick me clean after he'd fucked me. 'You bet!' I giggled, praying that Sally would make her timely entrance and catch Tony with his shaft buried deep in my bowels.

Stabbing his knob between my splayed buttocks, he drove gently into me. My small hole opened, my muscles yielding as he pressed his shaft further into the heat of my quivering body. The cucumber still filling my pussy, I felt as if I was going to split open as he pushed the last inch of his huge organ into my bum, his heavy balls brushing against my dripping labia.

Reaching beneath his balls, he worked the cucumber in and out of my vaginal sheath as he thrust his solid shaft in and out of my bottom-hole. I'd positioned myself over the table so that when Sally came in she'd have a perfect view of our obscene coupling – of her husband's penis buried in my hot bum. I'd expected her to scream hysterically when she saw us, to go wild – but she didn't.

I saw her from the corner of my eye, just standing in the kitchen doorway, watching us. Lost in his ecstasy, Tony obviously had no idea that she was there, and I grabbed the chance to kill their twisted relationship – to give the knife one last fatal twist!

'Fuck me harder with the cucumber!' I cried. 'Ah, yes, that's good! Come in my bum and then you can fuck my cunt and then shoot your sperm into my thirsty mouth!'

'God, you're a sexy little bitch!' he gasped. 'Christ, your bum's hot and tight!'

'If Sally takes you back, this will have to stop,' I giggled.

'No, it won't! Even if the prudish bitch does take me back, I'll still come round and fuck your lovely arse! Ah, God – I'm coming!'

Thrusting for all he was worth, Tony filled my bum-hole with his come, gasping his illicit lust for me as Sally stood quietly in the doorway, witnessing her husband's blatant adultery. Quickly slipping his penis out of my hot bottom-hole, he wanked himself off, spraying my buttocks with the last of his sperm before standing back and admiring me.

'There, I've covered your pretty bum with my cream!' he laughed, rubbing his sperm into my buttocks. 'I'll lap it up, and then fill your tight pussy-hole!' Pulling the cucumber from my burning cunt, he licked my juices from the green shaft. 'Mmm, you taste good!' he gasped, smacking his lips.

'Better than me?'

Tony turned to face his wife as I rose from the table. Her face flushed, her hands trembling, tears flowing from her tired eyes, she just stood there gazing at the pair of us. She said nothing – she was beyond pain, now. Her expression was blank, as if she'd taken so much that she was now incapable of feeling hurt.

Tony had really done it this time, I knew as he began his stammered explanation. As his sad, silent wife turned and left the room, he chased after her, his limp, adulterous penis swinging from side to side.

'Oh dear, that's torn it!' I laughed as he returned to the kitchen.

'Torn it? That's fucked it good and proper!' he bellowed.

'I wonder how she got in?' I mused. 'Sharon's not here, so I wonder how the hell she got into the house?'

'The bloody door must have been open! Shit, now I've really fucked up my chances!'

'I'm afraid you have, and she won't be speaking to *me* again, that's for sure!'

'Shit! One thing goes wrong after another! It's as if someone's deliberately trying to destroy me!'

'Of course they're not! It's just bad luck – fate,' I decreed, slipping into my bikini. 'So, what will you do now?'

'Nothing. There's nothing I *can* do, is there?'

'No, I suppose not. Anyway, you'd better get dressed, I've got things to do,' I said, wanting to get rid of him and prepare for my evening with Tom.

Pulling his clothes on as I wiped the cream and sperm from my buttocks, he cursed me for leaving the front door open, and Sally for spying on him. 'You've no one to blame but yourself!' I returned angrily. 'You can't blame me – and you certainly can't blame Sally for your infidelity!'

'No, I suppose not. Anyway, I'll come and see you again.'

'Yes, do – but ring first, won't you?'

'OK. Oh, well, it's back to the rented accommodation, I suppose! See you, Sue – and thanks.'

'You've nothing to thank me for!' I called as he mooched down the hall. 'Do come again!'

That was that relationship dead and buried! I felt some guilt, a little remorse over the way I'd treated Sally, but it only lasted for a few minutes. I was becoming used to the mental pain I was inflicting on others. More than used to it – I was enjoying it!

I didn't really want to see Tony again. My job finished, there was little point in seeing him again. Besides, I had Tom's demise to look forward to, which excited me – and Jim's second death! My mind reeling with exhilaration, I went up to my bedroom to change.

Glancing out of the open window as I slipped my bikini top off, I noticed Tom gazing out of his window. But more than gazing – he was looking at me through binoculars! How long he'd been spying on me, I had no idea. It could have been days, weeks! Christ, Tom had said that he'd turned the spare room into an office several months ago! I never drew the curtains at night during the summer. And, not dreaming that I was being spied on, I rarely used my dressing gown in the mornings, wandering around my bedroom naked until I went downstairs.

Alive with lust, I paraded up and down my bedroom, my firm, rounded breasts on show, knowing that Tom's penis would be hard and ready for the evening. Was that why he'd turned the spare room into his office? I wondered. Had he seen me and decided to install himself in the room so that he could spy on me?

Contemplating my bed, I realized that he wouldn't be able to see me sleeping – or masturbating! My clitoris stirring between my wet and swelling pussy lips, I repositioned the dressing table, adjusting the mirror so that I could see Tom when I lay on my bed. If I could see him in the mirror, then he could see me. I decided I'd give him a masturbation show – allow him to watch me bring myself off. But not now – I had other plans.

Slipping my bikini on again, I went out into the garden and lay on the lawn under the hot sun, knowing that his binoculars were focused on me. He'd said that he'd often seen me sunning myself – had he always used his binoculars to gaze at my bikini-clad body? Picturing him wanking, shooting his jism over the floor as he gazed at my bikini where it bulged over my breasts and pussy, I felt my own slippery juices oozing.

The hedge at the end of the garden was fairly high, but not high enough to block Tom's view, and I suddenly realized that he could see straight into my dining room. With the patio doors open, there'd be a clear view of the large mahogany table, and I imagined lying there naked, and Sandy using the binoculars to see her husband nibbling away at my delicious pussy! What more delectable way to destroy a marriage?

But she probably didn't know about the binoculars, and besides, the chances of her focusing on us eating each other in my dining room were slim, to say the least! I'd have to chat to her, mention that I'd seen Tom with his binoculars. Put it to her that he always seemed to be gazing at my house. But my words would have to be chosen very carefully. I didn't want to rock the boat too soon, arouse suspicion before the fun had even started!

Returning to the house, I grabbed the cucumber from the kitchen and went into the dining room. Opening the patio doors, I slipped my bikini bottom off, watching Tom out of the corner of my eye as I lay over the table, my legs open wide, my shaved cunt on display. Gripping the cucumber, I eased it between my ripening pussy lips and sank it gently into my hot cavern, imagining Tom's solid cock as he watched me fuck myself with the huge phallus. Opening my legs wider, I thrust the green shaft harder into my open body, gasping as my climax neared.

Knowing that I was being watched aroused me more than I'd ever have thought possible. My cunt burning, aching for relief, my clitoris throbbing in the beginnings of its climax, I tossed my head from side to side, lost in my obscenity before, finally, I shuddered and came.

The cucumber cooking now, my cunt gripping it like a vice, I made my last few thrusts before caressing the last waves of ecstasy from my solid clitoris. Stilling my shaking body, I relaxed, my sex-juices dripping from my used hole, running down the shaft of the cucumber to pool on the dark polished table.

Raising my head slightly, I gazed at Tom through my eye lashes. He was almost falling out of the window, the binoculars in his hands, as I pictured the view – my cunt stretched open by the cucumber, my fingers massaging my clitoris. He'd be ready for the seduction now, I was sure of that as I slipped the hot length from my vaginal sheath, licking my juices from the green shaft before climbing off the table. But he wouldn't be prepared for his ruination!

In my devilry, I slipped back into my bikini and picked the phone up. Dialling Sandy's number, my hands trembling with excitement, I asked how she was.

'Great!' she enthused. 'I'm sorry I've not been over to see you but . . .'

'Don't worry about it. I know it's awkward for other people when someone's had their husband walk out on them. Anyway, I'm fine now.'

'Yes, Tom said that he'd spoken to you and that you were OK. We'll have to get together for a chat.'

'Yes, I'd like that. How's Tom doing? I forgot to ask him.'

'Fine! He's been really busy. He's working from the spare room now. It's nice to have the dining room back!'

'It must be. I'm always seeing him gazing out of the window through his binoculars – he can't get much work done! Is he into bird watching, or something?'

'No, not that I know of! When have you seen him?'

'Evenings, mostly – when you're working at the pub.'

'He's always tinkering around instead of working! I'll ask him about it.'

'No, don't, Sandy. He might think that I've been spying on him.'

'Of course he won't!'

'Perhaps *he's* been spying on *me*!' I giggled, planting the first seed of doubt.

'I'm sure he hasn't, Sue!'

'You never know! I'll tell you what, I never draw my curtains at night – I wonder if he's been watching me get ready for bed?'

'What are you suggesting?'

'I'm only joking, Sandy!'

'I'll have to check up on him!' she laughed.

'You could always take a look through his binoculars when he's out one evening, on your night off perhaps, and see what it is that's taken his interest.'

'As it happens, he mentioned that he's going out to see a friend of his this evening. I haven't told him, but I've decided to swap my night off, so I'm free this evening.'

'I wish I'd never mentioned it now! Anyway, he uses binoculars for his work, doesn't he?'

'Yes, but what's that got to do with it?'

'Well, he's probably testing them out or something. God, I was only joking about him spying on me!'

'That's as maybe, but you've got me thinking, Sue. He spends an awful amount of time up there – and there's something else.'

'What?'

'I overheard him talking to your Jim, once. He was laughing and telling him about spying through bedroom windows with his binoculars. At the time, I thought he was on a divorce job or something, but now . . .'

'Now you're being silly!'

'Silly or not, I'll have to make my own investigations.'

'Oh well – you do whatever you think best. You might even see me getting ready for bed!'

'Of course I won't! Anyway, you should draw your curtains.'

'Yes, I think I will. Look, I must go now. Come over for coffee sometime.'

'OK, Sue. Take care – and draw your curtains!'

'I will – bye.'

It was easier than I'd expected. Her suspicion suitably aroused, Sandy would probably spend half the evening scanning windows for glimpses of naked women! What she'd do when she saw me lying over my dining room table with her husband screwing me, I didn't know. Shit, she might come screaming through the hedge and attack Tom with a carving knife! She might even attack *me*!

This was going to be an easy one, I was sure of that – but I was worried. Although well aware of the danger involved in breaking marriages up, I couldn't seem to help myself. I seemed to be driven on by something inside me – something evil. Satan? It had become a way of life now, seeking, luring, destroying – and I loved it! The danger was worrying but, at the same time, exhilarating! Anyway, I decided, if Tom had been watching me undress for bed every night, then he deserved to pay for it – with his marriage!

He slipped through my back door at seven o'clock, clutching a bottle of gin and wearing a huge grin across his face. Wearing my miniskirt and a very tight T-shirt – minus undergarments, as usual – I greeted him with a sweet smile. Wondering how long he'd been spying on me, I asked a few tentative questions as I poured the gin and tonic.

'Don't you get sick of being stuck in your office all day and night?'

'No, not really. It's nice sitting by the open window. It overlooks all the gardens, and I can see what people get up to.'

'Get up to?'

'Barbecues, things like that.'

'Oh, I see. You don't spy through bedroom windows, do you?' I giggled as he followed me into the lounge.

'Of course not!' he retorted.

'That's good, because I don't draw my curtains at night!'

'I know you don't!'

'So, you *have* seen me?'

'Only on the odd occasion. I don't spend my time spying on pretty young housewives in their bedrooms! Anyway, Sandy's gone off to work, and I've got the whole evening free, so what shall we do?'

Reclining on the sofa, I opened my legs and smiled. All too easily, I'd lured another married man into my lair, and I wondered again where it would all end. He was attractive, as they all were, and I wanted his lovely, solid cock fucking me, using my body for his sexual satisfaction – behind his wife's back! But where would it all end?

Wondering whether Sandy was at her post yet, I told Tom that I was going to get the gin from the kitchen, and slipped into the dining room. There she was, at the window, scanning the rows of houses with Tom's binoculars. The audience settled, the stage set – let the show begin!

I'd wanted to seduce Tom gently, watch his arousal build as the evening wore on, before moving in for the kill. But I had to act quickly. Sandy might well give up after a while – there was no time to lose. Slipping my clothes off, I returned to the lounge and stood naked before Tom, grinning wickedly as he admired my smiling slit.

'This is what you want, isn't it?' I giggled, placing the gin on the coffee table and moving closer to him.

'God, yes!' he breathed, reaching out and stroking my pouting cunt lips with the back of his hand. Delirious with lust, I stood with my feet wide apart, throwing my head back and gasping as he pressed his fingers into my hot, wet vagina.

'That's nice,' I murmured as he thrust and twisted his fingers, inducing my cunt milk to flow in torrents. 'You'd like to slip your cock into me and fuck me, wouldn't you?'

'Yes, I would!' he asserted, obviously stunned by my overt behaviour. 'Why have you shaved?'

'Because I like to see my cunt in all its beauty.'

'God, you're a beautiful woman! I've wanted to fuck you for months!'

'You'd better take your clothes off, then.'

Rising to his feet, he hurriedly unbuttoned his shirt, tossing it to the floor as he tugged his trousers down. His huge penis stood erect, the bulbous knob swollen, ripe – his balls heavy, full. Taking his hand, I led him to the dining room. 'You'll have to whip me first!' I grinned, taking the whip I'd left on the table. 'You do want to, don't you?' I asked as he took the implement and frowned.

'Yes, but . . .'

'No buts, just whip me!' I ordered as I lay over the table, my feet on the floor, my buttocks splayed before Sandy's wide eyes.

Tom began to thrash me, his penis waving from side to side as he lashed my burning buttocks harder and harder. 'You really like it, don't you?' he asked surprisedly.

'God, I love it!' I cried as the leather tails cut across my taut buttocks. Was Sandy dashing through the hedge with a carving knife? I wondered as the stinging pain, the danger, the excitement of being watched, brought me ever closer to my orgasm.

Or would she just watch from the window, and then lock Tom out of the house – for good?

Suddenly, Tom threw the whip to the floor and parted my taut buttocks. His huge knob quickly slipped deep into my vagina, causing me to gasp as he filled me, stretching my sheath wide open with his massive organ. Thrusting, grabbing my hips and fucking me as if there were no tomorrow, he gasped and grunted. Rocking as he pummelled my cervix with his solid knob, I cried out in my lust.

'Fuck me rotten, Tom! Fuck me rotten!'

'God, you're a right little tart!' he gasped, his belly slapping my stinging buttocks with every penetrating thrust of his rod. 'I watched you bring yourself off with a cucumber this afternoon!' he confessed. 'God, what a beautiful sight it was!'

'You sad pervy! I had no idea that you were spying on me!'

'I know more about you than you realize.'

The notes?

As our climaxes rose, mingling, taking us to our separate sexual heavens, I wondered again what Sandy would do. 'Coming!' Tom cried as his sperm gushed deep into my spasming cunt. We shuddered, our bodies locked in lust as he drained his heavy balls and my clitoris exploded exquisitely in orgasm. Panting, writhing, we fell to the floor, a tangle of limbs, our genitals still glued together. Prostrate on the floor, with Tom on my back, his huge cock still inside me, we rested as we drifted slowly back to our senses.

'That was something else!' he laughed as he finally slipped his beautiful length of male flesh from my vagina and stood up.

'God, it was!' I breathed. 'You're bloody good, Tom! The best I've ever had!'

As I climbed to my feet, I glanced at Tom's house to see Sandy leaning out of the window, the binoculars glued to her eyes. Sitting on the edge of the table, I lay back, my legs open, my pink cunt lips splayed to reveal my inner girl-folds.

'And now you can lick me out,' I goaded him, closing my eyes and waiting for his hot tongue to cleanse me.

'There's no satisfying you, is there?' he murmured as he knelt on the floor and kissed my inner thighs.

'No, there's no satisfying me! Now, lick me out and make me come in your mouth.'

Parting my pussy lips, stretching my delicate flesh wide open, he tasted my juice, his sperm, as it oozed from my hot sheath. His tongue brushed my clitoris, making me gasp with pleasure as he nibbled and tasted every inch of my glistening intimacy. Round and round he worked the tip of his tongue, stiffening my bud until I could take no more.

'I want to come!' I cried, all thoughts of Sandy fading as my mind began to swim in an ocean of lust. 'I want to come in your mouth!'

Suddenly, my entire being was engulfed in orgasm, locked in lust, and I shuddered violently, gripping the sides of the table as I released my juices, bathing Tom's mouth, his face, as he expertly sustained my incredible pleasure. I wanted him in my cunt, my mouth, my bum-hole – filling me with his gushing sperm, waking every nerve ending in my trembling body.

'Wank over me!' I gasped as he brought me down gently from my climax. 'Stand over me and shoot your come all over my body!' He needed no coaxing. Kneeling astride my breasts, his huge penis hovering ominously over my face, he grinned. Taking his shaft in his hand, he began wanking, watching me watching his knob expectantly.

His huge balls jerking, his shaft swelling to an incredible size, I waited for my prize, opening my mouth, hoping to catch a drop of his come as it shot through the air. Sooner than I'd expected, he grimaced, squeezing his eyes shut as his sperm jetted, landing on my face, splattering my cheeks. Pulling him nearer, I pushed my tongue out, catching his male fruits as he wanked and drained his balls yet again.

Finally taking his knob into my mouth, I cupped his balls in my hand and sucked the last drops of cream from his cock. Swallowing hard as he gasped and crumpled over my body, I was sure that Sandy and Tom had come to the end of the line – their marriage was over.

'What a woman!' he gasped as he climbed off the table. 'I've never known anyone like you!'

'What's Sandy like?' I asked, sitting up and licking his salty sperm from my lips.

'She's good – bloody good. But nowhere near as good as you – or as wet and tight!'

'I should be tighter, I *am* half her age! Do you come in her mouth?'

'Yes. But, I suppose, as with all women, there are certain things she won't do.'

'Such as?'

Tom appeared embarrassed as he ran his fingers through his hair and frowned. What wouldn't Sandy do? I wondered. She sucked his knob, so what was it?

'Come on,' I coaxed. 'You can tell me.'

'She won't let me do it from behind, if you know what I mean.'

'Yes, I know what you mean,' I smiled. 'Would you like to do that to me?'

'I'd love to, but I can't, not just yet, anyway,' he replied dolefully, looking down at his flaccid penis.

'There's plenty of time. Why don't you make me come again? That should stiffen you up nicely! I've got a fresh cucumber in the fridge, I'll go and get it.'

Retreating to the kitchen, I gazed at Tom's house, his office window. Sandy had gone. Was she on her way round? I wondered apprehensively as I strained my eyes to look for her.

My heart missed a beat as I caught a glimpse of her hiding in the hedge with the binoculars. What the hell was she doing? She'd had a perfect view from the window, so why creep around outside? Perhaps she was waiting for the right moment, when Tom was coming inside me, to leap through the patio doors and go wild.

I watched her creep across the lawn and crouch behind a large conifer by the patio, only yards from the dining room. She *must* be planning to pounce, I mused as I grabbed a cucumber from the fridge and returned to the dining room.

'What do you reckon you can do with this?' I asked Tom huskily, knowing that Sandy could hear every word.

'Quite a lot!' he laughed, taking the huge cucumber in his hand, his eyes fire-red with lust.

Leaning over the table, my feet wide apart, my buttocks facing the patio, I waited. On cue, Tom pushed the end of the phallus between my gaping labia and eased it gently into my hot cuntal sheath. Gasping as he opened my cunt wide, filling my sex-duct, I wondered what Sandy was thinking, what she was planning to do.

'It's in as far as it will go,' Tom declared, his finger exploring my bum-hole. Suddenly pulling the cucumber out, he pressed the end between my buttocks, locating my small hole and then gently twisting and pushing.

'Christ, it won't go in there!' I cried as he gently but firmly forced it past my tightening muscles. 'Tom, no!' Clinging to the sides of the table, I grimaced as he forced the massive green phallus deep into my bowels, opening me until I thought I'd split.

'It's in! Half of it's in!' he cried excitedly.

'God, it feels . . . it feels wonderful!' I breathed as he gently moved the shaft back and forth. 'God, that's good!'

Suddenly driving his solid penis between my inflamed pussy lips, his huge organ completely impaled me. My holes almost splitting, bringing me more pleasure than I'd ever have believed possible, I clung to the table as he fucked me, screwing my cunt as the cucumber screwed my tight bum-hole. Never had I felt so full, so completely sated, and I wanted more and more!

'God, I'm going to come!' I shrieked. 'I can't stop it! I can't stop it coming!' Rushing like a tornado, my orgasm ripped through me violently, shook my body to its core. My holes gripping the two shafts like vices, I cried out, forgetting about Sandy as I seemed to pass out in my multiple orgasm.

On and on Tom fucked my orifices until I thought I was going to die. My perspiring body rocking, taking the beautiful pounding, I finally begged him to stop. 'Please, Tom! I can't . . . I can't take any more!'

Ramming me harder, pumping his sperm deep into my quivering vaginal sheath, he finally stilled himself, relaxing, soaking up my inner heat before slowly withdrawing his penis, allowing my cunt, at least, to close.

'The . . . the cucumber!' I stammered. 'Take it out!' Gently twisting and pulling, he slowly extracted the green shaft from my aching bottom-hole, leaving me sore, stretched – satisfied.

'Nice?' he asked, massaging my bottom-hole with his finger.

'Yes, very,' I murmured, closing my eyes. 'But I thought you wanted to slip your cock into my bum, not the cucumber!'

'Later, my horny little angel – later.'

I couldn't understand why Sandy hadn't burst in, ranting and raving about divorce as I lay over the table with Tom's face buried between my thighs, his tongue lapping the sperm from my steaming sex cauldron. Surely, she was seething with anger? What was her game? Perhaps she was still waiting for the right moment to pounce?

I found myself wondering if she was crouching behind the

conifer, her knickers round her ankles, her fingers frigging her clitoris as she watched her husband drinking his sperm and my girl-come from my open cunt. Perhaps she was a voyeur? Christ, that would put paid to my plan of destruction!

When Tom had finished cleansing me, lapping the creamy milk from my pussy, he stood up. Smiling, he gently rolled me over and squeezed my aching nipples. 'You've a fine pair of tits,' he breathed, leaning over and sucking hard on each brown bud in turn. 'You're all woman, aren't you?'

'I am,' I sighed as my nipples stiffened. 'Tell me what Sandy likes.'

'Everything! In fact, she's often hinted at three in a bed.'

'What, you and another man?'

'No, another woman.'

'A woman? Christ, you mean that she's a lesbian?'

'She has tendencies, yes. She's a beautiful woman, and I love her very much.'

'She wouldn't think so if she could see you now!' I laughed, wondering, again, what she was thinking.

'No, but she might like to see us naked together – if we were in her bed.'

'Are you serious?'

'Yes, I am. Would you agree to it, if Sandy says yes?'

'I . . . I don't know. I mean . . .'

'I'll put it to her when she gets home. She'd like you in her bed, I know.'

I couldn't believe what I was hearing! Sandy wanting another woman to join her and her husband in their marital bed? I couldn't believe it! In all the years I'd known them, I'd never have dreamt that she was like that. Was she crouching behind the conifer assessing me, appraising my open pussy? Was she imagining me in her bed?

A stifled whimper came from the garden and Tom jumped up nervously to look out onto the patio. 'It was a cat,' I declared, leaping from the table and pulling him back into the room. 'It does that every evening.'

'It didn't sound like a cat,' he demurred.

'Well, it was. Anyway, do you want another drink, or are you ready to fuck my bottom now?' I asked, trying to keep him away from the patio where Sandy was obviously bringing herself off.

'I want to know what else you're into,' he smiled, squeezing my firm breasts.

'You name it, and I'm into it!' I laughed as another whimper came from behind the conifer.

'I've always wanted to tie a woman down and fuck her,' he confessed.

'Then you shall! Wait there a minute!'

Dashing upstairs, I grabbed the rope from my sex den and returned to the dining room. The whimpering had stopped and Tom was standing by the table, his huge penis stiff and ready for my hot body again. Tossing the rope to him, I lay on my back over the table and invited him to tie me down and live out his fantasy.

Wondering whether Sandy would join in as he bound my ankles and wrists to the table legs, I imagined her licking my cunt, bringing my climax out with her darting tongue as I lay defenceless across the table. The job of bondage done, Tom cupped my puffy pussy lips in his hand and smiled.

'Now that you're my prisoner, I can do what I like to you!' he laughed, a wicked glint in his eye as he eased a finger deep into my hot, yearning cunt.

'What *are* you going to do?' I asked, wondering whether or not it was such a good idea after all.

Leaving the room, I heard him rummaging around in the kitchen. What the hell he was looking for, I had no idea – until he returned wielding a bottle of wine. That's OK, I thought as he walked over to me – I've been *there* before!

'Do you think I can get this up your sweet little pussy?' he asked, brandishing the bottle and grinning wickedly.

'I *know* you can!' I laughed. 'Go on, do it!'

'Right, you've asked for it, so you'll get it!'

'No!' I cried as he tried to push the thick end of the bottle between my inflamed pussy lips. 'Tom, Please! You'll rip me open.'

'You wanted it!' he laughed as he peeled my sore lips wide open and pushed on the bottle.

Suddenly, I felt the thing slip into my body, forcing me open painfully but, at the same time, affording me beautiful sensations I'd never before known. Lifting my head, I watched as he sank the bottle deeper into my hot cavern, filling my pelvis, forcing my stomach to rise. Resting my head on the table again, I closed my eyes and bit my lip, imagining the walls of my vagina distending as he pushed the huge phallus in until it rested against my cervix.

'There!' he cried excitedly. 'I really didn't think I'd make it!'

'Neither did I!' I moaned. 'What the hell are you going to do now?'

'Massage a lovely orgasm from your clitty. Look at it – the beast's forced your cunt open so wide that your clitty's popped out of its socket!'

Paralysed with sex, with lust, as he began to massage my throbbing bud, I didn't look. Bloating my vagina like a massive penis, the sensations were heavenly as my sheath gripped and crushed the bottle, spasming in sympathy with my pulsating clitoris.

What the hell was Sandy thinking? I wondered in my sexual haze, my orgasm swirling deep within my contracting womb. Was she squatting behind the conifer, bringing herself off again? Would she go home and shove a wine bottle up her cunt, frig her clitoris to climax again? Perhaps she and Tom did this sort of thing regularly?

'God, I'm coming!' I cried as he expertly massaged my cumbud. 'God, I'm going to crush the bottle! Ah! Ah! Yes, coming!'

'Good girl! Keep it coming, feel it in your cunt, rising up to your clitty!' he encouraged.

'Yes, yes! It's here! Ah!'

Again, I experienced an orgasm of such intensity, such duration, that I thought I was dying. Again and again, the waves of sexual pleasure rolled over me – just as I thought that the tormenting taste of heaven was over, another series of waves would crash over me. Perspiring wildly, my head tossing, my eyes rolling, I garbled incoherently. 'Stop . . . St— . . . No . . . Can't . . .'

Ignoring my delirium, Tom continued to manipulate the bottle and massage my aching clitoris until I shuddered violently and fell limp, my consumed body half-comatose.

Slipping the bottle from my aching hole, Tom untied the ropes and allowed me to rest as he retrieved his clothes from the lounge and dressed. It seemed an eternity that I lay there – before I eventually managed to drag my abused body from the table and fall to the floor.

Crawling across the carpet to the patio, I hauled myself into a garden chair and wallowed in the cool evening breeze. Sandy had gone, Tom had gone. What were they doing? Had she gone home and confronted him? Or was she going to pretend that she'd been working at the pub?

Whatever they were or weren't doing, I was sure that I'd opened the coffin – prepared their marriage for death. But their relationship was weird, to say the least. I couldn't get over Sandy wanting another woman to join them in bed, and I began to wonder whether Tom had been fabricating to provoke a response from me. If not, and he asked her if she wanted me to join them in their sex games, would I say yes? I didn't know or care at that time. As I dragged my aching body up to my bed, all I wanted was rest.

Closing my eyes, I wondered whether Tom would return and take my bottom-hole. As I drifted off and slept as never before, I hoped so.

Chapter Ten

Lying in bed, the early morning sun warming my naked body, I turned to survey the dressing table mirror. I couldn't see Tom at the window. Perhaps Sandy had thrown him out? I reflected, hearing movement outside my door.

'Is that you, Sharon?' I called. Opening the door, she smiled at me – my breasts, my nipples, my naked pussy, as I kicked the quilt off the bed, complaining about the infernal heat.

'Morning!' she trilled, tossing her hair back. 'How are you?'

'Tired,' I moaned. 'Where have you been? I haven't seen you for a while.'

'Here and there,' she smiled, sitting on the edge of the bed and running her finger over my smooth mound.

Stretching my limbs out, I closed my eyes and sighed as she ran her finger up and down my opening slit. 'You're very wet,' she purred, slipping her finger between my inner lips and caressing the entrance to my vagina.

'I've been dreaming,' I lied. 'Dreaming of you making me come with your tongue.'

'Is that what you want me to do now?' she whispered as her finger entered me.

'Yes,' I breathed, closing my eyes and opening my legs further.

Leaning over, she kissed my pouting pussy lips, licking me, tasting me there. I breathed deeply and opened my legs wider as she parted my reddening folds and circled my clitoris with the tip of her tongue. As she thrust her finger deeper into my vagina, sucked my clitoris into her hot mouth, I shuddered, lost in my dreamy arousal.

My orgasm rose quickly from my contracting womb, emanating from my solid nodule and spreading over my quivering body. Expertly, Sharon flicked my clitoris with her tongue, sustaining my climax as she fingered my tightening cunt. Gasping, fantasizing about Sandy's wet cunt, I dug my fingernails into the bed as I rode the crest of my pulsating pleasure. Licking for all she was worth, drinking my come, sweeping her tongue over my throbbing bud, Sharon sustained my incredible pleasure until I gasped my last orgasmic gasp and crushed her hand between my twitching legs.

Slipping her finger from my drenched hole, she licked her finger clean and left me quivering with sexual satisfaction as my climax gently subsided. 'Was that nice?' she asked as I parted my thighs and she lapped the creamy come from my open hole.

'Mmm, lovely,' I murmured sleepily. 'Why don't you take your clothes off and join me?'

'I can't. I've got to be at college in half an hour. I'll see you later, though.'

'We'll do sixty-nine,' I smiled, closing my eyes as she finished cleansing me.

As she left the room, I turned my head and gazed into the mirror. Tom was there, his binoculars focused on my naked body reflected in the mirror. Had he seen Sharon licking me? I pondered as I massaged my stiffening clitoris. Raising my head, I lifted my breast and sucked my nipple into my mouth. Tom would soon be wanking, I knew, as I vibrated my fingertips over my throbbing bud and bit on my sensitive nipple. Watching me come, *he'd* soon be coming.

Within minutes, my shuddering climax came, exploding from my clitoris, waking every nerve ending in my trembling body, tightening every muscle as I caressed my beautiful sex-spot. Knowing that I was secretly sharing my experience with peeping Tom enhanced my pleasure incredibly, and I reached new sexual heights as my climax seemed to go on forever.

Frantically sustaining the pleasure throbbing between my open pussy lips, I craved sex with anyone and everyone. No longer the betrayed, cheated little housewife, I wanted Sharon's cunt, her nipples. I wanted Sandy in my bed with me, my fingers inside her tight sheath as I licked an orgasm from her lovely clitty. I wanted hard penises, sperming, penetrating every orifice – pouting pussy lips caressing my breasts, wetting my nipples.

As my incredible climax receded, I turned to the mirror to focus my eyes on Tom's window, but he'd gone – to masturbate, no doubt! Had he asked Sandy if she wanted me to join them in their bed? Surely he'd been making it up? Sandy wasn't a lesbian, and he knew it!

Climbing from my bed, I checked Tom's window again. He wasn't there. No point in parading my naked body, I thought as I grabbed my clothes and slipped into the bathroom. The phone rang as I was running my bath, and I dashed downstairs to answer it, noticing a white envelope lying on the doormat as I grabbed the receiver.

'Sue, it's Sandy.'

Oh, shit!

'Hi, Sandy!'

'You doing anything this morning? Only, I thought you might like to come round for a coffee – and a chat?'

'Oh! Er . . . Right. Yes, I'd love to. Give me half an hour, and I'll be with you.'

'OK.'

'Did you take the night off last night?' I asked, wondering what the hell she was thinking about my obscene sex session with her husband.

'Yes, and I didn't see anything through the binoculars.'

'There you are, then. I told you it was silly – I wish I'd never mentioned it.'

'There's someone at the door – I'll see you later.'

'OK – bye.'

What the hell was her game? I wondered. She watches her husband with me enjoying an evening of lewd, obscene sex, and then rings me to invite me over for coffee and a friendly chat! A bloody strange couple, to say the least!

Opening the white envelope, I unfolded the sheet of paper and, my heart filling with dread, read the familiar scrawl. *You're a destructive little tart! Your end is nigh!* Screwing the note up, I tossed it into the bin. How I hated the very thought of the evil notes! They were chewing away at my insides – destroying my mind!

Shaving the stubble from my mound as I lay in the bath, I ruminated, again, about Sandy's game. What was she playing at? Inviting me round for coffee after what she'd witnessed the night before was a completely abnormal reaction. Perhaps she really was a lesbian? I mused as the hot water lapped around my pussy lips. Perhaps she wanted my cunt lips over her mouth, her tongue inside me? Whatever her game was, I would soon find out!

Wearing a short skirt and blouse, I wandered out into the garden and slipped through the hole in the hedge, wondering if Tom was at home. Sandy greeted me as I stepped into her kitchen, her smile bright, her body slim, curvaceous beneath her short summer dress.

Her kitchen was new, fitted out with expensive oak units. Tom and Sandy seemed to have plenty of money. She only worked at the pub for fun, to meet people – it filled a void. Tom wasn't the going-out type, she'd often said. He was a homely, slippers-by-the-fire man – when he wasn't whipping and fucking his neighbour over her dining room table! His job as a private investigator hardly suited his image. But you never can tell what's beneath the exterior, I thought.

They were a nice couple – but, somehow, incongruous, I reflected. Both in their forties, they appeared happy enough, and yet there seemed to be something missing – something undefinable. Perhaps Tom hadn't been lying, and Sandy really did have lesbian tendencies? I hoped that I'd discover the truth as I sat at the table.

'It's good to see you again, Sue,' Sandy smiled as she sat opposite me. 'It's been so long.'

'Yes, it has. What with Jim going off and . . . I suppose I didn't feel like socializing for a long time, but now . . . Anyway, how's the pub?'

'Dreadful, I'm afraid! They got rid of two barmaids last week, leaving a young girl and me to cope. Cutbacks and all that. So, what have you been up to?'

Fucking your husband!

'Surviving. But I've been receiving awful notes telling me about Jim and Caroline in bed together – the things they do.'

'God, that's terrible! Who would do such a thing?'

'Someone with a warped and very twisted mind, I'm sorry to say. I can't take it for much longer!'

'You've no idea at all who's doing it?'

'I just want the notes to stop coming. Anyway, I'm over Jim now so . . . How are you and Tom?'

'In what respect?'

'As a married couple, I suppose.'

'We're all right, I guess. We're not ecstatically happy but, there again, we're not unhappy. Want some coffee?'

'Thanks.'

Could I come between these two and split them up? I pondered as I watched Sandy take the coffee cups from her new fitted cupboard. She was an attractive woman, and I found myself imagining her between my thighs, licking my opening sex-valley – making me come in her hot mouth. But why on earth hadn't she said anything about the previous night? I wondered as she filled the new kettle and plugged it in. *Lesbian*. The word played on my mind. *Lesbian*.

'Sugar?' she asked, turning to face me.

'No, thanks.'

Her short, dark hair shone in the sunlight, her glossy lips smiling, her blue eyes sparkling as she gazed at me. What was she thinking? About my pussy, perhaps? About Tom fucking me, more than likely!

'The weather's been good,' she said, filling the cups.

'Too hot for me! I can't take the heat!'

'I saw you relaxing on your patio last night – cooling down, were you?'

'Er . . . Yes, I'd got too hot during the evening and decided to sit in the breeze – naked.'

'I wasn't spying through Tom's binoculars!' she laughed. 'I just happened to notice you as I was drawing the curtains.'

'I often go around naked – it's really nice when it's hot.'

'So do I,' she smiled, sitting down. 'You've a nice body, from what I saw of it.'

'Thanks. Is Tom out?'

'He's in his office – working.'

'What did you do last night, then? I mean, if you weren't at the pub, what did you say to Tom?'

'I told him that I'd taken the evening off, that's all. He didn't say much. But he did ask me something.'

'Oh?'

'Something about you, Sue.'

Christ! Tom hadn't been lying! Looking into Sandy's eyes, I smiled sweetly, imagining her breasts, her long nipples – her cunt. My stomach swirled, my clitoris stirring as she reached across the table and squeezed my hand.

'We've known each other for some time,' she began. 'But we don't know each other very well, do we?'

'Don't we?'

'Not very well, no. Would you like to get to know Tom and me a little better?'

'How do you mean?'

'I think you know what I mean, Sue,' she murmured, squeezing my hand a little tighter.

'Er . . . Well, I'm not sure.'

'Why don't Tom and I come over to your house after lunch, and we'll spend the afternoon together?'

'All right – we'll have tea on the patio.'

Laughing, she released my hand. 'Yes, tea on the patio! That's *exactly* what I had in mind, Sue!'

Tom emerging from his den, I quickly finished my coffee, made my excuses and left. I wasn't sure that I wanted to come between a married couple – not in that sense, anyway! Bringing a husband and wife pleasure hadn't been part of my plan. Far from it, in fact!

Back in the security of my lounge, I retrieved my notebook from under the sofa. Derek and Jilly still hadn't scored any points, which didn't please me! Tony and Sally – ten. Jim and Caroline – ten. Craig and Tracy – ten. Dave the secondhand furniture man – nil. Sod Dave! Tom and Sandy – nil. Weird pair! There was one more hapless couple to add to my list of destruction – Jim and Mrs Wendy Dixon. And Mr Dixon!

I sighed as I pushed my notepad under the sofa. The day was young, and I was becoming bored. Housework? No! Sharon could do the housework. After all, she was living with me rent-free! And loving me.

Pacing the floor, I wondered about Derek and Jilly, and made a decision. I'd go round, knock on the door and . . . Sod it, I didn't have a plan. I didn't even know if they were in. Derek was probably working and Jilly was probably . . .

Answering my front door, I smiled to find Tracy standing on the step. She looked pale, tired – anguished. She'd lost her sensual air of femininity, and I wondered what on earth had happened.

'Come in,' I invited softly. 'I've been waiting for you to arrive.' To be honest, I'd quite forgotten about her in all the recent excitement.

'We need to talk,' she began. 'I know exactly what you're up to.'

'What I'm up to?' I echoed as I led her into the garden. Sitting on the patio, the atmosphere was awkward, tense.

'You're going round destroying marriages, aren't you?' she accused, wringing her hands.

'Of course I'm not!' I returned with a laugh. 'Whatever gave you that idea?'

'I've worked it all out, Sue, so there's no point in lying.'

'Worked what out? I'm sorry, but I'm not with you.'

'I've been speaking to Caroline.'

'And?'

'She told me what happened – about you and Jim.'

'Oh, that! Jim and I have been seeing each other for ages! He never wanted to be with Caroline in the first place. She kept pestering him and, in a moment of madness, he left me and went to her – he made a mistake, that's all.'

'That's not what *she* said. Anyway, the point is that you set it up so that she'd discover you and Jim and . . .'

'How on earth could I have set it up? I didn't know that she was coming round, did I?'

'She told me that you'd asked her round!'

'And did she not also tell you that she rang and cancelled?'

'No, she didn't. Anyway, you set it up – and you set it up with Craig and me, didn't you?'

'I don't know what you're talking about, Tracy – I really don't! Look, what I did with Craig was wrong, I accept that. He . . . This isn't an excuse but, on the first occasion, he seduced me.'

'You seduced *him* – *and* me!'

'When you and I were here, upstairs, making love . . . When Craig arrived, I thought that it would be fun to have the two of you make love, with neither of you realising who the other was. There was no way I'd set it up! I didn't know that Craig was coming round, did I? It was supposed to be fun, that's all!'

'You seduced him when he came here to fix your leaking pipe!'

'I seduced him? He has charm, Tracy, you can't deny that! He has charm, and I fell for it.'

'Did Tony seduce you using *his* charm?'

Christ! How the hell did she know about Tony? I hadn't even realized that they knew each other! I had to produce an instant lie. But what the hell could I say?

'Tony?' I frowned innocently.

'Yes, Tony – Sally's husband – soon to be her ex!'

'Oh, *that* Tony! I know that they've split up, but I don't see how I come into it!'

'You split them up, didn't you? The same way you split Craig and me up.'

'I don't know who's been telling you what, but they've got it all wrong, I can assure you, Tracy!'

'Sally told me all about it.'

'How do you know Tony and Sally, anyway?'

'We met some time ago at the local pub. We got chatting and . . . That's beside the point, Sue! I want to know what the hell you think you're playing at! How many more couples have you broken up?'

'You never told me that you knew Tony and Sally.'

'I hadn't seen you for ages, had I?'

'Anyway, I still don't know what you're talking about. Breaking marriages up – I ask you!'

'Three couples have split up recently, and what's the common denominator? You are, Sue!'

Things weren't looking good for me, but I didn't really care what Tracy did or didn't know. It was my business, and mine alone, I decided. There was nothing she could do about it, anyway. Sally had discovered me screwing her husband, so she knew that I was to blame. Caroline had stumbled across me screwing Jim, so *she* knew that I was to blame. Anyway, Sally had discovered Tony screwing Sharon well before he'd screwed me, so it was already over – wasn't it? Tracy could hardly threaten me – everyone knew that I was to blame!

'If you've finished, Tracy, I've got things to do,' I said, standing up.

'Why are you doing this, Sue?' she asked.

I sat down again.

'What I'm doing or not doing is my business, Tracy.'

'You've planned more break-ups, haven't you?'

'No, of course I haven't!'

'I'll be watching you, Sue. Every time a couple breaks up, or has a row, even – I'll be watching you!'

Storming off, she slammed the front door behind her, leaving me standing in the garden wondering what she was going to do. I'd been looking forward to tying her naked body over the exercise bench and bringing her to several massive orgasms, but not to worry. She'd be back for more sex, I knew. She no longer had Craig, not that she really wanted a man – so she'd be back.

But I didn't like the idea of someone knowing all the details of my game. If word got out, as undoubtedly it would, I could find myself in trouble! Still, I had the rest of the day to look forward to. Not that I was really looking forward to lying naked between Tom and Sandy! But I had Wendy Dixon coming round that evening – and that *was* something to look forward to!

Should I invite Jim round for the evening? Be screwing him as she walked into the lounge? No, this was the big one! I'd planned to wreck Wendy bloody Dixon's adulterous relationship with Jim – *and* her marriage! This one was going to have to be meticulously planned!

On the other hand, it was simple. Seduce Wendy's husband and have her find out, and then let her know that I'd been screwing Jim all along. It would have been nice for Wendy to catch me with her husband at her house. Yes, she'd walk into her lounge – and we'd be writhing in orgasm, naked, on the carpet.

Although Tracy's words played on my mind, I busied myself, passing the time, waiting for Tom and Sandy to arrive. I hadn't really made full use of my sex den, and I spent some time preparing it for an afternoon of rampant sex with both a man and a woman. The whip, rope, handcuffs, vibrator, KY-Gel all neatly set out by the bench, I wondered exactly what who would do to whom.

As the time passed, I found myself looking forward to sharing a man with his wife, and a woman with her husband. Although I'd been present when Craig had crudely fucked Tracy, it wasn't the same. This was going to be completely different!

When Tom and Sandy appeared in the kitchen doorway, my heart leapt. Christ, this was it! I wasn't ready! I was ready! Sandy smiled as she wrapped her arms around me and kissed my mouth, her husband grinning as he placed a large bag on the floor and unashamedly ran his hands all over my body. Before I had time to think, the two of them had slipped my clothes off, their hands everywhere as I stood naked in my kitchen.

'Doesn't she look pretty without her pubes?' Sandy asked, turning to Tom.

'Yes, very nice! Why don't you taste her there while I undress?'

'I'll slip out of my clothes first,' she replied.

They were talking as if I wasn't there, for God's sake, and I began to wonder what the hell they had planned for me! 'Shall we go upstairs?' I invited my guests. 'I have a special room for . . .'

'Lead the way,' Sandy smiled, stepping out of her summer dress.

I watched as Tom unclipped her bra, freeing her full breasts, her ample nipples, before grabbing the bag from the floor. His huge penis was already stiff, ready for . . . Christ, ready for what?

Sandy had a good body, and my clitoris tingled expectantly as I cast my eyes over her stomach and down to her bulging panties, speculating on her pussy. Leaving her panties on, she followed Tom and me to my sex den – Tom kneading my buttocks as he climbed the stairs behind me.

They both gasped at the sight of the equipment. Not losing any time, Sandy immediately laid me on my back over the bench and bound my wrists and ankles to the tubular frame. As I lay there, my head resting on the floor, my naked body tethered, my young cunt wide open to their every whim, I wondered whether I had seduced Tom, or he had seduced me the previous evening. Had Sandy known all along? He'd probably told her that he was seeing me, knowing that she'd love to watch us. If so, then why hadn't she joined in?

'She really does have a wonderful pussy!' Sandy beamed as she slipped her panties down to reveal her own delicacy – nestling beyond a black bush, a huge, swollen, pinken, gaping slit!

'She does!' Tom enthused, running his hand up and down his solid shaft. 'The usual?'

'Yes, the usual,' she smiled, moving towards me and settling on the floor between my thighs.

'What's the usual?' I queried, to silence. 'What's in the bag Tom?' I persisted, somewhat fearfully. There was no answer – just a salacious grin.

The usual? They'd obviously done this before! Tom hadn't been lying! How many women had they shared? I wondered as Sandy pushed her finger deep into my open vagina. How many women had she watched her husband fuck? The thought struck me that they might be willing to help me in my quest to wreck marriages – but no, maybe not! They didn't want to wreck marriages, they wanted to join them!

'She's nice and wet, Tom!' Sandy observed as she forced three fingers deep into my vagina, peeling my pussy lips wide open with her other hand.

'Good, I like them wet and juicy!' he enthused as he reached for his bag and knelt beside me. 'I'll fix her up, and then we'll start,' he added softly, taking something from the bag.

'I know you like them wet, Tom, you naughty boy!' Sandy giggled. 'When her juice is flooding out, you can drink it!'

'You're good to me, Sandy – you look after me.'

'And I always will, my love! Don't forget, there's another treat in store – we've got that young girl coming over this evening.'

'How could I ever forget?'

Christ, what was this? The odd couple, to say the least! A young girl coming round? Perhaps, if more women were like Sandy, more marriages would last? But what sort of relationship was this? There was no way I could destroy it, I knew that!

Raising my head, I watched as Tom fixed two metal devices to my long nipples and tightened them, squeezing my brown buds until I grimaced. Happy that my nipples were suitably, and painfully, crushed, he reached into the bag again and pulled out two large steel rings.

'What are they for?' I asked apprehensively as he placed them over my breasts. He just smiled as he tightened them, forcing my breasts to balloon out. 'That hurts!' I protested as he tightened them a little more before licking the sensitive brown skin of my areolae. My breasts forced painfully out of shape, I winced, looking to Sandy for sympathy as Tom tongued around my contorted nipples. But to no avail – still fingering my cunt, making the odd comment to her husband, she was busy examining my intimate inner folds, my erect clitoris.

Suddenly, she reached for the bag and pulled something out. Dreading what it could be, I closed my eyes, knowing that my fate was sealed, that words would be futile. Feeling something long, hard and cold sink deep into my tightening vagina, I gasped. It began vibrating, sending delightful sensations deep into my womb. Closing my eyes, my body felt vibrant with sex and, far from being averse, I knew that I was going to enjoy Sandy and Tom's attention's very much. Even my breasts, my squeezed nipples, were bringing me new and exciting sensations. I was in my sexual heaven!

Aware of Sandy kneeling astride my head, I opened my eyes to see her gaping cunt lips forced open by a thick banana. Lowering her body, she said nothing as she presented the fruit to my mouth. Tom moved behind her as I parted my lips and nibbled on the end of the hot, sticky offering. Suddenly, his purple knob appeared, slipping between her thighs, stopping only an inch from the end of the banana. His huge balls resting on my head, he began to slide his shaft back and forth as Sandy squeezed her cunt muscles and forced the baking banana into my open mouth.

Sucking, chewing, I savoured the delicacy with relish and was about to lick Sandy's pussy clean when Tom's huge knob exploded in a gush of cream. Sliding his throbbing plum back and forth between his wife's swollen labia, he showered me with his sperm before slipping the entire length of his massive shaft into her accommodating pussy.

Slurping, lapping up his come as I watched his penis

thrusting in and out of her wet hole, I became aware of the vibrator sending wonderful sensations deep into my centre, my cunt. Licking at Sandy's pussy lips, her husband's shaft, as it appeared and disappeared, my womb fluttering deliciously in response to the vibrations playing within my pelvis, I couldn't get enough of the lewd union.

Reaching down, Sandy gently massaged my clitoris while her husband fucked her, pumping his fruits deep into her quivering body. My beautiful orgasm rose and erupted in time with hers. Gasping as I watched Tom's organ slip away, leaving her pussy hot, wet and gaping above my mouth, I pressed my lips to hers, kissing her there, drinking the intoxicating cocktail of sperm and girl-come. Swallowing hard, I thought I'd never drain her sex geyser as my seemingly endless climax rode on and on.

Desperately, I wanted to escape the torturing pleasure! I knew that I couldn't endure any more. But there was no escape, and all I could do was lie there and take wave after wave of pulsating orgasm. Through my ecstasy, my torture, I saw Tom's penis reappear to drive deep into Sandy's dripping cunt. His balls slapping my head with every thrust, he was soon grunting and pumping more sperm into her ravenous hole.

Seeping between her rolling pussy lips and his huge shaft, his come dripped into my mouth, splattering my tongue as I licked and drank. Confident that he couldn't come for a third time, I closed my eyes and wallowed in my subsiding orgasm as his shaft disappeared from view. My beautiful ordeal finally over, Sandy moved away, leaving my face drenched with the odd couple's love juices.

I didn't open my eyes as they moved about between my legs. Whatever they were planning to do next was fine by me! Releasing my ankles, they held my feet high in the air, parting them to open my burning pussy-crack wide. Bringing my knees up to my chest, they ran a length of rope under the bench and over the backs of my legs, clamping my knees to my chest, exposing the entire length of my wet, open girl-slit. My body at forty-five degrees, my head dizzy with the weird and wonderful sensations the mysterious vibrator was bringing me, I gasped as someone slipped it from my cunt and began to stroke the crease between my splayed buttocks.

Suddenly, someone slapped my bottom, stinging me, making me wince as they slapped me again and again. 'She needs a bloody good beating for seducing you!' Sandy cried.

'She needs more than a beating!' Tom declared. 'She needs to be whipped until she screams for mercy!'

Opening my eyes, I watched Tom reach into his bag again and pull out a riding crop. My knees bound to my chest, my buttocks were exposed, vulnerable, and I watched wide-eyed as he positioned himself ready for the thrashing. Sandy moved aside, waiting for the punishment to commence, her eyes afire with lust, her long nipples standing erect – her cunt bush matted, dripping with her come and her husband's sperm.

'Fancy luring you to her house, Tom!' she cried. 'I really don't think that we can allow her to get away with that, do you?'

'No, I don't. And as for ringing you and suggesting that you spy through my binoculars! Well, I can only imagine that she wanted you to discover my adultery. Trying to cause trouble, I'd say!'

'Give her a good thrashing, that'll teach her to try to come between us!'

So, she knew all along! They'd set me up! Talk about the tables turning! Now I was in for the thrashing of my life, I knew only too well, as the crop struck my taut buttocks. Shrieking with glee, Sandy told Tom to look at the weals appearing across my pale flesh as he lashed me again and again. The searing pain spreading over my rounded buttocks, I winced every time the crop struck home, yelping like a dog as the thrashing continued.

'My turn!' Sandy shrilled, grabbing the crop. 'And now for a *real* thrashing, my girl!' she cried, landing the first stinging blow. Making himself useful, Tom tightened the steel rings and the metal clamps, causing my breasts to blow up like balloons, my nipples to send electrifying waves of pleasure through my tethered body.

Finally dropping the riding crop and releasing my right hand, Sandy instructed me to finger my bottom-hole. 'No, I won't do that!' I protested. But, grabbing my hand, Tom forced my finger out straight and pushed it deep into my bottom, moving it in and out as Sandy gazed on.

'That's nice, isn't it?' she asked, moving around my aching body and kissing my mouth. 'You love fingering your bottom-hole, don't you?'

'No, I don't!'

'Then, I'd better do it for you!' she giggled, moving away and pushing Tom aside.

As Tom retied my wrist to the tubular frame, Sandy pressed a finger deep into my bowels, exploring me there, massaging the velveteen walls of my anal sheath. 'Pass me that jelly,' she ordered her husband as she slipped her finger out. 'This will make it far easier for me,' she added, smearing the jelly around my aching bum-hole. 'There, now I'll be able to get three fingers inside her, or four, even! Why don't you give her a good fucking while I finger her bum, Tom? You look as if you're ready!'

'Good idea, my love! I'll fill her cunt with sperm, and then you can drink it from her!'

As Sandy forced three fingers deep into my aching bottom-hole, I sensed Tom's massive knob between my swollen pussy lips, stabbing me there, trying to gain entry to my tight vagina. Pushing his shaft deep into me, filling me with his huge organ as Sandy tried to push all four fingers into my bum, I gasped and cried out.

'No, Sandy! I can't . . . Christ, I can't . . .'

'Of course you can, my dear! There, four fingers inside your hot bottom. You should see it!'

'And you should feel *this*!' Tom breathed. 'God, she's tight!'

'That's because her bum's full, Tom!' Sandy giggled, thrusting her fingers in and out in time with Tom's pistoning shaft.

Another mind-blowing climax erupted from my aching clitoris as Tom thrust harder, driving his pumping knob deeper and deeper into my quivering body, splattering my cervix with his male come. Relentless, Sandy continued her thrusting, bringing me electrifying sensations, sustaining my orgasm as Tom filled my burning cunt to the brim with his sperm.

Another ordeal finally over, they allowed me to rest for a while, both licking and kissing between my legs, lapping up the mixture of sex as it oozed between my inflamed cunny lips. As I lay there, my body aching, my knees bound to my chest, tongues licking my cunt, my bottom-hole, I wondered just what the hell I'd let myself in for. What else would the perverse couple do to me? And for how long would I have to endure their debauchery?

'I expect she's hungry, Tom,' Sandy remarked, reaching into the bag again. 'Let's give her a banana to eat – after I've fucked her sweet cunt with it, of course!'

'Here, allow me,' Tom volunteered, peeling the fruit.

The large banana slipped deep into my drenched hole, soothing my inner flesh, cooling me there. Gently twisting and thrusting the fruit, Tom talked about my wickedness. 'She wanted me to have an affair with her, you know,' he said.

'That's not very nice, is it?'

'No, it's not. She thought that we could fuck while you worked in the evenings.'

'What, and leave me out of the fun? That's not very nice at all! And I always thought that she was such a sweet little thing.'

I could hardly believe what I was hearing! They'd always appeared such a normal, respectable couple. This was another side of them, and I wondered how many married couples harboured such hidden qualities. During my travels, my marriage-wrecking attempts, no doubt I'd find out!

Slipping the banana out of my vagina, Tom presented it to my mouth and instructed me to eat it. Opening my mouth, I began chewing the hot, sticky fruit, delighting in the taste of my own orgasmic cream mingled with his sperm. 'Good girl!' he breathed as I swallowed the last piece. 'Now, let's turn her over, shall we?' he suggested, turning to Sandy.

'I really do think that you should fuck her mouth first, Tom.'

'Whatever you say, my love.'

Sandy lifted my head off the floor and rested me in her lap as Tom settled by my side, his huge purple knob waving threateningly before my dilated eyes. 'Open wide,' Sandy breathed, taking her husband's penis in her hand and pushing the knob against my lips. 'You *are* thirsty, aren't you?' she asked as I parted my lips. I nodded, my eyelashes fluttering as she guided his knob into my mouth. 'She's a pretty little thing, Tom. Give her mouth a nice fucking, she'll enjoy that.'

'Why don't you wank me, my love?' Tom smiled.

'All right, if that's what you want,' she said obligingly, taking his shaft and manipulating his foreskin.

Breathing heavily through my nose, I could only wait for the inevitable as I lay there with my mouth full. Sandy gazed down at me, smiling benignly as if I were a babe in her arms. 'You're going to enjoy this,' she promised. 'Afterwards, you can suck my nipples, and then I'll come in your mouth. You'd like that, wouldn't you?' Sensing Tom's knob swelling, I nodded.

'Nearly there!' Tom cried, his face grimacing as he reached out and squeezed Sandy's nipples. 'Nearly, nearly! Ah! Ah, coming!'

Again, a married man was coming in my mouth, and I lapped up his offering, swallowing his come as his wife wanked him, cradling my head, smiling sweetly at me. 'Good girl!' she enthused as I choked and swallowed again. 'Good girl, drink it all up, now!' I had no choice! On and on Tom pumped out his male fruits as she wanked him until, at last, he stilled her hand, his huge silky knob resting against my tongue – done.

But Sandy wasn't! Positioning my head on the floor again, she squatted over my face, rubbing her drenched slit back and forth over my mouth as Tom moved down to my buttocks, stroking them, caressing the burning flesh. Choking on Sandy's copious juices now, I convulsed as Tom drove his penis deep into my bottom-hole, stretching my anal sheath wide open. Was there no end to his staying power?

Nearing her climax, Sandy ground her hard clitoris into my mouth, ordering me to lick and suck her cunt as Tom took my bum-hole with a frenzied vengeance. My whole body was on fire, burning with sex, lust, desire, as they reached their goals in unison. Tom pumping his sperm deep into my bowels, Sandy decanting her slippery come into my mouth, they filled me, used me like a blow-up sex doll.

Finally resting, Sandy squeezed her pussy muscles, her lubricous spend oozing, trickling into my mouth until she'd drained her vaginal sheath. Tom stilled his penis, absorbing the fiery heat of my bowels as the last of his sperm left his knob, baptizing our illicit union. Had they finished with me now? I wondered as Tom slipped his weapon from my bowels and Sandy moved away. God, I hoped so!

Releasing me, they turned me over, positioning me with my head resting on the sloping section of the bench, my bottom jutting up shamelessly in the air. Now what? I wondered apprehensively as they tied the ropes. Not up my bum again, surely?

'This looks interesting,' Tom observed gleefully, grabbing my leather whip.

'Is that what you whipped her with last night?' Sandy asked.

'Yes, and she loved it, so we'll give her some more, shall we?'

There was little point in my protesting as the first lash struck my burning buttocks. All I could do was let out involuntary yelps and pray that they'd soon be done and leave me to rest.

As Tom whipped me, Sandy pushed her fingers deep into my gaping cunt, thrusting them in and out, bringing me close to orgasm again. 'Come on!' she cried. 'Come all over my hand! Tom will thrash you until you come!'

'No!' I finally managed to shriek as the stinging sensations seemed to cut through me. 'Stop, please!'

'Only when you come!' she cried again, thrusting harder into my aching vagina.

I was amazed when my clitoris finally burst into orgasm. Searing pain in my buttocks, fingers thrusting deep into my cunt, I came. My eyes rolling, my body shaking violently, I swore to get my own back on Sandy. Capture her, tie her down and whip her!

'Keep coming!' she cried, thrusting harder than ever.

'No more!' I managed to scream as the leather tails cracked, landing across my fiery bum. 'Please, stop!'

'Keep coming!' she bellowed again. 'Keep coming!'

I thought I was going to pass out with the combined pain and pleasure. Whimpering, my used body twitching, my orgasm seeming to last forever – I thought I'd expire! Summoning the energy to beg for mercy one more time, the weird couple finally gave me some quarter.

'More in a moment,' Tom compromised. 'Rest now, and I'll thrash your bottom again in a minute.'

'Yes, relax for a while,' Sandy rejoined as she slipped her fingers from my hotpot. 'We'll be back to attend you again in a while.'

I lay there for what seemed like hours, my body aching, my cunt on fire. They'd gone, I knew. Gone and left me, most likely planning to return and use me again. Thinking that I lived alone, they probably planned to keep me tied up – to pop in for wild sessions of debauched sex as and when it took their fancy.

Sharon frowned as she finally came breezing into the room. 'God, who did this?' she demanded as she stood over me.

'Untie me!' I yelled. 'I've been fucked, fingered, vibrated, whipped . . . Just untie me!'

'And what if I don't?' she taunted.

'Just bloody well do it or I'll tie *you* down and whip *your* cunt lips!'

Releasing me, she helped me to my feet as I rubbed my aching limbs. 'Who did it?' she asked again.

'No one!' I snapped. 'Just mind your own business!'

'Sorry, I only asked!'

'Well, don't! Run me a bath, will you?'

'OK. What are you doing this evening – wrecking more marriages?' she spat as she turned in the doorway.

Shit, this evening! Mrs Wendy bloody Dixon! The way I was feeling, I didn't want to do anything. 'Just run me a fucking bath!' I snapped as I passed her and went to my bedroom.

Lying on my bed, I wondered what the hell I was doing with my life, to my body. Fucking anyone and everyone, using them, destroying all those who were unfortunate enough to cross my path – I wondered what the *hell* I was doing!

I thought of Jim, his downfall, as I drifted into a deep sleep, and realized that the destruction had to continue. I'd come so far, I couldn't stop now. I would never stop!

Chapter Eleven

I woke at seven that evening feeling awful. The bath Sharon had run for me was now stone cold, and I was in no mood for Mrs Wendy bloody Dixon! To make matters worse, Sharon had buggered off somewhere, leaving me alone in the house. I had been hoping for some moral support from her, but she never seemed to be there when I needed her!

I'd slung on my T-shirt and miniskirt and was munching on a jam sandwich, wondering whether to put Wendy off or not, when the doorbell rang. Seven-thirty. Shit, was that her? I was in such a state, I couldn't remember if we'd arranged a particular time or not. As I dragged myself to the door, my body still aching like hell, I caught my reflection in the hall mirror. My hair was all over the place, glued together with a concoction of sperm and fanny-juice. What a bloody mess!

Oh, well – I wasn't going to seduce the woman, I was only going to destroy her, so what the hell did it matter what I looked like? Taking a deep breath as I opened the door, I donned a huge, welcoming smile and invited her in.

'Sue, how are you?' she beamed, passing me a bouquet of flowers – bloody chrysanthemums! Wearing a red dress and matching hat, she would have been better off attending a stuck-up garden fête rather than coming round for a drink! What the hell Jim saw in her, I had no idea. There again, she had money – that would have been one attraction. And her pussy, of course!

She was youngish – early thirties, I'd say. Not unattractive, her brown hair, when not covered by a ridiculous hat, fell just below her shoulders. She had a wonderful mouth – her full lips curled into a sweet smile, almost child-like, and her eyes sparkled beautifully. She had a good body, too – slim, but with an ample bust, as my mother would have put it.

I looked at women in a different light now. Now that I'd had sex with other women, explored and examined the most intimate parts of their bodies, I found myself looking at them as I supposed men did – admiring their breasts, their feminine curves, imagining their pussies – hot, tight, wet. Wondering whether Wendy cried out during her orgasms or quietly whimpered, I thought of Jim between her legs. How many other women had he had? No doubt he'd fucked and licked dozens! Bastard!

'I'm fine, Wendy!' I replied. 'You're looking well.'

'Thank you. It's so nice to get out and see someone. When my husband's away, I feel so lonely!' she complained.

With my ex-husband screwing you, I'll bet you fucking do!

'Now that Jim's gone, I get pretty lonely at times, too,' I confided. 'Come into the lounge and we'll enjoy a glass of wine and a chat.' Dumping the flowers on the hall table, I led the way. Not that she needed leading round my house! *Bitch!*

As usual, I'd not formulated a plan. I was just going to play it by ear, drop a few comments about Jim, tell her a few home truths. Well, a few home lies! Pouring her a glass of wine and placing it on the coffee table, I sat opposite her in the armchair, wondering what to say, where to begin.

'It seems strange without Jim,' I said sadly, wondering how much she knew about Caroline, if anything. He'd have told her that he'd left me, of course, but had he told her that he'd been living with Caroline? And been thrown out? He must have said that he was living somewhere.

'It must seem strange to find yourself alone after years of marriage. What went wrong, if you don't mind me asking? What caused the split?' she asked sympathetically.

'He was cheating on me. He had several women on the go, and I found out and threw him out.'

'Several women?' she queried, almost angrily.

'Oh yes! There was Caroline, the one he moved in with when I chucked him . . .'

'Caroline? He moved in with another woman?'

So, she didn't know! How the hell could Jim have kept Caroline a secret? He'd been living with her for weeks on end! What horrendous lies had he been telling Wendy? I wondered.

'Yes, she was my best friend, or so I'd thought. He'd been seeing her throughout our entire marriage – *before* we were married, in fact! Anyway, she threw him out, as all his women do in the end.'

Frowning, she looked anxious, uneasy, as she rolled her wine glass between her palms. Was her stomach knotting in her anger as she thought of Jim – and his lies? I realized that, whatever I told her, Jim would lie his way out of it, probably turn it round and accuse me of making up stories. I had to come up with something really good. But what?

'I heard that you'd divorced,' she said.

'Oh, who told you that?'

'Er . . . It was . . . Oh, what's her name? The woman I used to see in the library. Never mind. So, where's your ex-husband living now?'

'Well, Caroline's only just thrown him out, so I don't know what arrangements he's made. He often comes to see me, but I haven't seen him since he left her place.'

'He comes to see you? What, even now that you're divorced?' she asked, her eyes filling with tears.

'Oh yes, we've been seeing each other for weeks!' I declared, pretending not to notice as she wiped her eyes discreetly. 'We get on so well now! It's funny how things work out. Our marriage was a sham, but since the divorce, things have been great between us – never better!'

That riled her! I was doing fairly well – the ball of deceit was already rolling, gathering speed. But I had to plant several seeds of doubt in her mind before she'd ask Jim awkward questions. And before he, no doubt, tried to lie his way out of them.

Her husband would be easy to deal with, as were all husbands! How I'd get to meet him, I wasn't sure. I could call in on the pretence of going to see Wendy, when I was sure that she was out, of course. Yes, that was the answer – and then flash my smiling pussy-crack to him. He'd fall for it, I knew only too well! We'd be screwing in their lounge one afternoon, gasping and writhing in orgasm – and she'd come home and discover us. Tears would be cried, the knife would twist, and divorce would rear its beautiful head!

'Jim asked me if I'd take him back the other day,' I continued, watching her face for a reaction. 'He wanted to leave Caroline and come back to me. I'm seriously considering it, now that he's not with her any more. We're so good together, physically, if you know what I mean.'

'Er . . . Yes, I suppose I do,' she smiled. Did I detect a tear roll from her eye? She was far from happy, I knew that!

'So, where's your husband gone off to?' I asked, wondering when he was coming back – when I'd have the opportunity to seduce him.

'France – on business. He'll be back tomorrow. He rang to say that he's tied things up earlier than he'd expected.'

'Oh, that's good! You must miss him.'

'Er . . . Yes, of course I do!'

'What's his name, by the way?'

'Stephen.'

I wasn't going to answer the doorbell when it rang, but it would have looked odd if I hadn't. I thought that it was probably Tony come round to complain about his situation, or Craig come to have another go at me, or Tom and Sandy – God forbid! But when I opened the door and saw who it was, I grinned inanely and thanked Lady Luck.

'Jim! Come in! I have company but, please, come in!'

'Who is it?' he frowned. 'One of your bloody men?'

'No, of course not!'

'I didn't ring – I was just passing and I thought . . .'

'That's OK. Come into the lounge and have a drink with us.'

I've never seen two people more embarrassed, more shocked, than Jim and Wendy when they saw each other. I was delighting in the game, and I couldn't believe how luck was on my side! Either luck, or the devil!

'This is Wendy, Jim,' I said, making the introductions. 'We know each other from the library. Wendy, meet Jim, my ex-husband.' Shaking hands, they offered weak smiles to each other. 'Sit down,' I invited. 'Jim, some wine?'

'Er . . . Yes – thanks.'

'We were just talking about you, Jim. How you were saying the other day that you wanted to move back in with me.'

That shook him!

'Oh! Er . . . Well, I have a nice flat now.'

'Yes, but I was telling Wendy that we've been seeing a lot of each other recently, and that we get on better now than we ever did. And now that Caroline's not on the scene any more . . .'

You could have cut the atmosphere with a knife! The seething anger on Wendy's face was wonderful! And even more wonderful was the way Jim did his best to appease her with his strange facial expressions. Again, I wasn't the little wife – I was the other woman!

'Who's Caroline?' Wendy asked accusingly, glaring at Jim. She was seemingly oblivious to the fact that I'd wonder why she was so interested in my ex-husband's mistress. But, in her anger, she couldn't help herself!

'Oh, no one special,' Jim mumbled.

'Sue was telling me that you've been seeing her for a long time. Before you married, even.'

'Well . . . She was Sue's best friend. You see . . .'

'Let me explain it, Jim!' I interrupted with a giggle. 'Jim had been seeing Caroline behind my back throughout our entire marriage – I found out, and threw him out. So he moved in with her and started seeing *me* behind *her* back, and she found out – and threw him out! It's hilarious, when you think about it!'

Cringing, Jim sipped his wine, not knowing what the hell to say or where to look. Wendy couldn't stop glaring at him so, to give the adulterous couple a few moments alone, I went to the kitchen to get another bottle of wine. The minute I'd pulled the door to, they flew at each other. Grabbing the Blue Nun from the fridge, I stood outside the lounge door and listened.

'What the hell are you doing here?' Jim whispered angrily.

'I could ask you the same question! So, you've been living with another woman, then? Why didn't you say anything about this to me? I thought that after your divorce you were staying with a friend – not another woman!'

'Caroline was nothing, she . . .'

'So you deny that you'd been seeing her throughout your entire marriage?'

'No! Yes! Take no notice of Sue, she . . . Look, we can't talk here. It's all very easy to explain, Wendy. I stayed at Caroline's place when Sue threw me out. I had nowhere else to go, for God's sake! She was just a friend, and nothing more.'

'An intimate friend, by the sound of it! Why did she throw you out? Was it because you were seeing your ex-wife?'

'No . . . Look, when I see you tomorrow, I'll explain everything.'

'I don't know that I *want* to see you now! Anyway, Stephen's back tomorrow morning so . . .'

'I'll meet you in the park in the morning, as we'd arranged, and we'll talk then.'

'If you've been . . .'

'More wine, anyone?' I trilled, grinning as I breezed into the lounge. 'Are you two getting on all right?'

'Yes!' Jim grunted. 'I've got to go now.'

'No, you haven't Jim!' I smiled. 'I was rather hoping that you'd stay with me again.'

'Again?' he frowned as Wendy pursed her lips in anger.

'Yes, we've had some good evenings together recently, so there's no need to dash off when we could have another one, is there?'

'But, don't you and Wendy want to . . .'

'Don't let me get in your way!' Wendy muttered under her breath as she stood up and moved towards the door. 'Thanks for the drink, Sue. I'll ring you sometime.'

'Where are you going?' I asked surprisedly.

'I don't want to stand in the way of true love,' she smiled ruefully as she left the room. 'You two have a nice evening together, and I'll ring you sometime, Sue.'

The front door slammed shut, and that was it – the beginning, at least, of Jim's second ruination! He was steaming with anger. Bulging like an old boiler about to burst! But he could hardly blame me! I was the innocent party, knowing nothing of his illicit affair with Wendy – as far as he was concerned, anyway.

'She left in a hurry!' I remarked as I sat down.

'Yes, she did,' he replied indifferently, his thoughts obviously on the horrendous lies he'd have to concoct.

'Do you know her from somewhere?' I asked.

'No, of course not! Why do you ask?'

'It's just that you seemed to recognize each other.'

'I've never seen her before in my life. She's *your* friend, and you've never invited her round, so how the hell would

I know her? Anyway, I'd better be going.'

'Where are you staying?'

'A flat. A poky bloody flat above the fish and chip shop in the High Street!'

'That sounds nice.'

'It stinks!'

'Any word from Caroline?'

'Hardly!'

'Oh, well – things will sort themselves out.'

'Why did you have to tell Wendy about us, me wanting to move back here and . . .'

'She's my friend, Jim. Women always natter about things like that. You'd be surprised how much women *do* tell each other! Anyway, what's it to you?'

'Nothing! I'm going!' he groaned, standing up. 'See you sometime.'

'OK, Jim, you can see yourself out, can't you?'

He sulked off, slamming the front door, and I wondered whether he was going to visit Wendy, to explain – to tell her more of his lies. Wherever he'd gone, I wasn't bothered as I felt sure that I'd done more than enough damage to rock their relationship, if not send it tumbling to the ground.

My thoughts turned to Stephen, Wendy's husband, and his return from France the following morning. If Wendy did meet Jim in the park, then Stephen might be at home, alone, and I thought again of calling round, pretending that I'd come to see Wendy. More planning, more scheming to be done, I mused as I heard shouting coming from next door.

Moving to the window, I saw Jilly stomp off down the path. Another row about money? I speculated. She'd be back, I knew. She was young and silly. As soon as she'd calmed down, she'd be back, and they'd put their loving arms around each other and . . .

Suddenly, I had a wonderfully evil thought. Was this the

time I'd been waiting for? A row, she stomps off, he's alone in the house . . . This was the time to move in for the kill!

My vagina, my bum-hole still sore and aching, I washed, did my hair, hurriedly applied my makeup and dashed round to their house. It was mid-evening and I was tired after a long day of sex, but I couldn't let this opportunity slip through my fingers – through my thighs!

Derek answered the door, his blue eyes frowning, his lips pursed, and I remembered that the unhappy couple had scored no points at all – yet! He looked tired, fed-up with the continual rows – fed-up with life.

'She's not here!' he grunted miserably.

'I came to see *you*, Derek!' I smiled, walking past him into the hall. 'I saw Jilly go out, so I thought I'd come and see how you are, how the decorating's going.'

Closing the front door, he followed me into the kitchen. He'd finished the decorating, and I gave him some male-ego-boosting comments, saying what a professional job he'd done and how nice it looked. Calming down, he smiled, gazing at my miniskirt as I sat at the kitchen table.

'We had another row,' he admitted dolefully.

'Oh, Derek, I *am* sorry. You're not having much of a time of it, are you? What with no sex life, and rows, you must feel pretty awful.'

No sex life, my pussy!

'The last time I had sex was with you,' he lied. 'I think my marriage is over, Sue.'

It bloody well should be!

'Why haven't you been round to see me?' I asked, reaching across the table and holding his hand.

'I don't know,' he sighed. 'I've been busy, I suppose.'

'Come here,' I murmured, smiling with my bedroom eyes and licking my full lips provocatively as I gently pulled him towards me.

Standing, he moved round the table to me, looking down as I unzipped his jeans. 'Let me wash away all your worries,' I whispered, pulling his stiffening penis out and kissing his silky knob. He breathed deeply as I squeezed his solid shaft and licked around his glans. 'You like it?' I asked huskily.

'Yes!' he gasped, pushing his hips forward, sliding his knob into the wet heat of my mouth.

Not knowing when Jilly would come back, I wasn't sure how far to go. I didn't want him coming in my mouth too soon – not until Jilly made her entrance. But when would that be? Taking an educated guess, I decided that she'd only be a matter of minutes. Putting myself in her shoes, I knew that she'd probably walk around the block, and then come straight back to her loving husband, expecting to make up – and make love.

With Derek suitably aroused, I tugged his jeans down, telling him to take all his clothes off as I slipped out of mine. Whether he had just come, was coming, or was about to come when Jilly made her timely entrance didn't matter. As long as we were both naked, entwined in lust when she walked in, my plan would work.

'The same as before?' I grinned as I leaned over the table, moving a bottle of ketchup and exposing my crimson buttocks.

'Christ, you've been well and truly whipped!' he gasped.

'Yes, and when you've fucked me, *you* can whip me, if you want to!' I giggled as he slipped his massive cock deep into my hot, welcoming cunt.

'Who did it?' he probed, stroking my burning buttocks as his knob caressed my cervix.

'A girlfriend I see from time to time!' I gasped as he began to thrust his organ deep into my trembling body, fucking me as hard as he could.

'A girlfriend?' he gasped.

'Yes, a lesbian girlfriend.'

I knew he was quickly nearing his climax, as I was, and I

prayed that Jilly would walk in – but she didn't. Suddenly pumping his sperm deep into my cunt as my clitoris exploded, he slapped my already stinging buttocks and rode me with a vengeance. Thrust after thrust, slap after slap, he took me to such a beautiful sexual high that I almost forgot about my plan – about his young wife.

Slipping his spent penis from my spasming sheath, he pulled the leather belt from his jeans and began his thrashing. I yelped, jolting with every wonderful swipe of the leather strap. My cunt squeezing out the cocktail of our come, my clitoris throbbing with anticipation, I wallowed in the painful pleasure until his penis had risen again.

Turning me over, he laid me on the table, my legs wide apart, my shaved cunt inflamed and open, wet with my juices of arousal – ready for another good fucking. As he stood between my thighs and entered me, I heard the front door open and slam shut. Locking my legs around his waist, I pulled him hard against me, his penis driving deep into my cunt, his heavy balls pressed against my buttocks. He fought to free himself as I moaned my sexual pleasure, but there was no escaping me – the serial marriage-wrecker!

'Give my beautiful hot cunt another good fucking!' I cried as he desperately struggled to break free. 'Fuck me like you did the other day, and then thrash me again with your belt!' I added for Jilly's benefit as she appeared in the doorway and shrieked.

Finally opening my legs, I released Derek, allowing him to slip his massive shaft from my wet vagina before his wife's dazed eyes. Gazing at me in bewilderment, she turned to her husband, a death-wish in her tearful eyes. Never had I witnessed such a look of complete and utter devastation, such agonizing pain, as she stood shaking in the doorway – a broken woman.

Derek said nothing as I slipped from the table, deliberately displaying my wet, naked pussy lips, pushing out my firm young breasts to show off my erect nipples. Jilly looked me up and down, eyeing my body, wondering, no doubt, what I had to offer that she didn't. Through my frozen emotions, I felt some empathy – I knew that devastating thought only too well!

Grabbing my clothes, I slipped into them, making sure that she had a good view of my wet pussy lips before pulling my skirt up. Flashing Jilly a nervous smile, I moved towards the back door and slipped out into the garden, leaving her alone with her adulterous husband – leaving her to squirm in her pain as I had once done.

Spying through the hedge, I watched, and listened, as they began their inevitable private Armageddon. Jilly slapped Derek's face as he tried to pull his jeans on, her tears streaming down her flushed cheeks, and I knew that they were finished. Their marriage had taken a fatal blow – suffered irreparable damage.

'Why?' she screamed. 'I thought we had everything together! I thought that we . . . Why?'

'Jilly . . . I . . .'

'You've ruined everything! Smashed all we'd built!'

'It was nothing! I love you, Jilly! We can . . .'

'Get out! Just get out! I never want to see you again!'

Oh, well! Another marriage in ruins, another couple to strike off my notepad. They'd scored ten points, gone straight to the top of the charts in seconds – amazing! It had been a good, clean fight, I mused as Derek dressed and fled the house, slamming the front door. A good, clean break, and I liked that. I was sure that, at their age – young and insecure in love and sex – there'd be no going back, no reconciliation. Jilly's heart had been broken – and that was that!

I was stunned when my doorbell rang and I found Derek standing on the step. His blond hair dishevelled, his face flushed, he smiled and apologized for what had happened.

'It's not your fault,' I consoled. 'You weren't to know that she'd come back and . . . What happened, what did she say?'

'She told me to get out. I think it's over – finished.'

'Oh, God! What will you do now? Can't you talk to her?'

'I'll try, when she's calmed down. But I don't think I'll get anywhere, do you?'

'No, I don't suppose you will. Come through and have a drink – I think you need one! Shame about the new pedal-bin.'

'What?'

'I was thinking about the wedding presents – it's a shame.'

'Oh.'

In the lounge, I explained that I hadn't seen Jilly standing in the doorway, and that's why I hadn't opened my legs and released him earlier – not that it would have made the slightest bit of difference! He seemed to be more upset for me than anything else, saying sorry all the time and asking whether I was all right.

'I'm fine! It's you I'm worried about, Derek!' I sighed, trying to show concern as I sat in the armchair. 'What will happen with the house?'

'We'll sell it, I suppose,' he said resignedly, settling on the sofa.

'But where will you live?'

'That's what I came to talk to you about,' he smiled.

Ah, I might have guessed! After telling him that my cunt would never be far away from him, that all he had to do was ask and my cunt would be his for the taking, I suppose he thought that he could move in with me, have some sort of permanent relationship. How wrong he was!

The truth was, I enjoyed the after-kill as much as the kill itself. When the men came to me, thinking that they meant something to me, I delighted in twisting the knife, telling them that I wasn't in the slightest bit interested in them. It was like a second killing – and I loved it!

'Talk to me about what?' I frowned, waiting for the inevitable.

'Well, I wondered . . . You said that you'd always be here for me, never far away and . . .'

'No – I said that my *cunt* would never be far away, and that it was yours for the taking.'

'Yes, that's what I mean.'

'What, you want my cunt again?'

'No . . . Well, yes, but . . .'

'What *do* you mean, Derek?'

'Can I move in with you?'

'Move in with me? What the hell for?'

His eyes opened wide in his confusion.

'What for? Because . . . We could be together, Sue. We could . . .'

'Come round and fuck me when you like, Derek – but you can't move in! What would be the point?'

He was visibly stunned.

'The point would be . . . A proper relationship, Sue! Isn't that what you want? You said yourself that I was the only one.'

Ah, so I did – but I lie!

'I have a girlfriend I see from time to time. I told you, she was the one who whipped me. I was expecting you to come round and see me but you didn't bother so . . . As I thought that you weren't interested, I found a couple of other men to have fun with – three or four, in fact. I don't want a permanent relationship with anyone. I'm sorry, Derek.'

Forlorn, anguished, he sighed. He'd lost his young wife, *and* his bit on the side! Better get rid of him before Jilly came round with a knife! I decided, hearing glasses and plates smashing loudly next door. So much for the marital home!

'You'd better go,' I said as another plate shattered.

'Go? Go where?'

Why was it always *my* problem when cheating men were thrown out of their homes? 'I've no idea, Derek!' I returned angrily. 'It's not *my* problem!'

'Can I stay for a while, just until she calms down, and then I'll go and talk to her?' he asked dismally.

'All right, but not for too long. I'll get some wine from the fridge.'

Jilly was having a field day, by the sound of it! Screaming and swearing, she must have been destroying the entire house! Poor girl, I mused, she didn't deserve it, really. There again, she didn't deserve to be with a two-timing shit like Derek! I'd saved her from that, at least.

'Here you are,' I smiled, pouring the wine and passing Derek a glass. 'Here's to the future, whatever it might hold.'

'Cheers!' he grunted, raising his glass. 'Some bloody future!'

'She's wrecking the house!' I almost giggled.

'Yes, I can hear her! All that work I'd done, for God's sake! Wrecked in minutes!'

'And your marriage wrecked in seconds!'

Opening my legs and reclining in the armchair, I burst out laughing.

'It's not bloody funny!' he groaned.

'No, it's not – I'm sorry.'

It's bloody hilarious!

He gazed at my naked pussy. Did he want more? I wondered. Might as well finish off what we were doing before his marriage fell apart, I mused. Resting my legs over the arms of the chair, my pussy gaping, oozing with the remnants of our fatal union, I smiled and licked my lips. Another plate smashed next door as Derek knelt before me and slipped his penis out. Rubbing his purple knob up and down my wet sex valley, stiffening my clitoris, he suddenly thrust into me, filling my drenched cavern with his massive organ.

Even when they've been thrown out of their homes, even when they find themselves out on the streets, men still want sex.

Sex was the last thing I'd wanted when Jim had told me that he was leaving me for Caroline. When I'd screamed at him, told him to get out and never come back, the last thing I wanted at that moment was sex. Why were men so very different?

'You'll let me come and give you a good fucking now and then?' he wheedled, peeling my pussy lips wide open and driving his huge penis deep into my hot hole again and again.

'Any time, but ring first!' I gasped, my body jolting. 'God, you're good!'

'You've got a beautiful cunt! You're the best fuck I've ever had in my life!' he breathed.

'And the last!' Jilly screamed hysterically as she flew across the room towards her husband, wielding a new frying pan above her head.

Another wedding present?

Ducking, Derek fell back onto the floor, his cock protruding, glistening with my juices as he rolled over, narrowly missing the frying pan as it hit the carpet with a dull thud. Leaping to his feet, his jeans around his ankles, he tore out of the front door with Jilly in hot pursuit.

Laughing wickedly, I gazed at my weapon, my ever-powerful pussy. 'You didn't get another drink of sperm, did you, my lovely?' I giggled in my mischievousness, closing my wet outer lips. 'Never mind, there are plenty more married men out there dying to get at you!'

'Hello, Sue,' Sharon droned, breezing into the lounge in an extremely short skirt.

'Oh, hi, Sharon. Where have you been?'

'Out – thinking,' she replied sullenly.

'What about?'

'You, and what you're doing. When I found you tied up earlier, I . . . Who did it?'

'A married couple, would you believe! I'd seduced her husband and, rather than come between them, excuse the pun, they both seduced me!'

'I don't like it, Sue. I mean, what you're doing is so very wrong. I've just been talking to the girl next door. She was walking back to her house crying, holding a frying pan. She told me what had happened – what you did with her husband.'

'Oh, that was nothing!' I quipped.

'Nothing! You've wrecked their lives! They'd only been married for six months! And who was that woman I saw leaving here earlier? Are you planning to destroy her marriage, too?'

'That was Wendy. Yes, I am, as it happens! Look, you don't know anything about her, what she's been doing, the sort of bitch she really is and . . .'

'Whatever she has or hasn't done, it's wrong to destroy her!'

'I'm tired, Sharon. I've had a long day and I don't need this.'

'And what about the girl next door? What had she done to you to deserve . . .'

'Her husband was a cheat! I saved her from the terrible pain of . . .'

'Saved her! You've as good as killed her! Anyway, I'm moving out.'

'Why?'

'I met a girl and . . . I'm moving in with her tomorrow. I don't want to live with someone like you, Sue. Your behaviour's despicable! I thought that we were going to be . . . I really don't know what I thought! I really liked you, Sue. I wanted us to . . . You need help! I'm going to bed.'

As she left the room, I was in two minds whether to tie her over the exercise bench and give her a damned good thrashing.

There she was, living in my house, rent-free – and complaining that she didn't like this and that!

Her words playing on my mind, I wondered what the future held for me. There'd be no going back now, no more friendly chats with Jilly and Derek – no more barbecues. Sally definitely wouldn't be calling in for coffee any more! And my relationship with Tom and Sandy would never be the same. Tracy . . . I wasn't sure about Tracy. I liked her very much, too much – but, it seemed, she was out to get me. What she would do about my *behaviour*, as Sharon had put it, I had no idea! I supposed that there was very little she could do.

So, Sharon was moving out. I must admit that I wasn't looking forward to living alone again. Although I had plenty of men friends, and women, it wasn't the same as having someone living with me. And I'd grown very fond of the girl, especially after her early morning visit to my bedroom.

Hearing her running a bath, I decided to punish her, teach her a lesson for disrupting my life! Although I was tired, I knew that this was my last chance to have sex with her – and I was determined to take it. Fortunately for Sharon, as I was creeping upstairs, the phone rang.

'Oh, Craig!' I replied with some surprise.

'I'm sorry I told you to fuck off,' he said softly.

'That's all right – I've been told to do worse. What's happening? Where are you, still at home?'

'No, no. I'm staying at a friend's for the time being. The reason I rang you is . . . Well, there are two reasons. Tracy and I have been talking, and she seems to think that she's got some kind of relationship with you. Is that right?'

'I . . . Well, yes, I suppose it is.'

'Oh. That answers my second question, then.'

'Does it?'

'Yes – I was going to ask if I could come and see you.'

'What, now?'

'Whenever.'

'Er . . . I don't know. What for, exactly – sex?'

'You're a very attractive and sexy woman, Sue. I'd like us to get together again, sexually, but there's something else I want to talk to you about. Tracy was saying that you're out to wreck marriages. I . . . I suppose Tracy told you about me having an affair some time ago?'

'I'm *not* out to wreck marriages! And, yes, she did tell me about your adultery.'

'Well, the affair never ended. I tried to end it several times but . . . you see, Tracy isn't exactly brilliant in bed. Now I've discovered she's a lesbian, I know why she wasn't into sex with me! Anyway, the woman I'm seeing, and have been seeing all along . . . I want her – permanently.'

'And?'

'There's a hitch – she's married.'

'That figures.'

'I just wondered – for a payment, of course – whether you'd consider . . .'

'Christ, Craig! I may have upset a few couples, but I'm not doing it for money! I don't wreck marriages to order!'

'So, you *do* deliberately wreck marriages?'

'Yes! No! I just upset the apple cart for certain people.'

'Why?'

'I have my reasons.'

'You won't help me, then?'

'Tell me more about her, this woman of yours.'

'Her name's Kirsty. She's unhappily married to a bastard twice her age, and she can't leave him.'

'Can't?'

'It's a long story but . . . They have money, both of them. She put as much into the house as he did. If she were to leave him, he'd make sure that she left penniless – and he could quite easily do it! I won't go into the details, but he's more than capable of ruining her, financially.'

'Does she *want* to leave him?'

'Yes, she does. I told her about you – it was her idea.'

'So, she's willing to pay me to . . .'

'Yes – five grand. Short of killing him, it's all she can do.'

God, I could have gone into business wrecking marriages! Five thousand pounds! All that money for screwing some old bastard and getting caught by his wife! That was a point – getting caught. What was the plan?

'Will I be cited in the divorce case?' I asked, not sure now whether I'd do it for any amount of money.

'Yes, 'fraid so. But you'd have five grand.'

'Come round sometime and we'll talk about it,' I suggested, hearing Sharon go to her room.

'She's here with me now. I know it's getting late, but can we come and see you now?'

'Er . . . I'm very tired, but I suppose so. I only want to *talk* about it, though. I'm not promising anything, Craig.'

'Great! We'll be with you soon.'

Replacing the receiver, I wondered what the hell I was letting myself in for. Destroying a marriage to order, for five grand! I felt like a criminal! But the money would come in handy, and I'd be destroying yet another marriage in the process. There was another bonus, too – when it was done, I'd wreck Craig's relationship with Kirsty! Befriend her, invite her round for a drink or something – and she'd discover him pumping his sperm into my mouth!

Sharon's punishment, I decided, would just have to wait. After all, I had more important things to do, and I had all night to thrash her for her ingratitude.

When Craig arrived with Kirsty, the adulteress, in tow, I was surprised by her tender age. As Craig had said that her husband was twice her age, I presumed him to be in his sixties – Kirsty could have been no more than twenty. Tall, and so slender that she was almost skinny, her long blonde hair and angelic face gave her an appearance of innocence, which I found quite appealing. Noticing her holding Craig's hand, I felt somewhat jealous – not because she had Craig, but because he had her!

'I want to make it clear that I don't do this for a living, Kirsty,' I asserted as we sat down in the lounge.

'No, I realize that,' she smiled, her hand still clutching Craig's as she sidled up to him on the sofa.

Ah, young love! Young lust!

'So, what's the plan? I'm to be caught rolling in sexual agony with your naked husband, yes?'

'Something like that,' Craig intervened. 'You see, Sue, we plan to marry and . . .'

'Oh, my God!' I giggled.

'Just because you don't like the idea of marriage, it doesn't mean to say that other people don't either!' he snapped.

'Sorry. Go on, please.'

'Well, Kirsty's husband, Paul, has been a right bastard to her. He . . .'

'Just get down to the nitty-gritty, Craig,' I sighed.

'This is what we'll do,' Kirsty began, suddenly finding her self-confidence as she released Craig's hand and began gesticulating. 'Tomorrow, you'll come to the house, my house, and I'll invite you in, as an old friend. I'll answer the phone and have to go out in a hurry, leaving you alone with Paul. You do whatever it is that you do, I come back with a witness, catch you red-handed and . . .'

'Hang on, hang, on!' I interrupted, trying to keep up with her waving hands. 'Firstly, who's going to phone you?'

'Craig will.'

'Right. Secondly, what if this husband of yours shows no interest in my sexual advances?'

'Oh, he will! Believe me, Sue, I know Paul!'

'OK, so you go off out, I screw . . . I do the biz with your husband, you come back and catch us – so who's the witness?'

'A friend of mine. She won't know what the plan is, but she'll witness . . .'

'What if she decides not to get involved? What if she won't back you as a witness?'

'Well . . .'

'I have a better idea. What does your husband do for a living?'

'He's a barrister.'

'Oh, great! Why couldn't he have been a bloody carpet fitter or something?'

'Well, because he . . .'

'Never mind. Is there any way you could get him to come here, to my house?'

'I doubt it!'

'That's a shame. I like to work on my home ground, you see.'

'I could always ask him to pick me up. Tell him that I'd been visiting you and the car wouldn't start and . . .'

'That's it! That's what we'll do. Now, I've already got one marriage to deal . . . I mean, I'm busy tomorrow morning, so is the afternoon OK?'

'Yes, what time?'

'Three o'clock.'

'So, when shall I come in and discover you with my husband? And what will you say when you answer the door to him and I'm not here?'

'I'll tell him to come in, get him into the lounge, and then say that you'd got the car going.'

'When do I come back? And why would I come back?'

'Give me half an hour, and then come back for your purse or something – I'll leave the front door open. Just walk into the lounge and, hopefully, you'll discover your husband . . . Well, you'll discover him fucking me, to put it crudely!'

'Right – but what about a witness?' she frowned.

'Leave that to me – I have just the man!'

'But where will the witness be?'

'Leave all the details to me, Kirsty. Just make sure that you ring your husband and tell him to pick you up from here at three o'clock – I'll do the rest. That just leaves the money.'

'Here's half of it. You'll get the other half when it's done,' she smiled, pulling an envelope from her bag.

'You've got the money? You were sure that I'd agree, then?'

'One hundred per cent!' Craig laughed.

'OK. If you decide not to give me the other half, I'll deny ever having seen your husband, and the witness will say that he witnessed nothing.'

'You don't trust her?' Craig asked angrily.

'Business is business, Craig. I'm just playing safe, that's all. Anyway, it's late, and I need my sleep.'

'OK,' Craig smiled, taking Kirsty's hand as he rose to his feet. 'Thanks, Sue. I hope it all goes to plan.'

'It will, don't worry.'

Seeing the happy couple out, I grinned as I thought how sweet they looked. They won't be holding hands for much longer! I mused, imagining Kirsty catching Craig writhing naked with me! One step at a time, Sue, I thought as I closed the door – one step at a time.

Sharon's punishment would have to wait until tomorrow. I was too tired, my body aching, my bum and pussy too sore for any more sex. Sharon would have the whipping of her life tomorrow! I promised myself. And the coming of her life!

Chapter Twelve

Sharon, the little bitch, was trying to sneak out of the house at seven the following morning, I was sure. Hearing noises, I thought that she was packing, and I slipped out of bed and threw my dressing gown over my shoulders. Creeping out of my room, I stood in the hall, frowning as strange noises emanated from the sex den – whimpering, buzzing, gasping. She was using my vibrator!

Spying through the crack in the door, I could see her lying over the exercise bench, naked, her legs wide, her fingers holding her pussy lips apart, the tip of the buzzing vibrator circling her clitoris. Seizing my chance for revenge, I inched the door open and slipped into the room.

Her eyes closed, her cunt wet and open, she was lost in her impending climax. Gasping, writhing as the vibrator stiffened her clitoris beautifully, she was oblivious to me – until I threw a length of rope over her young body, drawing it under the bench and tying it fast.

'What the hell are you doing?' she gasped, dropping the vibrator as she attempted to sit up. 'Sue, what . . .'

'Morning, Sharon,' I smiled, tying her ankles to the tubular frame. 'Enjoying yourself?' I asked, a wicked glint in my eye.

'I . . . I was just . . . Please, let me go!' she begged, her hands pulling on the rope across her stomach.

'Let you go? Now why would I want to do that? I thought I'd give you a leaving present. Something to remind you of me.'

'No, no!' she cried as I grabbed her hand and tied her wrist to the frame. 'You can't do this!'

'But I *am* doing it!' I grinned, tying her other wrist and standing back to admire the sensual beauty of her young body. 'Anyway, I thought you liked lesbian sex!'

'I do, but I don't want to be tied down! What's happened to you? You look different – you've changed.'

'Yes, I have. I'm going to give you something that you'll remember for the rest of your life, my girl!'

'What?'

'You'll see, my pretty little lesbian!'

Snatching the buzzing vibrator, I settled between her legs and presented the tip to her clitoris. 'I'll do it for you,' I whispered, watching her sex beast emerge from its hide as I pulled her outer lips up and apart. 'There, that's nice, isn't it?' I asked as she began to tremble.

'Yes, I like that. I thought that you were going to . . . Ah, that's good!'

'Going to what?'

'Use that whip on me.'

'Now, would I do that?' I giggled as her clitoris swelled and visibly throbbed.

Vibrating her bud, watching her girl-come ooze from her hot, yawning valley, I became overwhelmed by a rampant desire to use her young body, to defile her, lash her taut buttocks. Images of hanging the girl from chains and whipping her filled my mind as she cried out and shook uncontrollably in her sexual ecstasy. Watching her swollen cunt lips redden, her slippery juices decant, I decided to treat my prisoner as a sex-object.

Discarding the vibrator as her climax receded, I grabbed the whip and the KY-Gel. Rubbing the cooling lubricant between her buttocks, I felt my juices flowing, my cunt aching. 'You're going to lick between my wet pussy lips in a minute!' I promised as I smeared the gel around the delicate entrance to her tight bottom-hole.

'No!' she screamed as I pushed the thick wooden handle of the whip between her bum cheeks, forcing the hard end into her small hole, past her yielding muscles.

'Don't you want to lick my cunt?' I asked impishly.

'Yes, but . . . Take it out! Please, take it out!'

Ignoring her pathetic pleas, I gently eased the whip handle deep into her dank bowels, gazing at her intimate brown ring, stretched, dilated by the thick wooden shaft. How far to insert it? I pondered, wondering at the shape of her tight anal sheath. 'No more!' she suddenly gasped as I pushed another inch past her tight muscles. 'Enough!'

Her cunt milk coursing its way over her glistening flesh, running down to lubricate the wooden shaft, I knew that the sensations she was experiencing were more than pleasurable, and I made a mental note to indulge myself in the same treatment, once I'd finished with her.

'What does it feel like?' I asked, twisting the shaft a little as I pushed it deeper into her trembling body.

'It feels . . . I don't know. It's nice, but . . .'

'Then I'll make it even nicer for you!' I giggled, pushing another inch inside her bloated bum-hole.

'No, no more!' she cried. 'Please, Sue – no more!'

Five, six, seven inches embedded in her bum? I wasn't sure, but I decided that she'd taken all she could as I eyed her gaping cunt-hole – vacant, yearning to be filled. Looking round the room, I noticed the wine bottle that Tom had forcibly inserted into my tight sheath. That will do nicely, I mused, grabbing the bottle. Yanking Sharon's pussy lips open, I gazed at the pinken entrance to her vagina. The wet, juicy flesh formed a crater, reminding me of a flower with its pink petals converging in the centre where the delicate stamens lay – the remains of her hymen.

If only my tongue were longer, I mused, opening her inner flesh with my fingertips to expose her small urethral opening.

Further I stretched open her delicate girl-flesh, peering deep inside her wet cunt-hole at the creamy-soft walls. Placing the bottle on the floor, I used both hands to explore her inner depths, opening her, trying to see her cervix.

'Please, let me go, now,' she whimpered as I forced her pink flesh wide open, desperate to see what lay deep inside. 'Please, Sue, let me go!' Oblivious to her sobbed words, I held her portal open with one hand and grabbed the bottle by the neck. Offering the thick end to her open hole, I twisted and pushed on the huge phallus, forcing her swollen girl-lips apart. 'No!' she cried as the bottle slipped into her vagina, filling her pelvic cavity, forcing her wet flesh hard against her pubic bone.

I watched in amazement as the bottle slipped easily into her accommodating pussy, to be halted by her cervix. Her outer lips taut, stretched incredibly, rolled around the massive phallus, her clitoris forced from its hide, she begged me to remove the monster.

'Don't you like it?' I teased as I massaged her erect clitoris. 'You want to come, don't you?'

'Please, Sue! My bum . . . Please, I can't . . .'

'You can't what? Your bum's stretched wide open, your cunt's bloated with the wine bottle, so you can! Now I'll vibrate your clitty and make you come.'

'No, I can't . . .'

The buzzing vibrator shut her up as the tip pressed against her solid nodule to send soothing vibrations deep into her quivering pelvis. Gasping, she writhed and squirmed as I stiffened her throbbing budling. I was determined she was going to come and come and come until her cunt burned, her clitoris could throb no more! Giving her no mercy, I was going to bring her one multiple orgasm after another to see how many she could endure.

'God, I'm coming!' she murmured as her clitoris distinctly

pulsated with orgasm before my wide eyes. 'God, that's . . .' I watched the small protrusion as it exploded – throbbing, pumping, swelling beautifully. Working the bottle in and out of her tight orifice, I continued to vibrate her clitoris, taking her from one mind-blowing peak to another. 'Stop!' she managed to beg through her gasps as her abused bud receded, only to inflate again and pulsate against the tip of the incessant vibrator. 'God, not again!'

Thrusting the bottle between her twitching legs, moving the tip of the vibrator around the base of her clitoris, I knew that she was in her sexual heaven as again, she cried out in her coming. Her muscles forcing the whip handle out of her bottom-hole, I quickly pushed it back home, causing her to shriek with delight as it filled her anal sheath, stimulating the nerve endings there, bringing her more wondrous sensations of sex.

Her entire body shuddered violently as her climax rode on and on. Tossing her head from side to side, gasping, perspiring, there was nothing she could do to stop the beautiful sexual torture. 'No more!' she panted as her orgasm receded. 'Sue, please!' she cried as her clitoris swelled yet again, and another orgasmic peak neared.

Her cunt lips glowing a fire-red, her clitoris pumping in orgasm, I grinned as I turned the vibrator up to full power, increasing her incredible pleasure. Wondering how to keep the vibrator pressed against her cumbud while I sat on her face and forced her to drink the hot, sticky come from my burning cunt, I pulled the rope down from her stomach to her mound, securing it over the machine. Making a final adjustment, I sat back and gazed at the equipment between her thighs.

'I can't . . .' she whimpered as another peak shook her very soul. Slipping my dressing gown off, I knelt astride her head and lowered my open pussy over her pretty face, settling my sticky lips over her mouth. Coughing, spluttering, she pushed her tongue deep into my cunt, lapping up my juices as she trembled violently. I could feel her tongue exploring me, delving deep inside my vaginal sheath to seek out my inner nectaries – the source of my girl-flow. The sensations were mind-blowing, taking my lust for sexual fulfilment to giddy heights.

Swivelling my hips, I aligned my erect clitoris with her open mouth, gasping as she swept her tongue over my small protrusion, sending electrifying shudders of pleasure through my quivering body.

'Faster!' I ordered as her tongue circled my clitoris, swelling it until it was near to bursting point. 'Yes, that's it!' I gasped as my climax rose from my trembling womb and erupted in a powerful explosion of sheer lesbian lust. Rocking, sliding my drenched girl-slit back and forth over her hot mouth, I decanted my slippery come, lubricating our union as she trembled beneath me in her own bitter-sweet heaven.

My whole body afire with lesbian lust, I gazed down at her nipples, long, erect with arousal, and I reached out and pinched them, bringing her more sexual pleasure than she could bear. Spluttering through the wet cunt-flesh between my thighs, she begged me to release her. Sitting harder on her face, I rubbed my clitoris over her mouth, bringing out the final ripples of pure sexual ecstasy before falling to the floor, my aching cunt done.

'Please, no more!' she squealed as another wave of pleasure swept over her drenched body. 'Please, Sue, no . . . no more!' Lifting the rope, I removed the vibrator, bringing her down from her sexual paradise. 'My . . . my cunt!' she gasped, trying to squeeze her vaginal muscles to eject the bottle. 'God, take the bloody thing out!'

Slipping the hot bottle from her inflamed hole, I gazed at the whip handle buried deep in her bowels. The long leather tails hung ominously from the handle, trailing across the floor, and I decided to give her a good thrashing before freeing her. After deserting me, moving in with some young girl to enjoy long nights of lesbian sex, I might never see her again – she deserved a damned good whipping!

Gently pulling the wooden handle out of her tight anal sheath, I watched her brown ring gently close, guarding the entrance to her hot bowels. Untying the ropes, I helped her to sit up.

'God, I really ache!' she complained, looking down to her distended labia. 'You really are a bitch, Sue!'

'Here, let me help you,' I smiled, taking her arm and pulling her to her feet.

The time had come for the ultimate thrashing, and I prayed that she was in no condition to put up a fight. Twisting her round, I pushed her over the bench, pinning her down as I hauled the rope across her back, tying her down in readiness for the whipping.

'What the hell are you doing now?' she screamed as I pulled on her legs, forcing her to kneel and binding her knees to the frame. 'Christ, Sue!'

'Shut up, Sharon!' I hissed. 'Before you go and move in with your lesbian lover, I want to give you a bloody good whipping!'

'No!' she cried, struggling to free herself as I grabbed her wrists and bound them together.

When I'd done, I stood back, brushing the hair from my face as I gazed at her beautifully rounded buttocks, pale, unblemished – but not for long! Taking the whip, I dragged the leather tails over her pale orbs, teasing her virginal flesh.

'Unless you let me go, I'll . . .' she cried.

'You'll what?' I asked, dragging the soft tails up and down her dark crease.

'I'll . . . I'll come here with a friend and we'll whip you until you . . .'

'Until I come? I'll tell you what, I'll whip you until you come! Have you ever been whipped before?'

'No, and I'm not about to be!'

'But you are!'

'If you . . .'

The first blow shut her up, causing her body to jolt, her buttocks to twitch and contract delightfully. Swishing the leather tails through the air again, I watched as they cut across her taut buttocks, leaving thin, pink stripes in their wake. Incensed by a mixture of lust and anger, I continued to thrash her young buttocks, giving her at least fifteen good lashes before having to rest my aching arm. Glowing crimson, her burning flesh excited me, and I settled behind her and smeared more gel in her crease, wiping the cooling lubricant around the small, brown entrance to her bowels.

'You'll bloody well pay for this!' she threatened as I held her buttocks wide open and slipped the end of the whip handle into her brown hole, past her weakening muscles, driving it deep into her hot body. 'Ah! Ah, God, that's . . . You'll pay . . . Ah, no!' she cried as I slowly slid the handle in and out of her beautiful bottom-hole, fucking her there with the wooden phallus.

'Shall I call Jim and get him round here to fuck your bum?' I laughed as she began to quiver in her excitement.

'No, no . . . Just keep doing . . . keep doing . . . Ah, yes,' she murmured, pushing her bottom out to allow me better access to her hot depths.

'How about two men? That would be nice for you! One huge cock up your bum, and another up your pretty cunt, both fucking you?'

'Ah! No, just keep . . . Ah, God – yes!'

'Or three men! One creaming in your mouth as the others fill the pretty holes between your legs?'

The obscene image sent a wonderful shudder up my spine

and a delightful throb through my clitoris. Christ, three hard cocks all sperming into my trembling body at the same time! I knew then that that was what I wanted. I knew that I had to experience three penises buried in my young body, pulsating in orgasm, pumping my orifices full of male come.

The phone rang as I slipped the whip handle from her sticky anal sheath in readiness to give her another good lashing. It was persistent, and I had no choice other than to answer it. Leaving Sharon tied to the exercise bench, I bounded downstairs.

'Oh, hi, Tom!' I greeted, hearing his deep, sexy voice.

'How are you feeling?' he asked.

'Fine,' I replied, wondering whether he was going to propose another threesome.

'Are you doing anything this evening?'

'Er . . . No, I don't think so.'

'How about coming to dinner?'

'Oh, that would be nice.'

'About seven? And after we've eaten, we'll . . .'

'Er . . . I'm not sure about that, Tom.'

'Why, what's the problem?'

'Well . . . I don't know. After what happened . . .'

'You enjoyed yourself, didn't you?'

'Yes, I did. But you shouldn't have left me tied to the exercise bench!'

'Sorry about that!' he laughed. 'I was going to come back and . . . and release you, but I realized that a girlfriend of yours had beaten me to it.'

'How do you know that?'

'I have my binoculars! Anyway, what do you say about dinner?'

'All right, then, about seven.'

'Great! Until this evening, then.'

'Tom, there is one thing. Will you be around this afternoon?'

'I'm working, but . . .'

'Is there any chance that you could come over at three-fifteen and take a few photographs?'

'Photographs? What of?'

'It's a long story, Tom. Look, I'll pay you a couple of hundred pounds for creeping into my lounge and taking pictures of me and . . . of me and a man making love.'

'What the hell are you into?'

'I'll explain it all this evening. Just take some pictures, without him seeing you, if that's at all possible, and . . .'

'Without him seeing me? That won't be easy!'

'No, but seeing as you're a private investigator, I'm sure you'll manage it! Take some shots through the window or something. Anyway, if you want me to come to dinner this evening, then you'll have to do this for me.'

'Yes, all right. Leave your back door open, and I'll be there at three-fifteen.'

'Great! Thanks, Tom. When you've taken the pictures, hide the camera, and then wait in the hall for the man's wife to turn up – she'll be arriving at three-thirty. Both walk boldly into the room and make out that you're stunned. I'll take it from there.'

'I hope you know what you're doing!'

'I do, so don't worry. I'll see you later.'

'OK – and be careful!'

'I will – bye.'

Replacing the receiver, I wondered whether I was doing the right thing, agreeing to dinner at Tom's. I *had* enjoyed the sex session, but I didn't want it to become a regular thing. Tom and Sandy were weird, to say the least, and I wondered fearfully what they had planned for me. If they tied me up, there'd be no escape – no one would know where I was! They could keep me prisoner for days! I imagined becoming their sex-slave, having to perform anything and everything to order. That would be interesting!

But I was determined to split them up, ruin their strange relationship, so I had to go there and join in their sex games – whatever they were! If I could lure Tom away, enjoy secret sessions of perverted sex with him, suggest that he leave Sandy and come and live with me . . . I was about twenty years younger than her, my body was fresher, tighter. Yes, I was sure that I could take him away from her – and then discard him!

The afternoon planned, I wandered out into the garden and sat on the patio, my thoughts turning to Wendy's husband, Stephen Dixon. I didn't even know whether he'd be home or not. Wendy had said that he was arriving home in the morning, but what time? And I couldn't be sure that she'd go straight home after meeting Jim in the park. Whatever happened, if I could seduce her husband and get him to agree to come to my house for sex, I could plan Wendy's timely visit, and she'd catch him red-handed – and purple-knobbed!

God, two married couples in one day! But that was nothing, I reflected as I returned to the house to resume Sharon's beautiful thrashing. There were going to be dozens of the poor buggers coming my way!

Sharon, the bitch, had somehow managed to break free and escape. She'd taken her things, which she'd packed earlier, and fled the house before I could administer her full punishment. Oh, well – she'd had a couple of good lashings, at least. Besides, I couldn't dwell on her: I had other, more important things on my mind – namely, Stephen Dixon!

After a bath, I dressed in a loose, revealing blouse, and the shortest skirt I could find – a tight, red suede microskirt – and drove to Wendy's house. On the outskirts of town, the huge Victorian building could almost be described as a mansion. God, they had some money between them! No wonder Jim was sniffing around Wendy. Money had always attracted him – and other women's pussies, it seemed.

When a good-looking young man opened the huge oak door, I couldn't believe it was her husband. Probably the butler, I mused, asking whether Wendy was at home.

'My wife's out, I'm afraid,' the Adonis smiled, gazing down at my long, slender legs. 'Can I help you?'

Christ! Why was Wendy screwing Jim when she had this hunk?

'Er . . . I'm a friend of Wendy's, my name's Sue. I wanted to talk to her about something rather important.'

'I don't suppose she'll be too long. My name's Stephen, by the way. Why don't you come in and wait?'

'Yes, I think I will. I really do need to speak to her,' I replied, fluttering my eyelids as I smiled sweetly at him.

Leading me into the huge lounge, Stephen invited me to sit on the Chesterfield and offered me a drink. 'Vodka and lime would be nice,' I smiled as he opened a lovely antique drinks cabinet.

He was a huge man, tall, well-built – strong, muscular. His black hair was fairly short with a quiff above his forehead, his eyes dark, deep-set, his face rugged, weathered, reminding me of Heathcliff.

Oh to be fucked by Heathcliff on the windy moors!

'I've only just got back from France,' he began. 'I've been away on business. I only saw Wendy briefly this morning. She had to go into town for something or other.'

Yes, to meet my ex-husband! I thought as he passed me my drink. I suddenly felt rather awkward, unsure of myself, as he sat opposite me. He was wearing a crisp white shirt and tie and I suppose I felt somewhat belittled by him, his money and his huge house. But I had a job to do. Taking a deep breath, I sipped my vodka, convincing myself that he was a normal man, no matter how well-off, how well-dressed, and that he would have normal male thoughts – and fall prey to my abnormally perilous pussy!

'You have a lovely house,' I said admiringly, gazing round the room. 'Compared to mine, it's . . .'

'Never compare, Sue. There'll always be someone who has more than you, and someone who has less. It's what *you've* got, not what other people have or haven't got, that matters.'

'Yes, I suppose you're right,' I replied, wondering what the hell he was talking about.

'Tell me, what do you do for a living?'

Wreck marriages!

'I haven't got a job, I'm afraid. I used to rely on my husband but . . . I recently divorced and, sadly, I don't have a great deal of money.'

'Divorced? I'm sorry to hear that.'

'No, it's all right. I'm far happier now than I've ever been – apart from being broke, that is,' I smiled, parting my thighs a little.

'You're an extremely attractive girl,' he intoned sexily, gazing at my thighs. 'I'm sure you'll find yourself a partner, and a job before long.'

'It's nice of you to say that, but I don't want another relationship – not a permanent one, anyway.'

'It's a shame for someone as young and attractive as you to go to waste!' he laughed.

'I'm not going to waste!' I giggled, lowering my eyes to the slight bulge in his trousers. 'On that front, I lead a full and exciting life, I can assure you!'

'On which front?'

'Sex – the sexual front.'

His eyes widened. 'Oh! You have a boyfriend, then?'

'No, not at the moment. I suppose I'm looking for someone to enjoy a chat with, to spend the odd evening with, but nothing permanent – no strings. I suppose the only way to get that would be with a married man who wouldn't want strings either.'

'Well, I'm a married man, and I don't want strings,' he grinned. 'I'd love to spend the odd evening with you. The trouble is, Wendy would be bound to find out, and that would be that!'

Sounds promising!

'It would be nice to go out somewhere for a change. Due to lack of money, I haven't been out for so long . . . Anyway, you don't want to hear about my money worries.'

God, another typical man, I thought, parting my thighs a little further, displaying my femininity to his obvious appreciative gaze. Playing on being broke might be the answer. Perhaps I could entice him to see me regularly, take me out to dinner, to the theatre? Entice him away from Wendy. What to do? I wondered as he placed his glass on a low table and moved forward in his chair.

'If you really are that short of cash, I could always lend you a little to be getting by on,' he offered, his eyes transfixed between my thighs – on my hairless pussy-crack.

'Oh, I couldn't take money from you!' I exclaimed.

'Not take – borrow,' he smiled.

'Oh, no! It wouldn't be right! The only way I'd take money is if I'd worked for it. Besides, I'd never be able to pay you back.'

I didn't suppose that he'd dare to offer me money for sex, and I wondered how the hell to suggest it without appearing to be a complete tart. Mind you, with my shaved slit on show, he'd probably already gathered that I *was* a complete tart! Parting my legs even more, I smiled at him.

'There *are* ways I can earn money,' I began. 'A friend of mine has a photography business, and he suggested . . . Well, I'd only do that sort of thing as a last resort.'

'Pornography?' he queried.

'Well, not exactly. Just erotic poses, I think. I have a court case coming up soon and, to be honest, I'm in so much debt that I don't know which way to turn. I might *have* to take up my friend's offer.'

'Listen, Sue – why not do a little work for me? I could do with some help.'

'What sort of work?'

'I'm away a lot, and my paperwork tends to pile up. I have an office upstairs that I use when I'm here. Come on, I'll show you.'

Finishing my drink, I placed the glass on the table and followed Stephen upstairs to a huge study. The walls lined with books, a large, leather-top desk in the centre of the room, the place looked more like a library than what he'd glibly called his office! Sitting on the edge of the desk, displaying my shapely thighs as Stephen rumaged through a pile of papers, I wondered what Wendy would say if she discovered that I was working for her husband. There again, I had no intention of doing his paperwork. The only paperwork I was interested in was his divorce papers!

'This sort of thing,' he said, thrusting a sheet of paper under my nose. 'You see, this letter should have been answered two weeks ago. It refers to a deal I'm setting up with a Hong Kong company, but I just haven't had the time to do anything about it.'

'Doesn't Wendy help?' I asked, uncrossing my legs and parting my thighs.

'No, she takes no interest whatsoever in my work, I'm afraid,' he smiled, placing his hand on my thigh. 'You're very attractive, Sue.'

'You're full of compliments!' I giggled as his hand wandered up my inner thigh, causing my vagina to spasm delightfully.

'I mean it, you're a beautiful woman,' he said, his voice deep and soft.

'Is this what you do to all your secretaries?' I smiled as his fingers neared my naked pussy.

'I don't have a secretary. Well, I didn't, until now.'

I'd hooked him! Or perhaps he'd hooked me? He was the first man I'd met who *really* turned me on. His fingers exploring my upper thigh, nearing my wet pussy, excited me, aroused me, but it was his looks, his voice, his mannerisms, his charisma, that caused my stomach to swirl.

As I gazed into his deep-set eyes, he laid me over the desk, gently resting my head on a pile of papers. Opening my legs wide, I closed my eyes as I felt his hot breath between my thighs, on the soft skin of my swollen pussy lips. I sensed his tongue, licking, tasting, exploring my wet crack, and I gasped. Never had I felt so sexually stimulated, so alive with a burning desire for lust.

Wasting no time, parting my swelling outer labia, he pushed his tongue into my expectant hole and lapped up my cream. Rolling my head from side to side, I breathed heavily, arching my back as he moved up my sex valley and swept his hot, wet tongue over my hard clitoris. God, how the sensations gripped me, took me to strange new heights of arousal as my clitoris swelled and throbbed in the beginnings of my climax.

'Nice?' he murmured as he slipped a finger into my tight, vaginal sheath and massaged my creamy inner walls.

'Yes!' I breathed as his tongue repeatedly swept across the tip of my clitoris, rhythmically massaging, caressing my pleasure-spot until my body shook violently.

Gripping the sides of the desk, my skirt up over my stomach, my legs fully open, I squeezed my eyes shut as my climax exploded, sending electrifying waves of sex over my entire body. Panting, gasping for breath as the beautiful pulses of orgasm shook my very womb, I knew that I wanted this man all to myself.

Whatever I'd set out to do, and why, didn't seem to matter any more. I wanted Stephen to be my man, and mine only. Derek, Jim, Craig Tony . . . no one else mattered at that moment. I'd even forgotten about Wendy. All I wanted was Stephen inside me, fucking me with his beautiful organ, filling me with his gushing sperm.

As I gently floated down from my climax, I became aware of movements, trousers unzipping, a belt unbuckling. Opening my eyes, I gazed up at the huge chandelier hanging from the ceiling, waiting for the inevitable – for the beautiful penetration. Pulling my body along the desk, Stephen positioned my buttocks over the edge and parted my thighs. Standing between my legs, he ran his huge knob up and down my creamy slit, lubricating his glans in readiness to penetrate my yearning vagina. Suddenly, he was in, filling my pelvic cavity, stretching my cunt wide open with his massive organ. Shuddering, I clung to the sides of the desk, my body jolting with every ramming thrust of his massive cock.

I could feel the hood of my clitoris massaging me, my sensitive pleasure-spot, as he fucked me, rammed my young cervix, brought me untold sexual pleasure. I wanted his cock to stay there, deep inside my wet cunt, for always – fucking me for always.

'Ah!' he gasped as his sperm gushed. 'Ah, that's good!' I sensed his male come, felt the liquid squirting deep into my vagina, drenching me, lubricating our beautiful union as he thrust on and on until, again, my clitoris erupted. The sheer sexual bliss emanating from my tight cunt, from my pulsating clitoris, rippled over my entire body, gripping me in a heady lust – love?

'Fuck . . . fuck me!' I cried, although I'd no idea why!

'I am!' he gasped, making his final earth-moving thrust before stilling his huge piston. Both gasping, our genitals locked, absorbing the last sensations of sex, we breathed heavily, allowing the ripples to fade before gazing at each other.

'Is this the work you want me to do for you?' I asked.

'No . . . I mean, yes, if you want to,' he smiled, slipping his wet shaft from my hot, slippery sheath.

'Yes, I do want to,' I replied softly, sexily, hauling my perspiring body up and sitting, my skirt around my stomach, his sperm oozing, pooling on the soft leather desk.

'You'll come and see me again?' he asked, buckling his belt.

'Yes, whenever you want me to.'

'How much?'

How much? I didn't want money! Well, I did, but I wanted Stephen! 'Fifty?' he suggested, taking his wallet from his pocket. Fifty? Fifty pounds for a quick fuck? Was that it? Yes, I supposed it was. He had Wendy, he didn't want me! Well, he didn't want me to replace her, not permanently, anyway. All he wanted was my cunt, and he was willing to pay for it.

It was then that I realized that he was just another ordinary man. There was nothing special about him, nothing unique – apart from his money. I must have been mad thinking that he'd want to become my partner, to leave his wife and be with me!

'Yes, fifty,' I replied, slipping off the desk and pulling my skirt down.

'You shave,' he remarked, stating the obvious.

'Yes, I prefer it,' I sighed, taking the notes from his hand.

'It's nice, I like it like that.'

It? Yes, *it*! It, being my cunt, a hole – a hot, wet sheath between my legs to be fucked, paid for and fucked. Oh, well, I'd more than enjoyed being fucked, and I'd made fifty pounds, so I couldn't complain. It was a shame that Wendy hadn't caught us, though. Although I wouldn't have wanted her interrupting us, cutting short my sexual pleasure. But the time would come when she would catch us – discover her husband committing adultery. The time would come.

'Tomorrow?' Stephen began. 'Can you come round tomorrow morning?'

'No, I can't come here. Look, I'd better not come here to see you – it's not a good idea. Why don't you come to my house, we'd be safe there?' I suggested, just having had a brilliant idea.

'OK. What's your address?'

I told him, and he wrote it in his diary, saying that he'd call round at eleven the following morning. Well, that was it – I'd sold my body for sex. I was a prostitute! What the hell? He'd soon discover that all he'd paid for was a broken marriage, so what the hell?

'I'd better be going,' I said, adjusting my blouse, wondering why he hadn't paid any attention to my breasts, my erect nipples. A quick screw, and that was it – his penis satisfied, my cunt now discarded. Until tomorrow.

'Yes, Wendy will be back soon, so . . .'

'What's she like in bed?' I asked wickedly as we descended the stairs.

'OK, I suppose. Not as good as you, if that's what you mean.'

'No, that's not what I meant. Anyway, I'll see you tomorrow.'

He opened the front door and watched me walk to my car. As I started the engine, I became aware of his sperm oozing from my vagina, wetting my inner thighs, the back of my skirt. That was all I was good for, I reflected – being fucked, pumped full of sperm, before being deserted. I hated men – all of them!

Resting in my lounge, I thought about my plan. Get Stephen to come to my house and arrange for Wendy to call in and discover us screwing on the carpet. Better still, arrange things so that both Jim and Stephen were fucking me. What would Wendy say to *that*?

On the other hand, I'd be better off having Stephen discover Jim fucking Wendy, and then, get Wendy round to . . . Christ, I was complicating things unnecessarily! All I had to do was have Wendy discover her husband and her two-timing bastard lover, Jim, both fucking me at once. Kill two birds with one stone. Wreck two relationships with one explosive fucking session!

My thoughts turned to the second married man of the day, Paul. This one was going to bring me the second half of the payment, two and a half grand, and I was looking forward to the money, as well as the sex! But would everything go according to plan? Would Tom be able to take the photographs without being detected? Would Paul turn up when Kirsty rang him and asked him to pick her up from my house because her car had broken down? There were so many uncertainties that I was beginning to wonder whether I'd been meticulous enough in my planning. And, if everything did work out, would Paul succumb to my omnipotent pussy? Yes, that part of the plan was certain enough!

I must admit that I was apprehensive. After all, taking five thousand pounds and being cited in a court case wasn't something I was used to! Christ, I might have to stand in the witness box and relate how I'd fucked Kirsty's husband! I hadn't thought of that! I might have to go into explicit detail of how, where and when I met him, how many times he'd fucked me . . . Oh, well – what the hell? He might even cut his losses and agree to divorcing her and settling fairly rather than go to court – I bloody well hoped so!

I hadn't used the handcuffs yet, and I wondered whether Paul would agree to being cuffed and whipped. What a lovely set of photographs that would make for the family album! But how would Kirsty explain the photographs? Paul would know that he'd been set up and . . . Shit! I hadn't thought of that! She'd have to say that my friend, Tom, being the sad pervy he is, happened to discover me making love and thought that he'd take some pictures for fun. Weak though it was, that was the answer. Kirsty would just happen to get her hands on them, the evidence, and threaten her husband.

I was pretty sure then that there'd be no court case. The

photographs were all Kirsty needed to get whatever she wanted from her husband. Being a barrister, the last thing he'd want would be a set of photographs distributed to his colleagues showing him in an obscene sexual entanglement with the likes of me!

Anyway, that was between Kirsty and her husband – I had five thousand pounds to spend. God, all that money! I could buy some really elaborate equipment for the sex den, then lure hundreds of married men to my lair for perverted sex. But who would be next? I wondered. When I'd wiped out these two relationships, who next would fall under my evil eye?

Preparing a salad for my lunch, I wondered what Paul looked like. If he was half as good-looking as Stephen, I'd be more than happy to have him fuck me, use my body for his sexual pleasure. If he wasn't an attractive man, then I'd just have to close my eyes and think of the money. Either way, I'd get fucked and earn myself five grand!

Chapter Thirteen

Three o'clock, and I was ready, dressed for the kill. Six-inch red stilettoes, red suede microskirt, tight-waisted blouse, no bra or panties – and my sweet pussy, freshly shaved and juiced-up. What man could resist me? I mused as I twirled before the hall mirror. A real-life sex-doll!

Standing with my back to the mirror, my feet wide apart, keeping my long legs straight, I touched my toes. The upside-down reflection of my bulging pussy lips, my inner folds, pink and wet, protruding beautifully, excited me, roused my clitoris as I imagined Paul gazing at me in that provocative pose.

For years I hadn't realized the immense power between my legs. I'd never gazed at the reflection of my bulging cunt lips. I'd never seen the beauty there, nestling between my thighs. Stroking my inner petals, dragging the slippery juice over my outer lips, I felt a quiver in my womb. Was there time to masturbate, to appease my throbbing clitoris?

The front doorbell ringing startled me and I stood up, adjusting my skirt and tossing my long blonde hair over my shoulder as I walked to the door and took a deep breath. This was it – the seduction! Five thousand pounds!

'Oh, hello, you must be Kirsty's husband,' I greeted the middle-aged man dressed in a dark pinstripe suit.

'Yes, that's right. My name's Paul.'

'And I'm Sue. Please, come in.'

'I won't stay, I've got a lot on at the moment. I'll wait in the car for her,' he said abruptly, turning to leave.

Shit! What the hell do I do now? I wondered as he walked

down the path to the front gate. 'Hang on, Paul!' I called, stopping him as he opened the gate. 'Come into the house for a minute, I have to tell you about Kirsty!'

'What about her? She is here, isn't she?' he asked, frowning as he turned and walked back up the path, his mouth twisted as if every minute he spent talking to me was a minute wasted.

'Come through, and I'll explain,' I invited as he stepped into the hall.

Leaving the front door ajar, I showed him into the lounge, wondering why he'd taken little or no notice of my ultra-short suede skirt, my erect nipples pressing through my very tight blouse.

'Kirsty eventually got her car going,' I began. 'She's only just driven off and . . .'

'In that case, what the bloody hell am I doing here?' he complained. 'God, she really does waste my bloody time!'

Miserable sod!

'Hang on for a few minutes, just in case the car gives her trouble and she comes back,' I suggested. 'Would you like a drink?'

'No, I haven't got time!' he snapped irritably, eyeing my thighs for the first time as I switched the hi-fi on, hoping to drown out Tom's movements, his whirring camera.

'Sit down,' I invited as I settled in the armchair. 'Surely, you can wait for a couple of minutes?'

Reluctantly seating himself on the sofa, he ran his fingers through his thick, greying-black hair and looked agitatedly around the room. 'Scotch?' I smiled.

'No, thanks – I'm driving.'

'Oh, of course.'

The situation was awkward, the atmosphere tense. With the time running on and Tom due to take the photographs, I didn't know what the hell to do. I'd thought that I was well practised in the fine art of body language, exposing my smooth cunt lips to married men, but now I was beginning to wonder. There was only one thing I could do. Relaxing in the armchair, I went for it, opening my legs as I made myself comfortable.

'You married?' he asked, gazing wide-eyed at my alluring pussy-slit – pink, wet, and ready.

'No, recently divorced,' I replied.

'Did you leave him, or did he leave you?' he asked rudely.

'I threw him out. He had another woman.'

'He must have been mad!'

'Why?'

'Well, wanting another woman when he had you.'

I smiled, manoeuvring my body, pushing my breasts forward, stretching my long legs out and parting my thighs. He averted his eyes, then, drawn like a magnet, turned back to my femininity, my smiling girl-crack. What was he thinking? I wondered. Probably that I was some kind of tart! I suppose I was! But that didn't matter. I had to hook him – five grand was riding on it!

'I don't suppose Kirsty will come back now,' I breathed huskily, licking my lips and flashing my bedroom eyes. 'Why don't you come over here and get to know me a little better?'

'I suppose I've got some time to spare after all,' he smiled hesitantly, rising to his feet and standing before me. 'Do you always dress like that?' he asked as he knelt down and gazed up my skirt to my ever-powerful pussy.

'Only when I'm working!' I giggled.

'You're not a prostitute, are you?'

'What do you want me to be?'

He hesitated.

'I've got money.'

'Then why not spend some – say, fifty?'

'What will I get for that?'

'What do you want?'

'To fuck you.'

That was straight to the point! 'Then that's what you'll get.' *Another married man falls prey to my beautiful pussy*!

But better still, he was going to pay me fifty pounds for the pleasure – the pleasure of divorce! Feeling more confident as I watched him drop five ten-pound notes on the coffee table, I placed my legs over the arms of the chair, pulling my skirt up over my stomach. Losing no time, he homed in on my swelling cunt lips and planted a soft kiss in my sex-groove.

Breathing slowly, deeply, I closed my eyes, waiting for his tongue to explore my sex valley, my clitoris, my creamy love-hole. Opening my swelling hillocks of flesh with his fingers, he licked my pink, inner flesh – teasing me, skirting my clitoris and then moving away. I could feel my cunt tightening, my muscles tensing every time his tongue swept close to my vigilant bud. Moving forward in my chair, almost doing the splits, I offered him the open centre of my trembling body, allowing him to drink my juices of lust, praying that he'd attend to my aching nodule.

Taking my outer lips between his fingers and thumbs, he pulled them apart, stretching the delicate flesh until I winced and cried out. Decreasing the tension a little, he licked around my clitoris now, making my cherry swell, bringing me wonderful sensations of sex. Pulling my lips open again, he continued his caressing, sweeping his tongue around and over my clitoris, centring all his attention between my taut cunt lips. Further he opened me, until the pain became too much and I cried out again.

'What's the matter?' he asked, looking up at me.

'It hurts,' I whispered, running my fingers through his hair.

'Sorry, I'll be more careful.'

'There's some rope behind the chair, if you're into bondage,' I breathed, glancing at the clock. Three-twenty.

'All for fifty pounds?' he asked surprisedly.

'Yes, all for fifty pounds,' I conceded, smiling sweetly. 'Why don't you slip your clothes off?'

Standing up, he removed his jacket and hurriedly undid his tie. I glanced at the clock again as he unbuttoned his shirt and tossed it over the sofa – still three-twenty. His trousers around his ankles, he kicked them aside, standing in his boxer shorts and socks. 'Now let me see what you've got to offer *me*,' I grinned wickedly, massaging my clitoris as he slipped his shorts down.

His penis was long, stout – the biggest I'd ever seen! – his balls huge, hanging heavy below the thick root of his beautiful organ. Gazing at his silky, purple knob as he moved his weapon closer to my face, I gasped. 'God, it's big! I've never seen . . .'

His plum-like knob pressing against my mouth, I parted my lips and sucked him inside, rolling my tongue over his male hardness. 'You want me to tie you up?' he asked, gazing down at my bloated cheeks. I nodded as he pulled away and grabbed the rope from behind the chair.

Aware of Tom moving around outside the door, I prayed that Paul wouldn't hear him as he bound my wrists and placed my hands behind my head. Pulling me down, positioning me with my buttocks hanging over the edge of the chair, he tied the rope around my left knee, running the end around the back of the chair before winding it tightly around my other knee.

Then, taking a cushion from the sofa, he stuffed it under my buttocks, raising my hips, my open cunt in readiness to fuck me. My young body tethered, my stomach somersaulted with anticipation. I wanted his huge organ deep inside my vagina, pumping its creamy fruits over my cervix, taking me to a shuddering orgasm.

'There, that's better,' he smiled, pulling the chair into the centre of the room.

'What are you doing?' I asked as he tipped the chair up, resting the back on the floor.

'I can get to your pretty cunt far better with you upside down!' he laughed, settling at the bottom of the chair and stretching my pussy lips open until I cried out. 'It's all right!' he grinned. 'I won't split you open, I just want to see everything you've got – every fold, every intricate part of your lovely cunt!'

Gazing up at the ceiling, the blood rushing to my head, I prayed that Tom had some good shots of Paul fingering me. What a way to earn five grand! I mused, finding myself looking up at Paul's buttocks, his huge balls, as he stood with his feet either side of me, gazing down at my blatantly displayed girlish folds.

Leaning forward, he ran his hard knob along my open pussy-crack, lubricating his spearhead in readiness for the impaling. 'You won't get it in!' I sniggered. 'You're at the wrong angle!'

'Let me worry about that!' he gasped, forcing the head of his penis into my open hole.

'Agh, no! It hurts like that!' I protested as he drove his shaft into me, forcing my vaginal sheath into alignment with his solid rod.

His balls slapping my lower belly, I gazed up at his shaft, at forty-five degrees to my love-sheath, sinking deep into my cunt, thrusting again and again. It was certainly different, being fucked upside down by a man standing over me. Normally my buttocks were slapped by heavy, sperm-laden balls, not my belly! Still, the position was perfect for Tom, the photographer, and, I must admit, Paul's shaft screwing me at that weird angle, massaging my clitoris, aroused me incredibly.

Suddenly, he slipped his knob out of my quivering quim and massaged his shaft, bringing out his sperm. Splashing his come over my open pussy, he wanked his huge organ, draining his bouncing balls. Rubbing his swollen knob between my splayed cunt lips, soaking me with his come, he groaned as the last of his sperm dribbled into my open sex valley and trickled down my stomach.

'Now, suck it, you dirty little tart! And then I'll fuck your tight arse!' he bellowed, turning to face me, a frightening glint of evil in his eye.

'You fucking bastard!' Kirsty screamed hysterically, standing in the doorway.

Paul's face crimsoned as he turned his head to face his wife. A look of utter hatred in her eyes, she glared at him as Tom entered the room and gasped at the sight of my tethered body, my wet, open cunt.

'Sue! What the hell . . .'

'Will you be a witness to this?' Kirsty asked, turning to Tom. 'Will you tell the divorce court what you saw – my husband, naked, standing over this, this little . . .'

'Yes, of course I will!' Tom agreed readily as Paul grabbed his clothes from the sofa.

Setting the chair upright, Tom released me, asking me whether I'd been raped or had agreed to the weird sexual scenario. 'I agreed, Tom,' I replied shamefully, standing up. 'I'm sorry,' I half-smiled, gazing into Kirsty's eyes. 'Your husband . . . he . . .'

'Sorry? I was your friend, you bitch! And he was my fucking husband!' she blasted, running out of the room.

'I'll go and calm her down,' Tom said, leaving me alone with Paul.

Dressing, his face anguished, his forehead lined with worry, Paul cursed his young wife. 'Bloody woman! She's fucking well got me now! Who was that man, anyway?'

'My neighbour. He often calls round to see me. I . . . I must have left the door open.'

'Christ, she's got a bloody witness now!' he stormed, pushing me aside rudely as he left the room.

Yes, and she'll have photographs, too! I laughed inwardly as I pulled my short skirt down, covering my inflamed, sperm-drenched slit. That was that – mission completed! Five thousand pounds, and another marriage over! Plus fifty pounds thrown in for luck!

Things were looking up, I ruminated, leaving the room and stepping outside the front door. The battle was raging in the street – Kirsty swearing at her husband, thumping his chest with her clenched fists – Paul covered in guilt, Tom standing to one side . . .

Kirsty certainly put on a good show, I'll give her that! Quite the little actress, she even sobbed real tears. On and on she battered her husband's chest until Tom intervened, telling Paul to go. I watched him climb into his new Jag and screech off down the road – a fucked man. In her sheer delight, Kirsty turned to Tom and squealed with laughter before returning to the house.

'You did a good job, Sue!' she beamed as she approached the front door and passed me an envelope.

'You did pretty well, too!' I replied, grabbing the envelope and tearing it open. 'Do you want to come in for a drink?'

'No, thanks. I'm off to meet Craig to tell him the good news.'

'Oh, right. When Tom's developed the photographs, you can come round for them,' I smiled.

'Photographs?' Kirsty asked surprisedly.

'Oh, yes! I've done the job properly. Tom was not only the witness, but the photographer!'

'That's brilliant!' Kirsty cried. 'With photographs, I might not have to go to court!'

'That was the idea. Clever, aren't I?'

'Devious!' she laughed. 'I must go. Bye, Tom, and thanks – both of you.'

Yes, you go and tell Craig the good news, I thought,

wondering what her reaction would be when she discovered him fucking me! She'd be divorced, alone, single – and writhing in the pain of Craig's adulterous ways. *Wonderful!*

'Well, I'd better be going,' Tom said, taking his camera from under the hall table. 'I'll go the back way, through the hedge.'

'OK, Tom. Thanks for your help. There's two hundred, as agreed,' I smiled, passing him the notes.

'A nice little earner, I must say! Anyway, see you tonight for dinner.'

'Yes, I'm looking forward to it,' I smiled. At least, I thought I was looking forward to it! 'I'll see you later, Tom.'

'I'm looking forward to the afters!' he laughed. 'Anyway, until this evening.'

Watching Tom disappear through the hedge, I thought I heard a noise upstairs. Creeping through the hall, I was wondering whether Sharon had changed her mind, when I heard a dull thud. 'Who is it?' I called up the stairs. 'Sharon, is that you?'

'Yes, come up, Sue!'

Bounding up the stairs with images of the girl's naked buttocks, the leather whip reddening her already crimson orbs, I dashed into the sex den to find her standing by the exercise bench.

'So, you've had a change of mind?' I asked.

'Yes, I thought I'd come back and talk to you, Sue,' she said, a strange smirk across her face.

'Talk to me?' I queried, sensing that something was very wrong. 'Talk about what?'

'My threat to thrash you with the whip.'

'Oh, and how do you intend to do that?' I laughed uneasily.

'Simplicity itself!' she grinned. 'Come in, lads!'

On cue, two men in their late teens burst into the room, closing the door behind them. Both wearing tight blue jeans and open shirts exposing their hard, muscular chests, they were extremely attractive. One was darkish, suntanned, and all-man, with a mop of unruly black hair – while the other, blond and fair-skinned, was slightly effeminate. Both eminently worthy of a good screw! I quickly surmised.

'Undress her and tie her down for me!' Sharon ordered them as she picked my whip up, running the leather tails through her palm.

'It'll be a pleasure,' the darker man grinned, taking my arm and twisting it behind my back as the other yanked my skirt down, revealing my dripping pussy.

'She's got a nice cunt, hasn't she?' Sharon remarked crudely as I struggled to break free.

'Indeed she has!' exclaimed the blond man kneeling at my feet, pushing a finger deep into my vagina. 'When you've punished her, we'll have our fun with her!'

Sharon grinned evilly as they tore my blouse from my trembling body and fondled my firm breasts, tweaking my erect nipples before forcing me to kneel before the bench. As they pushed me down, tying my wrists and knees to the frame, I knew that I'd asked for this – that I deserved what was coming.

'Now!' Sharon bellowed, running the soft leather tails up my bottom crease as I tried to turn my head to look at her. 'I said that I'd thrash you, didn't I? So, here I am!'

'Not too hard, Sharon!' I pleaded as she raised the whip above her head.

'Not too hard? But I'm going to thrash you as hard as I can, Sue! Until your fucking cunt explodes in orgasm, or you die – whichever comes first!'

The first lash jolted my entire body and I yelped like a dog as the stinging pain engulfed my taut buttocks. The next lash would have sent me flying across the room, if it hadn't been for the ropes binding my naked body to the bench. Again, the tails cut into my tender flesh, the pain now flooding my mind.

Again and again they landed across my twitching buttocks, bringing me strange, unfamiliar sensations, bitter-sweet sensations of pleasure and pain I'd never known before.

'Please, Sharon!' I sobbed when I'd had more than enough of the torturing treatment. 'Please stop!'

'Never!' she laughed as she whipped me again and again.

'Christ! I can't take it!' I cried as the leather tails cut across my burning buttocks yet again. 'Please!'

'*I* had to take it, you bitch!' she screamed as she continued to lash me. 'I had to fucking well take it! And a wine bottle up my cunt, you dirty bitch!'

After what seemed like a thousand lashes, the young men halted her, grabbing the whip as she raised it above her head, insisting that I'd had enough. 'It's our turn for some fun!' one of them laughed, rubbing KY-Gel between my stinging buttocks. 'I'll take her bum-hole!'

Suddenly I sensed his knob, hard, solid, stabbing at my small brown hole as Sharon sat on the floor and lifted my head from the slope of the bench. 'You'll enjoy this!' she cackled as the man's knob slipped past my yielding muscles. 'While he fucks your arse, you can suck my cunt!' she added, yanking my head up and moving her bottom up the sloping, padded section of the bench, her legs wide open, her wet pussy lips only inches from my mouth. 'Go on, then! Lick my cunt!' she ordered crudely, moving her hips forward and lying full-length on the floor.

Her fanny wedged beneath my face, I could barely breathe as she swivelled her hips, rubbing her wet and swollen pussy lips over my mouth as the young man impaled me completely on his massive cock. Not wanting to be left out, his friend forced what felt like his entire fist into my hot cunt, filling my pelvic cavity to the brim. With my bum and my cunt bloated to capacity, the sensation was incredible!

Stretching my bum-hole open wide with his monster organ,

the man behind me began to thrust into my tethered body, gripping my hips and taking me as hard as he could, rocking my young body, forcing my face into Sharon's open crack.

Lying there with both ends of my body being crudely used, all three orifices employed for cold sex, I wondered what things had come to. Grief and self-pity had turned into a craving for revenge, but what had that led to? My whole life centred around sex now, around my naked body, my vagina. My very reason for living was to have sex, and more sex, with anyone and everyone – was that what I really wanted?

I didn't know what I wanted, whom I wanted. My life had changed so dramatically that I had become unsure of what I was doing, where I was going. Two men and a young girl using me, my naked, tethered body, for perverse sex – I wondered where life was taking me.

'Coming!' the man in my rear cried as his penis exploded within my ballooning anal sheath, lubricating our debased union. 'Agh, God, she's tight! I'm coming up her arse!'

Panting and gasping as I mouthed and sucked on her swelling clitoris, Sharon suddenly forced her open cunt hard against my face. The thought that I was being used by two people simultaneously to elicit their orgasms excited me and my own clitoris responded to the fist driving in and out of my vagina by erupting in a beautiful climax. Gasping, writhing, trembling, crying out our love of lust, like the Holy Trinity, all three of us came together.

'I'll have her cunt now!' the blond man said hungrily, slipping his hand from my tight pussy-hole as his friend pulled his cock from my bum. 'I'll take her cunt, and then we'll swap holes!'

Christ, where the hell had Sharon found these two? Probably from the college, I mused as my pussy lips were wrenched apart and my aching vagina suddenly inflated with the blond man's huge penis. The other man left the room as

Sharon quivered in orgasm again, pouring her sticky juices into my mouth as I licked and sucked her hot cunt-folds – mouthed her pulsating clitoris. But he soon returned!

As Sharon shuddered her last shudder and moved away, the dark man took her place, pushing his squeaky-clean knob deep into my mouth as he settled on the floor. Now I had two penises driving into me, using me, fucking my mouth, my cunt. I could barely take the pummelling as they thrust into me, finding their rhythm as they gasped their expletives, gave each other an obscene running commentary.

'Shame Phil couldn't make it!' one gasped. 'We could have fucked all three of her holes at once!' Yes, it was a shame that Phil, whoever he was, couldn't have made it! My dream, my fantasy of three cocks sperming inside my body would have come true. But I was receiving more than my fair share of pleasure, I decided, as the penis in my mouth swelled and pumped its first shot of come to the back of my throat. Both men coming together, filling my cunt, my mouth, as Sharon settled on the floor and massaged my clitoris – I was on Cloud Nine!

I knew then that the rest of my life would be spent enjoying one sexual encounter after another, one man after another, one woman after another. I wanted more penises, penises in all my holes, in both hands, two in my mouth at once – all sperming over me and inside me. I wanted wet cunts rubbing their juices all over my body, clitorises coming against my caressing tongue. I wanted sex and more sex!

As my climax came, taking me to an unprecedented sexual high, I fantasized, picturing twenty men all standing around me, over my naked body, wanking their stiff cocks, spurting their sperm all over me. Shuddering as my mouth overflowed and my cunt squeezed the sperm from the intruding, throbbing cock, I almost passed out with the intense pleasure between my thighs.

'I think it's time for another thrashing!' Sharon declared as she stood up. As the penises slipped from my body, her words reverberated through my mind, and I prayed that they'd leave me, allow me to rest – show me some mercy. 'OK, bitch!' she cried as the first lash cut across my taut buttocks. 'This is the *real* thrashing!'

I don't know how many times the whip swished through the air, how many times my buttocks twitched and I yelped. Thirty, fifty? It could have been a hundred! The men didn't stop Sharon this time. Laughing as they watched me take my gruelling punishment, they did nothing to save me. *Bastards!*

Finally coming to her senses, and running out of energy, Sharon dropped the whip to the floor. Virtually unconscious, I lay there, whimpering, trembling as my clitoris throbbed and my aching cunt decanted more girl-come than I'd ever have thought possible. Untying the ropes, Sharon released my abused, perspiring body. Aching, stinging, dizzy, I rolled off the bench and lay on the floor, Sharon standing over me, looking down at me, scowling. Gazing up at her now grinning face, the wicked glint in her eye, I wondered fearfully what was coming next.

'That'll teach you to whip me!' she spat. 'And think on this! We'll be back! One day, maybe tomorrow, maybe next week, we'll be back to do this again! I have a key, remember? In the dark of the night, or in the morning, or the middle of the afternoon, you'll never know when we'll come back. But we will be back – and Phil will be with us!'

Placing her foot on my stomach, she stood with her hands on her hips, leering at me. 'We're going now, bitch!' she hissed. 'Until the next time!' Closing my eyes as she put her full weight on me and walked towards the door, I knew in my heart that she would be back. I'd met my match – and a bolt of fear coursed its way through me, my tortured mind.

I heard feet thundering down the stairs, and then the front

door slamming shut – they'd gone. Climbing to my feet, I recalled Sharon's words, and wondered when she'd come back with her three insatiable studs. Despite my apprehension, I hoped it wouldn't be too long!

Sharon was a strange one, I reflected. I couldn't make my mind up whether she was just having fun with me, or if she really hated me. Who was using whom? I wondered as I grabbed the shower nozzle to douche the sticky juices from my inflamed sex-holes. Suddenly I remembered Tom's and Sandy's dinner invitation. I was in no fit state for an evening of sex – especially with a sex-mad man and his perverted, lesbionic wife!

But, washed and dressed, I felt much better, refreshed – and really looking forward to the evening's sex session. I seemed to have got myself back into gear as I answered the phone to Jim, a wicked plan forming in my mind.

'No, you can't come round now, Jim,' I told him firmly.

'But I have to see you, Sue!'

'Why?'

'I want to talk to you about the future. I . . . I'm on my own now – completely.'

'What do you mean, *completely*?'

'I was seeing someone, and she's dumped me. Well, not dumped me, exactly – but she's thinking about it.'

'Serves you right!' I laughed.

'Maybe. Anyway, I think it's time we talked, talked about the future – our future together.'

'*Our* future? What the hell do you mean – *our* future?'

'A lot's happened recently, and I, for one, want to make a go of it – of us. Let's make a fresh start together, Sue.'

A fresh start? God, was there no stopping him? Just because Wendy was considering dumping him, wondering whether to keep him on as her plaything or not, he was worrying about his future. He seemed to be so frightened of being left alone, without a woman, a wet pussy to screw. The bastard had given no thought for me when he'd left me alone and desperate.

'Come round tomorrow morning, Jim, and we'll talk about it,' I suggested, praying that Stephen would turn up as arranged. 'Say, eleven o'clock – OK?'

'Tomorrow morning, about eleven – OK, I'll be there.'

'I have to go now, Jim.'

'OK – and thanks, Sue.'

The plan was coming together nicely, I reflected as I dialled Wendy's number, praying that she'd answer the phone, rather than Stephen. If I could get her to call round at about eleven-thirty, she'd discover not only her husband fucking me, but also her lover! But would the men agree? Yes, of course the cheating, two-timing bastards would agree to fuck me!

'Wendy, it's Sue – how are you?' I trilled as she answered the phone.

'So so,' she sighed. 'How did you get on with Jim the other evening? Did he stay the night?'

'Yes, he did. We had a marvellous evening, we really did! He's going to come back, and we're making a fresh start together. Isn't that good news?'

'Er . . . yes, it is,' she agreed flatly. 'I'm pleased for you.'

'You sound down, Wendy. Is everything all right?'

'Yes, yes. I'm just tired, that's all.'

'Can you come round tomorrow morning?'

'No, I can't. I've got a meeting, I'm afraid.'

'Cancel it.'

'I can't do that.'

'Listen, I need to talk to you about the things your husband gets up to behind your back. He . . .'

'Stephen? But, you don't know him.'

'Yes, I do know him. Look, I can't say too much over the phone, but I know what he gets up to. Come round at eleven-thirty in the morning, and I'll tell you all I know.'

'Tell me now.'

'No, I can't.'

'It had better be good, Sue. I'm not cancelling my meeting if . . .'

'It'll be good, I promise you, Wendy!'

'How do you know my husband, anyway? And more to the point, *what* do you know about him?'

'His office is upstairs, isn't it? Lined with books, a huge desk in the centre of the room . . . I know who he's seeing behind your back, she told me everything about your house, about Stephen . . . I also know that *you've* been seeing someone, although I don't know who.'

'What *are* you on about? I'm not seeing anyone, and I'm sure Stephen isn't!'

'Come here tomorrow, and all will be revealed.'

'Yes, I think I'd better!'

'Get here at eleven-thirty. And don't tell Stephen.'

'All right. But I think you've got it all wrong!'

'We'll see. Bye for now, Wendy.'

As I replaced the receiver, the front doorbell rang. No peace for the wicked! What with married couples, separated couples, lesbian women . . . The thought struck me that they might all band together and come for me! A lynch-mob!

Tracy stood on the doorstep wearing a flimsy, see-through summer dress. Smiling as she stepped into the hall, she had a strange look in her eye. What had she discovered about me now? I wondered, following her into the kitchen. What was she up to?

'We need to talk, Sue,' she said softly as she sat at the table. 'I want to help you.'

'Help me?' I queried.

'Yes. As I told you, I know what you're up to, and I think you need help. I also know about the notes you've been receiving.'

'I don't care what you do or don't know,' I shot back gazing into her big, green eyes. 'I don't need help!'

My stomach somersaulting, I lowered my eyes to her rounded breasts, her long nipples, all clearly visible through the thin material of her blue dress. She was a beautiful woman, and I found myself wanting her – craving her mound, her pussy lips, so delicately seasoned with dark curls. She was sensual, feminine, and I pictured her naked, standing over me, her honeypot decanting its nectar over my face.

'You *do* need help, Sue,' she persisted. Images of her open cunt filling my mind, I began to wonder whether she was right!

'Listen, Trace. You know what I've been up to, I'll give you that – but you don't know why. What Jim did to me . . . He nearly destroyed me! Many times when I was sitting alone, I contemplated suicide. What I've been doing has . . . It's helped me, brought me out of that awful trough of depression. I have a new life now. I have a new and exciting . . .'

'That's as maybe, but you can't go around drowning people's marriages in adultery just to keep your own head above water!'

'Then how do I stop myself from slipping back into the mire? It's still there, lurking, waiting to suck me back in.'

'I don't know, but I do know that the way you're going, you'll end up in serious trouble!'

She was right, I knew that, but I couldn't stop myself now. It was too late. I'd carved out a new way of life, and I was enjoying every minute of it. Well, almost every minute! The sex I'd had with Jim during our marriage had been good, but the sex I'd discovered since he'd left me was incredible! I couldn't turn my back on that! And there was the money I'd been making – five grand. And the money to be made in the future.

'You're looking for a partner,' Tracy decreed. 'That's what you're doing – subconsciously, you're looking for a partner.'

'Don't talk crap!' I laughed. 'The last thing I want is a bloody partner! Besides, if I did want one, there are several men who'd jump at the chance!'

'Yes, but it's not a man you want, is it? You see, subconsciously . . .'

'Don't go all Freudian on me, Trace! My subconscious has nothing to do with it!'

'But it has! Don't you see, you're wrecking marriage after marriage because you're looking for a partner?'

'What are you, a bloody psychologist? Of course I'm not looking for a partner! Anyway, what do you mean, *it's not a man* I want?'

'Exactly what I say – you *don't* want a man. A man betrayed you, let you down terribly, and you'll never get that out of your subconscious. Like me, it's a woman you want. Admit it to yourself, be honest with yourself, Sue – you're a lesbian.'

Lesbian. God, the word haunted me. I'd had three lesbian encounters. Sharon, who'd initiated me in the fine art of lesbian sex, Sandy, who, with her husband, had brought me amazing sexual pleasure . . . And Tracy who'd . . . God knows what *she'd* done to me! Apart from the sex, she'd woken something, stirred something deep within my mind – my subconscious. *Bloody word!*

The sex with Tracy had been incredible, yes, but it went deeper than that. There'd been something more than mere physical pleasure, something almost spiritual. Was that what I wanted? Was she right? I didn't know what I did or didn't want. She was right about men, though. All I wanted from them was sex, and more sex – before I dumped them!

Leaning back on the sink, I surveyed Tracy, her curves, her full mouth, her long eyelashes. She was soft, sensual, warm – feminine. Was that what I wanted? I wondered as she stood up and walked over to me. Brushing my long, blonde hair away from my face, she kissed my mouth, caressing my tongue with hers. I melted, wrapping my arms around her to steady myself as my legs sagged and my stomach churned exquisitely.

Her hands wandered, feeling my body, stroking, exploring my breasts, her fingers pinching my nipples. Moving down over my stomach, she lifted my suede skirt and cupped my wet pussy lips in her palm. I felt dizzy with sex, intoxicated with lesbian lust, as her finger slipped into the wet heat of my young vagina.

'I love you,' she breathed in my ear. 'I want you.' I said nothing as she kissed my neck, licking me there, sending tingles of sex up my spine. Opening my blouse, she took my nipple into her hot mouth and gently sucked. I gazed down at her, her full lips engulfing my areola as her tongue swept over my sensitive breast bud. Breathing heavily, I closed my eyes as she slipped my blouse off my shoulders and squeezed each breast in turn. Her intruding finger still exploring the inner flesh of my spasming cunt, she licked my breasts, wetting them with her saliva, stiffening my nipples until they ached for relief.

Standing upright, she slipped out of her dress and stood naked before me. Since she was wearing no panties or bra, I knew that she'd planned my seduction. The thought excited me, and I smiled sweetly as I admired her nakedness. Her breasts were full, well-rounded, topped with long, brown nipples – erect, hard. Noticing my appreciative gaze, she moved towards me, cupping her breasts, pressing her nipples to mine. Our teats caressing, she tugged my skirt down and ran her hands down my spine and over my buttocks, sending thrilling sensations through my quivering womb as she ran her wet finger up and down my dark crease.

She was in control, leading me into yet another lesbian encounter. All I could do was stand there, quivering, trembling with lust as she moved down and licked the smooth skin of my belly, explored my navel with the tip of her wet tongue.

Leaning back on the sink with my feet wide apart, I threw my head back and gasped as she neared my naked mound, my shaved pussy lips. Her breath was hot, stimulating, as she clutched the back of my thighs and licked the soft skin just above my crack. The wild sensations of sex were incredible as she moved down and sucked my swollen outer lip into her hot mouth. *Was this heaven?*

I wanted her deep inside me, her tongue licking the wet walls of my vagina, tasting my cervix, drinking the life-juice as it flowed from my inner fountainhead. I wanted her very being inside my womb.

My head lolling forward, I looked down between my breasts at my lesbian lover, her chestnut hair parted in the middle, her full mouth engulfing my pouting cunt lips. Licking either side of my sex valley, her eyes closed, I knew that she was lost in her lust – lost in her love. This was what I desperately wanted – didn't want.

Holding her head, I gyrated my hips, moving my wet slit over her hot mouth, her inquisitive tongue. I wanted my clitoris in her mouth, pulsating in orgasm – her fingers inside my cunt, massaging my inner flesh.

A man or a woman? I pondered – which did I really want? A penis – long, hard, throbbing, pumping sperm deep into my cunt, was wonderful. But a girl's feminine curves, her firm breasts, her long nipples, her soft pussy lips, her wet vagina, her clitoris pulsating in my mouth, her cunt decanting girl-come over my tongue . . . Both? Perhaps I should enjoy both sexes, share my body with both men and women?

'Don't do it any more,' Tracy breathed as she lapped up my slippery, cuntal juices.

'Don't do what?' I gasped as her tongue snaked around the entrance to my tightening vaginal sheath, tentatively entering me and withdrawing.

'Go with all those men,' she replied.

'Why not?'

'I want you all for myself. Please, promise me that you won't be unfaithful to me, Sue. I want to live with you – I want us to be a couple.'

Unfaithful? God, was she serious? Did she really want a permanent relationship with me? A couple? What, live as man and wife? Wife and wife? *What would the neighbours say*? Well, what neighbours I had left after my escapades!

She looked up at me, half smiling as she parted my swelling labia, opening my inner folds, unveiling my very femininity. 'Well?' she murmured as she licked my wet, glistening flesh. *Well, what?* I thought. Was this a proposition? 'Do you love me?' she asked.

Love? What was love? Was it sex, sexual fulfilment? Lust was love, love was lust – what was the difference? But I didn't want to talk, to discuss love – I wanted to come, to feel my clitoris swelling in her hot mouth, her tongue sweeping over its sensitive tip, bringing out my desperately needed orgasm.

'Well?' she repeated, expectation in her exquisite jade eyes as she looked up between the swell of my breasts.

'I . . . I don't know what love is,' I smiled, stroking her hair. 'I'd thought I loved Jim but . . . I don't know what love is.'

'This is love,' she breathed, pushing two fingers deep into my wet cunt as she licked my glistening sex groove.

'This is sex, Tracy,' I sighed as powerful sensations rocked my womb.

'No, this is love,' she insisted. 'I love you, Sue.'

Throwing my head back, I parted my feet and jutted my hips forward, offering her my open body as she licked around my cumbud. Love, lust, cold sex, I didn't care – all I wanted was more! Her fingers exploring the hot depths of my spasming cunt, her tongue winding its way around my pulsating clitoris, I shuddered as my climax erupted, sweeping me off my feet, engulfing my mind.

My head lolling, my eyes rolling as I gasped for breath, I clung to her, forcing my open crack hard against her face, her full lips, as she sucked my girl-spot into her mouth and swallowed my climax. Licking my sex groove, lapping up my juices, snaking her tongue round my clitoris, she took me to one explosive peak after another. Barely able to stand, my head dizzy, I was swimming in a swirling sea of lesbian-induced orgasm.

Again, my clitoris swelled, taking me to yet another high, lifting my soul from my quivering body. 'Enough!' I cried as she thrust another finger into the hot depths of my yawning chasm. 'No more!' But she only continued her torturing pleasuring, sucking my pulsating bud into her mouth, flicking her tongue over the swollen tip as she finger-fucked my pussy-hole.

Finally pulling away, I crumpled to the floor, my body trembling uncontrollably, my cunt almost steaming, inflamed with sex, dripping with my sticky come. 'You liked that?' she breathed, taking my breast in her hand as I lay on my back, gasping.

'Yes . . . yes, it . . .'

'More?' she smiled, leaning over and licking my navel.

'No, not yet,' I sighed, trying to calm myself, to quiet my quivering body.

As I lay there, Tracy's tongue exploring every inch of my perspiring flesh, words drifted through my mind. Words that I didn't want to understand, words that I didn't want. Love, lesbian, female . . . My mind torn, I shuddered as she licked the length of my creamy slit, wetting me there with her warm saliva.

Trying to imagine myself in a lesbian relationship, living with Tracy as wife and wife, neighbours' fingers pointing, I realized that I wasn't thinking about my own needs – what *I* really wanted. What other people would or wouldn't say or do didn't come into it.

'I need to think, Tracy,' I said softly as she opened my swollen pussy lips and licked around my clitoris.

'Think about what?' she asked, slipping her slender fingers into my drenched vaginal sheath, tightening my muscles, inducing my slippery juices to flow.

'About . . . Ah, that's nice! About us, I suppose.'

'What is there to think about?'

'Everything! You talk of love, lesbian love, and I don't know . . .'

'What do words mean? *Lesbian* is just a word.'

'It means a great deal to me! I'm heterosexual, Tracy!'

'Are you? How can you say that?'

'I . . . I know what I am. Just because I've enjoyed sex with you . . . I'm heterosexual, Trace!'

I wasn't convincing myself – or her.

'You don't want me to come in your mouth, then? You don't want to love me, lick me, lick my pussy to orgasm?'

'Yes, no . . . I don't know *what* I want!'

Pushing her aside, I climbed to my feet and tottered to the table. My naked body turned me on – knowing that Tracy was a lesbian, that she was looking at my breasts, my nipples, my smooth cunt lips, my open slit, excited me. I *did* want her to come in my mouth, to pour her slippery, female juices into my mouth as I sucked an orgasm from her pulsating clitoris. But I was torn between . . . between what? Male and female.

'I have to get ready to go out,' I sighed as she stood behind me and stroked my hair, caressed my taut buttocks.

'Where are you going?'

'To see someone.'

'To destroy another marriage, you mean?' she asked sympathetically, as if she knew more about me, about my inner thoughts, than I knew myself.

'No, no . . . I have to go out to see someone, that's all.'

'Then I'll wait here for you,' she smiled, slipping into her dress.

'No, you can't . . .'

'All right, I'll go home and get some things, and then I'll come back.'

'But, Tracy . . .'

Watching her leave, I tried to call out, to tell her that I didn't want her to come back – but the words wouldn't come. Perhaps I *did* want her to come back? Perhaps, deep inside, I *did* want a permanent relationship with her?

But no, I couldn't allow myself to weaken. She would stop me destroying marriages, try to control me, ruin my plans – my plans of revenge. I'd have to consider her, her wants and needs – consult her as to whether or not we should do this or that. Marriage stifles, suffocates!

I was determined! No one would stop me, no one was going to get in my way! Not even Tracy – and her beautiful pussy!

Chapter Fourteen

After taking a shower and slipping back into my scarlet microskirt, I was ready to be wined, dined and, no doubt, screwed at Tom's and Sandy's. But I was still in two minds about Tracy, her words of lesbian love, and what the future held. At least there were no complications where Tom and Sandy were concerned. There were no words of love – only sex!

Did I need a permanent partner? I asked myself. If so, who? Jim would find himself without a woman after Wendy discovered him and her husband screwing me. But, whether he was eligible or not, I didn't want Jim back. Craig would find himself alone once Kirsty discovered his adulterous escapade with me, which I'd yet to plan. Poor Craig, he would have been a good catch, but for his cheating ways!

Tony? No, I didn't want anything from Tony – other than my bloody washing machine fixed! And as for Derek's idea of moving in with me – that was the last thing I wanted! Mind you, he was pretty good with his leather belt! Then there was Stephen. He was good-looking, wealthy, but he wasn't for me, either.

I didn't want a permanent relationship with a man – any man! Marriage suffocates the individual! Perhaps Tracy was right? I mused as I slipped through the hole in the hedge. Perhaps I *did* want a woman? I realized that I needed someone to share my life, my body with. Someone special – but not someone living with me, sharing my house, my secrets.

But, right now, I had Tom and Sandy on my mind. Was it

possible to divide them? I'd give it my best shot, I decided. Better to have tried and failed than not tried at all!

Sandy wasn't around when I stepped through the back door into the kitchen to find Tom, completely naked, standing by the sink. 'She's popped out for some more wine,' he explained, smiling at me as he poured me an extremely large gin and tonic. 'She shouldn't be too long. Come through to the lounge.'

'Tom, may I ask you something?' I said softly as I followed him into the lounge and sat in an armchair, gazing at his thick, hard penis, his heavily laden balls.

'Depends what it is,' he smiled, all too aware of my admiring gaze.

'I enjoyed my time with you the other night and . . . I realize that you've got plans for me this evening – you and Sandy. But it's *you* I want to be with, Tom – not your wife.'

'Sandy and I always do things together, that's the way we like it.'

'Yes, I know, but . . . Look, why not come and see me some evenings when she's working at the pub? Surely we can have some sexy fun together, just the two of us?'

'We have a golden rule, Sue. Sandy and I agreed long ago that we'd never lie to each other. If I have another woman, then I tell her about it and, hopefully, the three of us have some fun together. If she finds herself another man, from the pub or wherever, she tells me about it and, again, the three of us . . .'

'You join in with another man and your wife?'

'Why not? Usually, I just watch – but sometimes I join in. There's nothing I like more than watching Sandy being used and abused by another man!'

It was going to be impossible to break up this weird relationship! But, there again, if they had a golden rule, and Tom broke that rule . . . The only way to achieve my goal was to lure Tom to my place and have Sandy find out about our forbidden meetings – meetings that excluded her. What with me hinting that we'd been having secret sex sessions for months, I'd really upset the applecart!

'This golden rule, Tom – what if she caught you breaking it? What would happen if she found out that you'd been secretly enjoying my young body, keeping me for yourself?'

'God knows! She'd go mad, I suppose.'

'Would she divorce you?'

'Why are you asking all this?'

'Because I really enjoyed our time together – and I get lonely and I want you to come and visit me now and then. If Sandy were to find out, I want to know what the consequences would be.'

'Sandy did catch me once. Many years ago . . . I won't go into the details, but that's why we have this rule. We both enjoy sex with other people, it's fun, and the best way to do that, and remain faithful to each other, if I can put it that way, is to stick to the golden rule.'

Remain faithful?

'So, she would leave you, divorce you if you . . .'

'Yes, and I'd do the same if I found out that she'd been seeing someone behind *my* back.'

'So, you're saying that you don't want to come and spend the odd evening with me?'

'It's not that I don't *want* to. I . . . I'd have to tell Sandy about it, and she'd . . .'

'And she'd want to join in. I don't want that, Tom, so we'd better forget the idea.'

'What? You're staying this evening, aren't you?'

'Yes, but this will be the last time. I wouldn't mind all three of us having some sexy fun once in a while, but if I can't have you to myself sometimes, then we might as well forget the whole thing. Think me a spoilt bitch, if you like, but I want you, your lovely cock, all to myself.'

Frowning as he stood with his back to the mantlepiece, his penis like a poker, he sipped his drink, deep in thought. He was in two minds, I could see that. My young, naked body, my fresh, tight pussy-hole, all to himself, whenever he wanted it – or nothing. Surely, he couldn't refuse?

'Anyway, Sandy would never find out if you were to visit me on the odd occasion,' I added, smiling at him. 'I mean, she works most evenings, so there's no way she'd know. But, if you don't want me . . .'

'As I said, it's not that I don't *want* you, Sue! Look, I'll think about it. Anyway, I think she's back, so let's change the subject.'

Sandy entered the lounge wearing a long coat, which I thought odd, as the evening was hotter than ever. But I soon discovered why she'd covered herself up – she was wearing a red leather catsuit! Although in her forties, she had a damned good body, and the catsuit accentuated her feminine curves beautifully. My pussy already juicing up, I couldn't wait to get the meal over with and start the fun.

'I'm glad you could make it,' she smiled as Tom passed her a drink. 'The dining room's all set, so if you'll allow Tom to slip your clothes off, we'll go through.'

'What, we're eating naked?' I asked somewhat naively, eyeing Tom's erect penis as he moved towards me.

'You'll see!' she laughed. 'We have a surprise for you. Tom, will you do the honours?'

Taking my hand, Tom gently pulled me to my feet. Unbuttoning my blouse, he slipped it off my shoulders and smiled appreciatively at my breasts, my already erect nipples. 'And now for your skirt,' he murmured, tugging it down to reveal my hairless pussy to Sandy's wide eyes.

Taking my arm, Sandy led me from the lounge into the dining room and stood me before a large table. 'Lie on the table,' she instructed. 'And we'll get started.'

'But, I thought we were eating first?' I demurred, wondering why the table wasn't laid.

'We are, in a few minutes,' she replied mysteriously. 'Tom, I'll go and organize the food while you prepare Sue for the sex-banquet.'

When Sandy had left the room, Tom lifted me onto the table and spread my limbs. I didn't protest, thinking that they were going to eat my pussy for starters. But when he secured my wrists and ankles to the table legs with handcuffs, I became apprehensive and asked him what he was up to.

'You're going to enjoy this,' he grinned, running a finger up my wet slit. 'You'll see what we have planned for you in a minute,' he added as Sandy wheeled the food in on a trolley.

'Starters,' she smiled, placing two pineapple rings over my elongated nipples. 'You like bananas, Sue?' she asked, passing Tom the fruit.

As Tom pressed two or three bananas into my wet vaginal sheath, Sandy placed a cherry in my navel and poured cream over my breasts. The cooling sensation as the cream ran over my nipples and down my breasts was wonderful – but I hadn't expected to play the role of a plate! With Tom eating the bananas from my bloated pussy and Sandy nibbling the pineapple rings from my breasts and lapping up the cream, I knew that I was really going to enjoy this weird and wonderful dinner party!

'Pass me the cream please, Sandy,' Tom instructed as he finished off the bananas. Opening my pussy lips wide, he poured the cold delicacy over my inner flesh, cooling my hard clitoris. Taking a handful of cherries, Sandy stood next to her husband and, one by one, popped them into my creamy cunt.

'Drink, Sandy?' Tom asked, popping the cork from a bottle of wine.

'Mmm, thanks,' she replied, forcing more cherries into my bloated vaginal sheath.

The ice-cold wine caused my heart to leap as Tom emptied the entire bottle over my naked body. 'God, that's cold!' I gasped as Sandy lapped up the pool of wine from my navel, her fingers pushing the last cherry deep into my packed cunt. Both lapping the wine up, their tongues tantalizing every inch of my trembling body, they were obviously enjoying their kinky dinner party. But I was hungry and thirsty, too.

'Don't I get anything to eat or drink?' I panted as Tom tongued my wet slit.

'Oh, of course you do!' he smiled, climbing onto the table and kneeling astride my head. 'There, how's this for starters?' he asked, lowering his huge balls over my mouth as Sandy covered his penis with cream.

Lifting my head and lapping up the cream as it trickled down his hard shaft and over his hairy balls, I noticed Sandy slipping out of her catsuit. I knew that I'd have to eat my food from her pussy as part of their weird game. The mere thought tightened my cunt muscles, crushing the cherries.

'I'll give you a little wank in a minute, Tom,' Sandy promised as she stood by the table, naked, and thrust four bananas deep into her accommodating fruit bowl. Climbing onto the table, her knees either side of my head, she grinned at me as I gazed at the slimy phalluses protruding between her swollen cunny lips. 'Eat your food!' she ordered, lowering her body as Tom moved aside.

Hot, creamy, sticky, the bananas tasted delicious. Sucking them from her hot hole, I ate them all, licking her slippery cunt lips clean as I swallowed the last mouthful. Taking the cream, Tom poured a good quantity over Sandy's huge breasts. Coursing its way over her belly, it ran down her sex groove and dripped into my mouth, mingling with her sex-cream.

'Lick me clean!' Sandy instructed me as she lowered her dripping pussy over my mouth. 'And then you can drink from Tom's knob.' As I licked Sandy, Tom pushed his purple knob between our hungry orifices. Grabbing his organ by the base, he slipped his knob between Sandy's wet inner folds as I tongued his solid shaft. Sinking his entire length into his wife's body, his balls came to rest over my mouth and I kissed and nibbled them, gazing at the wonderful sight of his penis embedded deep inside his wife's cunny-hole.

His shaft gliding in and out of her hot hole, I felt my own cunt quiver, gripping the cherries, squeezing them out as my clitoris hardened. Desperate for Tom's sperm, I pushed my tongue out, allowing his hairy balls to slap against it as he thrust in and out of Sandy's yawning chasm. His shaft creamy, glistening with his wife's come, I opened my mouth wide as his knob slipped from her hole and spurted its offering over her gaping cunt. Rubbing between her pouting pussy lips, he massaged the sperm from his knob as I lapped it up, swallowing every drop as it dripped into my mouth.

Lowering her cunt, Sandy told me to lick her clean. Following her instructions as Tom opened her pussy lips to reveal her pinken folds, I wondered what the next course would be, and from where I'd have to eat it! As I finished cleaning my hostess, mouthing and sucking her rubicund sex-flesh, she climbed from the table, followed by Tom, and took something from the trolley.

I couldn't see what they were up to, but I was certain that Tom was easing something into his wife's ravenous pussy. As she resumed her position over my face and lowered her gaping crack over my mouth, I speculated on what delights could be hidden inside her wet pouch. I waited in anticipation as she squeezed her cunny muscles. Then, her inner petals opening like some exotic flower, I was presented with a small, *cordon bleu* potato.

'There are plenty more where that came from!' she giggled, squeezing her muscles again and popping another bechamel potato into my mouth. Next, she gave birth to a baby carrot, before another creamy potato was delivered from her pinken petals. On and on the vegetables emerged from her mobile oven, and I ate until she was empty.

Again, she slipped off the banqueting table for Tom to push more delicacies between her oily pussy lips. Back for the third course, she squatted over my face, contracting her cunt to expel a sausage into my mouth. Toad-in-the-hole! To my amazement, another sausage emerged, and then another.

'Still hungry?' she asked as Tom moved behind her and deftly slipped something into her empty love-tube. I nodded, gazing up at her as I licked my lips. 'Then here comes the next course,' she grinned, bearing down and pushing half an apricot from her hot hole. Sucking on the succulent fruit, I quivered as Tom mouthed between my pussy lips, eating the hot cherries from my burning cunt and licking me clean.

As Sandy manoeuvred her hips, aligning her stiffening clitoris with my mouth, Tom swept his tongue over my organic cherry. Sandy's marinade poured from her honeypot, drenching my face as I sucked and mouthed on her blossoming bud.

'That's it!' she whimpered. 'That's it, keep . . . Ah, yes!' My own clitoris near to orgasm, I licked and sucked between Sandy's open pussy lips until we both shuddered in our mutual coming. Expertly, Tom lifted me to my incredible orgasmic peak, stretching my inner labia wide open to expose the full length of my pulsating nodule to his caressing tongue.

'My cunt!' Sandy cried. 'Put your tongue inside my . . .' As she positioned her yearning hotpot over my hungry mouth, I pushed my tongue out and stirred, lapping the cream from her inner flesh. Writhing, grinding the open centre of her quivering body against my face, I thought her multiple orgasm would never end. My own clitoris still throbbing in response to Tom's oral attention, I sensed my juices pouring from my cunt, bathing the delicate crease between my buttocks.

Finally coming to rest, Sandy and I breathed heavily, allowing our bodies to recover, our cunt lips, our spent clitorises, to contract. In my sexual intoxication, I was vaguely aware of Tom, his fingers opening my vaginal lips, exposing the entrance to my womb.

'You'll enjoy this,' he whispered as he pushed something into my pinken hole. Suddenly, my cunt opened, filling with something cold. 'It's cream,' he grinned, gazing into my eyes for my reaction as Sandy climbed from the table. Gripping the aerosol can, the nozzle buried in my cunt, he filled me to the brim with cold cream. I could sense my vaginal sheath expanding as the cream bloated me and brimmed over, running down between my buttocks.

'And now for the other filling,' Tom announced gleefully, pushing the nozzle between my buttocks.

'No!' I cried as the aerosol hissed and my bowels ballooned.

'Nice?' he asked, holding my gaze steadfastly.

'Please, that's enough!' I begged as Sandy held my buttocks wide apart and Tom pushed the nozzle past my defeated muscles.

My anal tube dilating, my cunt quivering, I closed my eyes and allowed myself to drift in the delicious sensations. My entire being seemed to float as my pelvic cavity ballooned and the cream cooled my burning body. My mind brimming with carnality as a man and a woman worked between my thighs, I knew that I had become obsessed with sex, the sensations, the pleasure, the incredible orgasms. But still I didn't know what I wanted – male or female. I wanted only sex.

Tom's knob stabbed at my bottom-hole as Sandy parted my buttocks further. Releasing my muscles, I allowed his huge shaft to push its way deep into my creamy bowels. 'You're very cold,' he murmured as his heavy balls brushed my buttocks. 'I'll warm you up.'

His thrusting jolting my young body as Sandy sucked my

clitoris into her hungry mouth, I could barely believe the heavenly sensations emanating from deep within my pelvis. My cunt spewing out cold cream, lubricating Tom's shaft as it emerged and drove deep into my anal tube again and again, I sensed the birth of another orgasm deep within my contracting womb.

Sandy's fingers delved into my cunt, massaging, caressing, as she continued to suck and lick my clitoris as her husband pinched my nipples, bringing new sensations, adding to the incredible pleasure coursing its way through my entire body.

'Fuck me!' I cried through my sexual haze as Sandy's hand stroked my face, her fingers outlining my gasping mouth. 'Harder, Tom!' I ordered as she pushed her fingers into my mouth. Sucking, licking her fingers, her hand, as she sucked the orgasm from my clitoris, I sensed Tom's huge shaft swell, his knob pulsate as he gasped.

'Here it comes!' he cried, ramming my tethered body with his rock-hard organ. Mingling with the cream, his sperm pumped deep into my bowels as he thrust on and on. My climax exploded in Sandy's hot mouth as she fingered my vagina, expelling my girl-juice, rocketing my mind to dizzy heights of perverted sex.

'Pump me full of come!' I heard myself cry as Tom squeezed my nipples and continued to ram his weapon deep into my bum-hole. Arching my back, pulling on the handcuffs, I could do nothing to end the unbelievable pleasure a man and his wife were bringing me. They seemed to be inside my whole body, caressing, waking sleeping nerve endings, causing every muscle in my body to spasm with sex.

My legs spread wide, my cunt gaping, my bowels distended by an orgasming male organ, my clitoris coming in a woman's mouth, I gave my very soul to the carnal couple. I could feel Satan, close – coaxing, goading, driving us to the very limit of sexual perversion.

My body suddenly abandoned, I lay there, drifting in the welcoming warmth of sexual satisfaction. Murmuring voices floated through my mind as my eyes rolled and my head lolled. Distant, echoing voices breathing incoherent words of lust. Was I dead? I wondered as visions of Satan loomed.

Sex. Your body is for sex. More sex. Open your cunt to me. Give me your womb. Sex. Give me your very soul.

There were hands wandering, fingers fingering, tongues tonguing, mouths mouthing every inch of my perspiring body. It felt as if my very being was my cunt. No head, no arms, no legs, no torso. My body – perhaps even my soul? – centred on my cunt.

'Sue! Sue, are you all right?' someone called through the darkness. 'Sue! Say something!' Opening my eyes, I found myself gazing up at Tom and Sandy. 'Are you all right?' Sandy asked, stroking my forehead.

'Yes, I think so,' I whispered as Tom released the handcuffs and sat me up.

'We thought you were dead!' Tom laughed as he steadied my sagging body.

'So did I!' I gasped as my senses returned. 'Christ, what the hell did you do to me?'

'Brought you the best orgasm you've ever experienced,' Sandy smiled. 'I've never seen anyone come the way you did!'

'Help me. I need to get off the table,' I whimpered, my limbs aching, my cunt burning.

'Don't you want some more?' Tom asked, lying me down and rolling me onto my stomach.

'Christ, no!' I protested as they stretched my arms across the table and cuffed my wrists to the table legs.

'Of course you want more!' Sandy cried as she spread my legs and cuffed my ankles.

I think it was a leather belt that cracked loudly as it lashed my buttocks. Whatever it was, goaded by Sandy, Tom was about to give me the thrashing of my life. 'Harder, Tom!' she cried as he brought the belt down again.

'Please, no!' I screamed.

'Yes!' Sandy contended, seemingly in the grip of the devil.

Why Tom was thrashing me with a vengeance, I didn't know, but the sensations, the pain, the burning, quickly fused into immense pleasure and I sensed my clitoris swelling, throbbing, as I neared my climax. Dizzy, I lifted my head and opened my eyes to see Sandy sitting on the table, her open vaginal lips only inches from my mouth. Moving closer, she pressed her open crack against my face, ordering me to lick as my buttocks tensed with the hardest lash yet.

Pushing my tongue out, I licked the length of her drenched sex groove, drinking her juices as they spilled from her inner nectaries. Again, I felt my mind leave my body as my orgasm welled from my inner depths and erupted in an explosion of pure lust.

'Harder, Tom!' Sandy gasped. 'Give her the thrashing she deserves!' It *was* a leather belt, I was sure as it cracked loudly across my burning flesh, affording me a heady cocktail of incredible pain and sexual pleasure.

Intoxicated, floundering in a pool of sex, I lapped and tongued Sandy's cunt, stiffening her clitoris until she opened her legs as wide as she could and forced her open groove into my mouth. 'Coming!' she cried as she gyrated her hips, rhythmically working her clitoris against my probing tongue. 'Suck . . . suck it . . . Coming!'

Her wailing filling the house, she ejected a torrent of come, drenching my face as she writhed in her sexual heaven. With Tom still lashing my burning buttocks and his wife forcing her open cunt into my mouth, my own clitoris erupted yet again, taking me to a frightening new level of sexual consciousness.

Aware that I was riding the crest of my climax, Tom discarded the belt and groped beneath my bottom-hole, locating my pouting cunt lips and expertly massaging my clitoris. Waves of sex rushed through my tethered body, reaching out to the very extremities of my mind.

Gasping through mouthfuls of Sandy's cunt-flesh for Tom to stop, I thought that I was about to pass out. In the grip of a massive multiple orgasm, I fell limp, trembling as the electrifying ripples of sex bathed my entire body. Never had I known an orgasm of such strength, such duration. I'd given my soul to Satan, I was sure.

Finally relinquishing my throbbing clitoris as Sandy climbed from the table, Tom released me. Carrying me to the lounge, he placed my trembling, semi-conscious body on the sofa and allowed me to rest. Opening my eyes, I watched in amazement as Tom instructed Sandy to stand with her feet wide apart and touch her toes. Was there no stopping this bizarre couple? I wondered as I watched his solid shaft sink into her bottom-hole. No, there was no stopping them!

Slowly recovering from my ordeal, I watched Tom thrust into his wife's bottom-hole, gripping her hips and taking her from behind like a man possessed. His shaft finally withdrawing, he massaged his knob, spraying his sperm over her buttocks until he'd drained his huge balls and collapsed on the floor, entwined in Sandy's arms.

'I'm going now,' I murmured as I sat up, my head still dizzy with sex.

'So soon?' Sandy asked as Tom lapped up the sperm from her buttocks.

'Yes, so soon,' I echoed as I grabbed my clothes.

'You'll come again?' Tom called as I left the room.

God forbid!

Creeping through the hedge, clutching my clothes, like a thief in the night, I made my way across the garden and slipped into my house – aching, cream and sperm oozing from my holes and running down my inner thighs. Never had I had so much perverted sex in one day! Never had I been so fucked, used, whipped . . . I prayed that Tracy wasn't waiting for me as I entered the kitchen. The last thing I needed was her "love"!

Confronting the plain white envelope lying on the table, my heart leapt. Ripping it open, I absorbed the frightening words.

You're nearing the end. Too many ruined relationships, too many broken people around you, dying from the pain of adultery. Your turn is nigh!

Screwing the note up in my hand, I bit my lip. *Dying. The pain of adultery. Your turn is nigh.* I knew in my heart that what I was doing was evil, but I couldn't stop myself. I'd gone too far to turn round and come back. But the dreadful notes? At least they didn't expound on Jim's and Caroline's sex life any more. Wandering into the lounge, I decided to pour myself a stiff drink.

Your turn is nigh.

'Oh, you've decided to come back, then?' Tracy asked accusingly, looking up at my gaping slit from the sofa.

'I *do* live here!' I returned angrily.

'Wrecked another marriage?'

'No, as it happens, I haven't!'

'Failed in your mission, did you?'

'There *was* no mission! Look, Tracy, I've just about had enough of all this! Please, go now and leave me alone.'

'But I thought . . .'

'Please, Tracy! Don't think, just go!'

'What the hell's that stuff running down your legs?'

'Whipping cream, if you must know!'

'I've never known . . . What's that in your hand, not another note?'

'Yes.'

'How many more will there be?'

'How the hell do I know?'

'You definitely need help, Sue!'

'I need to be left alone!'

'You really do need . . .'

As I retreated upstairs to run a bath, leaving Tracy mumbling to herself, I wondered what the hell I was doing. Christ, how many marriages could I destroy before I destroyed myself? If I hadn't already destroyed myself, that was!

Sinking into the hot water, I thought of Jim, remembering our times together, wondering why it had all gone so very wrong. My body had been his, his and mine to share, bringing us both pleasure. But now it was a weapon to lure men and destroy them. The most powerful weapon mankind has ever known! I decided as I cleansed my burning cunt-crack.

Tomorrow morning, at eleven o'clock, I would use my weapon again – and destroy! Stephen and Jim would both fuck me, use me for sex, I was sure. I would stand in the middle of the lounge with Stephen fucking my bottom-hole and Jim thrusting his cock into my hot, tight cunt. And Wendy would arrive at the appointed time and finish with both her adulterous husband and Jim, her lying, cheating lover.

As I lay in the bath, soaking my aching body in the hot, soapy water, my fingers toying between my inflamed pussy lips, Tracy walked in and knelt on the floor. Leaning over the edge of the bath, she smiled sweetly.

'Want me to wash you?' she asked, taking the soap and lathering my breasts. Closing my eyes as she plunged the soap between my legs and massaged the entrance to my underwater cavern, I didn't answer. It was good to have someone wash me, attend my most intimate needs, as Jim used to. Relaxing, I listened to her ramblings as she gently massaged the bar of soap between my floating petals, stiffening my clitoris for the umpteenth time that day.

'I reckon that we'll be good together,' she said softly, parting my legs. 'I've been thinking. Thinking about us, the future, the things we can do together. Without men, and the inherent problems they have, we'll be happy. And you do realize that the notes will stop, don't you?'

Would they? I doubted it very much!

'I'll sell the house, and give Craig half, I suppose, so we'll have plenty of money. Just think, we'll enjoy holidays, the theatre, meals out . . . And we'll have each other, Sue.'

What the hell was it with her? What the hell was it with *me*? Why couldn't I just tell her, in no uncertain terms, to bugger off? My mind reeling with confusion as she massaged my clitoris, I tried to block out her words as she rambled on.

'By the way, I've shaved for you. I know that you'll like me shaved – you'll like my pussy naked, soft, smooth. I'll show you when we go to bed. There, is that nice? You like me massaging you there, inside your pussy? There'll be lots more of this, just you and me, caring for each other, looking after each other's feminine needs. Is that nice? Let me part your pussy lips, like this, and massage inside your beautiful cunny hole.'

As my orgasm approached, Tracy centred her attention on my clitoris, lathering me there, swelling my sex-button until, the hot water gently lapping around my pleasure portal, I cried out, shuddering as her vibrating fingers took me to my climax.

'There, that's nice, isn't it?' she murmured as I trembled and gasped. 'You're a good girl, letting me look after you. You love me masturbating you, don't you? I'll do this every day for you! Every day, I'll make you happy, make you come with my fingers, with my tongue. You'll like that, I know. We'll go to sleep licking between each other's pussy lips. Drift off to sleep sucking on each other's clitties.'

Finally, I relaxed, falling limp as my climax receded, leaving me warm, serene. Tracy's words drifted around me. Her words of love, lesbian sex, our future, wafted somewhere in the mist of my mind. When she left the room, I opened my eyes, more confused now than ever before about my sexual identity.

I was weakening, but I knew that I mustn't. I was falling, tumbling down and down, and there was nothing to grab, nothing to stop myself. Down, down, ever nearer to her web of lesbian lust. I had to stop myself!

Leaping out of the bath, I dried myself quickly and dressed in fresh clothes, wondering where Tracy had got to. Looking into my sex den, I was amazed to see that she'd set steel rings in the ceiling and walls. Heavy chains hung ominously from the rings, awaiting their victim – me. How the hell had she fixed the rings to the walls and ceiling, and why? What was she up to? Surely, loving, caring, gentle Tracy wasn't into bondage? I thought, pulling on the chains hanging from the ceiling. Or perhaps Sharon had returned with her studs and ordered them to prepare the sex den for my next gruelling punishment session?

Whoever the culprit, they'd done me a favour, I knew that! Now, I could have some *real* fun with my male conquests! Perhaps I should arrange for Jim and Stephen to chain me up during the double-fucking session? That would get Wendy knotted!

'Are you there, Sue?' Tracy called up the stairs. Bounding down the stairs to find her wandering into the lounge with a tray of coffee and biscuits, I realized that she was making herself at home. But where did she expect to sleep? In my bed, I supposed! 'I thought you were never coming down,' she smiled, placing the tray on the coffee table.

'Who's done that to the sex den?' I asked as I joined her on the sofa.

'Done what?'

'The chains.'

'I've no idea,' she smiled, passing me my coffee.

So, the young Sharon *had* called round and prepared the room for my next session with her studs. But when would she come back and administer the punishment? Midnight, midday?

Recalling her words, I realized that she could arrive at any time to give me a good thrashing – and a good fucking!

'What are your plans?' I asked Tracy as she made herself comfortable.

'I've already told you, Sue. I'll sell my house, and we'll . . .'

'That's rather rash, don't you think? I mean . . .'

'I've got to sell it, no matter what happens. Craig and I are divorcing, so we have to sell the house.'

'Yes, I suppose you do,' I replied, gazing at her shapely thighs and picturing her shaved pussy lips. 'Well, you said that you'd show me your pussy, so are you going to?'

'Yes, of course I will! After all, I did it for you. It's your pussy too now.'

Lifting her buttocks clear of the sofa, she pulled her short dress up to reveal her knickerless, hairless pussy-crack to my incredulous eyes. Pouting, swollen, smooth, her full outer lips invited my mouth, my tongue, and I couldn't resist leaning over her and parting her legs.

'Lie back and relax,' I ordered her, opening her thighs as I settled on the carpet between her feet. Peeling her soft vaginal lips back, I gazed at her inner folds – pink, wet, glistening, inviting. 'You'd like my tongue inside you, would you?' I teased. She murmured her inevitable reply as I tentatively licked her reddening flesh, breathing in her girl-scent, tasting her love-juices. 'If you want my tongue inside your sweet vagina, then ask me,' I taunted, licking around the entrance to her love-sheath.

She moaned something incomprehensible as I opened her inner flesh wider and peered into her tightening sheath. I would have her beg me to make her come, I decided, ordering her to ask me to push my tongue into her quivering body. Again, she moaned her incoherent words. Teasing the base of her clitoris, I was determined to have her plead for her sexual satisfaction.

'Beg me to fuck you with my tongue!' I ordered harshly.

'Yes . . . yes . . . Do it!' she gasped as I snaked my tongue around her wet entrance again.

'Plead with me! Beg me!' I demanded.

'Yes, please do it!'

'Do what?'

'Please, fuck me with . . . Fuck me with your tongue!' she finally managed to ask.

Opening her hole wide, I slipped my tongue inside, tasting her aphrodisiacal sex-juice, breathing in the heady scent of her open cunt. She squirmed and writhed, gasping as I repeatedly pushed my tongue into her sanctum and withdrew again. Her legs now wide like open scissors, I managed to drive my tongue deeper into her hot, quivering body, seeking out the source of her slippery flow.

'Let me do that!' she breathed, moving my hands aside and taking her fleshy outer lips between her fingers and thumbs. Pulling her womanhood wide open, exposing the stretched, delicate folds of her inner femininity, I thought she was going to split herself open. Never had I seen so deep, so intimately, into another woman's vagina, and I eagerly pressed my mouth against the rubicund flesh, pushing my tongue deep into her trembling body.

'Ah, yes! That's . . . God, that's nice! More, more, don't stop! Please, don't stop!' she cried as I repeatedly swept my tongue up from her open hole and across her swollen cumbud. Dragging her now copious cunt-juices up her valley and over her near-bursting bud, I knew that she was close to her sexual release. To prolong her pleasure, our pleasure, I continued my licking, teasing, tantalizing, now deliberately skirting her engorged bud with every long lick of her yawning crack.

'Please, Sue!' she cried, opening her reddening flesh even further to expose her throbbing clitoris to my darting tongue. 'For God's sake, I'm going to come! Please, make it good, lick my clitoris!' The poor thing deserved my tongue, and I gave it to her, bringing out her long-awaited climax. Writhing and moaning, she pulled on my head, forcing her open vulva into my mouth as she decanted torrents of girl-come over my chin. On and on her amazing climax rolled, shaking her entire body, gripping her in lesbian lust as I caressed her throbbing cherry.

'More! Do it more!' she cried as I was about to pull away. My tongue aching, my face drenched with her sex-juices, I licked and licked until I could barely breathe. Choking, I pulled away and watched as she frigged her clitty with her wet fingertips until she collapsed in a trembling heap.

'God, I love you, Sue! How I love you!'

'You love me bringing you off, you mean!' I giggled.

'No, yes . . . I mean, I love you!' she gasped, her fingers toying with her crimson inner lips as she rolled her head from side to side.

'I'm going to bed,' I said, staggering to my feet.

'No, not yet. I want you, I want to do the same to you.'

'I really can't, Trace! I'm knackered, I really am!'

Taking my hand, she pulled me over her lap and lifted my skirt, baring my buttocks. 'You will not go to bed yet!' she admonished, slapping my already stinging orbs as hard as she could. 'You will do as you are told!' she shrieked, spanking me harder and harder.

After what must have been fifty or so good slaps, she parted my buttocks, stretching them wide open and running her finger up and down my crease. Toying with my small brown hole, she pushed her finger just inside, bringing me wonderful sensations of crude, yet tender, female sex. Further she pushed her finger into my bowels, twisting, turning, thrusting, waking the secret nerve endings there until my clitoris cried out for her mouth, her tongue.

'Make me come! Please, make me come now!' I begged as she groped between my thighs with her free hand, thrusting her fingers deep into my aching cunt. 'My clit!' I cried. 'Please, it's coming, rub my clit!' At last, she located my clitoris and massaged it to a wonderful orgasm. My body shaking as she caressed me there, still fingering my bottom-hole, I felt faint with sexual euphoria. Again and again, waves of orgasm crashed over my trembling body, taking me higher and higher, until I thought that I'd remain forever in my sexual heaven.

Finally releasing me, she stroked my buttocks, circling her loving fingers around my small hole as I closed my eyes. 'There,' she whispered. 'That was nice, wasn't it? You can have some more later, if you're a good little girl.'

The encompassing sensations from her caressing fingers calmed my inner being, my very soul. As I lay contentedly across her lap, my naked buttocks bared to her loving caress, I fell into a deep sleep – serene, and satisfied as never before.

Chapter Fifteen

I woke in my bed with Tracy beside me, naked. How she'd managed to get me up the stairs was beyond me. I'd been so tired, mentally and physically zapped, that I remembered nothing about going to bed the night before.

Sinking my elbow into my pillow, I rested my head on my hand and gazed at her. Sleeping deeply, the quilt pushed down to reveal her full breasts, her long, succulent nipples ensconced by her dark brown areolae, I realized that I felt something for her. Something more than just sex – something deep. Was it love? I wondered. I didn't know.

As I lay there, dreamily gazing at her, my lesbian partner, I slipped my hand under the quilt and ran my finger up and down her creamy crack, thinking of the day ahead. At eleven o'clock Stephen and Jim would arrive, both expecting sex, rampant sex. But not expecting to share my body between them! I just hoped that they'd succumb to my alluring pussy, and both use me to satisfy their debased male desires.

I prayed that Wendy would turn up at eleven-thirty, as I'd sinfully arranged, and walk in on the lewd tableau – the vile act of my double-fucking. If she didn't, then I'd just have to plan the great event for another day. If she did, then all hell would be let loose! Satan himself would be let loose – if he wasn't already!

Turning my thoughts to the sex den as I slipped my finger deep into Tracy's hot vaginal sheath, I remembered the steel rings and the chains. When was that bitch, Sharon, planning to come back with her young studs to punish me, use me, defile me? I wondered. Not in the middle of my momentous morning fucking session, I prayed!

Tracy stirred and let out a deep moan as I pulled my finger from her tight hole and massaged her love juices into her swelling cherry. I needed her clitoris in my mouth, my clitoris in her mouth, both sucking out our orgasms, expressing our lesbian love for each other. But I had things to do, plans to plan – plans of destruction! 'Later, my angel,' I whispered in her ear. 'Later.'

Slipping out of bed, I glanced back at Tracy. It seemed strange having someone else in my bed again, especially another woman! But I found it comforting and realized just how many long, cold nights I'd spent alone in my loneliness. She'd moved in with me, it seemed. We were living as wife and wife. I still wasn't sure whether that was what I wanted or not, despite the wonderful sex and comfort she brought me.

Things to do and things to be done! I chided myself as I slipped my dressing gown on. This was my big day – the day when Jim would finally find himself completely alone in the big, cold world. I was nearly there, I'd almost won. I was about to destroy him – totally. Nothing would go wrong, it mustn't! Although the plan was somewhat precarious, I was sure that it would all come together. Stephen, Jim and I would come together, I knew that much!

No doubt Jim would come crawling to me as soon as the realization hit him that he had nowhere to stick his cock. In a grotty bedsit, without a woman, without a hot, wet, tight pussy to drive his cock into – he'd come whimpering to me, whimpering his words of fresh beginnings, new starts.

And, at last, I'd achieve my ultimate goal – the satisfaction of his long-awaited and very painful final downfall. I'd tell him what I'd done, how I'd meticulously planned his ruination, and expertly executed it! I'd tell him everything – everything! *Bastard!*

After a shower and a bowl of cornflakes, I tidied the lounge, wondering why Tracy was sleeping so late. All I needed was for her to come down and ruin things for me, so I woke her up and suggested – if she really did want to live with me permanently – that she go and get her belongings. Although somewhat suspicious of my motives, she was excited by the prospect and was washed, dressed and out of the house well before eleven o'clock, thank God!

I still wasn't sure whether I was doing the right thing having Tracy move in with me, but I couldn't think about that now. My mind was reeling, lurching between the excitement and the danger of my evil plan. I found myself knocking back the vodka – Russian courage, I presumed! Pacing the floor, I waited, my pussy juices flowing, my head spinning, my heart beating wildly. I was almost a nervous wreck!

Jim was early, unfortunately, as I'd rather hoped that Stephen would arrive first. I told him that I'd double- booked, which didn't please him, explaining that I was expecting not only another man to call, but a young girl, as well. After mumbling his disgust for me, he changed his tune and grinned when I invited him to join in the debauchery.

'You'll enjoy it, Jim!' I giggled. 'Imagine, you and another man both fucking me at once! And then the girl joining in, too!'

'I really don't know what's happened to you,' he sighed. 'You've changed so much, Sue! You used to be a . . .'

'What I used to be doesn't matter any more. The point is, I'm enjoying my life, the sex, the . . . Anyway, you'll stay, won't you? You'll stay and enjoy me, and the young, so very young, fresh, tight, wet girl?' I asked as the doorbell rang.

'Yes, of course I'll stay!' he smiled as I left the room, my heart fluttering, my stomach swirling.

What man wouldn't?

Praying that Jim wouldn't realize who Stephen was,

I opened the door to my victim. Stephen stood there grinning, holding a huge bouquet of flowers in one hand – and a fifty-pound note in the other. Pathetic figure of a man! Grabbing the note, I smiled sweetly, licking my full lips and inviting him in.

'Leave the flowers there,' I said, pointing to the hall table and pushing the front door to. 'I've a surprise for you, Stephen,' I grinned wickedly as I stuffed the money in the table drawer. 'Something that I know you'll enjoy very much.'

'Oh, what's that?' he asked, slipping his jacket off and hanging it over the banister.

'A young girl is going to join in – and another man.'

'Another man!' he gasped, hesitating as he followed me to the lounge.

'It's all right, he's perfectly straight! It's the girl and me you'll both be interested in, so don't worry.'

My lies about another girl weaving their magic, he smiled at the prospect. No doubt his male thoughts were bringing him visions of two tight, wet pussies – open, yearning, begging for his tongue, his cock, his sperm!

'Stephen, this is Jim,' I smiled as we entered the lounge. Shaking hands, they sat like Tweedledum and Tweedledee on the sofa, wondering, no doubt, who was going to instigate the proceedings.

The time running on, I couldn't waste a second. Standing before my audience, I peeled my clothes off, slowly, provocatively, until I was completely naked, my firm, rounded breasts, my elongated nipples, ready for sucking – my fresh, hairless cunt lips bulging invitingly. Their eyes wide, they watched as I lay on the floor, straddling my legs and slipping my fingers between my milky pussy lips. Slowly at first, I massaged my clitoris, masturbating, fingering my wet cunt.

Never had I thought that I'd be masturbating before two men, let alone a virtual stranger and my ex-husband! The obscenity, the pure crudity of the situation excited me, aroused me, as I held my pussy lips wide open and caressed my swelling clitoris, writhing, making the appropriate noises as they watched in amazement. Again, my cunt was in control. *Pussy-power!*

Opening my legs even wider, I reached under my thigh and pushed three fingers deep into my juicy cunt, bringing me wonderful sensations of lecherous sex – and stiffening my audience's penises, no doubt! When they were ready, when they'd witnessed me coming, writhing in my self-abuse, I'd invite them to use my naked body, to live out their wonderfully vile perversions – to fuck my holes, pumping the fruits of their realized fantasies deep inside me.

'God, I'm coming!' I cried as my clitoris swelled beneath my caressing fingertips. My girl-come flowing over my hand as I fingered my vagina, my outer pussy lips inflating, my nipples hardening, I reached my sexual heaven. Gasping my debased pleasure, I caressed the last ripples of orgasm from my beautiful cumbud before lying limp, my legs splayed, my cunt oozing, open wide in readiness for a huge male organ.

'You're some woman!' Stephen breathed as he slipped out of his clothes and joined me on the carpet, his penis long, hard, ready to penetrate my wet, quivering cunt – my every orifice.

'Where's the girl, then?' Jim asked as he, too, hurriedly undressed and settled by my side.

'She'll be here,' I assured him. 'While we're waiting, why don't you both pleasure me?'

'What would you like us to do?' Stephen murmured, sucking my nipple into his wet mouth.

'Let me suck you both. Let me stiffen your cocks with my tongue, get them really hard, ready for my cunt,' I suggested, grinning, licking my full lips.

Wasting no time, both men sat me up and knelt either side of me, their huge penises only inches from my face. Taking their organs in my hands, I pulled their foreskins right back and licked first one and then the other, causing my victims to gasp as they watched my tongue snaking around their bulbous purple knobs.

Pulling them closer, I pressed the silky heads of their weapons together and took them both into my mouth and gently sucked. Two swelling knobs pulsating against my tongue sent wonderful shivers of lascivious sex creeping up my spine, and I became lost in my sexual haze, dreaming of three, four knobs sperming over my tongue. In my dream – my subconscious? – I desperately wanted to experience the ultimate: twenty men sperming over my naked body. Twenty hard knobs pulsating in orgasm, jetting male come deep into my sex-holes, my mouth, over my aching breasts. I wanted to drown in a sea of sperm!

Mouthing, licking, sucking, I prayed that my men would come together, simultaneously shoot their lovely spunk deep into my thirsty mouth. Never had I had two penises in my mouth at once, two hard, silky knobs pressing against my tongue, two pairs of heavy balls to fondle, and I became delirious in my lust for sex.

Holding their hard cocks by the base, I moved my head back and forth, fucking them in unison, bringing them closer to their goals. Groaning in their ecstasy, the men shuddered, each reaching down and tweaking my nipples, kneading my breasts as they gasped their warnings of impending orgasm – impending sperm. *Impending doom!*

'Coming!' Stephen cried as his knob exploded, pumping cream over my snaking tongue as Jim erupted to unleash his first jet of salty come. Wanking their hard shafts, lapping at their swollen knobs, bringing out every last drop of their jism, I licked and drank, swallowing hard until I'd drained their heavy balls. Gasping, shuddering as I ran my tongue up and down between their knobs, they pulled away, leaving the remnants of their climaxes glistening on my lips, running down my chin, dripping onto my aching nipples.

'God, you know how to please a man!' Stephen praised as he sat on the floor, gazing at me.

'I know how to please *two* men!' I giggled, glancing at the mantelpiece clock. Eleven-twenty. 'How about both fucking me at once?' I suggested as I stood up and licked the sperm from my lips. 'Why don't you both fuck me together, come inside me together?'

'We wouldn't be able to!' Jim laughed, eyeing my tight pussy-crack.

'Oh yes, you would!' I grinned, kneeling with my knees wide apart. 'Come on, one in front, and one behind!'

They looked at each other and raised their eyebrows, probably unable to believe that this was really happening, that the ultimate male fantasy was becoming reality. Their cocks rising, stiffening at the prospect of penetrating my two love-holes, I prayed that Wendy wouldn't be late and miss the beautiful finale.

'Well?' I smiled as a car pulled up outside. 'Come on, then! If you're real men, then both fuck the holes between my legs and fill my young body with your sperm!' They moved towards me, Stephen behind me, parting my buttocks, and Jim in front, rubbing his knob up and down the length of my drenched pussy-crack. 'Come on, fuck me!' I ordered crudely as Stephen wrenched my buttocks open wide and stabbed at my small hole while Jim slipped the entire length of his massive organ deep into my spasming vagina. 'Come on, Stephen! Push it right up me!' I cried as his knob slipped past my yielding sphincter muscles and absorbed the fiery heat of my bowels.

As, inch by inch, he slipped his shaft deeper into my anal tube, I grimaced and quivered. The filling sensation was indescribable as my pelvic cavity gently expanded, bloated wonderfully with two massive dicks. They began their fucking motions, both slipping their hard cocks in and out of my love-holes. Increasing their rhythm, they used my defiled body with a vengeance, ramming into me as I flopped back and forth like a puppet.

'Both come in me at once!' I begged as my clitoris throbbed beneath my caressing fingertips with the beginnings of my orgasm. Hands wandered all over my body, my breasts, my nipples, exploring, waking every nerve ending as my cunt, my bottom-hole, were crudely taken by my victims. 'Both spunk inside me together!' I ordered, aware of someone moving about in the hall.

I gasped my pleasure, my obscenities, louder as my orgasm gripped me. 'Come up my arse, Stephen! Ah, yes, yes! God, I love two men fucking my sex-holes! Both sperm into my young body together! Use me, my body, my cunt, my arse! Fuck me harder! Fuck . . . fuck me harder! Ah, God! Yes, fuck me!'

'Coming!' Stephen cried as his knob pumped his fruits deep into my bowels and Jim's solid plum exploded within my tightening cunt-sheath.

My cunt burning, my clitoris pulsating in orgasm, my bottom-hole stretched to capacity, I felt dazed with lust. I wanted a cock sperming in my mouth, cocks sperming over my nipples – again, I desperately wanted to drown in a salty sea of bubbling sperm!

Through my lowered eyelashes, I saw Wendy standing in the doorway, her mouth hanging open, her face pale with shock as she gazed in horror at the three of us locked in orgasm.

'God, you've got a tight little arse!' Stephen cried as his belly slapped my buttocks again and again with his adulterous thrusting.

'We'll do this again!' Jim gasped as he found his rhythm with Stephen and finished draining his balls, filling my cunt with his treacherous come. 'We'll all do this again!'

As the two beautiful cocks gently slipped from my wet, inflamed holes of sex, deflating my pelvic cavity, I scooped the sperm from my cunt, licking my fingers as I smiled at Wendy. Stephen gasped as he turned to face his wife, his penis hanging limp, spent, dripping with spunk. Jim gasped, too, as he gazed in horror at Wendy – his mistress.

'Now I've seen everything!' she screamed hysterically as the men hurriedly pulled their trousers on. 'I want a divorce, Stephen!' she blasted. Glaring at Jim, she said nothing. She didn't need words to tell him that their illicit affair was over – dead.

As she stormed out of the house, I couldn't stop grinning. I'd done it! Executed my plan beautifully! The ultimate destruction – a man and his wife, a man and his mistress. They were finished, all of them! Ruined – fucked!

The guilt-ridden men grunted despondently as they dressed, Stephen complaining about his bloody wife divorcing him, and Jim mumbling something about being alone in the world. They knew that they'd come to the end of the line – Stephen had lost his wife, and Jim had lost his mistress. They'd both lost her tight cunt. And mine!

'That was bad timing!' I giggled as I sat in the armchair with my legs wide apart, exposing my inflamed, dripping pussy-hole to their wide eyes – their terror-stricken eyes.

'Bad timing?' Stephen bellowed. 'Christ! What the hell am I going to do now?'

'God knows!' I replied, catching Jim's eye and flashing him an evil grin. 'At least you're all right, Jim. You haven't lost a woman, have you?'

He glared at me, as if he knew exactly what I'd done. I smiled a sweet smile at him as Stephen left the room, his hair dishevelled, his face anguished, his future destroyed in seconds.

'It looks as if Stephen has problems!' I laughed. 'Anyway,

that's his business, isn't it? Did you enjoy it, Jim?'

'Suppose so,' he grunted as he adjusted his shirt.

'What's the matter? You've turned rather pale.'

'Nothing's the matter!' he snapped.

'Are you sure? You look awfully worried.'

'I didn't realize that he was Wendy's . . . that he was your friend's husband. *You* asked her round here, didn't you?'

'Now, why would I do a thing like that? Knowing that I was going to be screwing her husband, why on earth would I do a thing like that?'

His dressing completed, he sat on the sofa, a look of anger in his eyes. But he realized that he had to be very careful – I was the only woman he had left. Lose me, and he'd have to resort to wanking. Lose me – and he'd be cuntless!

'Sue,' he began, smiling at me, his tone changing, his thoughts turning to the future, his cuntless future. I knew only too well what was coming! 'Sue, I've been thinking about us.'

'Yes, so have I, Jim. And I think it's high time that we put an end to all this group sex.'

'So do I,' he smiled.

'Oh, I'm glad you agree.'

'Of course I agree! It's gone way too far, what with you screwing everyone who comes your way. I think, as you do, that it's time to put a stop to all this nonsense and get back together again.'

'No, no, Jim! That's not what I meant!'

'Then what did you mean?'

'What I meant was, I want to put a stop to all this sex with you. I want you to stop coming round here for sex.'

'But . . . but I thought that was what you wanted?'

'It was. But now . . . Well, I've had enough of it. What with you screwing Caroline, and then screwing . . .'

'There was only Caroline, you know that, Sue!'

'You've been screwing Wendy for God knows how long, Jim! I'm not stupid!'

'No, I haven't! I've never touched Wendy! The first time I ever saw her was when she was here the other evening, you know that!'

'I set you up, Jim. I've been playing games with you. I set you up with Caroline. I planned your downfall. I set you up with Wendy. I arranged for her to discover you, her lover, and her husband both fucking me. I've split you all up!'

He shifted uneasily on the sofa. He knew that if he lost his cool, he'd also be losing his cunt. He wanted to rant and rave, but he couldn't. Not if he was to win me over, secure his future – my pussy.

'I don't mind,' he smiled forgivingly. 'I suppose I'd half guessed what you were up to, anyway. Look, Sue, now that you're alone, as I am, why don't we start afresh? Let's put all this behind us and . . .'

'There's a problem, Jim – well, several, actually. One, I'm in love with someone else. Two, I don't want you anywhere near me. Three, after screwing so many other men, *real* men, I realize that sex with you is about as exciting as having sex with a rolling pin!'

'But you always said how good we were together!'

'Yes, that was before I'd had several other men's huge cocks up me! Yours is small, you come too quickly, you're bloody useless at bringing me pleasure, you . . .'

'God, you're a bitch, Sue!'

'That's me! I've been fucking you up all along! And, even though I say it myself, I did a bloody good job! What's it like, Jim? What's it like to be without a woman? What will you do alone in your bed at night, have a wank? You'll find out what it was like for me when you deserted me, when you went off with Caroline, hoping she'd give you the freedom you needed to screw Wendy. Oh yes, I know everything, Jim! Wendy was all set to leave Stephen and plan a future with you. But now . . . I suppose you'll be able to find a tart to use, some filthy little tart to fuck – for payment, of course. Mind you, I wouldn't take anyone back to a poky flat over a bloody fish and chip shop! I doubt that even a prostitute would want that!'

'You'll pay for this, Sue! You'll bloody well . . .'

'Pay? How, exactly, will I pay? I own this house. I have money, far more than you realize, in fact. I have someone moving in with me, my lover. What have you got, Jim? What have you got now? Apart from your poor little cock and your loneliness, that is.'

'Why, Sue? Why have you done all this to me? I don't understand!'

'No, I don't suppose you do. And I doubt very much that you'll ever understand. But understand this! I don't want you! I don't even like you, let alone . . . I never want to see you again, Jim! I hated you, despised you for what you did to me! You destroyed me, my very being! And now I've destroyed you!'

As he stood up to leave the room, he turned and gazed at my naked body. In a way, I felt sorry for him. But my sorrow soon faded when I recalled what he'd done to me, how he'd used me – and then tossed me aside. 'The tables have turned, Jim,' I smiled as I parted my swollen pussy lips and massaged my erect clitoris. 'The tables have turned!'

Saying nothing, he left the room, closing the door behind him. That was it – I'd closed the door on Jim. Never would he enjoy my young body again, my beautiful, powerful cunt – never would Caroline want him back, never would Wendy even speak to him again, let alone . . .

Answering the phone, I was surprised to hear Stephen's voice. 'I'm on my mobile,' he drawled. 'I just thought I'd ring you and tell you that the job offer still stands, if you want it, that is.'

Poor lonely man, thinking that he could fuck me as and when it took his fancy!

'Job offer? Oh, that! No, sorry, Stephen, I don't want the job!' I laughed.

'I'll pay you well, if you know what I mean?'

'Yes, I know exactly what you mean, but I've finished with all that.'

'But . . . When will I see you again?'

'Never, I should think! Anyway, I'm busy, so . . .'

'But I don't understand! I've got money, Sue!'

'Yes, so have I! I hope all goes well with your wife.'

'Did you know that she was coming round to see you?'

'Yes, I did. I suppose I forgot that I'd be fucking you. We all make mistakes.'

'Mistakes? Your mistake cost me my marriage!'

'Yes, I know. But you were the one who committed adultery, not me! Oh, by the way, your wife had been . . . No, I won't tell you.'

'Been what?'

'Nothing. Anyway, I must be going. Bye!'

As I was relaxing on the sofa, toying with my wet, inner lips, wondering what was taking Tracy so long, Craig rang, asking to come round and see me. It was as if Satan were working with me, rounding up his fallen angels for hell's fire! *Perhaps he was?*

'Yes, of course you can!' I replied enthusiastically. 'You know that you're always welcome to come and see me – *and* come inside me!' I laughed.

'I was hoping you'd say that!' he replied eagerly.

'I'll look forward to it, Craig. By the way, can you give me Kirsty's phone number?' I added. 'Only I have the photographs here for her.'

In his pathetic naivety, he gave me her number, saying he'd

be with me in fifteen minutes. Naturally, I rang Kirsty and asked her to call round immediately for the photos. She was busy but, desperate to get her hands on the evidence, she readily agreed. Satan *was* working with me!

I was still naked and dripping with sperm when Craig arrived. Inviting him in, I left the front door ajar. This was so easy! I couldn't believe how stupid he was, how stupid all men were, as he slipped out of his jeans and stood naked before me, his penis pointing skyward. I stroked his magnificent organ, running my finger over his silky glans.

'We'll do this every day, if you want to,' I smiled.

'Yes, I want to!' he breathed as I licked and kissed his bulbous knob.

'You'll have to lie to Kirsty, of course,' I added, sucking him into my mouth.

'That's no problem!' he laughed.

It will be!

Which would upset Kirsty more? I wondered. Me sucking her man's knob, drinking his gushing sperm, or him giving me the fucking of my life? Positioning myself on all fours, I projected my bum, inviting Craig to slip his length deep into my anal sheath. 'I love it up there!' I gasped as he parted my buttocks and slipped his bulbous knob inside my small hole. By that time, I really *did* love a hard cock up my bum! 'Really give it to me!' I cried as he grabbed my hips and thrust into me like a demon.

Lost in the beautiful pummelling, intoxicated by our crude union, I quickly reached my climax, shuddering as I sensed his sperm pumping deep into my defiled body. On and on he thrust his massive organ into my tight bottom-hole until I thought I'd expire with the obscene pleasure.

'Please, don't stop!' I begged as I sensed him withdrawing. 'Keep fucking my arse!'

'I'll fuck your arse every day!' he breathed as his penis

suddenly found renewed life and swelled inside me again. Groping between my swollen cunny lips, he massaged my stiff clitty, bringing me near to another exquisite climax. 'God, I'll fuck your tight arse every day!'

Kirsty's inevitable hysterical screams filled the house as she appeared in the doorway. Pulling his cock from my dripping anal sheath, Craig gazed in horror, first at her, then at me. He knew what I'd done as I rolled over and lay outstretched on the carpet, my creamy slit open before Kirsty's wide eyes. He knew that I'd deliberately destroyed him.

How many more would there be? I wondered as I watched Kirsty flee the house in tears with Craig in hot pursuit. How many more relationships would I destroy? How many more men would succumb to the mystical enchantment of my unveiled fanny?

Climbing to my feet, I thought of Tom and Sandy. The last on my list, I had to plan their divorce. But *were* they to be the last? There was a young couple who'd just moved into the house across the road who . . . There'd be more, many more, to add to my list, I knew as I heard the front door open.

Tracy. Oh, dear! What would she say when she found me standing naked in the lounge, sperm dripping from my two love-holes? What would she do? Move out? I didn't want that. I didn't think I wanted that, anyway. Shit! I *still* didn't know what I really wanted.

'God, not again!' she shrieked, predictably.

'Yes, *again*, Trace,' I smiled.

'If we're to live together, Sue . . . if you're genuinely serious about us, then I want all this to stop! Do you understand?'

'Yes, I understand,' I replied wearily as she brushed my nipples with the back of her hand and then squeezed my breasts, sending a quiver through my womb. She still wanted me? She knew what I'd been doing, screwing men, wrecking more relationships, and yet, she still wanted to be with me?

'I found this on the doormat,' she said, passing me a plain white envelope. 'The notes will have to stop, too, now that I'm living here. They will stop, won't they?'

'Will they?' I frowned, my mind troubled, my thoughts swirling.

'Yes, they will stop now.'

'How do you know that?'

Sitting on the sofa, she ran her fingers through her hair and sighed. I knew I was in line for a lecture as she looked up at me and patted the adjoining cushion. Joining her, my naked pussy-crack grinning as I reclined on the sofa and opened my legs, I smiled a sweet, inviting smile.

'What's on your mind?' I asked, taking her hand and placing it between my thighs.

'I know who's been writing the notes, Sue,' she replied softly.

'Do you?' I asked surprisedly.

'Yes. But what I want to know is, *why*?'

'I've no idea *why*! Who the hell's been sending them? That's what *I* want to know!'

'You have, Sue,' she sighed.

'*Me*? Of course I haven't! Do you think I'm completely mad?'

'I believe that you need help, if that's what you mean. Anyway, the notes will stop now, won't they?'

'I can't believe that you think that I've been writing those bloody notes to myself! Only a head-case would do something like that!'

'Not a head-case, Sue. But someone who's been tormented, psychologically disturbed by dreadful events. Someone whose husband left her for her best friend.'

'How long have you known?' I asked dolefully.

'I guessed some time ago. Why did you write them?'

'Because . . . I was suspicious of Jim. I don't know why, but I was sure that he was having an affair. I had no reason to think that he was seeing someone else. It was intuition, I suppose. In the back of my mind, I knew that he was up to something. I wrote the first note and showed it to him because . . . I wanted to test him, I suppose. I wanted his reaction. Anyway, it went from there. Had I never written that first note and confronted him, then . . .'

'Then he'd still be living here, with you – and screwing Caroline. It happened for the best, Sue. That first note you wrote . . . it was for the best.'

'Yes, I suppose it was,' I sighed, wondering how long Jim could have lived a lie – cheated on me.

'You won't write any more, will you? And all your escapades – they'll stop now, won't they?'

'Yes, I suppose so.'

'Now that I'm here, there's no need for you to feel insecure, to feel that you have to seek revenge, is there? And there's no need to send yourself any more notes. I realize that they helped you in your plight, that they made people feel sorry for you, that they somehow helped ease the pain. But there's no need for the notes any more, Sue.'

Her words rebounding off the wreckage strewn in the alcoves of my mind, I felt my face flush with guilt. I'd thought I'd won a battle against the pawns around me, taken revenge on those around me for the hurt and pain a man had put me through. But I realized that the only battle had been with myself. I'd fought myself – and lost.

'Let's go upstairs and make love,' Tracy suggested, running her finger up my sperm-drenched slit.

'Yes, let's,' I smiled as the phone rang. 'I'll join you in a minute,' I added, following her through the hall.

As she closed the bedroom door behind her, I lifted the receiver and grinned to hear Tom's deep voice. 'Tom, how are you?' I asked, massaging my clitoris as I leaned against the wall, my feet wide apart.

'Couldn't be better!' he replied. 'The photographs are ready for you. They've come out really well!'

'Oh, good – I'll pick them up later. Do you know what I'm doing while I'm speaking to you, Tom?' I quavered.

'No, tell me. What are you doing?'

'I'm standing in the hall, naked. And I'm fingering my tight pussy-hole. It's wet, hot – ready for you, Tom.'

'That sounds interesting! I don't suppose you want me to come over now and give you a hand, or a finger, or a tongue, or a . . .'

'No, not if you bring Sandy with you.'

'Ah, yes. That's why I'm phoning. I wanted to ask you something, Sue,' he said mysteriously.

'What?'

'Your proposition – does it still stand? Only Sandy's out tonight, working, and . . . I'd like you all to myself. I don't want to share you with Sandy any more. What do you say?'

'I say *yes*, Tom! I've someone staying with me but I'll get rid of her for the evening. Come round about seven – alone!'

'I'll be there, with some wine and a bottle of gin. And I've a nice cucumber in the fridge!'

'Be sure to bring it with you.'

'Oh, I'll bring it with me, all right!'

'Great! I'll look forward to it,' I giggled as I massaged my stiffening cumbud. 'I'll look forward to many evenings alone with you!'

'So will I! I just pray that Sandy doesn't find out I'm splitting my attention between . . .'

'Split . . .? Oh no, she won't find out, Tom! She won't discover us having our fun!'

Yet!

RAY GORDON

DEPRAVICUS

THE MISSIONARY POSITION!

The Reverend William Entercock is the highly – ah – *unorthodox* priest of Cumsdale church. As well as running various lucrative undercover commercial enterprises (from which the church gets a cut, of course) the randy rev also enjoys distinctly worldly relationships with a range of parish ladies, convent sixth-formers and young nuns. His confession sessions with the local lovelies are miracles of ungodly behaviour.

Bishop Simon Holesgood has his suspicions about the vicar of Cumsdale, despite finding no evidence of any wrong-doing on a visit to the crafty cleric. Joining forces with a vengeful Mother Superior, the Bishop is out to get Entercock defrocked. Worse, an attractive young tabloid journalist, Josie, wants to expose him for the sake of the sensational story that revelation of his excesses will make.

But William Entercock is far too clever to fall into their traps. In fact, with what he discovers about the secret lives of his hypocritical enemies, he's sure to come out on top. . .

DEPRAVICUS brings a whole new meaning to the phrase 'outrageously funny'. It is yet another triumph from one of the brightest talents on the modern erotic fiction scene.

HODDER AND STOUGHTON PAPERBACKS

RAY GORDON

HAUNTING LUST

House of Dark Erotic Pleasures

When twenty-year-old Tina Wilson left her job and moved into the old Victorian house that had been left to her, her life began to change dramatically. From the day she took up residence in the rambling building, she became aware of a heightened new sexuality flooding through every fibre of her being. Visitors, male and female, became the surprised and gratified targets of her surging desires.

At first filled with guilt at her predatory behaviour, Tina soon began to relax into her newfound erotic ecstasy. But the mystery of what had triggered the powerful change in her remained – until she discovered a torture chamber hidden in the attic and in it some old diaries that revealed the true nature of the occult force that had possessed her with this haunting lust . . .

Here is another totally compelling novel of sexuality's outer limits by one of the most inventive writers of contemporary erotic fiction.

HODDER AND STOUGHTON PAPERBACKS

RAY GORDON

HOUSE OF LUST

ALL THE WAY UP

Lady Hadleigh, the haughty mistress of the manor, likes to think that she can abuse anyone on her estate at will. But when she seduces Tom, the ambitious stable boy, she finds herself grappling with a ruthless adversary determined to rise in the world by mercilessly exploiting his tremendous sexual prowess at every opportunity. 'Breaking in' Lady Hadleigh's two teenage daughters is just the next stage in Tom's rapacious progress. There's a lot more to come as he thrusts his rampant way right to the top. . .

HOUSE OF LUST

is the surging, compelling story of the uncontrollable passions and desires seething behind the outwardly respectable facade of an 'aristocratic' household in the closing years of the last century.

HODDER AND STOUGHTON PAPERBACKS